W9-CFE-454

THE PURSUIT OF
TAMSEN LITTLEJOHN

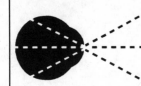

THE PURSUIT OF TAMSEN LITTLEJOHN

LORI BENTON

THORNDIKE PRESS

A part of Gale, Cengage Learning

GALE
CENGAGE Learning·

Farmington Hills, Mich • San Francisco • New York • Waterville, Maine
Meriden, Conn • Mason, Ohio • Chicago

GALE
CENGAGE Learning®

LIBRARY OF CONGRESS CATALOGING-IN-PUBLICATION DATA

Benton, Lori.
  The pursuit of Tamsen Littlejohn / Lori Benton.
    pages cm. — (Thorndike Press large print Christian historical fiction)
    ISBN 978-1-4104-7764-4 (hardcover) — ISBN 1-4104-7764-9 (hardcover)
  1. Large type books. I. Title.
PS3602.E6974P88 2015
813'.6— dc23   2015006076

Published in 2015 by arrangement with WaterBrook Press, an imprint
of the Crown Publishing Group, a division of Random House LLC, a
Penguin Random House Company

Printed in Mexico
1 2 3 4 5 6 7 19 18 17 16 15

For Brian

*And for those of my
maternal ancestors who
pioneered — Puryears, Hites,
and Amises — at least
one of whom became an
Overmountain Man.*

And I said, O that I
had wings like a dove!
For then would I fly away,
and be at rest.
Lo, then would I wander far off,
And remai in the wilderness. Selah.
I wou d hasten my escape
From the windy storm and tempest.

Psalm 55:6–8

FOR RICHER,
FOR POORER

1

Western North Carolina
September 1787

To Jesse Bird's reckoning, any man charged with driving forty head of Overmountain cattle to market best have three things in his possession — a primed rifle, a steady horse, and a heap of staying power.

Jesse had the first two, one balanced across his thighs; the other tired, fly bitten, and dusty between them. As for staying power . . . with miles to go before he'd be shed of those forty beeves, he was making a studied effort to let patience have its perfect work in him.

Looking back across their brown and brindled ranks, he spotted Cade and the packhorses rounding a bend in the river trace, where sunlight still speared the hazy air in moted streaks of gold. Riding behind the drove at the mercy of its dust, Cade had a kerchief tied across his mouth and nose, hat pulled low to shield his eyes. Though Jesse hadn't ridden rear guard since midday, the choke of that same dust gritted his throat. Grime coated the foot drovers too, spread out through the summer-fattened herd, armed with rifles and staves, eyes darting glances at the crowding wooded slopes.

Grasshoppers whirred beside the trace, leaping clear of trampling hooves that crackled the weeds. The sun hung to westward, its warmth fading, leaving rivulets of sweat drying on Jesse's neck, sticking his shirt where the straps of bullet-bag and knapsack crossed. He was thinking they'd reach their next camp a nip ahead of dark, with time to pen the cattle before swimming the dust off his hide, when something with the force of a slung stone clipped his hat brim. Thinking a deer fly had marked him for a meal, he reached for the hat, meaning to swat the pest.

The hat was gone clean off his head. It dangled from a nearby tulip poplar, pinned by a feathered arrow.

Jesse gave a whoop, then was out of the saddle and ducking behind a clump of rhododendron, putting his horse crosswise between himself and the beeves. From across the river came a spotty rain of arrows, pinging off rocks, thunking into trees along the bank. The drovers ducked behind the cattle on the hill-slope side of the trace, rifles shouldered.

Jesse's mind raced. Was it Creeks or Chickamaugas? Either held an everlasting grudge against the Overmountain settlers. Hang it all, it could be Shawnees. With a wordless prayer that it wasn't, Jesse aimed his rifle at a tawny flash across the river and fired. Powder smoke plumed out white from the barrel. On the tail edge of the report, he heard Cade's war whoop. An answering ululation came shrill and defiant from across the water, raising the hairs on Jesse's arms.

The cattle milled and bunched, kicking up a dust blind. One took an arrow in the flank and went down in the middle of the trace, bawling in pain but thwarting the bulk of the herd's bolting.

Rifle shot cracked. Powder smoke hung on both sides of the river now, sharp and sulfurous. For the moment they had the water for a buffer. The attacking warriors wouldn't risk exposing themselves to cross unless sure of taking them down. Surprise was a weapon spent.

A brindled cow broke from the jostling herd. It plunged down the riverbank and crumpled in the shallows, shot through the neck. The front of the herd not blocked by the downed cow pressed up against the hillside and then shifted in Jesse's direction, threatening to stampede off down the trace. More broke for the river. Busy reloading, Jesse could do little but pray his horse stood its ground.

A musket ball ripped through rhody leaves near his head. Back down the trace Cade's rifle fired. A warrior across the river fell through brush, lay thrashing, and was dragged back into cover. Another such loss and the warriors would likely break and run. If they could hold them off a few more seconds . . .

New voices shattered a lull in the firing. Tremolo cries like the warble of crazed turkey cocks sounded up the slope behind them.

Fear jarred through Jesse. Faster than thought, he yanked free his belt ax and whirled to throw it — and almost too late recognized the two Cherokee warriors. He shouted to the drovers to stop them firing on the blue-shirted figures leaping down the rocky slope, dodging frightened cattle. The Cherokees took cover on the bank, both with rifles, and commenced to putting them to use.

Jesse blazed a grin of welcome at the

younger of the two now at his side, rammed patch and ball to powder, and fired across the river.

A final arrow sailed over the cattle's backs. Then stillness fell, with smoke and dust drifting high on the river breeze.

The drovers moved among the beeves, soothing them with staves and words, settling their own nerves with rapid glances toward the river. The warriors had melted back into the forest, taking their wounded with them. It had been a hunting party, taking their chances on an unplanned raid. If it had been a tracking party out for scalps, there were far better spots to stage an ambush along their steep and winding route from Sycamore Shoals. A second attempt was unlikely. Jesse knew the thinking of such men as well as he did his own.

After sliding his rifle into its saddle sling, he mounted and wheeled his horse after the few cows that had bolted up the trace. By the time Jesse had them headed back, Cade had sorted the herd and ridden up through their ranks, leading the packhorses. His gaze raked Jesse head to heel, relief deepening the creases beside his eyes. He took in the cow with the arrow in its flank, then the dead one reddening the river shallows, and yanked down his kerchief to show a mouth narrowed in regret. "That dead one looks like Tate's."

" 'Fraid so," Jesse said. It was always a risk, pushing beeves down the mountains under the noses of Chickamauga warriors eager to cripple the Watauga settlers who depended on the sale of their stock. Jesse and Cade had hired on for this drove each September since the war with the British ended, tracing the Watauga River east to its mountain headwaters, then down to the Catawba River and the Carolina piedmont. The beeves were bound for the market cow pens, Jesse and Cade for Morganton to barter furs and hides for supplies and then hire on as guides for any settlers heading back Overmountain before snow fell.

"We'd have lost more'n cows had these wild turkeys not flushed from hiding." Jesse nodded at the late arrivals to the fray, both Overhill Cherokees. While the drovers cast half-wary looks at the two, Cade and Jesse slid off their horses to greet them.

"Friends of yours, Cade?" asked the white drover, owner of ten head of cattle and the two slaves helping drive them.

"Yours too, I'd say." Cade looped his mare's reins around a sapling and grasped the arm of the elder Indian, a stocky man with gray threading the hair flowing from under his turban. "Whatever brings you across our path, brothers, you've our thanks."

Despite Cade's half-breed Delaware blood, little distinguished his looks from the men he greeted, save that his black hair was tailed back, not plucked to a scalp-lock, as was the younger Cherokee's. Cade's hat brim, pinned with a hawk's feather, shaded eyes one expected to be as dark as the battered felt but were instead as golden brown as Jesse's — nothing to remark upon for a man of Jesse's coloring. In Cade's tawny face, they often drew a second look.

"Thunder-Going-Away," Cade said, naming the elder Cherokee first, by way of introduction. "And Catches Bears, his son."

The drover gave a wary nod. "Elijah Rhodes."

"Jabez and Billy," Jesse added, with a nod at Rhodes's slaves.

Billy, fourteen and on his first drive, was shaking in the wake of the attack — with excitement as much from shock, Jesse thought. "Think one them Injuns was Dragging Canoe? Them bad Injuns, I mean," Billy added with a sidelong look at the Cherokees.

"Doubt it." Jesse grinned at the boy,

who'd prattled on about the infamous Chickamauga war chief since starting from Sycamore Shoals. "Dragging Canoe would've crossed right over that river and lifted our scalps. Ain't you heard? He can swim like a fish and fly like a raven."

The boy's eyes whitened around the rims.

Jabez, an old hand at droving, slapped Billy's back, raising dust. "He pulling yo' leg, boy. Canoe ain't no demon-bird. Just a man like me and you."

"Huh," Billy said, looking unconvinced.

Cade was eying Thunder-Going, a question in his eyes. "You're a long way from Chota."

Thunder-Going raised his chin, nodding back toward the northwest. "Tate Allard said we missed you by three sleeps. We trailed you."

"Not hard to do," Bears said, nostrils flaring wide, "with the stink these cows leave."

Thunder-Going hid a smile in the lines carved beside his mouth. "We meant to catch you coming back from Morganton, to invite you to a feast. My daughter is to join blankets with a husband."

"White Shell? 'Bout time." Three pairs of eyes turned to Jesse when he spoke. The Cherokees and even Cade were looking at him as if he ought to say more on the matter. "What?"

Bears snorted. "You see? He does not know."

Jesse frowned. "What don't I know?"

"My sister wanted you," Bears said. "But you had no eyes to see her, so she chose one who does."

"My daughter was not the one for you," Thunder-Going said and shrugged away what looked to Jesse like mild disappointment. Then the Cherokee inquired of Cade, though he still eyed Jesse, "Is it to be Allard's girl, who follows this one like a puppy?"

Jesse cut in before Cade could answer that. "I have not found *the one.* I will know when I have, and maybe then I will tell you about it." They'd fallen into *Tsalagi,* the Cherokee tongue. Switching to English, he said, "Oughtn't we to be pushing on?"

Rhodes was in agreement. "How far to the next camp?"

"Mile or two," Cade said. "Have to tend the downed cows first."

Bears and his father exchanged a look. Thunder-Going said, "You go on with the herd. We will skin out the dead one. Better the hide than nothing, eh? For a share of the meat, we will bring that along as well. As much as we can carry."

The plan agreed to, Jesse mounted up. Behind him Cade said, "Where's your hat got to, Jesse?"

It still hung from the poplar, neat as on a cabin wall. Cade reached it first. He wrenched out the arrow, his face gone a shade like greened copper. In his eyes a heap of words clamored to be said, but he handed Jesse the hat and went to deal with the wounded cow on the trace. Fingering the hole in the hat's brim, Jesse watched Cade snap the arrow nearer the wound, leaving enough to grasp. Cade urged the cow to its feet. If the cow made camp, he would take the arrow out there.

Thunder-Going descended the bank toward the cow lying dead at the river's edge. With a wolfish grin, Bears drew the hunting knife from his belt. "If the other cow does not make it, leave it lying. We will see to it as well. Then you can tell Allard and the rest you got every one of their stinking cowhides to market."

Jesse came up from the river in darkness, rid of trail dust, hair dripping. Thunder-Going-Away and Catches Bears, having delivered the promised hide and meat — and having told them to come for the wedding after the corn harvest — had started the long trek back over the mountains to Chota, the Overhill's principal town. Billy slept, rolled in a blanket. Cade sat cross-legged on his bedroll, head wreathed in pipe smoke and the familiar smell of his blend of tobacco and *kinnikinnick* — red-willow bark and sumac. The sunken fire cast barely a glow but enough for Jesse to see the object lying across Cade's lap. The arrow that had pierced Jesse's hat.

"You only smoke that pipe when you've deep thinking to do." *Or praying,* Jesse didn't add. He unrolled his blanket, sat, and tied on his buckskin leggings. "You celebrating or brooding?"

Over by the brush pen, a cow bawled. An owl hooted in the distance, and the river chattered in its bed. Jesse rummaged out the cleanest of his shirts, then poked a stick at a slab of seared beef left on a stone in the embers. He glanced sidelong at a brief blaze in the pipe bowl. Cade blew a ring of smoke that rose and drifted, blending into the dark.

"I'm pondering the brevity of life."

Brooding, right enough. Jesse quit his poking and thrust the stick aside. "Look, what happened back on the trace, that was nothing compared to Kings Mountain." He and Cade both bore the marks to prove they had fought in that frontier battle, late in the war with the Crown. Along with the rest of the Overmountain militia, they'd whupped the redcoats under the command of an arrogant major called Ferguson, who'd dared threaten to come whup *them.* "We've nary a scratch between us to show for today."

"God be thanked." Cade looked away from Jesse, features glossed like beaten bronze in the fire glow.

" 'Sides," Jesse added, "you seen enough wounds to know they heal."

"And you've seen enough men fall beside you to know wounds aren't all we'll ever get. A bullet might've ended either one of us today. Or an arrow." Cade snatched the one off his lap and tossed it at Jesse, as if to underscore his point.

Jesse tossed it back. "Didn't, though."

Cade thrust the arrow into the fire, where it charred and smoked. "Tomorrow, maybe, or next year — if we go on like this. You ready for it?"

The night was cooling. Jesse pulled on his moccasins. "Ready for it? You fretting over the state of my soul or something, Cade?"

"Or something."

Jesse tried to quell a grin. "What for? Long as I do enough good to outweigh the bad, I'll wind up singing with the heavenly hosts. I don't aim to do nothing truly sinful, like steal my neighbor's wife or covet his rifle or —"

"Jesse!" Cade's brows were strongly marked, black and slanted as crows' wings. Even in the dark they glowered thunder.

Jesse kept his face innocent of mirth. "What?"

"Be serious about this." Cade was in no frame of mind for teasing, though Jesse couldn't hold back a chuckle.

"All right, then. Can't figure why you're fretting, though. You mind that day at the blue hole when the preacher put me under? I might've been all of twelve, but I meant every word I owned to. And aren't you the one always saying the Almighty has a plan for me? That's why you took me from —"

Behind them in the dark, a stick cracked. Cade and Jesse reached for their rifles but checked when Jabez came out of the dark, face glistening from his river dip.

"All well?" Cade asked.

"Even the shot one." Jabez toweled off with a shirt, then wadded it for a pillow and lay down next to Billy, who was still snoring like a hibernating bear. "Left Mast' Rhodes watching 'em."

"I'll stay up," Cade said. "Spell him in a bit."

In seconds Jabez was snoring in chorus

23

with Billy.

Jesse tugged on his shirt and lay back on his blanket, enjoying the cool, and being clean, and the blaze of stars overhead. Turning, he watched Cade tap out the pipe and stow it in a knapsack. "I'm glad you still worry for me, Pa," he said, knowing Cade liked it when he called him so, though he'd never once asked Jesse to do so.

This time Cade didn't soften right off. Whatever was eating at him, it'd bit down hard.

Jesse stifled the urge to sigh. One would think he was still twelve years old, struggling to hold his first rifle steady and making up his mind about heaven and hell. Best Jesse could figure, he was nearly twice twelve now. Cade ought to know he could manage this life and the next besides, having been the one to teach him the ways of both.

He waited, pondering if he ought to say more. Then Cade's big hand came down warm on the crown of his damp head, as it had most every night when Jesse was a boy and it'd been just the two of them alone in the world. Which it pretty much still was, all things considered.

"I do worry for you, Jesse Bird. Reckon I got my reasons."

Jesse half-smiled in the dark, but as Cade's hand lifted away, something he said before came back to niggle. *If we go on like this.* What *this*? Taking beeves to market each fall, or something else?

It couldn't be Cade was dissatisfied with the life they'd made for themselves — fur trapping half the year, deer hunting and a bit of farming the other half, living by the grace of neighbors on land they didn't own, accountable mainly to themselves. A good enough life. Maybe the best two rootless hunters could hope for, one a half-breed, the other half red on the inside. 'Course, such hadn't always been his life, or Cade's. Sometimes it was possible to forget that. But not lying on the edge of sleep with the fire crackling by. Never then.

Like most nights since he could recall, Jesse Bird closed his eyes, putting off sleep, and tried to conjure up a face, a voice, a place — anything — from that time before when he'd had another life, another name, another man to call Pa. And like every night before this night, he fell asleep still conjuring, staring into a void blacker than a starless sky.

2

Morganton, North Carolina

Tamsen Littlejohn peered through rippled window glass at the rutted street beyond. "I suppose this is entirely that painter's fault," she murmured and hoped her mother didn't hear the dread behind the words.

It had to be the painter. Mr. Gottfriedsen, a little mouse of a man, had barely spoken a word to Tamsen the day she sat for the miniature commissioned for her nineteenth birthday. While he hadn't flattered her with his tongue, he'd done so with his tiny brush strokes. Oval in shape, the miniature portrait showed her slightly paler than she was in truth, dark-eyed, shoulders clouded by coils of inky hair. Framed, it fit easily in the palm of a hand, even one as small as hers.

It also fit conveniently into Hezekiah Parrish's coat pocket. Tamsen's stepfather had chosen his moment well when, over cups in a Salem tavern, he'd *accidentally* brought out the miniature along with a shilling and allowed Mr. Ambrose Kincaid — nine-and-twenty years of age, unmarried, grandson and heir of a wealthy Virginia planter — to get himself a thorough look at her. Or Mr. Gottfriedsen's version of her. Thus was the unsuspecting Mr. Kincaid drawn like a rich fat fly into her stepfather's web of scheming to marry Tamsen up. Not sideways. Certainly not down. Everything must be *up* for Hezekiah Parrish, reasonably prosperous and immoderately ambitious Charlotte Town cloth merchant.

Tamsen and her mother had, of course, tamely done their part. They'd followed Mr. Parrish from Charlotte Town to this rustic outpost of civilization, where Tamsen was to wear the gown of blueberry silk that had cost her stepfather a small fortune, comport herself like a lady born, and, above all, charm a proposal of marriage out of Mr. Kincaid.

"Have you looked at this place, Mama? How can this be a county seat?" Tamsen figured she was standing in one of the few decent frame buildings in Morganton. The house belonged to Mrs. Brophy, an acquaintance of her stepfather's who ran her late husband's tavern. Tamsen, her mother, and Dell, their maid, had spent the night in the tiny parlor below stairs where the pine floors were uncarpeted, the plaster walls bare, the space crammed with a bed, a settee, a clothespress, and chairs. In one of the chairs, her mother sat, stitching at a heap of linen.

Exaggerated miniatures aside, between them Tamsen's mother held the true claim to beauty. The daughter of a Spanish merchant, Sarah Littlejohn Parrish, with her light olive skin and ebony hair, had once made Tamsen feel she dwelled in the shadow of Scheherazade, the exotic heroine of *One Thousand and One Nights*.

"However it may appear," her mother said in the cultured tone Tamsen had yet to perfect, "we've spent a great deal of effort to come here. I don't see any way around it, Tamsen. You'll simply have to meet the man."

And pray he isn't a younger version of Mr. Parrish, Tamsen thought as the butterflies in her belly took wing. If only her mother would stand up to her stepfather and thwart his overbearing designs — as Scheherazade had charmed and outwitted King Shahryar, turning him aside night after night from his wicked plans. Wit and charm her mother possessed, but the spirit to use them for such an end had long since been crushed by her stepfather's implacable will.

Tamsen wasn't quite ready to roll over without a fight. She longed for the freedom to choose her own path, to marry where she wanted. Or perhaps not marry at all. Or maybe . . .

But there lay half the problem. How could she demand — plead, bargain, beg for — the freedom to choose her path when she'd no earthly idea what sort of life she wanted? The one thing she did know: the life her stepfather had pushed her toward from the day he married her mother was one of the last she would have chosen.

Tamsen started to chew her lip, remembered Mr. Parrish's injunction against lip chewing, and crossed to the vacant chair to rest her feet.

"Don't sit," her mother gently warned. "You'll crease the gown."

Tamsen paced the room. "How does Mr. Parrish manage to get his way in everything?"

"He's a man." Sarah's needle pierced the linen in her lap with more than needful force. "And your guardian."

"He's never even adopted me."

Blinking away a shadow, her mother raised dark eyes luminous with sympathy. "You must marry, Tamsen, and soon. Resign yourself to it being a man of Mr. Parrish's choosing. Whatever burdens it may entail, your stepfather means to give you a comfortable life."

Tamsen refused to be placated. "Mr. Kincaid will be an ogre."

"A young ogre, at least."

"Nigh *thirty*. And a planter. He'll own slaves — or his grandfather will."

"We own slaves," her mother countered, but her shapely mouth stiffened around the words. Tamsen knew that if Sarah Parrish had her way, her stepfather would free every last one of his slaves that hour.

It often puzzled Tamsen that her mother's one strong opinion had to do with slaves. Mr. Parrish's treatment of the few he owned deeply upset her, and her objections still on occasion demonstrated her mother had a scrap of bone remaining in her lovely back. If only she'd use it for Tamsen's sake — not that it was likely to do more good than advocating for their slaves had done to improve their lot.

"Don't borrow worries," her mother told her now. "You've yet to meet the man. He may be far different than you imagine."

Reconcile yourself to endure what cannot be altered, her mother meant. Afraid such passivity was beyond her — and equally afraid it was her lot to suffer — Tamsen wanted to drop to her knees and plead with God next. But that would have soiled the gown. If only her mother —

She shook her head, breaking off the thought. If not for her mother, she might have acted upon the wild and frightening thoughts that had come into her mind since the name Ambrose Kincaid was first brought to her attention. Thoughts of slipping out to the stable one night, saddling her gray mare, riding away to some place of refuge. *Where,* exactly, remained undefined. She never got that far in her thinking because what was the point? If she fled like a runaway slave, she would have to leave her mother, because her mother wouldn't run.

Sarah Parrish was the true keeper of their jail, the one who held the key to the lock and would never hand it over.

"Will Mr. Parrish never arrive to escort me?" she inquired, not caring that she sighed over the words. "I promise to go meekly if I can but get it over with. As a lamb to the slaughter, I shall not open my mouth."

"Surely you aren't comparing your sacrifice to that of our Lord?" Her mother smiled despite the reprimand. "At least there is the gown. That's some consolation, yes?"

Before his death twelve years ago, Tamsen's father, Stephen Littlejohn, had been a cloth merchant like his cousin, Mr. Parrish. Tamsen supposed a love of clothing was in her blood, for standing in this strange house, in a strange town, preparing to meet a stranger who — should all go as Mr. Parrish planned — she would soon be obliged to call "husband," a part of her still could thrill to the rustle of brocaded silk, the striking contrast of blue skirts opening to reveal a cream petticoat embroidered in a garden of gold.

As for the gown's plunging neckline, her stepfather had debated whether she should show herself modest and wear a kerchief or go without and present the more alluring picture. He'd circled her at the final fitting, assessing the results of his design and her mother's labor as if she'd been a doll he'd taken pains to dress — and opted for the kerchief. A small, filmy one that covered little.

Such pleasure was fleeting. The beautiful gown enclosed her like a cage now. The boned stays beneath, drawn tight as she could bear, pressed in so snug that she couldn't draw a full breath.

Back at the window, Tamsen fingered the heavy curtain and stared at the wavering view beyond. Morganton wasn't the setting Mr. Parrish would have chosen for wooing a wealthy bridegroom. It was, however, the nearest Ambrose Kincaid meant to come to Charlotte Town while on business in Carolina.

"Why must we meet in a tavern?" she asked, simply because she couldn't bear the silence of the room.

"Mrs. Brophy's is a respectable ordinary," her mother replied predictably, "where women as well as men may dine. And you know Mr. Parrish's thoughts on the matter."

Having resigned himself to this meeting taking place where it was convenient to Mr. Kincaid, her stepfather had decided to bank everything not on their surroundings but on her face and figure bedecked in the blue gown. What better way to strike a contrast, to make an unforgettable impression, than for her to appear in all her glory in a public house? She would shine like a jewel in a pig's snout.

The idea revolted Tamsen, as it did her mother.

Glancing aside, she noticed what sort of needlework her mother was engaged in. Not

33

fine work for profit, of which her stepfather approved, but common mending. A shirt for Sim, their stable hand, the only other slave besides Dell spared from work at home in order to accompany them. Tamsen also noticed the purple blotches on the inside of her mother's wrist. Inwardly she cringed. She'd never actually seen her stepfather hit her mother, as he did their slaves, but he could be rough in his handling even of her.

"Oughtn't you to let Dell see to that?"

Sarah lifted her gaze — and tucked her wrist from sight. "Dell has enough to do. We'll hear your stepfather coming."

Before her mother ceased speaking, the front door opened and a boot struck the floor of the entry hall. Tamsen's stomach lurched. Her mother dropped the mending on the floor beside the chair.

Tamsen flew to her side. "I don't want to do this, Mama."

In the room beyond, footsteps crossed the floor. Her mother clasped her hand. "I know, baby. 'Twill be all right."

"Will it?"

There was no time for her mother to reply. Hezekiah Parrish stood in the doorway, hat in hand, brows drawn, forehead rising like a piled thundercloud to a receded hairline. He'd have seemed a nondescript man —

neither tall nor short, handsome nor ill made, overly lean nor fleshy — were it not for the force of resolve behind his middling appearance, refusing to be disregarded. Or disobeyed.

"It's time," he said, his gaze pinning Tamsen.

"Yes sir. I'm ready."

"Let me judge that. Turn."

With a swish of silk, Tamsen stepped away from her mother and turned, knowing every lock of hair was pinned and curled to perfection, every inch of her below the neck cinched or padded to best advantage. Knowing she hadn't, against all odds, stained or creased the gown.

Knowing her mother was fervently praying.

"Good." Mr. Parrish clapped his hat on his head. "He's waiting."

Tamsen moved toward her stepfather's proffered arm. Never mind *she* had been waiting nigh the day long, too sick with dread to force a bite of food past her lips. Such a notion wouldn't register with her stepfather. Nor with Ambrose Kincaid, she was willing to wager. Fully prepared to loathe the man, she touched her fingertips to her stepfather's coat sleeve.

At the front door, Mr. Parrish glanced at

her and frowned. "Smile," he said.

Tamsen smiled. Braced to be paraded through Morganton in all her finery, she stepped across the threshold, wondering as she did so whether those mute lambs Scripture mentioned ever screamed on the inside when they saw the altar.

3

No one could have been more astonished than Tamsen when, moments after setting eyes on Ambrose Kincaid, her internal screaming ceased. *Not an ogre, after all* had been her first grudging admission as she passed between benches in her rustling silk and he'd risen to stare like a man vision struck.

Mr. Kincaid went on staring while her stepfather barreled into formal introductions. Finally the man blinked, very nicely thanked Mr. Parrish, and requested they be left alone to conversate. With thinly veiled reluctance, Mr. Parrish complied, leaving Tamsen to settle her stomach, gather her wits, and bring herself to bear on making a favorable impression on this man her step-father meant her to marry.

Seated at a secluded table — within sight of Mr. Parrish, if not hearing — and served what Tamsen admitted was a respectable cup of tea, Mr. Kincaid had yet to look away from her. His Adam's apple bobbed above a neat cravat as he swallowed. "Miss Littlejohn, forgive my boldness in declaring you more beautiful than your portrait promised. I did not think that possible."

It was a pretty thing to say, made prettier by his refined Virginia accent. No matter, she supposed, that it was utter nonsense.

"Thank you kindly, Mr. Kincaid." Tamsen thought better of saying she found his looks less displeasing than she'd feared. His hair was unfortunate — blazing red — but his eyes were a clear and pleasing blue. He wore a waistcoat fancifully embroidered with dragonflies but had paired it with a coat of sober green that complemented his coloring. He took some thought for his appearance, but not excessively so.

Angling a glance across the taproom, she spared her stepfather a small but genuine smile — and almost laughed at the startlement on his face.

Mr. Kincaid had begun telling her of his business in North Carolina, something to do with a parcel of mountain land on the Yadkin River, left to him by . . . She reined in her attention in time to realize he spoke of his father.

". . . buried him late this spring, at Long

Meadows."

"Long Meadows?" she asked.

"My plantation on the James River, near Lynch's Ferry — Lynchburg, it's now called." He smiled then. "Truth be told, it belongs to Alexander Kincaid, my grand-father. It shall be mine, though I admit it already owns my heart."

"It certainly has a lovely name." It was out of her mouth before she realized she ought first to have acknowledged his father's passing, a recent and tragic loss, however well Mr. Kincaid concealed his grief. But his face lit at her praise of his plantation.

"It is the most beautiful tract on God's earth," he said, and went on to speak at length of acreage, crops, river frontage. And slaves. "We've eleven Negroes to the house alone, counting those in the kitchen. It is a comfortable home, Miss Littlejohn."

Comfortable. It began to seem an abomi-nable word. A comfortable cage was yet a cage. Tamsen schooled her face to pleasant interest. "Then you've no plans to home-stead above the Yadkin?"

Mr. Kincaid's russet brows rose. "None at all. The land's gone too long untended. What improvements my uncle once made are hardly to be distinguished from the wilderness encroaching upon it now."

"Your uncle? I thought your father . . ."
Warmth crept into her cheeks, having revealed her earlier inattention.

If he noticed, Mr. Kincaid overlooked her
lapse. "Yes, my uncle, but I see I have failed
to make the situation clear. My only excuse,
Miss Littlejohn, is that your presence has
me thoroughly rattled."

Or perhaps the scanty kerchief was working, she thought, as his gaze dipped below
the level of her throat.

Blushing now in earnest, Tamsen glanced
around. Few of Mrs. Brophy's patrons were
within hearing. Mr. Kincaid had chosen a
table secluded by the placement of a tall
cupboard. Still she could see nearly the
whole taproom. Her glance snagged on a
man standing at the rear door, a young
mulatto who was scanning the room. He
caught her gaze, which she quickly returned
to Mr. Kincaid, to whom she said what her
stepfather would have wanted her to say at
this pass.

"Do forgive me. It was never my intent to
rattle you so."

She smiled. Ambrose Kincaid's jaw fell
slack.

Mr. Parrish would like the way this was
progressing. How unfortunate for him that
he must sit at a distance and wait — on *her.*

She felt the sparkle that thought put in her eyes.

"Let me attempt to clarify," Mr. Kincaid said, back in possession of his jaw. "The homestead was originally my uncle's. Bryan Kincaid was my father's younger brother. I'm sorry to say there was bad blood between the two. Uncle Bryan and his wife, Fiona, left Long Meadows to homestead above the Yadkin in . . . '63 or '64, it was. Just after the French war."

Tamsen leaned forward, clasping the table's fringed cloth. "What happened to him? Your uncle?"

"He died. He and his wife. It fair broke my grandfather's heart."

Tamsen sat back. "How very tragic. How did they die?" she asked, feigning neither sympathy nor interest. Mr. Kincaid seemed flattered by both.

"That is still a mystery. Neighbors said it was raiding Indians, but we cannot be sure. Uncle Bryan took along one of my grandfather's slaves when he left Virginia. Theo, his name was. My father particularly despised him — which wouldn't of itself offer any proof of wrongdoing on Theo's part. But it is true that after Bryan's and Fiona's deaths, Theo was never heard from again." Mr. Kincaid paused, leaning across the table. "Miss Littlejohn, would your step-father approve the lurid topic of our conversation, could he hear it?"

The glint of conspiratorial humor in his eyes gave Tamsen a small thrill. "He most certainly wouldn't, but never mind him. Is there more to your uncle's story?"

"Only that Uncle Bryan surprised everyone by leaving his land to my father, after having quarreled so bitterly in the past. My father had grand plans for it once upon a time, but of course he never followed through. I'm amazed he never sold the tract. But I shall. What need have I of it when there is Long Meadows to hold me to Virginia?" He paused again, holding her gaze. "I think you would like it there."

His eyes were telling her he wanted her to like it. She thought she liked the man. At least she didn't loathe him as she'd feared. "Your father passed just this spring? I'm sorry for your loss."

"You needn't be," Mr. Kincaid replied abruptly. He must have seen her startlement. "I beg your pardon. That must sound a terrible thing to say, especially when clearly you once lost a father."

Surprised by the observation, she said, "When I was seven years old."

"And you admired him?"

"He was the light of our lives, mine and Mama's."

Mr. Kincaid reached across the table and took her hand with a boldness that stole her breath. His eyes were very blue and disconcertingly direct. "I envy you that, Miss Littlejohn. My father, in contrast, was a man to engender neither admiration nor respect. Collin Kincaid was a drunkard who brought grief to father, brother, and sons alike. I daresay most egregiously to my mother, God rest her soul. But this one good he did me — he left me land in Carolina, which in turn has brought me to you."

Tamsen saw the turning of his thoughts in his eyes, felt it in the pressure of his hand. Her stomach gave a lurch. This time her heart matched it. It was what her stepfather wanted, why she was here. She simply hadn't expected it to come to the boil so swiftly.

"Mr. Kincaid," she began, but he was already speaking.

"I cannot be anything but forthright with you, Miss Littlejohn. When I saw your portrait in Salem, I was certain you couldn't be half so beautiful, and if you were, you were bound to know it. It would have made you haughty, cold, to think all men your devoted worshipers. Instead, I find you nothing of the sort, but tender-hearted and warm. So I warn you, I am about to throw caution to the wind and —"

"Mast' Ambrose. Sorry to trouble you now, sir."

Like a fraying thread, the tension between them snapped. Tamsen looked up to find the young mulatto she'd noticed earlier standing at their table, battered hat clenched between work-scarred fingers. She looked to Mr. Kincaid. High color flamed in his face as, scowling, he said, "I asked not to be disturbed while I met with Miss Littlejohn. I was very clear."

"I ain't forgot, sir." The slave's hat was getting a thorough mangling. "But something —"

"Let it wait, Toby." Dismissing his slave with an abrupt shoulder, Mr. Kincaid reached for her hand again.

But Toby hadn't left, only taken a step behind his master, clearly too distressed to obey. Tamsen glanced across the taproom. Mr. Parrish had allowed himself to be engaged in conversation and wasn't for the moment watching. "Please, Toby? Tell us what's wrong."

"Thank you, ma'am." Mouth trembling, the slave stepped forward. "It be Tess, Mast'

44

Ambrose. She done them errands you sent her on, but some men catched her on the way back, drug her off to the woods, and took turns —"

Mr. Kincaid lurched to his feet and back-handed Toby across the mouth. The slave cringed, eyes flaring with shock. His master's face had gone chalk white. "How dare you speak such filth in front of Miss Little-john?"

Nearby conversations faltered while Mr. Kincaid, low voiced, ordered Toby from the taproom and reclaimed his seat across from her. With a kerchief from his coat, he wiped his slave's spittle off his hand.

Witnessing a lap cat transform into a panther and proceed to attack an unsuspecting passerby could not have been more shocking. Voices around them rose again, but Tamsen's ears rang as if she'd been the one struck. She looked toward her step-father. Somehow he'd missed the entire episode. She forced herself to face Mr. Kincaid. Her voice shook.

"You needn't have done that. Didn't you hear what he said? Your slave —"

"Hasn't anything to do with us," Mr. Kincaid finished for her.

"How can you say so? Of course she does."
The true cause of her distress seemed

45

finally to register: not the interruption, but his reaction to it. "Miss Littlejohn . . . I only meant *you* needn't be concerned."

"Yet I am — and you should be." This wasn't what she was meant to say now. She was meant to smile and nod and suppress whatever opinion she might hold on the matter. But she could not do it. "The people whose lives and bodies you own, those whose burden it is to see to your every need, they are your responsibility to protect."

These were her mother's words, spoken often in years past in timid counter to Mr. Parrish's callous dealings with his slaves, but she wasn't saying them in any tone of voice her mother had ever used.

"Yet you hear of such cruelty done to a woman you call your property and cannot be bothered to go to her aid? Because of *me*?" She stood so abruptly that her chair rocked back and would have hit the floor had she not caught it. "If I'm to be your excuse, Mr. Kincaid, then allow me to excuse myself from your presence. Please, go and see to her."

The faces in the taproom were a blur, all turning to gape at her flight. At the door she glanced back to see her stepfather — very much aware of her again — hurrying to where Ambrose Kincaid still sat, staring

46

after her more stunned than when she'd entered.

4

With the cattle down from the mountains, Cade and Jesse had parted with the drovers and now had only their mounts and the packhorses to manage. Or so Jesse had assumed. Turned out Cade was carrying around some peculiar notions in his head. Not till they'd reached Morganton, leading the horses, did he let on about them.

"What would you say to us getting a milch cow this trip — and some extra seed corn, more'n last year? I talked with Tate before we left. He don't mind us planting another acre or two."

"Milch cow?" Jesse halted between an oak-shaded frame house and the trade store, where the beaten path between met the town's main street. "You take up courting some woman without telling me? She got you flirting with the notion of settling down?"

A pace ahead, Cade stopped his horse and

48

said something to that, but Jesse never heard his answer, since that was the moment he saw the girl in the blue gown.

She was crossing the lane where they'd halted, moving fast and looking straight ahead, heedless of left or right — till her stride hitched like she'd put a fancy heel down wrong and she staggered smack into Cade. She'd have gone sprawling over those yards of silk petticoat had Cade not loosed his horse and snaked an arm around her slender waist to catch her.

Jesse caught the horse as Cade released the girl — a dark-eyed, dark-haired beauty, dressed finer than any female he'd ever set eyes on. Next to him and Cade, both topping six feet, she seemed as neat and tiny as a doll, and somehow not quite real.

"I — I beg your pardon," she said, not how Jesse expected such a girl would speak to a trail-begrimed stranger in buckskins who dared put his hands on her person. More like she meant it.

She looked up at Cade, and her eyes rounded. Then she looked at Jesse, who promptly forgot everything else about the girl save what was staring from her eyes — fury, fear, resolve, all in a stunning flash as real and raw as the earth beneath his moccasins and the sun beating on his back.

A shout rose from the direction she'd appeared. "Tamsen!"

The girl flinched. Breaking their gaze, she swept up her skirts and was across the lane in a blink, making for the house next door. Jesse watched her mount the steps, fumble at the door, and vanish in a swirl of blue. He barely registered the glowering man that hurried past and followed her inside. Behind the door a shout rumbled through the walls of the house to worry the street like distant thunder.

Jesse had dropped both horses' reins to gape. "Did you . . . ? Have you ever . . . ?"

Cade fetched the reins and looked down his long nose, taking full advantage of the inch of height he had on Jesse. "Did I? Have I? All that book learning I got you, and you can't find a single word to describe a chit of a girl?"

"A chit of a . . . ? Did you *see* her?"

"I saw a fancy gown, a pretty face. What'd you see?" Cade's eyes danced with amusement. "Give me *words,* boy. Or did she knock 'em clean out of your head?"

She doth teach the torches to burn bright.

Not a chance he'd stitched such words together of his own wits. He must have read them somewhere. But if he spouted them now, Cade would think him addled, right

50

enough. What, then, could he say? He'd read himself a heap of books, and the Good Book twice through, but heaven help him could he call to mind another phrase better fitting what he'd just seen. Or thought he'd seen. *Could* you glimpse a woman's soul with one look into her eyes?

"Never mind," he said, still sounding pole-axed to his own ears. "Weren't we talking 'bout cows . . . or corn?"

While her stepfather raged and her mother pleaded, Tamsen huddled in the parlor bed with a door shut between, pouring out her misery and resentment into the muffling pillow. On a pallet by the fire, Dell prayed, calling on the Almighty and His angels to hold her stepfather in check.

They'd never heard him quite this angry.

It was near dark before the front door slammed. Mrs. Brophy's house shuddered with the silence. Moments later her mother entered the parlor. Candlelight wavered, steadied. Tamsen feigned sleep, listening as Dell rose to the nightly ritual of removing her mother's gown and stays and brushing out her thick black hair.

"Law, Miss Sarah," the maid hissed through her teeth. "Look what he done to —"

51

"Hush, Dell."

"But he never —"

"The gown tore when I tried to pull from his grasp. That is all."

"He sounded terrible worked up," Dell ventured after a moment. "Ain't laid a hand on you nowhere?"

"Thank the Lord, no. Now hush."

Eventually the candle was snuffed and the bed tick sagged beneath her mother's slender weight. Tamsen faced the wall, holding herself rigid. Her heart thumped ten slow beats before reaching fingers curled around her shoulder. A smell almost of cinnamon — her mother's smell — filled her next breath. She knew what was coming.

The sense of betrayal choked like bile.

"Tamsen . . . please. Won't you give Mr. Kincaid another chance? He was so taken with you." Her mother stroked the tear-wet hair back from her face. "Mr. Parrish says he was set to propose when . . ."

When he showed his true nature, Tamsen wanted to say. A nature as mercurial as her stepfather's. Only difference being, Mr. Kincaid possessed a veneer of charm, something her stepfather lacked entirely. But charm was deceitful, and despite what the man said of her better nature, his reaction to her beauty had made her vain enough to *be* deceived. Nearly.

"Mr. Parrish means to smooth things over," her mother said into the dampness of her hair. "Convince Mr. Kincaid to see you again."

Tamsen pictured her stepfather out in the night entreating the man, making excuses, promising all manner of reform to her behavior. She was young. She was malleable. Mr. Kincaid could make of her what he wished, once the union was legal. Hezekiah Parrish wouldn't scruple to interfere with his methods, however stiffly they be meted.

And here was her mother, cowed into persuading her it was something for which she ought to be glad. It was all Tamsen could do to bear her touch, her pleading breath.

"Tamsen?"

Swallowing back the gorge of humiliation and fury, Tamsen said what she knew she must, though the words came out stiff as whale boning. "All right, Mama."

Sarah Parrish pressed a kiss behind her ear and retreated to her side of the bed. Tamsen heard the tiniest of shuddering sighs. Resentment cooled enough for concern to thread its way in. She turned in the bed. "Did he do more than shout at you,

53

Mama?"

The hesitation lasted a breath too long. "I'm fine, Tamsen. Don't worry for me."

Tamsen rolled away and lay in darkness. Listening. Waiting. Begging the Almighty to forgive her for what she was about to do. Had to do. She could bear a lot of things, she'd decided, but ending up like her mother, crushed and caged in a life too miserable and loveless for words, wasn't one of them.

An hour passed, best she could judge. Mr. Parrish didn't return. Nor did Mrs. Brophy, who kept her customers' late hours. Not until she was certain her mother and Dell both slept did Tamsen begin the measured process of easing from the bed, taking up the bundle she'd hidden at its foot, and slipping out of the room, out of the house, out of the yard.

If there was to prove a hitch in her plan, it would involve the horse. As had her stepfather, Tamsen had ridden to Morganton rather than endure the jouncing wagon ride with her mother, Dell, and Sim, but less than a mile from their destination, her mare had gone footsore. Not badly, and Sim would have seen to it in the days since. She hoped the mare had had time to heal. She also hoped wherever Sim slept, it wasn't in the stall box.

The large public stable spanned the yard behind the trade store, next door to Mrs. Brophy's house. The night was moonless. With her eyes still growing accustomed to the darkness, Tamsen felt her way past the stable's unlatched door.

Outside the air had been clammy, cool after a warm day, but the thick scents of hay and manure enveloped her as she passed the stabled mounts of Morganton residents, and of those just passing through, the air on her face warm with the heat of so much horseflesh. Snorts and shufflings followed her along the row. She found her dappled mare in the last stall but one. The horse's nose thrust over the gate, nudging Tamsen's reaching hand.

"It's me, sweet girl," she said, just above a whisper. With one hand she fondled the mare's nose, with the other groped for the sidesaddle she hoped was close to hand. The bridle and reins were there, hanging from a post, but not the saddle. She felt along the gate of the empty box at the end, peering within to see if it contained what she sought. The box was black as pitch. She banged a knee against the boards and froze, heart slamming. Sim had to be somewhere near. In the loft above?

The mare nickered. Tamsen hurried back and grasped the horse's head between soothing hands. "Hush now. We have to be quiet."

And quick. She hadn't wanted to risk dressing in the house. She'd brought the rust-brown linen petticoat and matching jacket worn on the journey to Morganton, bundled in a summer riding cloak. She opened the mare's box, set the bundle on trampled straw, and dressed clumsily in the dark. She bent for the cloak to shake it free of straw. When she straightened, a man stood in the half-open box gate.

Tamsen jumped back, dropping the cloak, startling the mare. The figure, tall and featureless, loomed closer. A hand clamped her arm.

"They're liable to hang horse thieves in these parts."

It wasn't Mr. Parrish. That brought a flare of relief, despite her heart's crazed hammering. For a second she thought it was Ambrose Kincaid, but the voice was too deep — and too unrefined. She found her voice in a rush of outrage. "I'm no thief — release me!"

"Give me good reason," said the man, sounding, of all things, amused. His grip sent panic coursing through her.

"You're hurting me!" He was, but only because she fought his grasp. He was strong, and he smelled of horses and dressed hides, and since she couldn't break his hold, she stopped struggling. He relaxed his grip.

"All right, then. If you're not set on thieving, what'd you aim to do with this fine mare?"

"Who are you, Mrs. Brophy's stable guard?" She'd edged her voice with mockery, keeping fear and desperation at bay. Whoever this interloper was, he was dangerously nigh to ruining her escape — one she was already starting to regret — but that wasn't the salient point just now.

Tamsen stepped back, nearly tripping over the cloak tangled at her feet.

The man caught her again and set her to rights as if he could see perfectly well in the dark. He made no effort to curb his voice. "I guard what's mine and Cade's. Not everyone sneaking 'round in the dark is to be trusted, are they?"

Tamsen reached for calm. "Please, keep your voice down or —"

"Miz Tamsen? That you making a racket?" Sim emerged from the shadows.

"Tamsen?" echoed the interloper, the spoiler of her plan.

"Sim . . . yes, it's all right," she said, thankful for the darkness when she felt the burn of helpless tears. "I-I heard something in the stable and . . . Where did you come from?"

"Mast' Parrish got me sleeping in the loft. But I didn't hear nothin' save you tromping about."

"Go on back to sleep, then." *And forget you saw me,* she added silently. Precious time was ticking past. Oh, what was she even doing here? What had she been thinking?

Sim hadn't budged. "You sure you all right?"

Tamsen, better able to see now, caught the glint of his eyes. He was glaring at the stranger. "I'm sure. Now go before —"

"Who is there?" a voice called down the stable's length. The voice she'd dreaded to hear.

"Go," she hissed.

Sim went, scurrying up the loft ladder, sending down a sifting of hay as light spilled through the stable door.

5

Hezekiah Parrish strode down the aisle, a horn lantern lighting his way and, incidentally, bringing out of shadow the face of the stranger who'd spoiled Tamsen's escape. It was the man she'd collided with after fleeing Mrs. Brophy's tavern. His hair was brown, tailed back none too tidily, his jaw lean and in need of a razor. He wore the same dusty buckskins and fringed linsey-woolsey shirt she'd seen him in before, with a beaded Indian belt cinching his waist.

But he wasn't the one she'd collided with, she realized. That one had been older, darker. This was the younger one who'd gaped at her as if he'd never seen a woman before. He was looking at her so now, with eyes of a peculiar golden brown. He didn't retreat before her stepfather's advance. In fact, as the lantern light swelled around them, he moved nearer.

"Get away from her." Mr. Parrish halted

nose to nose with the young man.

Nose to chin,' rather, for he was inches shorter than the stranger, who said, "Why? She got something that's catching?"

Mr. Parrish grasped her arm. "Because I'm her stepfather, impudent whelp, and I bid you do so." He turned on her, fingers biting hard. "Has he molested you in any way?"

She tried not to wince. "No sir."

"He's frightened you," her stepfather said, as if he blamed her for this state of being. "You're shaking."

She was. She was also painfully aware of the cloak in the straw that she dared not glance at, and of the young man gazing between them, eyes watchful, unreadable.

No. There was something in those eyes to be read. A brief, flaring intensity, as if he meant to communicate a thing to her alone. Before she could fathom it, her stepfather demanded, "What business have you in the stable at this unseemly hour? Have you no sense of propriety? Of what you risk?"

Risk? If he only knew.

The grip on her arm tightened. "Answer me, girl."

"No. I . . . yes." Flustered, she glanced again at those golden eyes.

"Your daughter thought she heard a

ruckus. I was bedded down with my gear." The young man nodded toward the empty stall box. "I came out when I heard her."

"Plainly all is well," Mr. Parrish said, unappeased by the explanation. "You can go back to your . . . stall."

Unruffled by the implied insult, the young man stepped forward, standing square in front of where the cloak lay. He looked down at Tamsen, ignoring her stepfather. "My apologies, miss, if I frighted you."

Tamsen risked a glance at the cloak but didn't see it. She looked up at the man in time to catch a hint of a nod that might have been meant to accompany his apology but she sensed was meant to convey something else.

"I thought I'd be safe enough to check on the mare," she choked out. Thankfully her stepfather forbore asking how she could have heard anything at the stable from Mrs. Brophy's parlor.

He reached to shut the mare's stall. "Return to the house," he bid her. "At once."

Tamsen spared the young man a look, with no idea whether she despised him for the ruination of her plan or was grateful for his inexplicable assistance in the wake of that ruination. Anger at her mother's weakness was cooling, cracking, showing her its selfish core. She wanted to run from the stable, back to her mother in their bed, tell her she didn't mean it, that she was sorry, but couldn't with her stepfather hard on her heels.

Hezekiah Parrish disapproved of females running.

"I presume your mother spoke to you of the other matter," he said as they reached the stable doors.

Ambrose Kincaid. And she could tell by his tone Mr. Parrish was certain of getting his way in the end. The desperate spark that had carried her into the night sputtered out, leaving no more than a trailing wisp of its memory.

"Yes sir," Jesse heard the girl tell her stepfather. "I've agreed to see him."

Likely she meant to sound compliant. What Jesse heard was despair.

Neither noticed him dogging their steps, quiet as a hunter. He let the stable door shut in his face, waited a breath, then opened it to peer without. The pair made for the house next door, the man with his hand clamped to the girl's arm, still berating her with words like *unseemly* and *risk*.

Jesse reckoned he was the unseemly. As for risk . . .

A shadow under the stable eave peeled away from the dark — Cade, rifle and knapsack slung at his side. "Jesse?"

"Pa. How much of that did you hear?"

"Enough to make me wonder why you lied for that girl. The only thing disturbing the horses was the two of you."

"I gave him the tale she gave. I'd no call to be saying different." He didn't mention he'd caught the girl trying to slip away into the night. That was her secret to tell.

Cade lit a lantern in the back stall. Since he was one of the few men Jesse knew who never touched hard liquor, there was little call for their crossing a tavern's threshold. Cade would've slept happy under the stars if a stall hadn't been free.

"Why'd you figure you had call to say anything — to either of them?"

Jesse lay back on his bedroll, caught Cade's gaze, and flicked his eyes toward the ceiling. Above them was the loft and the one called Sim. A groom? Whatever else, a slave with a healthy fear of his master. Jesse tapped his ear.

Cade nodded, then asked in an undertone muffled by the rustle of rolling out his blanket, "It was the girl from before? The one in blue?"

Jesse propped himself on an elbow. "Her name's Tamsen. Pretty name, huh?"

He'd been startled to find it was *that* girl banging about outside the stall where he'd just drifted to sleep. Not till the first beam of lantern light struck those dark eyes scowling up at him had his blood quickened with recognition. Seeing her out of that fancy gown and closer up than she'd been on the street, it was clear she had a decent height to her. It must have been that tight-cinched dress and Cade's nearness that made her seem so tiny. Not that she wasn't slight as a wisp. His skin still tingled with memory of her slender arm beneath his hand . . .

"Jesse." It was a chiding growl.

"Yeah, Pa?"

"What are we in Morganton for?"

"I know what we're here for."

"Salt, sugar, lead . . ." Cade reeled off the list as if Jesse hadn't spoken. As if they hadn't done this trek years running. "And to hire on with the next crop of wagons headed west — which I may have found while you were dallying with a girl you'd no business looking twice at."

"Tamsen," Jesse said again, liking how it felt to say it. "Don't know her back name. Yet."

"Don't matter. That girl's the last thing you need to be thinking on." Cade settled and snuffed the lantern candle. "You hear me, Jesse Bird?"

In the darkness Jesse smiled. "I hear you."

"You best."

"G'night, Pa."

After Cade slept, Jesse got up and opened the neighboring box to retrieve the cloak he'd hidden in the straw. The mare had put a hoof on it. He ran his hand down a foreleg, urging it to lift, and felt the telltale heat and swelling above the fetlock as the mare obliged. Had the girl made good her escape, she'd not have gotten far. Jesse would've thought her foolish for trying had something in her stepfather's eyes not sent a cold stake through his belly. He hadn't known he was thwarting an escape when he rose to investigate her noise, but now it was done.

What had he sent her back to?

As he bundled the cloak among his belongings, there came a rustle from the loft above. On the morrow, Jesse decided, he'd have himself a talk with Sim, the groom.

6

After breakfast, Tamsen's mother retired to the parlor with Dell to see the blue gown freshened. Her stepfather, having failed to speak with Mr. Kincaid the previous evening, went out again in search of the man. Mrs. Brophy went to see to her tavern. Tamsen, seizing the moment, slipped out to the stable to retrieve her cloak.

Dressed in her riding clothes, hair pinned under a cap, she drew little notice in the yard, though here and there men and women were going about their business. Inside the stable a man was shoveling manure into a cart, halfway down the aisle. Morning shadows showed her no more than a long back and broad shoulders that strained against a shirt.

She pressed on, hoping he'd ignore her while she found her cloak and hurried out.

Hearing her step, the man rested the shovel, propped a moccasined foot on its blade, and boldly watched her approach. Tamsen glanced aside and met the eyes of the man who'd sabotaged her escape in the night. Startled, she stumbled into the cart. He thrust the shovel away and moved to catch her.

Blushing at the memory of his hands on her in the darkness, she caught herself and stepped back from his reach. "I never took you for a stable hand."

A corner of his mouth lifted, as if in amusement. "Clever of you, since I ain't one."

His voice was well timbred, if uncultured. Aside from his eyes, it was the only true impression she'd carried from their midnight encounter. He was taller than she recalled — her eyes were level with the sun-browned hollow of his throat, visible since he wore no manner of neckcloth. His hair was tied back but seemed barely tamed. The brown of it was sun streaked, putting her in mind of a hawk's variegated feathers.

There was something hawklike in all his features. His thin-bridged nose was slightly aquiline, the nostrils curved in faint echo of a raptor's beak, narrowly flared as though he'd just scented something — prey perhaps — on a breeze. He'd shaved off yesterday's beard stubble, leaving clear the lines of cheekbones and jaw slanting forward to a chin indented by a slight cleft, kept from sharpness only by the wide, full-shaped mouth above it. Taken with those gold-brown eyes, the total effect wasn't so much displeasing as disconcerting. It was a wild face. Maybe a reckless one. And she hadn't liked his tone.

"If you aren't a stable hand, what business have you mucking stalls?"

"Those lacking coin to pay their way use what they got. In my case, time and muscle."

Muscle he had, especially through the shoulders, though the shape of him under shirt and buckskin trousers was lean.

Not trousers, she realized, catching a scandalizing glimpse of skin below his shirt-tail. He wore a breechclout, embroidered at its edges, and leggings that left his upper thighs bared. She dragged her gaze back to his face to find him smiling, boldly return-ing her inadvertent scrutiny. Did he pre-sume what passed between them in the night gave him the right to ogle her so?

She was scouring her mind for a recrimi-nation withering enough to suit when he said, "You'll be wanting your cloak back, I reckon."

The cloak. Reminded of her errand, she pushed past him and headed for the stall.

Her mare thrust out a dappled head, which she pushed aside as well. The straw beneath the mare's hooves was freshly strewn. There was no cloak. She turned to confront the man, to find he'd followed her silently. She stepped back, lifting her chin. "What did you with it? Return it at once — please."

"I'd aimed to." He tilted his head, beckoning her. Warily she followed him to the last stall. Stacked therein were bundles wrapped in oilcloth, two saddles, packsaddle frames, rifles, and other sundries she supposed men needed when traveling long distance by horse. But a bow and quiver of arrows? She narrowed her eyes at the man as he moved among the stacks.

"You're a white man, aren't you?" she blurted before thinking better of it.

"Guilty as charged." He turned with her cloak in hand and, as if to reinforce the observation, made her the mock of a courtly bow as he handed it over. "Your cloak, miss."

The dark wool had been brushed and folded. "Thank you." The words nearly stuck in her throat.

He crossed his arms, studying her. "Is this you thanking me for the cloak or for saving you landing in a worse shambles than it seems you're already in?"

She felt her brows soar. "Saving me? Are you under the delusion that you rescued me last night? If I'm in a shambles, then it's your fault, in the main." It was a ridiculous exaggeration, but she fixed him with a glare she hoped would put him in his place.

"Hold on now," he said, arms uncrossing. "I lay no claim to having aught to do with whatever drove you out here in the dark last night. But I did have a talk with your groom this morning." He jerked his chin at the neighboring stall. "That mare's lame."

"Still?" A stab of guilt deflated her pride. She hadn't spared the horse a thought since her flight was curtailed. The man's mouth twisted, sparking her to add, "I'd have checked had I not been interrupted."

"I checked. It'd be plain cruel to ride her again inside a week. Whatever your scheme was, reckon it's good I interrupted it."

"Good?"

"For your horse. She needs time to heal. Time to herself, to recover."

It was disconcerting the way those golden eyes looked straight into hers as he spoke. He was still talking about the horse, wasn't he? Only *time* was the very thing she desperately needed. Her stomach rolled, thinking of what was yet to come that day. Another meeting with Mr. Kincaid, if her stepfather arranged it. Even if not, there would be some other rich prospect eventually. Another sprawling plantation, worked by more men and women bound to servitude than Mr. Parrish could hope to own in a lifetime.

The man in the stall had crouched to fold up the oilskin bundle where he'd put her cloak. "Where'd you aim to go," he asked, "had you got away?"

"I hadn't thought that far." To whom could she have fled? There was no one in the world she trusted who wasn't under her stepfather's influence. No place of refuge. Nowhere to hide.

She'd never felt so great a fool. Maybe she ought to be grateful for this interfering —

"Then tell me this." Crouched still, he looked up at her, balanced on the balls of his feet. "What's gone so amiss for that blossom-eyed girl I saw yesterday, the one all decked in blue, that riding off alone in the night seems a better prospect than sticking with her kin?"

For all it was gently voiced, the question cut a swath across her heart. "I see myself becoming my mother," she whispered.

"Is that the worst thing you can imagine?"

Why she should think so was beyond her, but Tamsen sensed the man knew more of her situation than she'd revealed — and that he'd help her, if she asked. The impulse to do so swept over her in a dizzying rush. His sharp eyes must have seen it. A hand, big, soiled from mucking, rose as if he meant to take hold of hers.

Tamsen stepped back, cloak clutched to her chest, fingers digging into the wool. She could never ask this man for help. What could he possibly do for her? Frustration and despair surged up, and there was nowhere else to vent it.

"Why did you have to interfere?"

He unfolded his tall self with a dignity she hadn't suspected he possessed. "To spare your poor horse. If you lack the sense to consider the needs of those that serve you, reckon someone has to step up and do it in your stead."

The indictment stung. That this uncouth, rustic white *savage* had the audacity to reproach her with the very shortcoming she'd laid at the feet of Ambrose Kincaid —

"How dare you say such a thing to me?"

"Well, now. I've faced down charging bears and starving wolves and murdering Chickamaugas. Reckon the pique of a pretty miss ain't like to daunt me." Those striking amber eyes twinkled — with laughter.

Tamsen had no memory of whirling on

her heel and exiting the stall. So complete was her fury at his impudence, his unfairness, not a single thought of her stepfather, the blue gown, or Ambrose Kincaid crossed her mind for the half minute it took her to reach Mrs. Brophy's back door.

7

Torn betwixt amusement at the girl and regret for her unhappiness, Jesse Bird went back to shoveling dung. He'd only meant to tease, not offend, but had to admit the snap in her dark eyes before she'd flounced out of the stable had set his blood to racing. Fragile as a broom twig she might look, but she had spirit, and boldness to speak her mind — to him at least.

Tamsen Littlejohn. He'd gotten her full name out of Sim, and that of her stepfather, Parrish. He knew they'd come from Charlotte Town so the girl might secure herself a bridegroom, a planter from Virginia besotted by a portrait of her he'd seen. And he knew Tamsen hadn't taken to the man, even with riches to sweeten the pie.

'Course she hadn't, Jesse thought, piling the last of the manure into the cart. Back on the trace he'd told Catches Bears and Thunder-Going he'd know *the one* when

he found her. He'd said it to hush their fool talk about White Shell, was all. Twice now he'd seen Tamsen Littlejohn to talk to. Neither conversation had ended well. Still he couldn't shake what he'd sensed at that first meeting of their eyes. Tamsen Littlejohn just might be the woman the Almighty intended for him.

Jesse wheeled the cart outside. In the yard behind the trade store, he spotted Cade, talking with the clerk and three men he took on sight for poor farmers with big dreams of Overmountain land, looking for a guide to take them west.

Cade nodded him over.

Jesse paused at a rain barrel to wash, wiped his hands on his shirttail, and strode over to the men. He shook hands and set names to memory, marking the one who put himself forward as leader of the trio, each head of a family, with stock and canvased wagons camped outside of town.

Jesse knew his part. He was the white face, the one to ease whatever qualms settlers had in putting their safety in the hands of a man who looked too much like the Chickamaugas they feared. Sure as sunrise, once Jesse made it clear he'd be along for the crossing, their wary faces eased. The lead man voiced his intention of settling along the Nolichucky.

"Hear tell General Sevier's got himself a brand-new state yonder. The State of Franklin."

"The back country is in a state," said the store clerk. "Though whether it ought to be called Franklin or the Great Divide, I'll leave it to you folk to reckon. Politics runs high t' other side o' these mountains."

Jesse watched their faces as the clerk described the situation Overmountain, where many of the leading men like John Sevier had formed a separate state after North Carolina ceded her western lands to the Union three years back, not knowing till after they'd set up the Franklin government and shaken hands and signed their names that the General Assembly had snatched back those lands in a repeal of the cession. Now everyone's hackles were up, and neither side was backing down in their say on who should claim, protect — and tax — the Watauga settlers. North Carolina or Franklin. Old State or New State.

"God alone knows where the confusion will end," the clerk said. "A man might do better going right on through the Cumberland Gap, follow Boone and his lot up into Kan-tuck-ee."

"What of the Shawnees up along the Ohio?" the lead man asked. "We hear tell that's a bloodier ground by far."

Cade and Jesse exchanged a glance. "If you're fretted over Indians, you'd best keep east of the mountains," Cade said. "Forting up from time to time, having a crop or a cabin burnt, that's going to be a way of life once you cross over."

Jesse knew Cade didn't like seeing so many settlers heading west, filling up the coves where the Cherokees and Shawnees once hunted. But settlers were coming whether he liked it or not. What bothered Cade more were tales of women and children scalped in the passes before ever setting foot on the land where they hoped to prosper.

Movement glimpsed sidelong made Jesse turn to see Sim outside the stable, with him a dark-skinned woman he recognized as Parrish's maid. The two had their heads together. The woman cast a glance toward the Brophy house, where Tamsen was staying. Sim looked toward the store yard, catching Jesse's eye. Taking hold of the maid's arm, Sim drew her inside the stable.

Jesse knew the look of two people conspiring. Over what, he couldn't say. Much was amiss in that household.

"Mata-howesha," he murmured.

"What isn't good, Jesse?" Cade's Shawnee was still as fluent as his own, but Jesse shook his head, thinking it best he held his tongue — in any language.

The settlers were saying they'd wait and see the lay of the land and decide whether they meant to file a claim on the Nolichucky or head to Kentucky instead. "All we're asking of you is to get us over safe," he said, nodding toward the blue rise of foothills to the northwest. "Help us keep our scalps and stock and young'uns along the way. You swear to that and we'll talk about compensation."

"I can avow," the store clerk said, "not a man, woman, or puppy dog has regretted placing their lives in the hands of Cade and Jesse Bird."

The light slanting through the window heralded sunset; still Mr. Parrish had not returned. With pins and combs and the hot iron, Dell had swept back Tamsen's heavy curls and tamed them into ringlets, secured at the crown with a lace pinner in place of a cap, to show off more of her handiwork. Tamsen was dressed to stays and petticoat, hose and heeled silk shoes but didn't want to don the blue gown until certain a meeting would take place.

"Dell, I think 'tis time. Why don't you go on out to Sim?"

Tamsen turned from pacing the room to stare at her mother, dressed in nutmeg silk, then at Dell, who'd just set the cooling iron on the hearth. She'd heard her mother dismiss their maid after a thousand hair dressings, yet never in such a manner. *Go on out to Sim?* And what did that sorrowing look coming over Dell's face signify?

"Go now," Sarah Parrish said. "If this is still what you want."

"Miss Sarah . . . thank you." Dell cast her mother an anguished look, then hurried from the room, tears spilling down her brown cheeks.

Tamsen stared after her. "Mama, what's upset Dell?"

Her mother was inspecting the blue gown, hung from one of the bedposts, though there couldn't be a crease left hiding in its folds. "Never mind Dell. 'Tis you we must speak of now. I've been informed of what you tried to do last night."

Tamsen sank onto the foot of the bed, twisting her fingers together. "I'm sorry, Mama. I don't know what I was thinking."

Another lie. She'd let desperation drive her to attempt something that, had it suc-

79

ceeded, would have haunted her the rest of her days. Abandoning her mother. Yet remorse ran countercurrent to resentment at being trapped by the person she loved best in the world.

Her voice shook as she asked, "Does *he* know?"

"You'd know if he did. Sim was circumspect."

More so than she'd been, apparently. Her mother had been unusually silent the day long. Tamsen, stewing in her misery, had left her to Dell's company, the pair often whispering together. About what?

"And there is no need to tell me you are sorry. 'Tis I should be saying that to you."

Tamsen frowned at the back of her mother's neck, at the coil of black hair swept up sleek and elegant, the crown of it decorously covered. "What do you mean, Mama? What are you sorry for?"

"For every choice I've made since the day your father died. For standing by while Mr. Parrish has done all in his power to see you make the same choices." Despite her words, Tamsen's mother turned with her beautiful face serenely calm. "There is one thing more on the subject of Mr. Kincaid I need to ask you, Tamsen. Have you considered there is occasion for you to do great good

80

in all of this, in marrying that man?"

"Good for whom?"

"For Mr. Kincaid's people. They will have a mistress eventually, and there are far less kind ones than you would make. Your presence in his house could mean all the difference in their lives. That is no small thing to which to devote oneself."

Tamsen had begun shaking her head before her mother finished speaking. "If that's what you think, Mama, then answer me this. Did marrying you make a difference in how Mr. Parrish treats his slaves?" *Look how he treats us,* she wanted to scream.

Her mother must have plucked those stillborn words from the air and taken them to heart. Her face drained of color, yet it held its resolve. Moving as if in a daze, she drew Tamsen to the chairs by the hearth. Her hands were cold.

"Not a blessed difference," she said, with a conviction all the more startling for its suddenness. "Still, Mr. Kincaid may prove more open to influence. Aren't you willing to give him that chance?"

"Not unless I'm forced to it. Mama, is there a way out of this? If Mr. Parrish doesn't know I tried to run away, maybe *we* could try . . . together?"

Her mother drew a shaky breath. "I have

81

little doubt of it coming to that, Tamsen. And I believe 'tis here, in Morganton, where we must make the attempt. But not in secret. It must be done openly, with as many as we can muster to bear witness."

This wasn't making sense. At long last her mother wanted to break free of Mr. Parrish, but she didn't want to run away in secret? What other option was there?

Her mother read her bewilderment. "There's something I have never told you, Tamsen. Something that could prevent your marrying Mr. Kincaid, or any man like him. But more importantly, it should free us both from Mr. Parrish, if we can convince the right people to believe it. But 'tis a risk, all the same."

Tamsen could barely catch her breath. She grasped her mother's wrist. The pulse beneath her fingers beat hard. Her mother's dark eyes met hers, wide with fear but something else that made them shine. Hope?

"Mama, tell me."

"Where do I start? There's so little time. First I must tell you about your father, about what Stephen did for me when —"

"Shut — your — mouth!"

Unheralded in their distraction, Hezekiah Parrish had returned. He crossed the room, snatched her mother's arm from Tamsen's grasp, and with the sound of tearing seams, yanked her to her feet.

"You swore to me, Sarah. Why are you breaking your word?"

Pain thinned her mother's lips. "We were speaking of Mr. Kincaid's slaves. I was explaining to Tamsen —"

"You were speaking of *Stephen Littlejohn.*" He spat the name as if it tasted foul. In its wake fell a silence so complete Tamsen heard her heart slamming against her tight-drawn stays. She stared, a coldness in the pit of her belly, as her mother smiled.

"I made you no promise never to speak of my husband," she said with a calm that raised the hairs on Tamsen's arms — in the seconds before Mr. Parrish drew back his fist and hit her mother full in the face.

Her fall toppled the chair on which she'd sat, her heavy petticoats tangling with its legs. The crack of her head hitting the hearth was audible over the chair's crash.

For an instant Tamsen couldn't move, so cruel was the blow, so shocking its results. She gaped at her mother, sprawled and still. "Mama?"

Sarah Parrish made no sound. Blood spilled from her nose, running rivulets across her mouth and chin.

"Stephen Littlejohn is dead," Mr. Parrish shouted at her mother. "You are mine, and you will do as you are bid. You and your daughter are *mine.*"

While behind her Mr. Parrish raged, Tamsen stared at her mother's blood, a red stain that blossomed until it filled her vision. Filled her soul. With a screech of rage, she flew at her stepfather, fingers clawed to rake his face, gauge his eyes, tear him into a thousand pieces.

She never even scratched him. He caught her neatly, thick fingers closing over her wrists with appalling strength. Their faces were inches apart, his dark with fury. He freed one hand and clouted her, just above the ear. Where a bruise wouldn't show.

Tamsen plowed into the bed. Grasping the coverlet, she pulled herself onto the tick and rolled over, head ringing. Her stepfather hadn't pursued her.

"Repair your hair. Put that on." Issuing orders as though his violence against them had affected him not in the least, Mr. Parrish shoved a finger toward the gown hanging from the bedpost. "Ambrose Kincaid will see you. You're to apologize for your previous indecorous behavior. If he should offer again, you will accept his proposal of marriage."

"I won't." It came out a sob, not the blazing defiance she'd intended. "He's the one who should apologize."

Mr. Parrish advanced to the bed. Leaning over her, he grasped her chin with squeezing fingers, forcing her to look at him. To her humiliation, a whimper escaped her lips. "I'm sorry."

"I am not the one who cares to hear that lie out of your pretty mouth." He released her and withdrew, leaving behind a cloud of stale breath. "You will make your apologies — convincingly. You will give him every encouragement to repeat his offer of marriage. *Every* encouragement. Should he do so, you will answer him with an immediate acceptance. Am I clear?"

Tamsen risked a glance at the hearth. Her mother hadn't moved. "Yes sir. But . . . Mama."

Hezekiah Parrish was already at the door, too consumed with the fly at the edge of his web to concern himself with the one long caught. "Let the maid see to her. You've an hour to make yourself decent."

8

Unsteadied by the ringing in her head, Tamsen lurched across the room before the front door had shut. "Mama!"

Conscious now, Sarah Parrish's mouth sagged as she gasped in breath, a wet, labored sound, more alarming than the blood seeping from her swelling nose.

"Mama, you're choking. Can you sit up?" Tamsen slid a shaking hand behind her mother's head to help raise her. Seeming dazed, her mother pushed herself off the hearth to sit, slumped in a tangle of petticoats. Blood spattered the nutmeg silk.

"I'm all right." Her voice was as thick as her breath.

Tamsen stared at the hand that had cupped her mother's head. Blood slicked her fingers. "You aren't all right, Mama. Look."

Sarah's head swayed like a flower too heavy for its stem. She put a hand to her temple. "I don't know . . ."

Tamsen got her mother on her feet and half-carried her to the bed. She lowered her head to a pillow, smearing blood over the coverlet and her embroidered petticoat. "You need help, Mama. I'll find Dell."

Where was the maid?

Go on out to Sim. The stable. Before she took a step, her mother grasped her hand. "Dell's gone her way."

"Mama —" Tamsen faltered, looking back at her mother's battered face. At first she thought it was the light — the sun was setting, casting the room in a swelling amber glow — for a youthful gloss had flushed her mother's skin despite the cruel effects of her stepfather's blow. A gloss she hadn't possessed in years. But it wasn't the light. It came from within.

It was joy. Her mother glowed with it, smiling through the blood on her mouth and chin.

"Has Stephen come? Where is your papa?" Her mother was staring at a corner of the room, as if Dell, their troubles, and her injury were matters too insignificant to concern her now. As if something long anticipated was about to transpire there. Fear slipped cold down Tamsen's spine.

"What are you saying? Mama, look at me.

Where is Dell?"

"Tamsen . . ." Her mother's voice was losing strength, though her grip still anchored Tamsen to the bedside. "Get the box."

"What box?"

Sarah's fingers fluttered to the bodice of her gown, fumbling for something tucked beneath her blood-spattered kerchief. There was a cord around her mother's neck, tucked into her bodice. Tamsen pulled it free. On it hung a key, small and dark. From the clothespress Tamsen grabbed her mother's scissors, left out for repairs to the gown. She snipped the cord. The key dropped into her hand, warm from her mother's body.

Sarah's eyes strayed again to that corner, seeing something Tamsen couldn't. Behind their almost feverish glow, urgency glittered. "In my trunk . . ."

"Mama, whatever this is, it can wait —"

"You have to know. *Hurry* . . ."

Sick with dread, Tamsen went to her mother's trunk, pushed against the wall where Sim had left it. She knelt and rummaged among the few contents still unpacked until she found what she thought her mother meant — a box the size of a bread loaf, dark with age, hinged with iron. She set it on the floor and fumbled with the key. The lock was rusted. The key wedged tight. She wrenched it sideways. Finally it sprang. Inside were papers. Letters with broken seals. She fingered through them, heart hammering, the need to dump them in a heap and run for help all but overwhelming. How long had her stepfather been gone? Five minutes? Ten?

"Mama, what is all this? Why —" A paper caught her eye, silencing her. The name *Sarah* was penned near the top, under a date. April 1767. Tamsen snatched it from the box and skimmed the first lines.

I, Stephen Joseph Littlejohn of the Colony of North Carolina and County aforesaid, owner & possessor of Sarah, a female slave of mixed blood . . .

It was a request for manumission. The petitioner was her father.

Hands shaking, Tamsen checked the date again. A year before her birth. She rifled through the papers, coming up with a more official-looking document bearing the seal of the North Carolina Assembly, dated later that same year.

The petition of Stephen Joseph Littlejohn praying that the petitioner may have a license to set free and liberate from slavery a certain female slave of mixed blood named Sarah, owned by the petitioner, was preferred and read to the Court, and it being also certified to the Court that the said Sarah is of good and meritorious character; the Court after taking the same under mature consideration do allow the said petition, and do grant the said Stephen Littlejohn license to set free and liberate the said Sarah agreeably to the prayer of said petition.

Tamsen raced through the convoluted words, trying to make sense of them. *A certain female slave of mixed blood.* Seconds passed while her mind spun on the edge of an abyss, scrabbling for denial.

Then her breath caught. Her mother's arduous breathing had quieted.

Tamsen lurched for the bed. "Mama?"

The sunset glow had fled the room, stealing with it the rich hue of her mother's skin. The flesh across her graceful bones had turned the gray of ashes, the blood on her face darkening to brown. Her eyes were closed, save for slits through which their darkness gleamed, no longer with joy.

She hurtled into the dusk and crossed the yard to the stable. Inside she halted and looked to the loft ladder down the shadowy, deserted aisle. "Sim — are you there?"

No reply came, save the ruckle and champ of horses that peered at her over their boxes.

"Dell," she hissed, fearing every shadow lest Mr. Parrish step from it.

Her fear materialized in a tall form coming at her through the stable door, from outside. With a cry she whirled and struck.

He moved fast, catching her upraised hand. "Easy there."

Captured by a man's grip for the second time that evening, Tamsen yanked with all her might. Pain seared her bruised wrist, making her cry out. Her captor stepped back, opening the stable doors to the failing light, showing her the disconcerting face of the young man in deerskins — this time complete with fringed coat.

Recognition lit his features. "I didn't aim to hurt you, miss." He reached for her, but she cringed back, raising a hand smeared with her mother's blood. Seeing it, his gaze scrabbled over her as if seeking its source. She'd fled the house in her fine embroidered petticoat, now a bloodstained ruin, nothing up top but her shift and stays. "Are you hurt?"

"Mama — She —" Desperation tripped her tongue. "She won't wake up, and I can't find Sim or Dell."

"I doubt you will. You aren't hurt?"

"No. Mama is!"

His eyes swept her once more. "Take me to her."

It wasn't the help she'd sought, but she needed no persuasion to accept it. "Hurry."

Her mother lay as she'd left her, battered and still. Wincing at the sight of her, the man pressed his fingers to her neck. He waited, leaning close, an alien presence smelling strong of horse and wood smoke, pines and sun. Yet his calm was some re-assurance. Until he straightened and met her pleading gaze. Despair swallowed hope as she saw in his eyes what he had no need to say.

She tried to push past him. He caught her shoulders between strong hands. "Did your stepfather do this?"

"Yes."

His eyes were stricken with shock, outrage. The muscles in his lean jaw hardened, but while she was fast losing her head, he kept his. "Are you in danger?"

Tears pooled, running from her eyes. She pressed her hands to them. "He means me to marry Mr. Kincaid. Mama was going to tell me a way out of it all, only *he* came before she could." She was babbling but couldn't stop. "He hit Mama for it and she fell. He's killed her and now . . . I'm supposed to be getting *dressed.*"

With that last word burning her throat like bile, she wrenched out of his grasp and lunged for the blue gown. She ripped it from the bedpost with bloodied hands and hurled it into the dying hearth fire. It caught flame at once. Still she went after it, kicking its silken folds onto the grate.

The man stood back, staring at the burning gown, and her, in something like awe. "You aren't minded to marry this Kincaid fellow?"

"I'd rather be dead."

She turned to stare in horror at the bed. Had she said such a thing, with her mother lying dead right there? Time and the world and her heart shattered, falling to pieces.

The man was speaking again, but his words were slow to penetrate. "Is there somewhere you can go? Kin to take you in, protect you?"

Tamsen stared at him. She was alone. The friends she had in Charlotte Town wouldn't be her friends if the truth she'd just discovered was made known. What was the truth? That her mother hadn't been the daughter of a Spanish merchant, as she'd always believed, but a slave? She looked down at the innocuous little box, its key still protruding from the lock. She'd always known her mother held the key to their freedom. She hadn't imagined a literal key. And the box, the papers. Whatever was she to do with them? What *could* she do? Whatever plan her mother had for the box's contents, it had died with her.

"There's no one." She clamped her hand across her mouth and fixed her gaze on the only person left who seemed to care about her plight. The young man's chest rose and fell beneath his deerskin coat, as if his heart pounded like hers, as if he, too, sensed the world knocked off kilter. But when he spoke, his voice was steady.

"Tell me how to help you. What do you want to do?"

To be given that choice now, after the one person she'd wanted to make it with was snatched away . . . It was too cruel.

"There's nothing I *can* do." Except bury her mother and marry Ambrose Kincaid, and spend the rest of her life trying to lessen the misery of everyone around her . . . if not her own.

The man took a step nearer, his eyes holding hers, something growing in them at odds with her panicked, spiraling thoughts. Something strong and calming. "There's one thing. I can get you away from Heze-kiah Parrish. And that planter. You don't have to marry him. Not if you don't want to."

"You mean run away . . . with you?" As she said the words, realization burst upon her. "That's what Sim and Dell have done — run away together."

Her mother had known. Her mother had been complicit. *Go on out to Sim.*

"I think so," the man said. "But it's you I'm worried for. Listen. I can take you where you won't be found, but it's got to be now. Right now. If your stepfather gets hold of you, I misdoubt I'll get near you again."

Fear clawed at her. "What about Mama?"

Compassion moved his face, but his voice held firm. "She'll be seen to. There's good people in this town. If I judge your step-father right, he'll make a decent show of things."

The injustice of it was a wailing in her soul. "He did this."

"I know he did. But the truth will keep. Right now we've got to get you someplace safe."

Tamsen glanced aside at the box her mother had spent her last breaths to tell her of, its soul-rattling contents spilled across the floor. Then she looked back at the man watching her, earnest and ready for anything, it seemed. "You'll help me? Truly?"

"I will." A simple answer, unadorned with explanation, yet it had the power to dispel all but one clear thought: *escape.*

"All right."

He blinked, as if he hadn't expected her trust. Then his jaw firmed. "Your stepfather said he'd be back for you? How long since?"

She couldn't think. The past moments were stretched and blurred.

The man reached for her, his grip on her shoulder urgent. "Tamsen, how long have we got?"

"Half an hour? I don't know." She started moving about the room, gathering up a hairbrush, a set of pockets, heading for the clothespress for her riding gown.

From the doorway he called to her. "What're you doing?"

She turned, petticoat and fitted jacket draped over her arm. "Packing."

"No time. Just get that cloak. By morning you'll want it. I've all else we need."

Dumbly obeying, she stuffed the hairbrush into a pocket and snatched her cloak from the clothespress.

The box. She couldn't leave that. Rushing to it, she scooped the papers inside and jammed it shut. The key rattled loose and fell to the floor. She shoved it back into the lock.

"Tamsen, hurry!"

She gathered up her clothing and the box and started for the door, only to lurch back to the bed to kiss her mother's brow. With the faintest scent of cinnamon lingering behind her, she stumbled toward the outstretched arm of the last man on earth she'd have expected to take her away from Morganton.

9

Having spent the better part of an hour shifting horses and supplies to the settlers' camp, Jesse had been returning for his own horse when he'd encountered Tamsen Littlejohn in the stable. He brought the horse, saddled, to the back door of the house where she waited. She'd stripped off the bloodied petticoat and donned the plainer clothing he'd seen her in once before.

It was near full dark. The town folk's comings and goings centered on the tavern — too close for Jesse's comfort. He led the horse till they were into the woods, Tamsen holding tight to his coat sleeve all the while, clutching the cloak she'd bundled around her box.

He stopped beneath a spreading oak. "All right, you mount up. I need to fetch my kit, tell Cade I'm bound away."

The girl didn't raise a foot to the stirrup.

"I can't."

In the dark under the tree, he made out the oval of her face, those big eyes staring at him, unblinking as an owl's. "You were keen to ride last night. You have ridden a horse?"

"Yes, but I can't ride astraddle. My ankles will show."

Had his heart not been banging into his ribs, Jesse might've laughed. "Where we're headed no one's gonna see 'em but me — and I've seen a woman's legs before."

She hadn't liked his answer. She backed away.

Before she eluded his reach, he bent, grabbed the front of her petticoat at the knee, and drew the hunting knife from his belt. "Don't move."

She made a sound like a mouse-squeak as he thrust the knife tip through the linen and slit her petticoat, knee to hem. He sheathed the knife, swooped her into his arms — cloak, box, and all — and hoisted her into the saddle. She clung astride, too shocked to lash out. All the same he backed out of reach of the blue silk shoe dangling below the torn petticoat.

"I'll be back by the time you get yourself sorted. Don't ride off without me." He didn't wait for protest but ran into the night, moccasins striking loamy earth. There wasn't time to lead the horse through the maze of brush and forest and back again before her stepfather found her gone. Still he hated to leave her adrift, mind filled with turmoil and the image of her dead mother. That last haunted him, pumping rage through his blood, tempting him to hunt down Parrish. He sheathed that urge and ran on, skirting yards, passing privies and wash kettles, praying no dog scented him and raised a ruckus. At last he sighted firelight through the trees, shining off faces, canvas. The settlers' camp. Cade sat at the head man's fire, sharing supper. He'd been welcomed at their board, such as it was. It eased Jesse's guilt over what he was fixing to do. But only a bit.

Sweating under his coat, he circled around to where he'd left their kit. A wagon stood between their small camp and the others. Jesse slipped in. Half by feel he collected rifle, bullet-bag, bow and quiver, knapsack and bedroll, slinging everything crosswise over his shoulders. He circled the camp till he was behind Cade and made a wood thrush's fluty call. Cade's head lifted.

Jesse waited, fretting. Would Tamsen spook? Steal his horse and take off for parts unknown? She'd no reason to trust him. That she'd given herself into his care spoke only of desperation. Her life in his hands felt fragile as a bird's. *Lead me on from here. Guard and keep her . . . even if it's from my best intentions.*

He quit praying when Cade rose from the fire. Like a man heeding nature's call, he came toward Jesse's place of hiding. Jesse waited till he was far enough from the fire, then said with a half breath, "Here."

Cade's sharp ears found him in the dark. "Jesse? What're you doing? Come on in —"

"Can't, Pa." A breeze threshed the hardwoods, sound enough to cover their talk. "I'm heading out, going to scout the trail."

Cade was a shadow at his side. Jesse sensed him stiffen. "You hear tell of trouble? Thought we'd head out on the Catawba trace, then aim for Roan Mountain —"

"No trouble. Leastwise not on the trace. Can't tell you why, but I got to start tonight."

Cade had him by the arm now, as if trying to sense in his flesh what he couldn't see for the dark. "You get yourself into mischief back in town?"

"There's mischief right enough, but none of my doing." Parrish had seen his face by lantern light but didn't know him from Adam. Even if he fell under suspicion, the man hadn't seen him with Cade. The less

Cade knew, the less he'd have to conceal. "You trust me, Pa, that I ain't done wrong?"

"If you say so, then it's so. But what of this company? These men expect you to be part of this crossing."

"Tell 'em what I'm doing — scouting the trail. I'll meet up with you. Say, 'round back of Bald Mountain to begin with."

"After that?"

"Depends. I may need to lay low for a time." A squirrel chittered in the boughs above. An acorn dropped through the branches, skimming Jesse's shoulder. There came a space of pounding heartbeats while Cade made up his mind.

"All right, Jesse. Just be where you say you'll be."

Cade's gruffness told Jesse how far he was reaching to let him go without explaining himself. Jesse felt the burden of that trust as keen as that of the woman waiting for him under the oak, doubtless holding by a thread. He grasped Cade's arm, felt the sureness of the hand gripping back.

"I will be. Pray for me." Jesse broke away, trying for a grin, though it was too dark for Cade to see it. "I'm thinking, after all, you might want to get that cow."

Jesse chose a trail out of Morganton unsuited to wagon travel. Few were so, being old Indian traces or buffalo paths that migrated about for miles to vanish high among the rocks and rhododendron, or down in the canebrakes thick along streams. Jesse planned to make confounding use of them.

Hours later, with the moon risen at their backs, he halted on the steepening trace and dismounted. "I'll lead us for a bit. Horse can't go all night carrying double." When Tamsen said nothing to this, he hesitated, wondering at her mettle. "We got to get deep in the high country before dawn. If'n you need to see to things, now's the time."

Seeming to grasp his meaning, she cast a look into the nightblack foliage crowding close. Something rustled in a nearby thicket. She said a hasty, "No."

It was past midnight, by his reckoning, first time she came sliding out of the saddle. He'd been picking their way up a stony incline, alone with his thoughts but wide awake with caution. It was her box tumbling from the saddle that alerted him. He let that fall with a clatter, reaching for her instead.

She was awake by the time he set her on her feet.

"What?" she yelped, then groaned and swayed, bumping into his chest.

Jesse gripped her tighter. "Careful. Mountain's steep here."

Even with the cloak she was slender in his arms, pressed so close that the lacy bit pinned to the crown of her head snagged in the stubble under his chin. She pulled away from him, groping for the saddle. Then she turned, face pale in the moonlight.

"My box. Where is it?" Panic laced the words.

"It fell. Hold the horse; I'll hunt it up."

She grasped his coat sleeve before he could move. "Please. It's everything."

He put a hand to hers. "Calm yourself now. I said I'd find it."

Her hand under his, small and cold, eased its grip and slid away.

After a quick search, he decided the box had gone over the trail's edge. Grasping at brush for support, he felt his way down the pine-needled slope, praying it hadn't fallen far. Praying he wouldn't go sliding off the mountain in the dark.

He found it lodged against the pine under which they'd halted. Back on the trace, she took it from him with quiet thanks. He wondered what it was she deemed so precious, but didn't ask. He got out the canteen and handed it to her. "Want to walk a spell? It'll help you keep awake."

Sleep was what she needed, but she gave him back the canteen and said, "I'll walk."

Pleased with her fortitude, he took the horse's bridle and started.

Not a dozen steps on, she gave a little cry. Jesse turned back to find her hunkered on the trail, rubbing at her foot. He'd forgotten she wore those dainty-heeled shoes. He'd have to do something about that. Ahead lay stretches they'd both have to manage afoot. But not yet.

He went back and offered her a hand. "Come on. Let's get you up on that horse."

He caught her falling from the saddle twice again before the stars faded and the trail grew clear enough to follow without his senses focused on every stone and root and knife-edged drop. A mist had crept up from the hollows. Chill tendrils of it nipped at his heels. They were deep in the mountains and high, with rank on rank of giant hardwoods crowding in, here and there dark pockets of spruce and fir. They hadn't been seen — by human eyes — but with dawn coming, a change of direction seemed in order.

Ahead the trace crested. He and Cade had hunted these mountains in autumns past. If memory served, it dipped into a meadow where a stream flowed. Along that stream ran another trail, overgrown but passable. He'd make for that, find Tamsen a place to lay her head for a spell.

Glancing back at her, he reckoned they could be tracked by the hairpins she'd been losing through the night. Her hair spilled down in an inky thicket across her shoulders, halfway to her waist. The lacy bit hung askew. So did her head, lolling toward her chest. Shadows underscored her eyes, and her face showed the strain of fatigue and grief and fear. Still she was so beautiful that Jesse had to remind himself to breathe.

Then he looked past her, and his chest filled at the sight that greeted him. He brought the horse to a stop on the sloping ground. She jerked in the saddle. He moved to her knee in case she fell, but she didn't. Getting her bearings, she blinked down at him with dark, suffering eyes.

"Morning," he said, with a searching smile.

She shut her eyes, as if the sight of him and the horse and the world was too much misery to bear. He wanted to give her something to hold against the dark tide of memories sure to be pressing in on her.

"Tamsen." When she opened her eyes, he nodded toward their back trail. "Fetch a look."

Clearly she was weary beyond caring, but she turned to look and caught her breath.

They were too hemmed by trees for the grandest view, but a gap in their ranks below gave prospect of a limestone cliff rising sheer from a dark wave of forest crashing, mist-foamed, against its stony face, ablaze in every shade from rose to ruddy gold, giving back the colors of sunrise. Above it in the clear-washed air an eagle turned, catching fire in its wings. Jesse drank it in with the joyous relief that always accompanied his leaving the piedmont behind — though this time he'd brought along more than a few of its complications.

The horse shifted, breaking the moment. Tamsen Littlejohn had put her back to the view and was looking up the trace, eyes wary as a deer's. The same alarm jolted down Jesse's spine when he followed her gaze.

Where the trace crested, there now stood a string of pack mules with a man at their head, looking back at them.

The lean little trapper with a scruffy beard was headed to Morganton to divest himself of the hides his mules conveyed. There'd been room for horse and pack train to pass on the trace, which Jesse had hoped to do with no more than a how-do. But the trapper, who'd camped the night past in the meadow beyond, proved inclined to conversate.

"Charlie Spencer," he said by way of introduction. "Where ye folks headed?"

"Homebound." Jesse berated himself for not abandoning the trace sooner as Spencer took in the drooping horse and Tamsen — more drooping still — with her ripped skirt, tumbled hair, and haunted eyes. Below a stocking cap worn low on his brow, Spencer's gaze was friendly enough. It was also keen.

"Where might home be?"

"West by a bit, then south." It was as far from the truth as Jesse could deliver on short notice.

"Over on the French Broad? Ain't ye taking the roundabout way?"

Jesse forced a smile. "I'm showing my bride a bit of the country." He put a hand to Tamsen's knee. It jerked under his touch.

"Anything you folks needing? I got coffee, food — nothing fancy, mind, just trail vittles," Spencer offered, while his eyes pursued another line of questioning with Tamsen, who looked less like a bride than a woman abducted and ravished.

A sudden baying of hounds made Jesse's

guts seize. Parrish couldn't be tracking them so soon, unless . . . Were they seen leaving Morganton despite his care?

Spencer emitted a piercing whistle. The barking escalated in pitch. The trapper grinned. "Them's my dogs. Hope they ain't treed another bear. I got all the skins my mules can tote. If'n I add one more, I'll be hauling on the ropes to stop 'em sliding down the mountain like tin on grease. You folks out from Morganton?"

Jesse cleared his throat. "Speaking of skins, I could use me a sturdy hide — for footwear," he added, then wished he hadn't when Spencer's gaze went to the ripped, dirty silk shoe on Tamsen's foot. "I can pay you for it."

Amenable to the notion whatever his suspicions, Spencer moved to the first mule and worked loose a hide from its burden. Six shillings was the going rate for a good deerskin. This one was well cured. Jesse dug inside his knapsack, searching for his coin pouch, praying he'd enough. He and Cade didn't do much trade with hard money.

Spencer held out the skin, neatly rolled. "Take it, with my compliments on your nuptials." Though he spoke to Jesse, he'd been looking at Tamsen.

"You sure?" Jesse asked.

109

Spencer hesitated a beat. "Certain sure, on both counts."

Disinclined to argue, Jesse took the skin. "My wife and I thank you kindly."

A crashing of brush heralded the arrival of Spencer's hounds, a lanky trio of spotted hides and lolling tongues. Jesse's horse shied at their milling. The mules barely twitched an ear.

"Best be pushing on," Spencer said, giving up trying to catch Tamsen's gaze. "Good luck to ye, folks."

At the stream that wound through the sloping meadow, Jesse halted. The rising sun spangled the dew clinging to grass and brush, save in the flattened place of Spencer's camp, set back off the trace. The fire ring emitted faint warmth beneath Jesse's outstretched hand. Crouching over the blackened remains, he looked back to where the trace crested, but he saw no sign of the man. He stood. "Sorry 'bout the wife talk. I had to think quick."

Tamsen's haggard eyes beseeched him. For rest.

Concern tightened in his chest. "Reckon you can make it another half mile?"

She bowed forward in the saddle, a study in misery, but clung on as he turned the horse along the stream, following it into cover.

10

Lulled by the monotonous sway, Tamsen fought to stay in the saddle. She didn't want to fall again into the arms of the man to whom she'd recklessly entrusted her life. She didn't want him getting ideas, alone as they were in that wilderness . . .

"Tamsen?"

Would the rocking never cease? And the weight on her chest, would it never lift? It stole her will to breathe and pushed her down . . . down to some mired place, black with shadow, where unseen things chittered and rustled and swooped at her head.

"Tamsen. You got to wake up now."

She woke up. She wasn't on the horse. The rocking was a hand, shaking her. Under her was hard ground. She hurt all over. And her mother was dead. That was the weight. Not on her chest. In it. As though her heart had been replaced in the night by stone, her ribs by iron bars. She had a powerful thirst

behind her, startling her out of a near doze. "Indians say they're bred from horses left behind when Spaniards come through these mountains, long time back."

Spaniards. Tamsen's throat closed tight as images of her mother careened through her mind, memories tainted by violence and lies. Sarah Littlejohn Parrish hadn't been Spanish after all . . . or had she been? A Spanish slave? As dusk gathered and clouds came up over the mountains, covering the few stars already burning in the luminous sky, Tamsen stared at the backs of her hands as if they belonged to a stranger.

They had corndodgers again for supper. Though it seemed wrong somehow to eat, she choked down one of the dry cakes, then sought refuge in her cloak, only to toss and turn at the painful pressing of her stays. The air had chilled. Her nose ran. Her feet ached.

Her guide said, "You awake?"

She rolled over, showing him her eyes in the firelight.

"Can I borrow your shoes?"

With no idea what he could want with her shoes, she sat up and handed him the battered things. As he reached past the fire to take them, a long howl pierced the darkness. She dropped the shoes at the flames' edge. He was quick, dragging them out before they were more than scorched. It hardly worsened their condition. One heel was all but fallen off. The silk uppers were in tatters.

Another wolf answered the first. At the edge of the firelight, the horse nickered. The man spoke to it almost chidingly, in a language unrecognizable: *"Meshewa. Nooleewi-a."*

Tamsen edged closer to the fire. Her guide was doing something with the deerskin he'd gotten from the trapper. He sat cross-legged, firelight catching sparks in his strange eyes as, at a rustle in the brush or another howl, he'd look out into the vast dark that pressed in close. His hands stayed busy with the deerskin, cutting it with his knife. Other tools came out of his bags. An awl. Beeswax. A sturdy needle. Something coiled like thread, only thicker.

He made no attempt to engage her in conversation, though she was sure he knew she watched him. Had she not heard him speak it often enough, she could almost imagine he had no English. Though his coloring wasn't an Indian's and he claimed to be white, she might as well have thrown in her lot with one of that race. Was she one of that race? There was one place she might look for answers. She hadn't yet read all the papers her mother's box contained. But she wasn't ready for the whole truth yet, or learning the box held only part of the truth, leaving her forever with questions unanswerable.

She shivered.

Golden eyes flicked to her. "Cold?"

He got up to put his blanket over her.

When she woke next in the lifting darkness, the first thing she saw was his face in profile, very near her own. She'd scooted up against him in the night, despite having his blanket and her cloak and sleeping closest to the fire. He lay on that big black fur, face upturned to the fading stars, hands folded on his chest. One gripped his rifle.

She eased away and only then saw the moccasins tucked between them. They were small and neat, with a center seam stitched of that thick thread, and the flaps . . . They were cut long enough to cover her ankles if she tied them up.

Sight of them caused a tightening in her chest, separate from the stone of grief lodged there. She reached a hand from her warm nest to stroke the supple leather, finding it buttery soft. Tears stung her eyes. She blinked them back and pillowed her head on her arm and watched the man beside her sleep while morning swelled around them, closing her eyes when the tightening of his lips warned her he was about to open his.

A mist had risen by the time Jesse checked his snares, cleaned the rabbit caught in the night, and made his way back up the mountain. They'd been blessed in the weather, though it was a blink and a sneeze till autumn. Some of the hardwoods were already tipped in red. The sun and warmth couldn't last.

Left to himself, he could be down on the Watauga in a day. Two at most. With Tamsen it would take longer, but not by much. Ought he to make it take longer? Could she bear it if he did? The shattered look of her, sick with grief in the clearing by the stream, haunted him still. Even had she been whole in spirit, she wasn't used to such exertion or rough living. He knew it by that blue gown, her soft hands.

He'd left her sleeping, yet to find the moccasins he'd made. Would they please her?

He was wondering that as he came over a rise into their camp and stopped in his tracks. She was kneeling by the fire with her back to him, and the mist wasn't so thick that he couldn't see she'd taken off the jacket of her gown and was tugging at the laced-up thing she wore beneath it.

Stays. He'd seen them on the bushes at their neighbor's cabin, washed and spread like the wings of a desiccated bird. He'd never seen them on a woman. Was she trying to get at the ties in back? How tight did women lace those things? For a second or two, he admired her trim shape, then cleared his throat. "You needing help with that?"

With a yelp, she scrambled back into the jacket, thrusting her arms into the sleeves. She flipped her braid over her shoulder, head bent to fasten up the front.

"Guess that's no," he said under his breath.

While he skinned the rabbit and whittled green sticks to spit it, she fidgeted, trying to adjust her various layers without seeming to do so. Finally she gave it up and reached for the moccasins he'd made. Halfway through tugging them on, she glanced at him from under her lashes.

"Thank you for these."

He nodded, watching her through drifting smoke. "Best wrap your feet in the hose. Loose-like, to cushion things. There'll be some walking again today." The hose had dried, spread by the fire in the night. "I got a pair of breeches you can slip on under that skirt." She shook her head at that, and her cheeks pinked up. "We're headed higher today. Weather can turn in a blink this time of year. Could get chilly."

Still no. She'd maybe change her mind, later. At least she seemed to like the moccasins. She stood and took a few steps. He noted she didn't limp. "I put the fancy shoes in the fire. Hope you don't mind."

"They were ruined."

It was all the talk he got from her while the rabbit cooked.

Keeping company with Cade all these years, he was used to silent stretches. But he'd seen enough of Tamsen Littlejohn before her mother's death to guess this wasn't her usual way. He trusted she'd talk when she was ready. That she hadn't cried a tear since leaving Morganton . . . that concerned him.

He couldn't read with certainty what lay behind her guarded face, but the transformation happening on the outside was encouraging. Only a day on the trail and she was already taking the sun, taking it well. He'd feared her skin would burn, adding to her misery, but it was coming up golden across the bridge of her nose and brow.

They ate the rabbit unseasoned with talk, till out of the fire-hissing silence, she said,

"It occurs to me you haven't . . . I haven't asked . . ." She faltered when he looked at her. "What is your name?"

He'd almost told her a time or two but reckoned his name, or anything else about him, was the last thing on her mind. Still he'd hoped she'd come 'round to asking. He savored the moment now, along with the last bite of rabbit, while the flames fluttered and the mist swirled down the mountain at their backs.

"That's a good question," he said. "But I answer to Jesse Bird."

11

Jesse had left Tamsen Littlejohn with everything but his rifle and his horse. He'd
loaded his pistol, showed her how to cock it
and squeeze the trigger. "A precaution. I'll
just be down the mountain, gone an hour
and a bit."

He was uneasy going out of shouting
distance, even for an hour. He was uneasy,
too, about the clouds piling dark above the
mountain. He'd settled her under pines and
tied up an oilcloth shelter, explaining while
he worked about the wagon party Cade was
guiding. "They need to see me, know I'm
still part of their outfit. It's no more'n a
mile or two to where we aimed to meet up."

Tamsen had stood before the makeshift
tent, under which he'd piled their kit, frowning at the loaded pistol set atop her little
box. "Why can't we both go?"

"We can't know if the hunt's on, or if your
stepfather's learned I helped you away. Be-

ing seen together is too risky. There'll be no one along this trail, and if there was, they won't see you if you stay put in these pines."

Lord Almighty, let her stay put in those pines. He offered the prayer a dozen times before he struck the rutted trace the wagon party would be traveling. Thunder rumbled a few ridges over, menacing the air like war drums, but barely a sprinkle had overtaken him in the time it took to find Cade, camped with the settlers in the green cup of a meadow off the trace that skirted Bald Mountain. Women tended fires and young'uns at the wagons. Smells of cookery thickened the air. Jesse dismounted near the roped stock pen where Cade stood solitary guard, a grim knowing tight across his face.

"I didn't want you having to lie for me," Jesse said straightaway. Thunder murmured while Cade digested that, brows pulled in fierce enough to scare a painter-cat up a tree. "You know 'bout her ma?"

"All Morganton knows."

"It was her stepfather done the killing. Tamsen saw it."

"I figured as much, once I put it all together." Cade's eyes held worry, though he tried to hide it. "Tell me this, Jesse. You see this ending well?"

"I'll make sure it does — for her." Jesse

glanced at the wagons. Having come at the camp from behind, his arrival had gone unmarked. "Tell me quick what's passed. Then I could use some provisions. A blanket if one's to spare."

Cade gave him what news he had. Parrish had wasted a day chasing the slaves he'd brought from Charlotte Town, thinking their flight had to do with his stepdaughter's. He'd lost that trail and turned back to Morganton, in time to meet a trapper come down from the mountains.

"Charlie Spencer." Jesse rubbed the back of his neck, cursing himself for letting the man set eyes on them.

"They were heading out toward the French Broad country when I started these folk on the trail," Cade said. "Spencer seemed of a mind that's where you were bound with the girl."

"He named the place. I didn't correct his guess." What else Cade had said registered. "What d'you mean 'they'?"

"Parrish and that redheaded planter the girl refused."

"You get his name? The planter?"

Cade looked at him warily, then arched a brow. "She hasn't told you?"

"She ain't doing much talking yet."

Cade wasn't liking the situation. "She'd

best get to talking because folk in Morganton are. Word's gone 'round an Overmountain man abducted Tamsen Littlejohn."

Back in the room where her mother lay dead and he'd offered his protection, Jesse had considered such a charge might come of it. It didn't make it easier to hear. "I was there, Pa. I saw what was done to her ma. I had to —"

"It may be you did," Cade cut in, "but you need to know what else is being said." The rain came harder now. Over at the wagon camp, folk were taking cover. "Parrish has put it about that whoever abducted his stepdaughter also killed his wife."

The earth seemed to tilt. Raindrops smacked Jesse's face, cold and clammy. Cade gripped his arm.

"They don't know your name. Only one man knows your face. But he's lent himself to the hunt, as guide."

Jesse knew he'd made a poor impression on that man. Add to that word of Tamsen's disappearance from Morganton, a murder besides, and he could imagine the trapper feeling moved to help Parrish track down his missing stepdaughter — the only other person who knew how her mother truly died.

But what of her thwarted suitor? Parrish

131

wouldn't have told him the truth. Not if he still had his sights set on the man's wealth as a prize in trade for Tamsen.

"His name's Kincaid" was the clipped answer Jesse got after asking a second time. "He hadn't much to say, just watched our faces while Parrish asked his questions."

His pa's face was guarded, strained no doubt by Jesse's tangling them in the girl's messy plight.

"Why wouldn't she have him?"

"She took a powerful dislike to the man is all I know." It was a thing Jesse aimed to find out.

Cade looked like he wanted to utter a few choice curses — most of them aimed at Jesse. He breathed hard through his nose, then met Jesse's gaze with resignation. "Keep her from him, then. Keep her far away."

Keep her from *him.* Oughtn't Cade to have said *them?*

Jesse hadn't time to question. One of the settlers, braving the rain, was heading over from the wagons. They had seconds to themselves. "How're these folk settling in?"

Cade's mouth quirked, but there was no humor in it. "They say with an Indian guide they figure they've less to fear from Chickamaugas, though their eyes sometimes say

132

different. They'll be glad to see you."

The settler reached them, rain sluicing off his drooping hat brim. While Cade went to gather provisions, Jesse talked about the trail ahead — hoping his memories of last autumn would hold true, with no new slides or trees down or streams overrunning their banks. He came into camp, greeted the watchful men, the women busy keeping all and sundry dry as possible. He'd no more chance for a private word with Cade before he was back on his horse, provisioned and riding up the trace Cade would follow come morning.

Clouds hugged the ridges, ragged as old men's beards. Lightning sheeted the landscape, thunder cracking on its heels. A fresh torrent of rain overtook him as he left the trace, slowing his progress. Though barely evening, under the forest canopy twilight lay thick.

Way he saw it, he'd a choice to make. Get Tamsen to the Watauga and hole up, hope for a respite, be ready to bolt again at sign of pursuit, or lose themselves in the mountains for an indefinite spell, wait out the hunt until her stepfather gave her up for lost. There were places he could survive on next to nothing, even in winter. But Tamsen?

He'd lay it out to her, let her have a voice

in deciding.

Just let her have stayed put. He hurled the prayer heavenward again as his horse threaded a stream already swollen from the trickle of half an hour past.

From childhood Tamsen had thrilled to the clash and drama of a thunderstorm. Until now. With nothing but an oilcloth above her head, every flash of lightning prickled her scalp. Every wet wind gust stippled her arms with gooseflesh. Rain drummed, pounding in its fury. Thunder rolled down the mountain like cannon blasts. Hunched low, hardly able to draw breath for the press of her stays, she put her back to the driving rain and covered her mother's box with her bedraggled petticoat.

Had Mr. Bird found his settlers? She'd no idea how long it had been since he abandoned her — half the promised hour? Nor did she fathom how he could make his way with such confidence through these jumbled mountains, riddled with creeks and bluffs, impenetrable thickets and brakes, and trails all but invisible to her eyes. She felt herself folded into their savage embrace, swallowed by their immensity. If he never made it back to her . . .

Before the fretful thought was finished,

the wind fell off. The rain slackened, then ceased with a suddenness as unnerving as its violent falling had been. Runnels spilled down the oilcloth and dripped from laden pines. Light beneath the trees was dim and green. Thunder rumbled, but the storm was moving off, leaving her a scrap of muddied flotsam in its wake.

She needed to stand up straight, but dared go no more than a step or two from her shelter. Having removed the moccasins Mr. Bird made and tucked them into one of the bags to keep dry, she stood barefoot on soggy pine needles. The back of her gown was soaked to the waist. Mr. Bird had used a branch as a rooftree to ensure the sides of the shelter shed the rain, but runoff had created a rivulet on the uphill side of the tent — which her gown had wicked up. Trickling through unhindered now, the water nipped at the corner of her mother's box. Ducking down to rescue it, she saw something that alarmed her as deeply as the storm had. The lock was empty, the key gone.

Fallen under one of the bags, perhaps? She crawled beneath the oil-cloth and shifted the knapsack, the bow case and quiver, their bedding, frantic fingers scrabbling through wet pine straw.

135

"No — no." The key had to be somewhere.

She'd worked up a sweat in her search despite the chilling air. She unpinned her jacket, then untied the petticoat with its ripped hem soiled and sopping. She shook out the grubby linen, but no key tumbled free. She dropped the garments onto the bags. She checked her pockets. No key.

She tried to think. And breathe. Wretched stays . . . Could she have slipped the key down inside them and forgotten she'd done so?

She yanked. Tugged. Slid her hand down the clammy front of her chest but could barely wedge her fingers a few inches in. Her mother, in anticipation of her winning back the approval of Mr. Kincaid, had drawn the lacings of her stays as tight as Tamsen could bear them, squeezing her into the narrow shape required by the blue gown. There was nothing between her flattened breasts save the sweat-sour linen of her shift.

She must have let the key fall on the trail.

Mr. Bird had told her to stay put. Told her most emphatically. But all her mother's secrets were in that box. She had to have that key.

Leaving the camp barefoot, she descended from the pine thicket and searched with care

136

along the faint path they'd followed, among weeds and rock crevices, anywhere a key might have tumbled from the back of the horse.

With her eyes on the ground, she heard the rushing creek before she saw it, at the bottom of a winding draw. It had widened since the storm, moving faster over its rock-tumbled bed. Mr. Bird had led the horse across at that spot, but it didn't look safe for foot crossing now.

She climbed a few yards up the draw over stone outcrops, fingers and toes grasping the wet surfaces. Not far above was a level stretch where the stream widened into a pool, before rushing off over rocks and flood-washed limbs, but just above the pool, matters proved more promising. A few stones, evenly spaced, spanned the creek. With only her shift to hamper, Tamsen thought she could cross. Then it would be a matter of climbing back down to the path on the other side.

Trying not to think of the possibility that the key might have fallen into the creek, she stepped out onto the first stone. It wobbled, but she kept her balance. Three more stones lay between her and the far bank, which rose to an overhang of berry shrubs. Huckleberries, she thought, catching sight of a few clinging late to their stems, peeking dark through leaves tinged with autumn scarlet.

The second stone was lower, cushioned in moss that squished between her toes. Water foamed an inch below her heels, cascading over submerged tree limbs. She glanced down, but the pool below was too brown and churned to judge its depth.

The third stone wobbled worse than the first. Her arms flailed as fear shot up the backs of her knees, but she steadied herself — in time to see the thicket above her on the bank erupt with a shedding of leaves. A bear, big and black, stood up among the berry shrubs and looked at her with its small, startled eyes.

With a cry she stepped back. Her foot landed in the creek, shot from under her, and she pinwheeled over the edge into the pool.

It was deep and shockingly cold. Her head went under before her foot touched bottom. She kicked up from pebbly silt, thrashing, and broke the surface. She choked on water that rushed straight into her mouth and was dragged under again.

The current swept her into something hard. Her fingers clawed it, but the surface refused her a hold. She pushed off from it, hoping she was propelling herself up and toward the bank, not into deeper water.

Her shin struck stone. She scrabbled for it with her toes, finding purchase enough to launch herself out of the sucking, swirling hole. Still in water above her waist, she floundered for something to catch hold of.

A shape loomed above her. With the bear still lurking at the edges of her panic, she screamed and flailed. Something closed over her wrist, clamping hard.

"Tamsen — take hold of me!"

"Mr. Bird!" She gulped down water as she cried his name and came out of the creek retching it back up as he hauled her to safety.

12

Flat on his back and half-soaked, Jesse sprawled on the creek bank while Tamsen Littlejohn coughed up half the mountain's runoff. His hands and knees shook with the aftershocks of finding her gone, tracking her to the creek and hearing her cry, hurtling up the stony draw to find her thrashing in the pool. Had he been seconds later . . .

He sat up and faced her, nigh as angry as he'd been scared. "Didn't I tell you to stay put?"

Creek water spiked her lashes and streamed from the hair clinging in black tendrils to her waist. His eyes raked lower. Below the stays her wet shift molded to her hips and thighs and . . . He saw her shin, scraped and bleeding.

"You're hurt." He clasped her leg, meaning to get a better look. She jerked out of his grasp.

"Let me be!"

140

Anger sparked again through the fear and concern still shuddering through him. "Good thing I didn't let you be a minute ago. What in the nation were you trying to do?"

A possibility hit him square. Had she been escaping again, from him? Why? Had she lost all confidence in him? Lord, had he got this all wrong?

No. He was meant to help her. That much he knew. And he sensed that something more was there between them. Or might be. Could be. But what had she been thinking, taking off barefoot in her shift?

He tried not to let it — he did try — but his gaze went over her again, down to her bared, comely ankles.

She was raw voiced as she said, "I was crossing the creek just fine when it startled me. I lost my footing."

His gaze snapped to her face. "What startled you?"

"A bear."

That jarred him. He raised himself, looking up and down the draw. If there'd been a bear, she'd spooked it with her flailing. "You sure?"

Her dark eyes were stones. "I'm sure."

"All right," he said, hands raised. "But answer me. Why were you trying to cross

141

back over in the first place?"

"I was looking for the key."

The pulse in her neck beat as crazily as his own. He could see it. "Key?"

"To my mother's box. It's gone — and I didn't know if you were coming back."

Now he was just plain insulted. "You thought I'd ride off and leave you stranded on this mountain? What sort of man d'you take me for?"

"I don't know what sort of man you are."

The unfairness of it stung. Jesse drew breath to retort, then realized she had a fair point. She didn't know him. She'd barely looked past her own misery to see him as anything other than a means of escape. It had taken her days to ask his name.

As if by mutual impulse — the better to square off perhaps — they got to their feet, but when she started for the creek again, he grasped her arm. "What're you doing?"

She yanked free. "I told you. I need to find the key."

She needed no such thing. He could smash the fool box to get at whatever was so all-fired important inside it but thought it best not to say so just now. What he said was "All right," which didn't help, for no sooner had he said it than she was clambering up a boulder, sopping wet and stubborn

142

as a mule. A mule with the sweetest wet-shift-molded curves he'd ever seen . . . Lord help him. He had to think.

"Think for moment. When's the last time you mind seeing the key?"

That checked her. She turned to meet his gaze. "I put it in the lock before we left Mrs. Brophy's house. It might have fallen out anywhere."

In that clinging shift, perched on the rock, hair streaming wet as pond weed, she looked like a nymph stepped out of a tale.

Again he forced himself to think. The key . . . to her box . . . which had tumbled over the trail-side that first time he caught her pitching out of the saddle, barely out of Morganton. He knew what had happened to the key but said, "You can't go looking for it sopping wet. Let's get you dry — me too — then we'll talk about what to do. All right?"

He waited, eyes fastened on her face and not an inch lower. Finally she nodded. Relieved, he held out his hand. She hesitated, then took it.

But she couldn't keep up. The going wasn't that steep climbing out of the draw, but he heard her breath shortening, the pull on his hand increasing with every step.

"Mr. Bird," she gasped, a thin and

strangled sound.

He turned in time to catch her in his arms, a tangle of wet hair and linen and clammy skin, and eased her down on a stone beside the muddy trail. "What's wrong?"

No more'n a trickle of blood seeped from the scrape on her shin, but her color — or lack of it — alarmed him. When her head came up, he drew his arms away, leaving a hand on her shoulder to steady her.

"My stays. They hardly . . . let me . . . breathe."

"Then take 'em off." He spoke sharper than he'd meant to but couldn't fathom why she'd torture herself wearing a garment made for fancy gowns, not crossing mountains. "Wearing 'em seems foolish. Can't you —"

"My mother tied them."

He stared at her trembling mouth, her quivering chin, started to say, "Why does that matter?" when it dawned on him why it mattered. He held his peace a moment, then said, "I'm sorry for it, Tamsen. But it'd make things easier if you could draw a full breath."

She didn't fall to crying, but the look on her face wrenched his heart. "Nothing can make this easier."

144

She didn't mean trudging up and down mountains. "I know it. But you'd be able to breathe, at least." He waited, not knowing what she meant to do next, what he was meant to do.

She looked at him, chewing at her lip. "Will you help me?"

She scooted forward on the rock, put her back to him, then gathered up her mass of dripping hair and pulled it forward over her shoulders. The nape of her slender neck was whiter than her face now, the skin so smooth he longed to touch it. More than touch it.

"What do I do?" The words might've been a prayer.

She turned her head, giving him a view of her graceful jaw, long sooty lashes brushing her cheek. "The laces tie at the top. I think they've knotted."

A tide of pink rose up her neck. If he'd never been presented with a pair of stays to unlace, he reckoned she'd never asked a man to unlace them. His heart beat hard again.

Perched behind her on the rock, he put his hands to her. The rigid garment was only slightly darker than the bleached shift beneath it. Against it his hands looked big and brown as bear paws. With the point of his knife, he worked loose the knot. The wet lacing took some doing to pull through the tiny holes, but he'd tackled swollen rawhide more stubborn.

He'd reached the center of her back before her shoulders curled forward. He felt her shaking, though she made no sound as she wept. Feeling wretched for her, he loosened the stays to her waist.

"Lift your arms." When she did, he pulled the stays over her head, resisting the urge to toss them down the draw into the creek.

She bent over, crying into her hands. Jesse sat behind her, wanting to hold her while she grieved for her mother, who would never lace her stays again. He put a tentative hand to her shoulder.

She sat up stiff. "Don't touch me!"

He sprang off the rock. She set her hands to her ribs and smoothed them down her shift, then yanked at the fabric where the stays had molded it to her sides. Jesse watched, pulse hammering, as her hands went to the small of her back, fingers groping upward, seeking to soothe.

"How'd you stand it so long? You must've been in torment since the night we left Morganton." He hoped she never put the wretched things on again.

She didn't answer, but his words seemed to distract her. With her back to him still,

146

she said, "You keep saving me."

The words were thick with tears.

Thinking how much she'd been through in the past few days, thinking how close he'd come to finding her drowned just now, Jesse came around to crouch beside her, looking up into her tear-swollen face, framed in wet tangles.

She looked back at him, desolate. "I thought I was going to die."

"I know it. I think you scared ten years off of me."

Wordless, she raised a hand to his face and held it there, cupping his rough-bearded jaw. He was so startled by the gesture that he couldn't breathe, much less speak. Their gazes held, hers welling with gratitude.

He was the one drowning now.

Around them the birds, quiet since the storm, broke into song again. At last he choked out, "I wish I could've stopped what happened to your ma, but I'm not about to let you die."

She took her hand away, still holding his gaze, eyes red from weeping but clearer now than they'd been since fleeing Morganton. "I believe you mean it."

"I do. But it'd be a help to me," he added shakily, "if you don't try crossing another creek — or taking on any more bears — at least while I'm not by to lend a hand."

13

It was some sort of wheaten loaf. Baked by whom, Tamsen didn't ask. Nearly drowning had quickened her appetite. With her mouth stuffed full of bread, she looked up to see Mr. Bird poking a stick at their small fire, watching her across the flames.

"You're enjoying that a sight more'n you did my corndodgers. Ought I to take offense?"

She could tell he was teasing her, was pleased to see her eating; still she flushed as she swallowed her mouthful.

She'd had plenty cause to blush since Mr. Bird pulled her from the creek. With her shift soaked and her petticoat and jacket in little better state, she'd let him talk her into draping them to dry on the shelter he'd constructed above the draw, meantime donning his spare clothes. A makeshift belt of leather whang cinched a pair of homespun breeches that fell nearly to her ankles. His linsey hunting shirt — taken warm off his body — was so voluminous that she'd had to roll the sleeves half their length to keep them above her wrists. Her nakedness under the shirt had mortified her at first, but Mr. Bird, dressed in a buckskin shirt and those scandalous leggings, took her appearance in stride.

He smiled at her now. "I ain't offended 'bout the bread. Cade got it back at the settlers' camp, so 'course it's better'n any vittles I'd cobble together."

She'd been about to pop the last of the bread into her mouth. Now she lowered the morsel, wondering what her mother would say to see her sitting on a mountainside wearing a man's clothes, moccasins on her feet, damp hair drying in the fire's warmth. Would it shock her, or would the sight have made Sarah Parrish laugh?

Tamsen closed her eyes, grief swelling thick in her throat. She didn't want to cry in front of Mr. Bird again. She looked up from the bite of bread. "Who is Cade? You've mentioned his name . . ." She flushed, feeling she ought to know the answer.

"Cade's my pa."

That surprised her. "Your father was in Morganton? Did I see him?"

"You fell into his arms, first time I laid eyes on you."

"Oh." Memory of the man she'd collided with in the street had fragmented until only scraps remained. A tall, hard shoulder; startling eyes netted with creases; tawny skin and sculpted bones and rather alarming black brows. She searched Mr. Bird's features for an echo of those looks, some indication of mixed blood. Then she met his gaze.

"I'm a white man like I told you — far as I know. Cade's my foster father. He's half Delaware. *Lenni Lenape,* they call themselves."

"What do you mean, far as you know? How could you not know?" The question was barely out of Tamsen's mouth before she wished it back. Her glance strayed to her mother's box, tucked under the shelter.

Mr. Bird followed her gaze. "You don't need the key, you know. I can get it open for you any time you want." His hand stretched toward the box, just within reach.

Tamsen half rose to intercept him. "No, please."

Mr. Bird looked at her questioningly. Though she'd taken time to scour the trail through the draw again, and Mr. Bird had crossed the creek and looked on the other

151

side, they hadn't found the key. She'd hidden her disappointment. Told herself the key was not her mother. Only a keepsake. But it felt like losing her mother all over again.

"Not now, I mean," she said, unable to explain.

In the storm's wake, the sky was clearing, the air taking on a chill. She wore her summer cloak over Mr. Bird's shirt, which drooped low on her shoulders. Still he rose, took his sleeping fur from under the shelter, draped it around her, and settled across from her again.

"When you're ready, I can get into it without much damage done. Nothing that can't be mended."

The gesture, and his words, brought her to the edge of tears again. From barely being able to acknowledge the man, she'd swung to wanting to thank him with every other breath. She ran a fold of the fur through her fingers, fixing her attention on it instead. It was old, worn in spots, black . . . and familiar. "This is a bear's fur, isn't it?"

"Sure is. My first bear."

She looked up, meeting his gaze across the fluttering flames. "You shot the bear? How old were you?"

152

" 'Bout thirteen."

Tamsen thought of what she'd been doing at that age. Embroidering sleeve cuffs. Learning to bone a set of stays. Nothing that could help in her present circumstances.

Down in the draw, the creek rushed over rocks, its noise magnified in the darkness. A breeze caressed the trees in the black above the firelight's reach, ruffled the flames below, whistled now and then through some stony fissure out in the dark.

In scant grass nearby, the horse grazed. With the bearskin around her, a roof of pine boughs to shelter her, a fire to warm her, Tamsen felt remarkably snug.

Once they'd given up the key for lost, Mr. Bird had gone to work on the shelter. She'd returned to the creek to rinse her filthy petticoat and came up the draw again in time to see the clouds part and the sun setting behind dusk-purpled mountains, peak piled on peak like jumbled ribbon, strewn westward as far as she could see, vast, brooding and ancient. She'd stood staring, caught small and helpless between the terror and the grandness of it, until Mr. Bird, soft footed as usual, came up beside her.

Looking out over that howling wilderness, he'd said, "The Cherokees tell a story of a

153

great vulture creating these mountains, back when the earth was new and wet as clay on a wheel. Ever hear tell of that?"

"No," she'd said, wondering if he'd heard of Genesis.

"It was the bird's wings dipping as it flew that scooped out the coves and swept the mountains high."

As he spoke, she drew a shuddering breath, unable to look away from the dreadful beauty stretching before them.

"Are ye afraid?" he'd asked her. Then, upon her admission that she was, "Of what? All those mountains?"

"And what they hide." Bears. Wild Indians. Her future.

"I've long acquaintance with what those mountains hide," he'd said. "You needn't go in fear of it with me."

They'd stood, side by side, until the light went. Now the sky loomed black, with stars strewn in a glittering net that showed in patches between the rustling trees. She was still reaching for the courage he'd promised to lend her.

"Whither shall I flee from thy presence?" she whispered, gazing at the stars, breathing in the tang of pine and rain-soaked leaves and something strange and subtle beyond that — maybe the smell of the mountains

154

themselves, like the distant exhalation of a cavernous sigh. "If I ascend up into heaven, thou art there."

Above the flame's crackle Mr. Bird's voice rose. "If I take the wings of the morning, and dwell in the uttermost parts of the sea; even there shall thy hand lead me, and thy right hand shall hold me."

Surprised he'd recognized the psalm, much less could quote it, Tamsen dropped her gaze to him. Mr. Bird sat cross-legged, rifle at his knee, looking back at her. She swallowed and said, "Do you mean to answer my question?"

"What question was that?" There was a smile in his voice.

"Why aren't you sure about being white?"

"Truth to tell, I'm as much Indian as Cade is, never mind my skin's not brown."

It was such an outright contradiction of his earlier profession that Tamsen frowned. Mr. Bird held a hand toward the flames, staring at the back of it. Then his mouth crooked, like he knew he was confusing her, enjoying it, even. But he didn't leave her puzzling for long.

"I had maybe three years on me when Shawnee hunters found me somewhere in these mountains. Wasn't a war party. Hunters. They heard screaming and cut over a ridge to have a look. Found a white man dragging the bodies of another man and a woman into a cabin, which he set fire to. The Shawnees — there were three of 'em — hid in the trees while the man got on his horse and rode off like the hounds of hell pursued him. He took nothing, far as they could tell. Didn't touch the stock in the barn. That's where they found me, hiding in the hay while all this was going on."

Mr. Bird kept his eyes on his hand while he spoke, turning it over and back in the firelight, as if it held some mystery he longed to fathom. Just as she'd looked at her hand, she realized. He had large hands, well-shaped, though callused and scarred. Tamsen glanced at his face. He showed no sign of grief as he related the horrific tale, but the ache of her own loss twisted tighter. "They were your parents?"

"Reckon so." Mr. Bird took up the stick and poked the fire, sending sparks high in a bright swirl, before reaching for more deadfall laid by. "Truth is I don't recall any of what I've told you. First memory I'm sure of is crossing the *Spay-lay-wi-theepi* — the Ohio — heading north by canoe into Shawnee lands." He sat back, watching the wood take flame. "Once they got me to their town — Cornstalk's Town, it was — I was

156

adopted by a couple whose children had died, and I became Shawnee. They called me Wildcat."

"I'd have thought Hawk," Tamsen said before she could stop herself.

"Would you?" Mr. Bird rubbed a fingertip along the bridge of his narrow nose, looking as if she'd paid him a high compliment. "Maybe now. Back then I was still a snub-nosed baby. Cat-That-Scratches is another way of saying my name. When they found me, I was curled up with a batch of half-wild kittens and fought like one when they took me up. They fed me, and soon enough I settled down to purring — or that's the tale they liked to tell."

Tamsen fingered a lock of drying hair. She'd spotted a sizable gap in the story, between the tiny child he'd been, adopted by Shawnees, and the man sitting before her now. "Shawnee warriors found you? But you said your father — Cade — is Delaware. Where does he come in? Why is your name Jesse Bird now? And how —"

"Hold on," he said, stemming her flood of questions with a laugh. "This is where it gets twisty. Cade's pa was a white man, his ma full-blood Lenape, but he'd got himself adopted by the Shawnees too, a grown man. Wolf-Alone, they called him. Cade's a good hunter, even better in a fight. He was thought highly of for one adopted after running the gauntlet." He paused, then with a cautious look asked, "You know what that is?"

She'd heard of it. "They — the Indians — line up and make a man run past while they hit him with sticks?" The night breeze gusted, tickling the back of her neck. She suppressed a shiver at the thought of such cruelty.

"Sticks, whips, other things," he said. "Sometimes war clubs."

A horror dawned in Tamsen's mind. "Not you? They don't make children do that, surely?"

"Not small children, no. But I've seen older boys, women . . ." Mr. Bird searched her face, then redirected the conversation. "Anyway, by the time I was four, maybe five years old, Wolf-Alone took to spending time with me, teaching me to track and set snares, even made me a little bow so I could practice. My Shawnee parents were older, so he stepped in and taught me like an uncle would've done. But he also spoke English to me on the sly, when it was just the two of us. Didn't want to forget it himself, he's told me. So I grew up knowing how to speak it, more or less, though for years I was more

158

conversant in Shawnee."

That answered a question Tamsen hadn't even thought to ask yet, why he had no trace of an accent, save the drawl of an Overmountain man. "Why did the two of you ever leave the Shawnees?"

She wondered if he minded her questions, but he didn't appear displeased. She was glad, for she wanted him to go on talking. The sound of his voice was a comfort, a shield. Like the firelight, it was helping hold back that vast unknown looming dark around her. Besides, he had a remarkable story, and he told it well.

She knew now she'd misjudged him, based on their first meetings in the stable. Not only was he brave and kind, but watching his face now, she glimpsed an intelligence and wit that his rustic manners and speech at first had obscured. Or perhaps it was his eyes that masked the depth of thought behind them. Such an unnerving shade . . .

"I suppose the blame lies with Virginia's governor at the time, Lord Dunmore," he said in answer to her question. "I'd been seven years with the Shawnees when the Virginians made war on the people. This was a year or so before the colonies rebelled, the autumn of '74. Dunmore's War, they call it now. My adopted pa, Split Moon, was too old for battle but not too old to hunt, and at ten I was finally big enough to go along and not be in the way. We'd thought it safe, since the fighting had stopped back in October and our chief, Cornstalk, was talking peace with the Virginians. We hadn't crossed the Ohio — it was too dangerous, with our old Kan-tuck-ee hunting grounds filling up with settlers. The Ohio was meant to be the new boundary between the red man and the white. But that didn't stop hunters, even settlers, from crossing over onto our side. Three days out, a party of white hunters stumbled onto our camp. There were four of us — Split Moon, a warrior called Falling Hawk, Wolf-Alone, and me. It was early morning. I'd just woken up and gone off a ways to a creek to wash. Wolf-Alone had gone with me. We heard the shots, could see through the trees, Split Moon and Falling Hawk were down, hit before they could reach their muskets. Dead."

Instead of fighting on after Split Moon and Falling Hawk were shot, Jesse told her, Wolf-Alone had snatched him up as if he were a flour sack and fled, getting shot at for a mile over trackless ground before outrunning the hunters, with Wildcat struggling all the while, wanting to go back and avenge his fallen father.

"Wolf-Alone was a sight bigger'n me then, and about five times stronger." Mr. Bird gazed past the fire, as if beyond its light, he could see that boy he described for her, furious with grief and bloodlust. "He told me plain weren't no hope in going back, and he wasn't minded to let me throw my life away afore I'd lived it. He told me God — the white man's God, the Christian God — had a plan for me and betwixt him and whatever angels were lent to guard us, Wolf-Alone meant to see it unfold."

Wildcat hadn't much cared for those words, and soon, Mr. Bird went on, it was clear that Wolf-Alone had no intention of returning him to the Shawnees at all. He was taking the angry, grieving boy south, to the hated whites. Wildcat, feeling himself and their people betrayed, escaped him twice before injuring himself in a fall from a ridge.

Mr. Bird stroked his right shin, as if feeling the echo of an old wound. "I'd broken my leg and was out of my head with the pain of it when Wolf-Alone caught me the second time. He picked me up, and eventually we came stumbling, me dangling in his arms, into a clearing in the wilds of Kan-tuck-ee, found a cabin with folk not inclined to shoot every Indian they saw on sight — a miracle, Cade likes to say. They gave us shelter in their barn while my leg healed. Their name was Bird."

It wasn't until they'd left that place that Wolf-Alone started calling him Jesse Bird, after the youngest boy in that family. " 'They were good people,' " he told me when I asked why he was calling me so. " 'They won't mind you borrowing the name.' "

"And Cade?" Tamsen asked. "Where did he get that name for himself?"

Mr. Bird shrugged. "Picked it out of the air, I reckon. He's never said. Anyway, by then I'd grown used to the idea of being with him. He'd been like an uncle to me for years, after all. Cade took me on south, hunting along the way, working the hides to trade for things we needed. One of those things was a Bible. After that it was reading lessons along with the hunting. We moved around the back country, Virginia, Carolina, sometimes farther west. After a time we came down the Watauga to Sycamore Shoals. Reckon that's as much home now as any place."

Mr. Bird fell quiet, elbow propped on a knee, chin braced in his hand. Tamsen was holding on to the end of a braid she didn't remember plaiting. He bestirred himself, drawing one of his bags close to take out a coil of rawhide. With his knife he cut a piece and held it out. She tied off her braid, still caught up in his story. "Have you tried to learn who your parents were?"

"Split Moon and Red-Quill-Woman were my parents."

"I meant your white parents."

He smiled faintly. "I know who you meant. Mind you, I was only ten when we left the Shawnees. Too young — or too Shawnee — to care about white parents I couldn't recall."

"Don't you wonder now?"

" 'Course I do. But Cade reckons anyone — anyone Shawnee — who knew where I came from is likely dead."

Leaving him with a borrowed name and no ties to his blood kin, whoever they had been. Tamsen couldn't help thinking it might be best he never knew the truth. Though she understood the burning need to *know* — raw and new as that need was in her own soul — she was tempted to ask if he'd ever thought he might not like what he found.

He was watching her, looking as though he, too, debated saying something more.

"Aye," he said. "I do wonder. Some nights

I lie awake trying to grub up those memories. Anything that came before . . ." He didn't finish but dropped his gaze.

"Before Cade?" she asked, thinking she knew why he'd faltered. He looked up, surprised by her question. Maybe even chagrined.

"He's been good to me, has Cade. He told me once . . . something out of the Bible. Goes along the lines of 'The LORD is my inheritance' or maybe 'my portion.' *Therefore will I hope in him.*"

It was a consoling thought. Even so, he'd admitted to wondering after all these years.

"How long ago was it," she asked, "when you stopped being Shawnee?"

"Lenawe nilla," he said, his golden eyes fixing her across the fire. "I never said I stopped being Shawnee."

She stared, thinking he jested. He held her gaze, letting her see he didn't.

"It's going on thirteen years since we left them. More'n half my life ago."

He was only three and twenty. She'd thought him older.

"Why didn't —," she began, but Mr. Bird cut her off.

"Let the past bide. Now you're dry and fed, there's a talk more pressing we need to have."

14

"He's saying you *abducted* me?"

"Does it surprise you all that much?"

The blood had drained from Tamsen's face, hearing what Mr. Bird had learned from his foster father, detained in Morganton with their settler party long enough to be questioned by her stepfather and Ambrose Kincaid. She was pursued, but at least Mr. Parrish hadn't learned Mr. Bird's identity — only what had been told him by the trapper who'd given them the deerskin.

Mr. Bird was watching her across their little fire while she absorbed the news.

"What must we do?" she asked, feeling the dark press in with more malevolence than moments ago.

"I take it you still don't want to be found?"

As if there could be any doubt. "Not by either of them."

"Then there's two things we can do," he said, so readily she knew he'd been thinking hard on the subject. "Make for our place, mine and Cade's. It's off the beaten way. We'd be safe there for a time, at least. Or we can stay in these mountains, hide out, let the snow seal us in somewhere. It'll be rough, but I'd look after you, keep you warm, fed."

"Would it be just the two of us?"

"Aye. Like as not. Unless Cade finds us."

Tamsen drew her knees up, hugging them close, sobered by the realization of how much Mr. Bird had risked in aiding her. That he'd offered his help before she'd thought to seek it didn't ease the sense of obligation rising up through her grief and fear.

"Back in Morganton . . . why did you help me?"

"You needed me." His reply came quick enough, but not before she caught something guarded sliding across his eyes. She waited, but that seemed all he meant to say on the matter.

Did he see himself a knight to her rescue? A knight in greasy buckskins? The price he could pay for his chivalry must be a mite higher than he'd bargained for.

"We're not going anywhere till morning," he said. "Let's see what wisdom the sun brings. You be praying on it, all right?"

He would be, his expression told her plain.

Wrapped in her cloak and a blanket sent by Cade, Tamsen lay curled on her side beneath the pine shelter, still damp around the edges from the rain. Mr. Bird stayed by the fire. For a time she watched him through half-lidded eyes. The shirt she wore smelled of him, and his horse. She turned her face into the arm cradling her head, cheek against the rough sleeve, and stared at the strip of starry sky visible above distant peaks.

Somewhere far off, a wolf howled. Closer by, an owl screeched. Neither gave her more than a start. Not when Mr. Bird didn't flinch or even lift his head as the fire sank to embers at his feet. She felt safe with him, in a way she hadn't under the shingled roof of her stepfather's house in Charlotte Town. It was long since she'd trusted in a man, but she hadn't forgotten what that felt like.

Did she trust Mr. Bird, upon so brief an acquaintance? He'd snatched her out of a horrifying situation, risking his own well-being. He'd guided her across mountains, fed her, comforted her, saved her from drowning, and at every turn given her the thing she'd longed for since her stepfather first mentioned the name of Ambrose Kincaid in the same breath as marriage —

freedom to choose the shape her future would take. Or as much freedom as circumstances allowed.

Yet still . . . there lay the problem. Long before she'd understood the purpose, she'd been shaped with one aim in mind: marrying above her station in order to improve Hezekiah Parrish's lot. In the dark above the draw where her life had nearly ended, she lay thinking that, if not for Mr. Bird, she'd have died without ever truly knowing herself, what she was capable of becoming. She felt a stirring at the core of her being. What it was exactly she couldn't yet say. It was fragile, still encompassed by grief. But it was there, taking root inside her like the tiniest of promising seeds. Maybe it was hope.

And there was another stirring. One of obligation, tinged with guilt. Willing or no, Mr. Bird had been dragged into her sorrows. The threat of an abduction charge overshadowed him now. In her choosing which way they went from there, could she do anything to help him in return?

Opening her eyes a last time before sleep claimed her, she saw him by the firelight, still sitting. Maybe still praying.

I do trust him.

Perhaps it was this revelation coming on

the edge of sleep that sparked the notion, which in turned kindled a plan. A plan that — if Mr. Bird could be made to agree to it — might save them both from the pursuit she feared was bound eventually to overtake them.

Tamsen Littlejohn was silent through breakfast. She was silent when she went into the trees to don her clothing while he dismantled the shelter and covered all trace of their camp. Though the day promised fair, she came back swathed in her cloak, returning his shirt and breeches. Still she said not a word.

When the horse was loaded and there was no more to do but put her in the saddle and start out, Jesse handed her box into her keeping. "You decide what you want to do?"

"I have." She licked her lips and raised her chin, dark eyes wide and direct. "But first I need to ask you a question or two."

"All right," he said cautiously.

She pulled in a breath, then asked, "Are you given to hard drinking, Mr. Bird?"

He raised a brow. "No ma'am. Cade don't touch the stuff, and I rarely do."

She gave a nod, as if his answer satisfied. "Have you ever hit a woman?"

Both brows soared. "Never in my life. And

never mean to."

"Good," she said, leaving him mystified as she plowed ahead. "One thing more. You've quoted Scripture and told me Indian legends. Does that make you a Christian or a heathen?"

"I know for a truth it don't make me either one. A man can be a Christian and tell the stories of another people. Or a heathen and quote Scripture, for that matter."

She considered that, her full bottom lip drawn between pretty teeth. "But are you a Christian?"

"With all my heart, soul, and strength," he said. "Now how 'bout you answering my question? What have you decided?"

She raised her chin a fraction higher. It gladdened him to see her spirit emerging from the shock and grief that had wrapped her like a mountain mist since Morganton, but she had him flummoxed if he could guess what the next words out of her mouth would be. Would she choose west to Sycamore Shoals? North into —

"I've decided I want you to marry me — if you would, that is. If you think it would help matters for the both of us."

Good thing he'd already handed her the box, else he'd have dropped it where he stood. "You . . ." He sucked in air, having forgotten to breathe. "What?"

Her cheeks bloomed, but her tone held firm. "You can't be charged with abducting me if I'm your wife — by my consent."

"But we don't . . . I never thought . . ." Words failed him. The plain truth of it was he had thought — someday, God willing. But he'd imagined himself doing the proposing on that someday. While he admired her gumption and plain speaking, she fair made his head whirl. There she stood like a storm's calm center, while the mountains and their future and his heart spun 'round her. And he hadn't even brought up the murder charge. Maybe she didn't need to know about that. Not if the thought of him branded a kidnapper had brought her to this.

The spinning stopped, leaving his heart thumping out an eager beat like the call of drum and fire. He closed his eyes for a ten count, gathering his wits.

"Can I ask you something afore I give an answer? Why didn't you want to marry that planter?"

Her brows flicked in surprise. "He reminded me too much of Mr. Parrish."

"In what way?" Jesse's mind darkened

with suspicion. "He didn't hurt you, did he?"

"He struck a slave in front of me. Struck him for seeking his aid to help another of his slaves, one who'd been badly harmed." She opened her mouth to say more, then closed it and looked aside at the horse, raising a hand to stroke its flank.

"Your stepfather owns slaves," Jesse said. "I saw 'em."

"Dell and Sim. They ran away."

"Still running, to Cade's knowing." He saw her satisfaction at the news, a bright flicker amidst the shadow of more troubling thoughts. "Is it the violence you objected to or the slavery?"

"Both. You don't own slaves, do you?" She narrowed her eyes, as if to shield them from his scrutiny. He couldn't guess what she might be holding back on the subject of slaves, but he sensed there was more.

"I don't. Wager you'd reckon me a poor man."

"There is worse than being poor, Mr. Bird." She drew nearer, close enough that he could have touched her had he dared. "Is there a church or courthouse west of these mountains?"

"Several of both," he said, feeling the spinning start again.

"Then I'll stand in whichever you wish and say that marrying you is my choice."

She pressed her lips tight. Her fists curled at her sides. Jesse drew a steadying breath. He wanted to take her in his arms and show her in no uncertain terms the choice his heart had made in Morganton, seconds after meeting her gaze. But there was nothing intimate in this for her. Every resolute inch of her warned him to not presume otherwise. Even so, how was he to say no to this? Ought he to say no? Or was this the Almighty's doing, bringing them together this way?

He liked that last thought. Liked it with all his might.

"All right, then. My answer's aye. I'll marry you."

His heart gave a heady thump as relief flooded her face, and all he could do for a moment was suck the air into his chest, and look at her, and marvel that she'd come up with such a plan, and hope the feelings she'd stirred in him weren't showing on his face. She started to speak, but he raised a hand to stop her.

"We'll do this, but it ain't going to be a simple undertaking."

Her chin stayed raised. "Simple or not, it's what I choose."

Still stunned as a bear clubbed in its den, Jesse held the stirrup for her and gave her what he hoped was a reassuring smile. "Reckon, then, you and me are headed for Jonesborough."

■ ■ ■ ■

FOR BETTER, FOR WORSE

■ ■ ■ ■

15

Western North Carolina

Four days out from Morganton, Charlie Spencer stared into the forest gloom and cringed at the sound of two flatlanders tromping through the underbrush. Seeing to the necessary, quiet as a pair of buffalo.

Nell, lying against his thigh, raised her head at the ruckus and gave him a look of pure disgust. He grunted agreement with his hound, gripped his rifle, and went back to scanning the shadows thickening among the trees.

Charlie had made a habit out of not tangling himself in the affairs of strangers. As a rule, it kept his nose clean and got no man, or woman, riled enough to come hunting his hide, or those hides he spent half the year harvesting to keep body and soul together the other half. A confirmed loner he was — aside from the dogs and mules. But critters were easy company. They let a body go where he aimed and didn't pester him as to why. Just how it fell out he'd agreed to guide Hezekiah Parrish and Ambrose Kincaid Overmountain to the French Broad River settlements, when he'd meant to be making for his fall camp above the Holston, still had Charlie scratching his head like the dogs had shared their fleas again.

He'd scarce set foot in Morganton afore hearing of the Parrish woman's murder and her daughter's kidnapping. In the trade store, swapping hides for cornmeal, bullet lead, coffee, and sugar, he'd no more'n half-listened to the tale — till it reached the particulars of the missing girl. That's when he knew. He'd seen that girl with her dazed dark eyes. He'd seen her kidnapper, who'd said he was her husband, taking home his bride. Worst of it was, he'd known it wasn't one of those times he could shoulder on past, leaving folk to their own messy affairs.

He'd found the fellow called Parrish and told what he'd seen above his meadow camp. Before Charlie knew it, the girl's would-be suitor had joined them, seizing on this lead to her whereabouts, as fired as his red hair to be after her. That's when the whole thing went sliding out from under Charlie like a pig on a pine-needled slope.

Plans were made, avowals of rescue and reprisal uttered. Then all eyes turned his way. He was last to see the girl. He knew the mountains. Surely he wouldn't abandon the refined Miss Littlejohn to the mercies of a murdering backwoodsman out in the perilous wilds.

Sitting now, the fire warming his side, he reminded himself it was a good thing he was doing, the right thing, even if the search had so far turned up nothing. If the kidnapper had taken Miss Littlejohn to the French Broad country like he'd claimed to be doing, someone ought to have seen them by now. She wasn't a woman easily put out of mind. Even he'd seen that. But their failure to find trace of her wasn't what was plaguing Charlie most grievous as night closed 'round the camp.

"I've lost my razor strop to that foul stream!"

Charlie's shoulders hunched as Parrish fought his way out of a laurel thicket into firelight, coat creased and patched with damp, hose stained, brow dark as clouds fixing to spit hail.

It had been a trying day for Parrish. The only settlement they'd come across since breaking camp that morning had been burnt and abandoned. At the outset Charlie had cautioned they'd be traveling through Chickamauga-ravished country and such was to be expected. Still the sight had set Parrish on edge. Not that he was ever what you'd call sanguine.

Next they'd crossed a tributary to the French Broad, in full spate on account of rain upslope. Parrish's horse balked midway, dumping him and the contents of a poorly tied saddlebag into the creek. Charlie had hitched his lead mule and went back to help, while Kincaid dismounted to do likewise.

Despite the dogs romping through it all, thinking it a game, they'd saved most of what the creek snatched, including Parrish, who kicked one of the dogs in a fit of temper. Hearing Tuck's yip, Charlie had — behind Parrish's back — reached for his belt ax. Spying Kincaid's look of warning, he'd recalled himself and let the incident go. But it rankled.

In the end Parrish lost a tinderbox, a pair of thread stockings too fine to be of use, and apparently a razor strop. Though they'd built the fire on the spot to dry his things, Parrish still looked put out as he unrolled his bedding and tossed stones from beneath it into the brush.

Pelting how many Injuns? The thought

made Charlie grin, till a voice hailed from out of the dark.

"Cease! I come in peace." Kincaid stepped from the trees, rubbing a spot on his forehead blooming to match his hair.

Parrish stopped hurling stones and sat to tug off his boots, looking disgusted at the sucking sound they made coming free.

At the start of this business, Parrish had shown more'n a smidgen of deference to Kincaid, the young Virginia gentleman. But strain had frayed the merchant's regard till plain civility was wearing thin as threadbare linen.

Maybe he could be excused. Parrish had buried his wife in a hasty grave back in Morganton and must be out of his mind with worry for his stepdaughter.

Or not. Heck if Charlie could tell. Give him a dog any day. A mule, even. People had too many layers to work through to get at their truth. Charlie Spencer mistrusted layers, and Parrish seemed possessed of more'n his fair share.

Ringo, his old dog, yawned. The mules and horses, hobbled in grass near enough to guard, swished their tails and scented the camp with their droppings. Tuck lay at the edge of the firelight, eyes shining. Nell pressed her bony spine against his leg and sighed.

"You may borrow mine as needed," Kincaid said after a prickly silence.

Parrish looked across the fire. "I beg your pardon?"

"My strop. You may borrow it."

Though he'd taken to roughing it with somewhat better grace, Kincaid was no gladsome companion either. Around the fire at night, he mostly brooded — or stared at that tiny portrait of the girl they were tracking, though he tried to do the latter on the sly. He had it bad for Miss Littlejohn, and intentions dark as Parrish's for the man who'd murdered her ma and taken her Overmountain. Stringing him from the nearest tree was the favorite means of reckoning he'd heard the two discussing.

"Vile roots." Parrish got up to drag his bedding to another spot and commenced flinging stones again before finally lying down.

Kincaid caught Charlie's eye. "Will you turn in as well?"

"Aiming to keep watch long as I can. One o' ye gents of a mind to spell me?"

Parrish had gone still. Asleep, or letting on to be. Kincaid got up and retreated to the edge of the firelight, saying neither aye nor nay.

Charlie turned his gaze back into the dark, longing to find the girl and be done with the business. And present company.

The pairing of them was what confounded him most — men who'd likely never rub shoulders in life, brought together by that pretty face in the portrait Kincaid was even now slipping out of his coat pocket to moon over.

Women. Too much trouble to fool with, if you asked Charlie. A few more days, maybe a week, they'd find the girl, part ways, and he'd hightail it to the Holston, get back to blessed solitude. Or maybe . . . maybe he'd go visit that piedmont land in the Carraways, hilly acres back east he'd laid down shillings for years back while caught up in the notion he might make a farmer — a delusion half a summer shook him free of.

Just as well. A farmer needed sons. To get sons he'd need a wife, and Charlie Spencer was more sure now than he'd been in his six-and-thirty years that he could get along fine without one of those.

16

The State of Franklin . . . and North Carolina

It was morning, and Mr. Bird had left her again. This time he'd left the horse too, promising to return before she'd time to miss him. He'd set off at a lope into the trees, so Tamsen supposed he meant it.

Since that frightful day of the rainstorm, he'd met with Cade and the settlers twice, leaving her within shouting distance concealed along the wagon trace. This time he'd been evasive in his going, saying he needed to speak to someone before they continued on — the first indication Tamsen had that they were near wherever he called home. Good thing he knew. She was truly and utterly bewildered as to where she was.

For the past two days, they'd avoided farms and settlements when they could. From high trails that wound through massive hardwoods, Tamsen had glimpsed scattered homesteads carved from wooded coves, each with acres of standing corn, a cabin with a chimney wafting smoke into the vibrant blue of early autumn.

Or was it yet summer? The mountain ash and maple had been tipped with scarlet on the heights, the great chestnuts flushed with gold. But around her now all was green. The air had warmed as they came down off the windy balds. Before her lay a rolling country, hemmed by lesser ridges. It looked a peaceful land, nothing to indicate the strife transpiring there.

"Tell me if I have this straight." Tamsen had looked down from the saddle at the tail of Jesse Bird's hair, bleached to a shade nearly blond at the ends, as they'd made their way across another of the seemingly endless ridges. "There's the Old State faction — those who think this land west of the mountains is still North Carolina — and the New State faction, who call it Franklin. Both maintain a court in each county, and both expect the people to pay them taxes?"

"Right enough. You got Governor John Sevier and his ilk on the Franklin side. Colonel John Tipton at the head of the North Carolinians. Jonesborough is Franklin's town. Ten miles away, Tipton holds sessions for North Carolina. I figure we best marry under both states — so we wind up legal in the end." He'd looked up at her briefly. "Cade and I, we keep out of that fray. Not hard to do when you spend half the year roaming for furs."

Roaming. Maybe his use of that word had been the start of it, the first layer of uncertainty sifting down like silt over the choice she'd made. Would he still want to roam once they were married? If so, what would she be expected to do? Stay behind in a cabin somewhere, not even certain what state she was in?

Surely he'd exaggerated the situation. People couldn't live under such confusion. Or had he understated it so as not to frighten her?

His horse, waiting more patiently in the little clearing than she was doing, chose that moment to ruckle down its nose — a sound befitting thoughts of Jesse Bird's delicacy in sparing her feelings at this point. She couldn't be more unnerved by the unknown stretching before her, and she wasn't thinking primarily of land. Or politics.

Standing by the stream, alone with her thoughts for the first time in days, she confronted the doubts that had built up since she stood above that draw and asked Mr. Bird to marry her.

Mama, what would you have done?

The answer hit her so square that she dropped to her knees, sick in her stomach. Her mother would have gone through with this risky marriage. Her mother *had* gone through with such a marriage so that Tamsen would have a decent roof over her head, security, comfort. Instead of repaying her mother's sacrifice by doing what her stepfather wanted of her, Tamsen had broken the bars of that cage, and her mother had paid the price.

She bowed her face into her hands. "Mama, I'd undo it all if I could. I'd stay at that table and smile at Mr. Kincaid no matter what I was thinking. But it's too late, and I don't want them to find me — or Mr. Bird. Or taking me away if they do."

By what means could she keep that from happening save marrying Mr. Bird?

With empathy for her mother like she'd never known, Tamsen willed her stomach to settle and rose to make use of what time was left her.

Never mind the State of Franklin. It was the state of her clothing that presently grieved her. Her torn petticoat and jacket were too bedraggled for a rinse in the stream to improve matters, had there been time for the garments to dry. Mr. Bird had seen her in worse — his own clothes — but even while dreading marrying Mr. Kincaid, this wasn't how she'd pictured herself on The Day. Then, at least, there had been the consolation of her stepfather's finest silk. Pearls sewn on her bodice and entwined in her hair. And lace. Rivers and falls of lace. And she'd been clean, not soiled head to toe from crossing mountains and sleeping by open fires.

Kneeling at the stream, she washed her face. There was little help for her hair beyond brushing it out and coiling it off her neck, secured with the ivory combs. That left her pinner, which she anchored with the carefully hoarded hairpins. One bit of lace, soiled as the rest of her.

Somewhere near, a branch snapped.

Tamsen's heart skipped as a deer stepped from the brush across the stream, saw her, and bounded off again, white tail high. Nothing else moved among the trees except the birds. Their songs filled the air, shrill above the stream's chatter. Like the frantic voices still clamoring inside her, for all her willing them silent.

There was no turning back time, no making things as they were before she walked away from Mr. Kincaid. She told herself marriage to Jesse Bird was a better prospect than marriage to any man her stepfather would have chosen. At least Mr. Bird didn't own slaves.

Did he own anything at all? He hadn't pressed upon her any knowledge of himself that she hadn't sought to learn, save that he'd called himself a poor man. She wished she'd sought a little more diligently.

"Lord, have mercy," she said, rising from the stream. As she did, Mr. Bird stepped from the trees.

He hadn't worn his breechclout today but the breeches and shirt he'd briefly lent her, with the buckskin coat. His hair was damp, tied back at his neck. His lean jaw, fresh shaven, had a scrubbed look. His features were a careful mask. He'd heard her prayerful plea. She was sure of it. Had he heard, or seen, anything more?

"It's early enough we can reach Jonesborough," he said through tight lips. "Get the Franklin marrying done today. But first," he added, and his mouth softened. "I fetched these for you."

A petticoat and matching bodice draped his arm. Tamsen, her jaw slackened, came forward, reaching for the garments. They were linen — fine woven, not homespun — died the warm brown of pecans, a lighter shade than the rags she wore. They boasted no adornment. No pearls or lace. But —

she raised them to her face — they smelled of lavender and cedar, and they were clean.

Mr. Bird was watching her. "I thought Janet Allard was about your size. Will they do?"

Tamsen held the petticoat to her waist. It fell a tad long, but she could tie it high. The sleeves of the bodice cuffed below the elbow, an inch or two long, but it looked to be a passable fit. The garments were so much better than what she'd expected to be married in that it took her a moment to find her voice.

"Thank you. What made you think to do this?"

"I saw you in that blue gown, remember?" He gave her a crooked smile. "Though far as I'm concerned, you could drape yourself in sacking and still be pretty as a speckled pup."

Speckled. She raised a hand to her cheek. "Have I acquired freckles?"

"Well . . ." He pretended to peer at her, then broke into a full grin. "Not nary a one. But I wish you could see yourself, the way you've taken the sun. You've colored up the prettiest shade of gold."

"Mr. Bird . . ." Heat rose to her cheeks at his open admiration, but something more serious had her crumpling the garments he'd brought her, all but wringing them in sudden nervousness. Was she as olive skinned as her mother now? She touched her fingertips to her face again, then whipped them away as Mr. Bird's eyes rested on her, questioning.

She had to tell him. The last thing she wanted were secrets between them, secrets that might one day come to light and cause her to suffer the way her mother had . . . because she'd married Mr. Parrish without telling him she'd been a slave.

That was what her mother must have done. But somehow Mr. Parrish had found out the truth and punished her for it ever since.

"There's something I need to tell you."

Mr. Bird looked mystified. "All right."

Praying those words would still be on his lips once she was through, Tamsen closed her eyes and said, "My mother was a slave, Mr. Bird. Papa — my real father, Stephen Littlejohn — freed her, and married her, and to my knowing didn't tell anyone the truth. I only found out right before . . ." She clenched her teeth, willing her mind away from that room in Mrs. Brophy's house. "If this changes your mind about marrying me, I'll understand."

There was the smallest silence before he

spoke. "Is that what's in that box of yours? Something to do with all this?"

Tamsen nodded, opening her eyes to see him looking at her with the last expression she'd expected, a wry smile.

"If my own upbringing hasn't put you off marrying me, then I don't aim to let your mother's having been a slave keep me from" — he seemed to change what he'd been about to say — "from doing whatever you need me to do so you feel safe."

She worried over that pause. "You're certain? I mean *certain,* because this isn't just about me. I'm doing this for —"

"I'm certain," he said with firmness. "But, Tamsen?"

She waited, her stomach turning flips at the change in his expression. There was warning in his face.

"Don't go telling anyone else what you just told me. Leastwise, not in that courthouse we'll be standing in later today."

"But you said you don't mind it."

"That's not it. I don't know about Franklin, but North Carolina has laws against some folk marrying on account of things like blood."

"Oh." She felt the biggest fool. It had never once entered her head, those laws against interracial marriage. Of course she'd known they existed, but it wasn't something she'd ever thought about as having any bearing on herself. Even if Mr. Bird wanted to marry her — and he looked for all the world as if he did — was this going to help the man, repay him for all he'd done for her, or make it worse for him? If Mr. Parrish knew the truth about her, couldn't he simply declare the marriage illegal once he found them, lay claim to her again, bring that abduction charge against Mr. Bird?

If she was legally a person of mixed blood. Her father had been white. Had her mother a white father as well? At what point did a person stop being too mixed to marry white?

There was her mother's box, tied behind the horse's saddle. Its contents might settle the question . . . or might not.

She didn't look at the box, and Mr. Bird didn't seem to think of it. "If that's settled, go put on those clothes, and we'll see to getting this union made legal — at least as far as anyone else is concerned."

She swallowed further protest, her stomach doing a different sort of flip. "I'll need to wear my stays again for the gown to fit. Will you tie them for me?"

"Do I have to?" He was trying to look disapproving, but humor lurked in his eyes. If he aimed to calm her nerves, he'd struck the right note.

She drew herself up straight, matching his gaze. "Yes, Mr. Bird. Unless there are more mountains to climb betwixt here and Jonesborough?"

"No ma'am. Not from here on."

"Then, if you please, I prefer to be married in my stays."

17

In the log-built structure that served as the courthouse in the hamlet of Jonesborough, faced with the sheet of foolscap he was meant to sign to post a marriage bond, Jesse Bird felt the spit dry in his mouth.

"You're telling me I'm liable for how much?"

"Five hundred pounds." The clerk, a tall, bony man, angular as a wading heron, shuffled through a stack of papers on the table, then turned to call a question to someone in a back room.

Till today, Jesse had never stepped foot inside a courthouse, Franklin or otherwise. A sense of urgent business taking place just out of sight, of nerves stretched taut behind harried gazes, had infected him the moment he entered the confined space, rifle slung at his shoulder, Tamsen Littlejohn at his side. Forced to wait while an older couple saw to some matter of a land deed, he'd been edgy to have the proceedings over long before he was called by the clerk. Tamsen, lovely in her borrowed gown, still occupied the bench beside the door, along with several later arrivals, all within hearing of every word Jesse uttered.

"I'm back from east of the mountains, all my furs turned to winter supplies. Not hard coin."

The clerk jerked his chin at the crowded bench. "Post bond or don't. I haven't time to jaw over your private business."

Jesse's frustration must have shown in the beat of silence when the clerk finally met his gaze.

"You don't have to do it this way," the man informed him. "Find a minister. Have the banns read. But you'll have to wait three weeks in case anyone objects to the union."

Jesse glanced at Tamsen. Her eyes had widened at the clerk's pronouncement, reflecting the unease that had coiled inside him when he learned they'd have to put their names in writing. He hadn't thought through the details of what two people had to do to be married legal, never having the need. Signing their names seemed like leaving a trail a crawling babe could follow. But having banns read three weeks in a row was nigh as bad. Parrish and Kincaid might spend those weeks nosing along the French Broad, or they could show up in Jonesborough by suppertime.

The clerk waved away a fly that had come in through the open door. "I can't see what the problem is. You do want to get married?"

The man didn't need to know the worst of it. "The problem is I ain't got five hundred pounds to lay down. I'd like to know who does."

The clerk's brows shot high. "You don't have to pay it *today*. You're only pledging that price to your wife if some impediment to the marriage should arise after the fact."

Far from reassured, Jesse asked, "What sort of impediment?"

"You don't have another wife stashed away somewhere?" The clerk gave him a looking-over and leaned close. "I don't mean an Injun. That don't count."

Hot blood flooded Jesse's face. Tamsen's gaze bore hotter into his back. He ground his teeth. "She'll be my first. And only."

"Well, then, is she twenty-one, or have her parents' consent?"

"Her parents are deceased," Jesse said, skirting the former question which he couldn't answer. Tamsen might be twenty-one. Or eighteen. Why hadn't he asked?

197

Sweat was gathering on his brow. The clerk batted the persistent fly.

"If you mean to sign, I suggest you make it fast on account —"

"Amis!" Another man stuck his head around the doorway of the adjoining room. "Need you in here to witness."

"Sign or make your mark — there." The clerk jabbed a finger at the paper, then ducked into the back room.

Jesse beckoned Tamsen to his side.

"What's wrong?" she asked.

Outside the courthouse voices rose and there was the stamp of horses hooves. Was this why all the tension and hurry? Some big proceeding set to get underway?

"Just need to sign this. Then we stand before the justice of the peace, who I'm guessing's in that back room." The blood pounded in his temples. Every instinct was telling him this was a mistake.

The clerk poked his head in view, shot a glance toward the door. Not a harried glance this time. One of plain alarm. Anxiety leapt from the back room, licking like flames at the edges of Jesse's mind. They had to do this. They'd ridden half the day into Jonesborough. They had to be married, for both their protection. Hadn't they?

He took up the quill, dipped it, but had

198

written no more than *Jesse* before the disturbance outside escalated to shouts.

"We aim to enter the premises of this unlawful court. Stand aside!"

"Over our rottin' corpses you're coming in here!"

"If needs be —"

"Ye got no right!"

Two men waiting on the bench leapt to their feet as the doorway darkened. A scuffle ensued, men pushing in, others pushing back, then the tangle burst like a festered sore and bodies spilled into the courthouse. A dozen men, armed and grim, fanned out through the front room. Jesse knew the figure at the center of the throng — Colonel John Tipton. A big man with a big voice, Tipton raised it above those clamoring for his immediate removal from the Franklin court premises. "By the authority of the State of North Carolina, I demand all records of this illicit court be remanded into my keeping."

"Absolutely not, sir!" The shrill rebuke belonged to a gray-haired man who charged out of the back room, riled as a fighting cock and nigh as small. "How dare you insult this honorable court with such outrageous accusations and demands?"

Jesse calculated their escape. A few paces

of open floor space separated them from the confrontation — one balanced on the blade of a knife, violence a word or misstep away.

"It's this so-called *court* that insults the General Assembly and the good order of the State of North Carolina." Tipton motioned to his men, three of whom headed for the back room with rifles ready.

The older man flung his short arms wide. "Calumny — thievery!"

Tamsen clutched his arm. "Jesse, are they going to —"

"Come on." He snatched the bond paper off the desk, cramming it inside his coat, then grabbed her hand and edged toward the door, glancing back to see the clerk lunge from the room and throw a wild punch at one of Tipton's men.

Whatever restraint had held till then evaporated. Others rushed toward the back of the courthouse, leaving the door temporarily clear. Jesse hurried Tamsen through it.

Behind them a brawl erupted.

From cabins, smithy, stores, stables, and tavern, men came at the run, dodging wagon ruts and stumps left standing in cleared lots. Jesse recognized faces in the crowd but hoped stranger and acquaintance alike were too set on the melee to pay them any mind. He unhitched the horse, took the reins in hand, and made for the edge of town, Tamsen trotting along on the horse's other side, clinging to the stirrup. They'd reached the tavern on the track leading out of town when a familiar voice cried above the commotion.

"What's this? Jesse Bird down out of his holler?" It was Dominic Trimble, sandy headed, blue eyed, slowing his dash for the courthouse, grabbing at his brother as he did so. "Lookit who's graced Jonesborough with his presence."

"Jesse!" Seth Trimble, younger of the two, called. "Where you going? Fun's this a'way."

"Not for me." Jesse turned the horse so it blocked their view of Tamsen, praying she'd stay behind it. "Some other time, boys."

"You been saying that for how long? Too good for the likes of us!" Dominic waved him off like a lost cause, grinning as he followed his brother and half the town toward the courthouse. Jesse hurried on, sweating in relief. Beyond the last cabin on the outskirts, he slowed the horse.

Tamsen came around to face him, breathless and worried. "Friends of yours?"

"Just a pair of rascals from back in Virginia."

"They seemed to know you."

"We're acquainted, aye. I let them lure me into betting on a horse race once, over in Sycamore Shoals — lost what little coin I had and found out later they likely fixed the race ahead of time. Cade was furious with me for mixing with 'em at all. He's heard tell they came Overmountain on account of trouble with the law back east."

"What sort of trouble?"

"No idea, and they aren't likely to say." Jesse tried to smile, though his heart had yet to cease its pounding. He didn't think the Trimbles had taken note of Tamsen. Not even a courthouse brawl would've pulled Dominic away had he seen her.

She glanced back the way they'd come. "The clerk . . . that little judge . . . Will they be all right?"

"I couldn't linger to get drawn in."

"I know." She met his gaze, knowledge that he'd fled for her sake clear in her eyes. "That's not what I asked."

"If it ain't come to shooting yet, it won't." Even the shouting had died down. "What you saw wasn't the start of things, and it won't be the end. It'll be Franklin men storming Carolina's courthouse next, or something like it."

Tamsen's breathing slowed. He could see

her coming to grips with the scuffle they'd narrowly evaded. "I'd hoped you had exaggerated."

"Wish I had. But I don't know . . . It might've been for the best."

That surprised her. "You've changed your mind?"

"No." *Lord, no,* he had to restrain himself from saying. He took out the crumpled bond. "It's only that our names would've gone on record with this. Maybe not the wisest notion, all things reconsidered." It wasn't till he glanced again at his half-signed name that it hit him, what she'd called him right before they fled the courthouse. Not Mr. Bird. *Jesse.*

He couldn't suppress his grin even when she shook her head as if he'd lost his mind, confusion in her searching eyes.

"What do we do now?"

He didn't have an answer yet, but he was already working on it. "Let's go." Putting his back to Jonesborough, he led his horse and his almost-wife toward a new plan taking shape.

It had turned into another wearisome day of traveling. They'd ridden double for a time, but now Mr. Bird led her on the horse, the borrowed petticoat rucked up above her moccasins. He hadn't said much since leaving Jonesborough, though plainly he was thinking hard. Tamsen had held her peace, chary of asking the questions swirling through her head. How many miles they'd come, heading roughly north, she didn't know. They were traversing a hilly track that passed an occasional cabin, a plot standing in corn and tree stumps, sometimes a fellow traveler. Mr. Bird trudged on like a man with a destination in mind and precious little time to reach it.

Curiosity at last surmounted Tamsen's weariness. "Exactly what are we doing?"

He glanced up at her. "We're going to be married. If that's still what you want."

She nodded, bereft of any other course. "A North Carolina court?"

"Same problem there — our names on record."

"Then where? How? We can't wait three weeks for a minister."

"There's one other way. If I can get him to agree to it."

"Who?"

"We're nigh there." He nodded ahead and pulled in a deep-chested breath.

The homestead they were making for just off the track they'd followed looked like others they'd passed — a cabin, corn scattered through girdled trees, a garden, outbuildings — except for the large log structure at the edge of the skirting forest opposite the cabin. At the garden's edge a flock of yellow finches darted among tall sunflowers with heads bowed like a congregation at prayer. The sun was in the west, casting the clearing in a green, peaceful light. No outward sign labeled it so, but Tamsen, gazing from the back of the horse as they passed, might almost have guessed the larger structure to be . . . "Is that a church?"

Jesse nodded. "It is. Mine and Cade's. It's a fair piece to travel from our place, though, so we don't make meetings often."

Mr. Parrish didn't go in for religion, so she and her mother hadn't set foot inside a meetinghouse in years. But when her father was alive, they'd attended Anglican services. She felt an ache of longing. "What sort of church is it?"

"Bible-preaching, deep-water Baptist." They stopped in the cabin yard, where Mr. Bird hitched the horse to a post. "He might be tending his other flock, over to Doe Creek. I'll see if he's about the place."

Mr. Bird helped her out of the saddle before she could ask a single question. She was brushing down her rumpled skirts when he spoke, but not to her.

"Reverend." His tone — an odd mingling of warmth, respect, and apprehension — more than his address made Tamsen look up.

A man stood in the cabin doorway. He was of middle height, thick waisted, with a head of dark curls heavily silvered, cropped at the collar of his shirt. His gaze rested on Tamsen before darting with the quickness of the finches to the man beside her. The lines of his face deepened with welcome.

"Jesse. This is a surprise. Aren't you meant to be shepherding cows back east?"

"Aye sir." Mr. Bird swallowed. Hard. "Had us a minor set-to with some Chickamaugas, but Cade and I got the cows and the drovers down to market. All but one — cow, I mean. Rhodes, Billy, Jabez, they all made it fine. Cade's heading back with a passel of settlers, but I — *we* come on ahead."

Tamsen had never heard Mr. Bird chatter so nervously. He touched her elbow, and she jumped.

"Tamsen, this is Reverend Luther Teague, our preacher."

Mr. Bird urged her forward as Reverend Teague stepped into the yard, reaching out a hand. Whether by design or instinct, Mr. Bird raised hers and placed it in the reverend's, who clasped it warmly.

It was the only hand he had. The man's left sleeve dangled empty from the elbow. Tamsen looked away from it, into a pair of deep-set brown eyes as kind as they were keen.

"This is Tamsen Littlejohn," Jesse Bird said, his voice dry-sounding at the edges. "She and I aim to be married, Reverend — today, if you'd oblige us."

18

"There now. That's everyone settled, is it?" Molly Teague stood back to survey the table laid with tea, shaved from a brick of pressed black leaf. "Saved for my most special guests," she said, then brushed her hands down her apron's ample front, beaming at them seated in the cabin's homey front room.

Jesse glanced across at Tamsen, who cradled a china cup between her hands as if its contents were too precious to bring to her lips. Finally she took a sip.

"Mrs. Teague, this is — heavenly." She closed her eyes. Her mouth trembled, and she crumpled into tears.

Jesse half-rose from his chair, uncertain what to do, but neither of the Teagues showed the slightest upset while Tamsen sniffled and gulped and tried to stem the tide of emotion.

The preacher, seated at the table's head,

grasped his wife's hand. "Thank you, Molly. You'll join us?"

Molly slid into the last empty chair, giving Tamsen's shoulder a squeeze and offering a ready handkerchief. "It'll all work out, my dear, and for the good. You wait and see if it doesn't."

The gesture and words brought on a new freshet, but Tamsen put the kerchief to use. "I didn't mean to spoil such a pretty tea."

Reverend Teague took a swallow. "Molly's tea tastes just fine. Nothing's spoiled that I can tell." His eyes twinkled at his wife, then at Tamsen, till she returned a watery smile.

Jesse settled back in his chair, too wretched over Tamsen's misery for tea drinking. Her sudden upset perplexed him. He stared at the delicate, rose-patterned teacup still cradled in her graceful hands. It was a far cry from canteens and creek water. She wouldn't have seen a thing so fine since . . .

Understanding dawned. The kindness of the Teagues, the china, the homey comforts of the cabin — she was thinking of her mother and everything she'd lost, sitting there grieving while he studied on how to talk his preacher into pronouncing them man and wife. He wanted more than ever to go 'round the table and console her, but before he could budge, Luther Teague got down to business.

"Jesse, Tamsen, the two of you wish to marry, do you?"

Jesse bit back a hasty *aye,* waiting for Tamsen to speak.

"We do," she said, with far less certainty than he'd hoped for.

"Today," Jesse added, with enough to make up for her lack.

Reverend Teague shared his gaze between them. "Is there some reason for haste?"

Tamsen colored like a ripe strawberry. Jesse was a beat behind in comprehending.

"No sir. Not that. We haven't . . ." Face warming, he leaned forward, hands fisted on the table's checked cloth. "It's complicated, Reverend. Tamsen's parents are both passed. Her step —" He glanced at her, then hastily away. "We met in Morganton after Cade and me got the cows to market. Tamsen was in a spot of trouble and needed the protection of a man not bent on using her for his own gain."

He couldn't meet anyone's eyes now. He stared at his hands, sun-browned and clenched. That he'd fallen head over heels for Tamsen at sight of her, had his head filled with notions of the Almighty meaning her for him, didn't seem a piece of news liable to aid their cause. More likely to color every action he'd taken since — and not in a becoming shade. "Our marrying now is part and parcel of me assuring her safety." And his own, he might've added.

"I see," said Reverend Teague, leaving Jesse wondering how much the man did see. "Does Cade give his blessing to this union?"

Jesse chose his words carefully. He hadn't told Cade about the marrying. "Cade knows about Tamsen and the need to keep her safe. He's in agreement with me on that."

The preacher seemed to weigh Jesse's answer with equal care. "Wouldn't you rather wait, so Cade can be here to stand up with you?"

"With respect, Reverend, I'm well over my majority and don't need any by-your-leave for this, from Cade or anyone."

Reverend Teague blinked. "I meant his blessing, Jesse. Not his permission."

This wasn't starting well. Jesse knew it by the guarded look stealing over Molly's pleasant face, the set of the preacher's mouth. He was digging them a hole he might never climb out of if he didn't hit on the right words, and quick. He drew breath, hoping they'd be there when he opened his mouth.

"It was me," Tamsen blurted. "I asked Mr.

Bird — Jesse — to marry me."

Jesse risked a glance at her. The strain on her face was anything but reassuring. "She did, Reverend, for a fact. But it's my choosing too. And if you'd consider marrying us today, without reading the banns —"

"Jesse?" Reverend Teague stood from the table. "Might I ask you to step outside? If Miss Littlejohn is agreeable, I'd like to speak with her and Molly. Alone."

Jesse froze, then looked at Tamsen. Her eyes held trepidation, but she nodded. "You sure?" he asked her, not at all certain this turn was for the best.

She looked at the preacher and his wife, then reached across the table and touched his hand. "It's all right, Jesse."

Luther Teague waited, no telling from his face whether he meant to talk Tamsen out of the whole idea of marrying, urge her to wait, or something else entirely. But the jolt that went through him at her touch left him so befuddled that he found himself outside the cabin without knowing quite how he'd gotten there.

Beside the door was a bench. He sat on it, leaned over his knees, and put his head in his hands. He scrubbed his fingers back through his hair, pulling it free from the whang he'd tied it with that morning — a morning that seemed weeks ago. He captured the bit of leather and picked at the knot. Above him stretched a sky half-clouded in mare's tails beginning to pink with sunset. Would he and Tamsen be married come nightfall? Or would she bid him leave her with the Teagues and go his way?

It shook him to the core, how much it mattered. What he'd seen in her that day in Morganton when she stumbled into Cade, again during that first encounter in the stable — determination, yearning, fragile hope — it was coming back to her again, though he knew she still had grieving to do.

What was it she hoped for? What did she want for herself? Apart from keeping shed of her stepfather. She had courage to have come this far. And, he dared believe, some small faith in him.

Enough to convince the preacher they did no wrong in marrying?

The murmur of voices wafted from the cabin like a teasing aroma. Banished from the conversation, unable to settle within hearing of it, he stood. Across the clearing the meetinghouse door stood ajar. It was almost always left so, for anyone to enter.

He was striding across the clearing before he knew he meant to do so, lips moving on a soundless prayer.

Within moments of Jesse's leaving, Tamsen had poured out her tale, from the portrait's commissioning, to Ambrose Kincaid, to her mother's death and the flight from Morganton, including the charge of abduction that hung over Jesse.

"That's why I asked him to marry me. To protect him, like he's protected me."

The Teagues had listened, asked a few questions to clarify matters, then bowed their heads as if by mutual consent. The reverend prayed aloud to the Almighty for comfort for Tamsen, protection for her and Jesse, finally for guidance. At last Luther Teague raised his deep-set eyes and smiled in a way that made Tamsen weep again. Silent, cleansing tears.

He reached out his hand, covering both of hers clasped tight on her knees. Rather than addressing any of the things she'd told him, he said, "Tell me, my dear. What do you make of our Jesse Bird?"

Tears still wet on her cheeks, she glanced toward the cabin door. "He's a good man. And a God-fearing man, I think."

"He is that. Is it important to you that he be both?"

"Yes."

"Yet you don't love him?" It was Molly who asked the gentle, probing question.

Flustered, Tamsen managed a strained whisper. "He's been kind and brave, but . . . I barely know him."

"Molly and I have known Jesse a good many years," the reverend said. "What has he told you of his history?"

"That he was raised by the Shawnees. And by Cade." Tamsen frowned. "If you think I should be concerned about that, I'm not. We were alone in the mountains for days and not once did he misbehave toward me. He's been a perfect gentleman in all the ways that matter. More than my stepfather ever was — and him I wish never to see again, or give any right to me whatsoever. I will never again live under the roof of the man who killed my mother. Not for an hour."

While her words rang in the quiet cabin, Tamsen straightened her shoulders, drew back her hands from the reverend's clasp, and waited.

"And yet you might have stayed," Molly said. "Married the man your stepfather chose for you, and escaped him just as well."

Tamsen shook her head. "Mr. Kincaid was no better than my stepfather. I saw him commit violence against one of his slaves. My mother taught me to treat our slaves with kindness. She —" Tamsen met their gazes, hands fisted in her lap. "Jesse told me not to speak of this, but I see he trusts you, and maybe you can tell me whether our marriage would even be legal. We'd need it to be legal, you see."

Their puzzlement was plain. "Legal in what way?" Molly asked.

Taking a deep breath, Tamsen explained. "My mother was born a slave. I don't know how she and my father met, but he obtained her freedom, and he married her — or pretended to. I was born after her manumission, but . . . I don't know what I am."

Nor did she know what her mother's having been a slave meant to her, or should mean. Perhaps, eventually, it wouldn't matter, but right now it did. Very much.

"Mama *looked* white, you see."

"And you wish to know how white a woman need be to marry a white man?" Molly asked.

"Yes." She waited what seemed an interminable pause, while Luther Teague considered.

"As I understand the laws of North Carolina," he said, "if a person is known to have one great-grandparent of the African race,

216

then that person is considered of mixed blood."

"One eighth," Tamsen whispered.

Molly took her hand in hers, gripping it gently. "Is marrying Jesse that important to you?"

Tamsen looked down at the hand gripping hers. An older hand, not smooth or firm. Yet there was no difference in the color of their skin, hand to hand, aside from Molly's having a spattering of brown spots. It was the blood beneath that mattered to those who made and kept the laws. "What's important is that he not suffer for helping me. I'd thought if we married, there would be no grounds for an abduction charge."

"That's as may be," the reverend said. "But have you considered what you might feel a year from now? In five years? Or twenty?"

Twenty years? She hadn't yet dared look beyond that day.

Molly squeezed her hand. "What Luther means is, have you thought that one day you might regret not marrying for love? That's something most young women hope for, is it not?"

She was fighting tears again. She was so weary of tears. "But I don't have a choice, do I?"

"Perhaps you do."

She looked at the reverend, who'd made the statement. "What do you mean?" An idea struck her. "Oh . . . that maybe I can stay here? With you and Mrs. Teague?"

The couple exchanged a glance heavy with unspoken words. Tamsen felt the hope the idea had kindled flicker. It was Molly who quenched it, though she did so kindly. "Luther and I would certainly not object, but from what you've told us thus far, it seems to me that staying here, where our meeting gathers, would place you in great danger of discovery."

Tamsen bowed her head, staring at the tea gone tepid in her cup. "What, then, should I do? I won't go back."

"No one is saying you should," the reverend assured her. "What we're saying is this: Don't make a decision now that you cannot undo, though you spend the rest of your life regretting it. Take the time you need to be certain — which I don't think you are just now."

Tamsen had been leaning forward, listening with all her might. At this pronouncement, she sat back in her chair. She tried to force her mind ahead that twenty years the reverend mentioned, tried to see herself with Jesse Bird . . . and knew that Luther

218

Teague was right. She was far from sure about anything, except not wishing to be found by the men who pursued her.

She'd wished for freedom, yet the reality of it was proving more complicated than she'd ever imagined.

Reverend Teague's gaze was gentle in its scrutiny of her — but thorough. "Do you remember what Molly said, before we sent Jesse out to bide his soul in patience?"

She almost smiled at the twinkle in his eyes. "Something about everything turning out all right."

"Do you know why I said that?"

She looked at Molly. "To make me feel better?"

Molly chuckled. "That's one reason. But they weren't empty words. Our Father in heaven works all things for good, for those who love Him and want to see His will done in their lives. Do you believe this?"

Tamsen chewed her lip. Dared she be honest?

"I want to believe, but . . . how can what happened to my mother be *good*?"

Compassion filled the reverend's eyes. "Not everything that happens to us in this life will bring us joy. Certainly not the grievous death of your mother. But in time God will work even the worst things men do to us for our lasting good. Eternal good. Trust in the Almighty, in His love for you, and you'll have no need to dread anything He allows to befall you. For with a test, a trial, He gives an equal measure of grace to bear it and the comfort of His fellowship as He strengthens us. He is acquainted with suffering."

Tamsen dropped her gaze to the reverend's empty sleeve, mute testimony to his own suffering. "Would you tell me . . . ?" She put a hand to her mouth, appalled at her forwardness, but Luther Teague showed no sign he felt himself intruded upon.

"It was during the war for our independence, at a place called Kings Mountain. Our Overmountain militia — including Jesse and Cade — took prisoner a whole company under British Major Ferguson. It was quite the victory, but we had our losses. I took a musket ball in the elbow, and my arm couldn't be saved."

"I'm sorry for it," Tamsen said, meaning it.

"We also lost a son. Mine and Molly's only child."

Tamsen felt her heart squeeze tight. She looked at Molly, whose eyes were moist. This loss went beyond frail words of condolence, but it seemed none were needed.

Peace dwelled in both their faces. Sorrow too, even after all these years, but the peace was stronger.

"We'll see Liam again," Luther Teague said. "As I'm sure you shall one day see your mother, if I judge anything about her trust in the Almighty after talking with her daughter."

Tears were a fountain, hot and stinging. Tamsen wondered if they would ever stop. "Yes," she choked out. "Mama's in heaven. With Papa. I think . . . I think she saw him in the end. Waiting for her."

They let her cry, unflinching in the face of her emotion, and when she had control of herself, the reverend took her other hand in his. "Have faith that God has you right where you need to be, though all around seems bewildering. Have faith that He sent you help when you needed it, that He will guide you on from this moment too. One step at a time. You don't have to figure it all out now."

She wanted such faith. She wanted to believe that in the same hour the Almighty allowed her mother to be taken away, He'd given her Jesse Bird to deliver her from her stepfather and Mr. Kincaid. But delivered unto what?

"I will try," she said.

221

"Good." The reverend's eyes held hers, steadying. "Now, there's a young man out there waiting to know what it is you truly need from him. Tell me what that is, and I'll go have a talk with him about it."

You know my heart better'n I do. If this is all for me — my wants — then turn her path another way. Don't let her yoke herself to me if it'll bring her nothing but regret . . . Jesse hadn't approached the front of the church, where the simple wooden pulpit stood. He'd done his talking to the Almighty from a back pew, forearms on his knees, the hardwood seat pressing into his thighs, the building's musty scent filling his nose. *Cover her. That's all I'm asking now. If not through me, then some other way. But if it can be me . . .*

After a stretch of praying in circles, he could bear it no longer. He stood, thinking they had to have gotten something sorted between them by now. Opening the meetinghouse door wide, he found himself face to face with Reverend Teague.

"Jesse. Thought I'd find you here. Walk with me?" Luther Teague's face was relaxed, welcoming, which told Jesse nothing since that's how the man most always looked.

In silence they strode toward Molly's garden, where the sunflowers stood like spindly women in yellow bonnets, heads bent. The finches took flight at their coming. Jesse's heart fluttered in his chest. "Well, Reverend?"

"I'm going to explain why I won't be marrying you and Tamsen today."

Jesse didn't know if he was more dismayed or — and this was odd — relieved. "Reverend," he started in knee-jerk protest but checked at a lifting of the older man's brows.

"Hear me out first, Jesse. Please. Tamsen has told us everything, and there's nothing you've done that strikes me as misguided, as best I understand this situation."

That sounded good, but there was one thing the preacher couldn't know. "With respect, sir, Tamsen didn't tell you everything because she don't know everything." Though they were a distance from the cabin, he lowered his voice. "There's more'n just a kidnapping charge hanging over me on account of all this. I'm accused of murdering her ma — by the man who actually did the violence that killed her."

If he'd thought this might shock the preacher or convince him to reconsider his decision, Jesse was disappointed. "That only confirms to me that allowing Tamsen to make this sacrifice for you is something I'm not prepared to do."

223

Jesse started to speak, then clenched his jaw and pleaded silently with the man who'd been his and Cade's preacher for years, had put him under the waters of baptism when he was still a boy.

Reverend Teague smiled, in sympathy rather than amusement. "Jesse, too much has happened to her in too short a time. Time — maybe a lot of it — is what Tamsen needs."

"And protection."

"True. But you can give her that without the pair of you committing yourselves until death do you part. Besides, this is her choice."

Jesse sucked hard on his lip to keep from saying anything too hasty. Where had that fleeting sense of relief gone? He wished it back. "What does she want to do, then? Stay here with you?"

"As I explained to Tamsen, that won't do. She'd be too easily found." The preacher fell silent. Still thinking this through. Or maybe listening for the path to be shown him. Jesse reined in his impatience, let the man gaze at his wife's sunflowers, and waited.

"Here's my suggestion," his preacher said at last. "Take her home. She'll last longer in anonymity with you and Cade than she would here." He gestured at the church, deserted now, but it wouldn't always be.

Jesse thought of Tamsen sleeping in his cabin, sharing meals, seeing her day to day but forbidden to touch her. *Not married.* Cade would be by. They wouldn't be alone all the time . . . but there were limits to a man's strength.

Luther Teague was watching him close. "Do you feel more for that young woman than the need to protect her?"

What was the point in denying the obvious?

"Aye sir. I do. A heap more. Reckon I'm more'n halfway to being in love with her, to tell the plain truth."

"If that's the case, wouldn't you rather marry knowing she loves you in return? She trusts you and seems to care a great deal that you not pay a price for coming to her aid."

"But that ain't love." Jesse looked away, coming to terms. "Back in the mountains, when she came up with this scheme, part of me knew it wasn't right. Not like this. I just . . ."

"Couldn't say no." Luther laughed softly when Jesse looked sharp at him. "I remember how it felt, meeting Molly." His gaze grew sober again. "You'll be called on to say no to yourself, many times over, if you take her home. My feeling is she's lived a sheltered, probably restricted life till now. Though she's of an age to have done so, she's yet to learn who she is, what she wants in life."

The words were ringing true, though Jesse didn't like their tune.

"Can you give her that time, Jesse? Can you lay down your desires and be for her the friend, the brother, she needs, and no more?"

"I want to, sir," he said hoarsely, then cleared his throat and said with force, "And I will. I'll do all in my power to protect and provide for her, long as she needs me to. And I'll ask nothing of her in return. I vow it, Reverend — God and you as my witnesses."

For the first time since their arrival in his dooryard, Reverend Teague seemed taken aback, maybe a little amused, and — Jesse hoped he wasn't imagining this part — impressed. But when he spoke, it was to caution, "This isn't a wedding, Jesse. You understand that?"

"I do, sir. But I meant what I said, and I needed you to hear it." To keep him honorable. Accountable.

It wasn't the vow he'd hoped to make this

day, but it was as binding as the other would have been. Tamsen would have what she needed, time to decide whether she wanted the life he could provide her — and him with it — or something else entirely.

He'd give her that freedom, whatever it cost in the end.

19

With the distance home too far to travel so late in the day, they'd spent the night with the Teagues, Jesse in the barn, Tamsen on a quilt by the hearth. The next morning Molly Teague accompanied them the few miles to Sycamore Shoals, where she went into the trade store and obtained for Tamsen items neither Jesse nor Cade could have known they'd need back in Morganton — things it wouldn't raise an eyebrow for a woman to purchase.

Molly wasn't much of a horsewoman. It had taken them the morning to reach Sycamore Shoals. Jesse and Tamsen ate a bite of dinner while they waited, concealed along the Stony Creek trace. Jesse was thankful for the reverend's offer to extend him credit for the purchases, as well as his promise to keep Tamsen's presence a secret and hold his peace about the murder charge. Luther Teague wasn't happy about that last, but Jesse had insisted. Tamsen didn't need another reason to feel obligated. If ever they married, he didn't want it to be out of duty on her part, or fear, or anything but . . .

He hobbled that thought as Molly came riding along the trace with the purchases, bid them blessing, and they were on their way. Up the creek without a paddle, or much of a plan for what came next, it seemed to Jesse.

October was upon them. The air had a tang of autumn. The press of Tamsen's arms around him as they rode double for the first stretch was both pleasure and torment. She didn't ask where they were headed. He was too busy running the vow he'd made over in his head to say much of anything. He wasn't surprised when she fell asleep against his back, about the time he turned the horse away from Stony Creek to make their way along a feeder creek, closed in by wooded slopes.

The sun was an hour or more away from setting, but the western slopes lay in dusk, when he felt Tamsen stir.

"Jesse? I need to find a spot."

He looked ahead along the trail. "There's a likely thicket, other side of that rock."

She leaned around his shoulder, saw the boulder he meant, tall and mossy. "You

229

know this place that well?"

He stopped the horse and slid to the ground, reaching up to help her down. "Every rock, tree, and bush along this creek. Every game trace, salt lick, and fishing hole too."

She looked about her, still blinking sleepily. "Has this creek a name?"

"Tate Allard's the only one farming up this way. He calls it Greenbird Creek. Guess that makes this Greenbird Cove." He gestured at the tree-thick hills. "It opens up some, 'bout a half mile on, where Tate's land starts."

While she saw to the necessary, he filled the canteen.

She came around the rock at last, drooping with fatigue, still the loveliest sight he could imagine. It struck him with fresh wonder, as if she came walking to him out of a dream and might vanish did he dare touch her. But she was real, and plain worn from the journey they'd made, and now he was taking her to stay with him and Cade, and he couldn't guess what the coming weeks would hold. She wasn't his wife. Wasn't his in any way, save to protect.

He cleared his throat. "Not much farther now. You want to walk a spell? Horse is tired, so I'll be afoot."

"I can walk." She surprised him by wrapping her arms around the chestnut's neck, patting the horse with affection, then planting a kiss on its velvety nose. He took up the reins and led on, hiding how much that gesture pleased him.

There was room on the trail to walk abreast, but minutes passed before she broke the silence. "What crops do you raise on your land, or do you raise cattle?"

"We grow some corn. It's not our land, though, where we're living."

"You aren't squatters, are you?"

"No ma'am. When we aren't on a long hunt, we live on the edge of Tate Allard's land — by his leave. In return we share what meat we bring in, drive Tate's cows to market in the fall, lend our backs when needed. Neighborly stuff."

It had proved a fitting arrangement for the past four years. Cade had raised him thinking it best not owning land, staying free to pick up stakes when game grew scarce or a place got too tricky to live in — like the State of Franklin was fast becoming.

Now, though, contrary notions were swirling through Jesse's head, laying waste to old thinking — thoughts of digging in more permanent-like, acres of his own in a hollow somewhere, land he could make yield a living. He looked down at Tamsen trudging along in the clothes he'd borrowed and the moccasins he'd made, dark hair falling in a thick braid, sun-glossed features set in weariness. Was she disappointed he hadn't land of his own?

"I'm thinking . . . ," he began, but stopped. Thinking he'd left the Watauga country content getting by the Indian way, with enough to eat and some to share with his neighbors. Thinking he'd come back more a white man than he'd ever been, with a heap of new concerns on his shoulders.

She cut her eyes toward him. "Thinking what?"

"Lots of things, but never mind. Let's not think beyond getting home so you can rest." He couldn't be sure but thought he heard her mutter "amen" under her breath.

The hollow opened up as Jesse said it would. They passed a sloping field standing in corn, fenced with rails. Beyond it, forest rose again in a leafy wall, running up to the crest of a ridge where the trees were tipped in gold, save for a natural bald midway up catching the westering sun.

It was a wild, isolated place where squirrels and jaybirds protested their passage and the tracks of deer and bear crossed the dim trail. Once, passing a break in the trees, she glimpsed smoke drifting over a rise and supposed it was the home of Janet Allard, to whom she must return the pecan-brown petticoat and gown as soon as she could ply her new needle.

At Sycamore Shoals, according to Molly Teague, all the talk had been about the Jonesborough courthouse raid. She'd heard no mention of a missing woman, abducted or otherwise, or talk of men called Parrish or Kincaid while she'd procured yards of striped homespun, bleached linen, thick-ribbed stockings and other sundries, including the sturdiest, ugliest pair of shoes Tamsen had ever owned, all wrapped inside a quilt behind the saddle.

After she saw the smoke, the trail curved back into forest, climbing along the meandering creek that tumbled over stones and deadfalls, lively and pretty. The sun was setting, and her legs burned with the strain by the time they emerged into a clearing nestled between the shoulders of a low mountain. Trees ringed three sides of the clearing. A cornfield edged the fourth. Where the ground rose toward a wall of forest stood a cabin built of peeled logs, squared and fitted.

It was smaller than the Teagues' cabin, with a door in the center and a covered window to one side. Because the land lay lower to the west, the cabin caught the burnished light of sunset, making it look as if it hadn't lost the luster of new-cut wood. She licked her lips, aching for the comfort of a feather tick — though straw would do, she'd not be picky — but hesitant to mention one.

They came first to a stable, just up from the creek bottom. Jesse stopped, untied the quilt bundle and handed it to her. He began unsaddling the horse, while she stood swaying, yawning. He was about to lead the horse into the stable when he noticed.

"Go on up; have a look at the place." He gave her a half smile. "I think we left it tidy, but don't hold me to it."

His eyes told her he wasn't worried, but she began to be — not about what she might find inside that cabin. What sort of role was she meant to play in Jesse Bird's life now? She was a guest, she supposed, but that notion didn't sit right. If the reverend hadn't talked them out of marrying, this might, in some ways, have been easier. More straightforward, at least.

Clutching the quilt bundle, she followed a path up to the cabin door, pulled the latch string, and pushed her way inside.

Her first reaction was relief. While the stale muskiness of hides lingered, the place didn't smell too bad. And the floor wasn't dirt. Puncheon logs spanned the space, fitted with hardly a crack between. Leaving the door open for light, she stepped inside.

It was two rooms, between them a wide stone hearth with a crane for cooking. A few pots and skillets lined the hearthstones. The ceiling was open beamed, but a loft reached by a pole ladder was built above the room behind the chimney.

A rough-hewn table with benches occupied the main room. Smaller tables and shelves lined the walls, holding possessions her eyes skated over until they landed on the books — half a dozen at least, lined up neat with their spines facing out. The sight was a welcome surprise.

Clothing hung on pegs — breeches, leggings, shirts — as well as traps and snowshoes. Heavy winter moccasins stood in pairs beneath. Everything was tidy. More surprising, the cabin bore a woman's touch. Checked curtains hung at the window, matching a runner that spanned the table under a burl-wood bowl heaped with red-striped apples. Fresh apples?

Frowning, she stepped closer, the quilt in

her arms.

"Well, forevermore. Where on earth did you come from?"

Tamsen's heart leapt to her throat as she froze midstep. Framed in the doorway between the cabin's rooms, hands on slender hips, a girl in faded blue homespun stood scowling at Tamsen.

20

The girl looked about fifteen. She was small boned and pretty — even with the scowl — with pale hair loose to her waist and eyes so blue Tamsen could see their color from across the dim room.

"We . . . Jesse and I . . ." It took a moment for a suitable reply to surface through startlement and weariness. "We've just come from Reverend Teague. Who are you?"

Tamsen set the quilt on the table.

"Don't put that there — I just prettied that table!" The girl rushed forward as if to snatch the quilt away. Tamsen placed a hand between it and the girl.

"You haven't told me who you are — or what you're doing here."

Fury twisted the girl's features. Instead of going for the quilt, she raised a hand to Tamsen, who stepped back out of reach.

"Bethany!" Jesse thundered from the doorway. He strode across the cabin and took the girl by the arm. "What in blazes are you doing?"

Instead of pulling away, the girl flung her slight person against his broad chest, one fist striking him, the other clinging.

Jesse got hold of her by the wrists. "What's got into you? Do Tate and Janet know you're here?"

She pulled out of his grasp, stricken face shining with tears. "I came to tidy the place for you, but . . . you got married? Why?"

Jesse's face drained of color. Ignoring the question, he crossed to Tamsen and touched her cheek. "What happened? Did you walk in and give her a fright?"

Behind Jesse's back the girl glared venom.

"I must have." Impulsively Tamsen took his hand in hers and heard a sound from the girl as she did so. Quite possibly a growl. "I'm all right."

Jesse's fingers squeezed. Then he drew a breath and glanced around the cabin. "Those are nice curtains, and the table looks pretty. It was kind of you, Beth, 'specially as you couldn't know I'd be bringing home . . ." Seeming at a loss for what to call her, he said simply, "Tamsen. But I'd take it kinder still," he added with an edge to his voice, "if you'd make your apologies to her."

The girl's face went a humiliated red. There was a moment when Tamsen thought she might actually say the words. Then her vivid eyes iced over.

"I shan't." She whirled toward the door, the movement fanning out her pale hair. On the threshold she looked back, gaze raking Tamsen. "And those are my mama's clothes you're wearing."

She fled as the last of the sun's angled light vanished, throwing the dooryard into shadow. Tamsen and Jesse stood in thundering silence, staring after her.

Tamsen heard him swallow.

"That," he said, "was Bethany. Tate and Janet's daughter."

Come morning, Jesse was wishing Cade hadn't hung a sturdy door between the cabin's rooms. Best he could tell, staring at it, Tamsen hadn't stirred off the bedstead that used to be his own. He'd gone down to see to the horse, come back up, fixed breakfast, and was just rising from the table when he finally heard the pad of feet behind the door.

He sat back down, rubbed a hand down his face. Waited.

A crash in the next room had him leaping up, heart doing a jig. At the door he stopped, chary of barging in.

"Tamsen? You all right?"

Silence. Then her voice, tear filled, muffled through the door. "I'm fine."

He took leave to doubt it. "You dressed decent? Can I come in?"

"No."

Presuming that answered both questions, he leaned against the doorjamb, hand hovering on the latch. "Don't reckon you'd come out?"

"Not now."

"You hungry?"

"Mr. Bird . . . Jesse. Please. I'm fine. Really."

Behind the cabin he split up a hickory trunk, hurling pieces into a stack. Time, the preacher had said. Time was what she needed. Time wore on, and the morning with it. He was sitting in the cabin threshold sipping from a canteen, sweaty from work, when Tate and Janet Allard came into view on the path that crossed the ridge to their homestead.

He leaned his rifle against the logs and rose.

Janet, blond as her daughter but nigh as tall as her husband, came forward holding out a pie, and an uncertain smile. Jesse took

240

the pie, never one to turn down his neighbor's cooking. It was apple.

"Thankee kindly. What a fine welcome home." Compared to the one they'd had last night, he didn't say.

Tate, toting a covered basket, darted a gaze into the cabin. But Janet took the basket and the bull by the horns, stepping inside and asking brightly, "What's this we hear of you bringing home a wife from back east?"

Tate followed her in, Jesse on their heels. He set the pie on the table while the Allards took in the barefaced lack of anything resembling a wife. Their gazes rested on the door beside the hearth.

A wife from back east. Bethany had rushed out before he could correct that misunderstanding. Till last night he hadn't credited that she'd fixed romantic notions on him. Of late she'd taken to dogging his steps more often than he liked — like a pesky little sister, he'd thought. He'd been patient, tried to be kind. Had he misled her in some way? Had Tate and Janet been thinking he was sweet on their girl?

Janet dropped her voice. "She sleeping this far up into the day?"

Jesse busied himself emptying the basket of cornbread, cheese, butter, and huckleberry preserves. "Tamsen's awake, I think. She just hasn't come out of that room to-day."

The Allards shared a look. "*Is* she your wife?" Janet asked. "We weren't sure Beth got the story straight."

Jesse's mind raced over how much truth to tell. While he trusted the Allards, and having Tate looking out for anyone asking after Tamsen might be the wiser course, there was another thing. Here was Tamsen living under his roof. Even if the Teagues knew about his vow to keep his distance, why should anyone else presume it?

"We saw Reverend Teague yesterday." Jesse watched those words do their work, expecting Tamsen to come barging out to dispute their implication. She didn't, though she must have heard.

Janet cleared her throat. "I was happy lending you my gown, but you didn't mention *you* were marrying the woman needing to borrow it."

When he'd run over the ridges yesterday morning to fetch something decent for Tamsen to wear, it happened a calf had busted its pen and Tate had taken Bethany and her little brothers traipsing after it, leaving Janet the only one home. She'd assumed one of Cade's settlers needed the gown for a hasty wedding. Jesse hadn't amended the notion.

Janet Allard had a sweet smile — and a forbearing nature. She graced Jesse with both now. "Not that I mind."

Knowing he was in the midst of deceiving her again, the tightness in Jesse's chest didn't uncoil.

Tate offered a callused hand to shake. "Think she'll come out so we can meet her?"

Tamsen had suffered enough to make anyone shut themselves in a room for a week. "It was a rough crossing. Reckon she'll come out when —"

The door opened, silencing him. All three turned to look.

Tamsen's hair was neatly parted, pinned up under a cap that covered the back of her head. She wore the top part of Janet's gown, with a petticoat made of the new homespun — basted, it looked like, and hastily hemmed. Janet's petticoat draped her arm. Her eyes were a bit puffy, rimmed in red.

"Tamsen." He wished mightily they'd talked before now. Last night she'd been so tired she'd fallen onto the bed tick with barely two words left to speak to him — a mumbled "good night."

She came into the room, eyes on Jesse's

243

tall blond neighbor. "Are you Mrs. Allard?"

Janet paused a beat before smiling in welcome. "I am. And you'll be Jesse's wife? Tamsen, is it?"

Tamsen's glance at Jesse was brief. She'd heard him tell the lie. "Yes," she said, and Jesse let out a breath.

"Tamsen Bird," Janet said. "What a lovely name. This is my husband, Tate."

"Mr. Allard." Not quite hiding her startlement at the sound of Jesse's name paired with hers, Tamsen dipped a curtsy to Tate, who whipped off his hat.

"Pleased to meet ye, ma'am. I'm Tate to my neighbors."

Jesse had never seen Tate blush, but in that rough-hewn cabin, Tamsen was as dazzling as an angel come to earth, even if she'd spent the morning in tears, which he feared was the case.

"You been in there sewing all this while?" he asked her.

"Part of the time." Tamsen spared him a nod, a small smile, before turning back to Janet. "Thank you for lending me your gown. I can return the petticoat now, but I've yet to sew a bodice. Or launder my own." She handed the petticoat to Janet, then touched the waist of the borrowed bodice, a short gown of looser fit than the clothes she'd worn over the mountains. "Would you mind my keeping this a bit longer?"

"Keep it as long as need be. I don't wear it save for go-to-meeting. With harvest nigh, that won't be for a spell." Janet moved so Tamsen could see the table. "We brought along a little hearth warming."

Tamsen stared at the table's bounty, clearly moved by the kindness. "Thank you. That's . . . that's lovely."

"No one makes a better pie west of the mountains," Jesse said.

"Bethany made that one." Janet glanced guardedly at Tamsen, who managed a smile.

"It's kind of Bethany. Please relay my thanks."

The relief on his neighbors' faces filled Jesse with warmth. They weren't disappointed, just surprised.

Tate and Janet made to take their leave, the petticoat folded inside the empty basket. Jesse stepped from the cabin with them, leaving Tamsen inside. Having decided on enlisting Tate's eyes and ears, after all, he took him aside long enough to tell him Tamsen's story and his part in it.

"Kidnapping?" Tate's face darkened at hearing the charge laid against Jesse — the only one he chose to share. "Parrish and

Kincaid, eh? I'll keep an ear out, 'specially down in Sycamore Shoals."

"Tell Janet," Jesse added, glancing at her waiting at the head of the path. "If you think she ought to know. But let's keep this to the four of us — and Cade, of course. All right?"

Jesse watched them go, torn in his soul over letting the world beyond the Teagues and Cade think them married. And he'd completely forgotten to mention Tate's cow shot dead by Chickamaugas on the drove.

Maybe he'd let Cade deliver that news.

Back inside, he found Tamsen in her mismatched clothes, staring at the feast spread on the table.

"I was getting worried over you." He longed to talk with her, hear what was going on in that pretty head of hers — better, her heart. "Want to sit and have us some pie?"

She grimaced, as if thought of eating soured her stomach, then chewed her lip in indecision. "There is something I want to talk to you about." They sat across from each other. Neither touched the food. "You let them think we're married."

"I was minding your reputation, staying here with me . . ."

"And Cade?"

"Aye. He'll be along." Jesse paused, uncertain how to proceed. She looked unhappy, but like she was trying to choke it down. To go along. "We can tell the Allards the truth, down the road a piece." He'd hoped to reassure her, but his words brought on a frown.

"What about my reputation when I leave?"

Beyond not liking her choice of words, Jesse felt frustration rising up. "We had us a plan, but it changed. I'm sort of making this up as we go along now. If you'd come out and talked to me before they arrived, we might've gotten all this straight betwixt us."

They sat, staring at each other warily across his neighbor's food, until her expression softened.

"I didn't mean to make more trouble for you, Jesse."

He wanted to reach across and take her hand, but she held them in her lap. "You're no trouble."

She gave him a look as if to say she knew better.

"No trouble I didn't take on willingly, all right? And let's not use that word. That's not what you are to me." He knew he'd best stop there or he'd be telling her just what she was to him.

"All right," she said. "But I don't mean to be waited on. I want to do my part, whatever that is, while I'm here."

"Fair enough."

Awkwardness hung between them. He needed to clear the air about one more thing, but worried how she'd take it.

"I want to be sure you understand. There was nothing to Bethany's little tantrum last night. Not on my side."

Her face closed up, so he couldn't tell what she thought about the girl. "You don't owe me an explanation, Jesse. We aren't married."

"No. But I promised the preacher to protect you, shelter you, for as long as you need me, and I keep my promises. But I've never made a single one to Bethany Allard." Worried he was back on the brink of revealing too much, he reached for the pie.

She watched him slice into it with his belt knife. "Bethany isn't what I wanted to talk to you about."

He fetched a pair of spoons, setting one before her. "I'm listening — but eating too." He smiled at her and dug in, but she didn't join him.

"A bit ago," she said, "I opened Mama's box."

Jesse had stopped eating after the first bite. "That crash? It worried me some."

"I'm sorry. It was something I needed to do alone." Tamsen found it hard to meet his gaze, still a little rattled by his letting the Allards think they were married — though she understood why he'd done it. "There was a letter to me, from my father."

"Not Parrish." It wasn't a question. Even so, she shook her head. She couldn't help the tears that welled, but her voice stayed steady as she explained.

She'd awakened with vague memories of the room she'd fallen asleep in, of crickets chirping beyond the logs, and the specter of a girl spitting-angry over her very existence. Sitting up in half light, in one of two narrow beds built into opposite corners, she'd had herself a look at her surroundings. Along with the beds, the room boasted a small table with a basin, tapers in wooden rings, the means to light them. A trunk at the foot of one bed. Pegs on the walls. More clothes. Her own things.

Her mother's box.

She'd risen, lit a candle, then brought the box to the bed. Standing barefoot on the edge of the frame, she raised it high as the ceiling allowed and slammed it to the puncheon floor, bursting its rusty hinges.

She'd found the letter beneath the petition for her mother's manumission and the

249

General Assembly's reply. Like the petition, it was written in her father's hand.

To My Darling Daughter upon the Advent of her Birth . . .

Dated the week she'd been born, the letter told a story. Her parents' story. How her father met her mother, enslaved on the plantation of a Spanish merchant, a man he had dealings with in his business. Struck by her appearance, he'd pursued her in secrecy, learning that she was, as he'd suspected, her master's offspring.

Her mother, Mariah, had been a house slave. Though I never saw her, she being in her Grave some years before I encountered Sarah, Mariah was what is commonly referred to as a quadroon — a person of one-quarter African blood — which makes your Mother an octoroon. Such Distasteful Appellations I despise to use in connection with the Woman I love and call my Wife. Yet they may be of Importance to you one day, our Daughter, so I state them plainly here.

Stephen Littlejohn went on to tell how, upon subsequent visits, he'd come to love her mother, and she him. How after a time

250

he persuaded her master to sell to him his daughter.

He let her go as though she meant no more to him than one of his Carriage horses, though to me she is all the World, notwithstanding our Marriage is unrecognized in the State of North Carolina. Sarah was reared in the house of a Gentleman, serving his wife and legitimate offspring. She can present herself as polished as they, and so it is believed we met far off in Georgia, on one of my Sojourns, were married there, and she, bereft of Family, consented to travel North with me to Charlotte Town . . .

There was more to explain — or excuse — the elaborate courtship story Tamsen had grown up believing in, but too little of the truth the story concealed. Not even the name of the plantation where her mother had been born, enslaved, and sold. The name of a grandmother, a long-dead slave, was all she had.

Maybe that was as her father had wanted it.

"Oh, Papa." Even with her hands shaking and the truth — the little of it he'd given her — washing over her in waves, she missed her father with a love that had survived these revelations unscathed. She remembered Stephen Littlejohn as a tall man, slender, with dark hair and kind eyes. Hazel eyes, she thought. Lighter than hers and Mama's, anyway.

Jesse was gazing at her, pie forgotten. "I understand wanting to know where it is you come from. Reckon you wish there was more. But you have his letter. You have that much, at least."

So much more than he had, from his parents.

"Yes." She wondered if he realized what her father's letter implied. Two days ago she'd asked Reverend Teague whether their marrying would be legal. Her blood was no longer at issue, though of little consequence now.

"There was something else in the box," she said. "I don't know how Mama managed to hide it." A leather wallet had been hidden under a false bottom, which had sprung open as the box hit the floor. Pressed inside the wallet were more than twenty silver dollars. All whole. "I can repay the Teagues. I'd have done so at once had I known about the coins."

Jesse's mouth firmed. "Those coins are yours to keep."

"I mean to pay my way. You weren't expecting this . . . me." Despite her protest, his face remained set. She couldn't budge him to accept her money. "If not that, what can I do to be of help?"

Jesse glanced around. "What do you want to do?"

She followed his gaze, looking about the cabin. They had food in front of them. Nothing needed cleaning — Bethany had seen to that. There was no stock to tend save Jesse's horse. "I haven't much experience with cooking."

She could have added to that washing, scrubbing, and sweeping. She'd rarely been allowed to do those things after her mama married Mr. Parrish. Surely an able-bodied woman could take care of two men and a cabin.

"But I'll learn. For now, I suppose I should finish my gown. And then . . ." She bit her lip, unsure where best to begin her domestic education.

"Never mind *and then.*" Jesse took up his spoon as if he'd remembered the pie in front of him. "And never mind the gown — for the present. Pick up that spoon and eat. I insist," he added with mock severity.

She complied. It really was good pie.

■ ■ ■ ■

After they polished off the pie, Tamsen bent over her sewing until her neck ached, finishing the petticoat and making a start on a plain serviceable jacket. The main cabin was empty when she stepped from the room. Embers glowed in the hearth. Over them a pot of water steamed.

She went to the door.

Jesse was down at the stable, along with another man in leggings and a long blue shirt. He was as tall as Jesse, maybe a tad taller, with a tail of black hair falling below his hat. Though busy unloading packhorses, one with a cow hitched to it, both sensed her watching and glanced up toward the cabin. Jesse raised a hand, beckoning.

"I don't aim to tell Tate about it," Cade was saying as she came within hearing. "His share's what it would've been had we got the whole cow to market, 'stead of just the hide. Tate don't need to know."

"He won't hear it from me." Jesse was unhitching the cow, a brown creature with gentle eyes and a full udder. Holding the lead, he turned to her. "Tamsen, this is Cade, my pa. 'Course, you saw him in Morganton."

He didn't explain her uncertain place there or that their neighbors thought she was his wife; Tamsen guessed he'd done so before she came down to them. She met Cade's gaze and found herself riveted. His was a strong face, with a broad brow and eyes that were, surprisingly, near the same shade as Jesse's, arresting in his darker face, arched over by brows as sweeping as crows' wings. What the mind behind those striking features made of her, she couldn't say.

Cade nodded, touching his hat, which had a hawk's feather thrust through the brim. "I've news for you," he said. "About your stepfather."

21

Jesse watched her with eyes that asked a dozen silent questions. "We mainly put supplies in the loft. But put them wherever suits you, since you'll be taking over the cooking."

Tamsen caught the smile tucked into the corner of his mouth but pretended to survey the bundles and casks heaped near the loft ladder, as if she knew what to do with it all.

"Won't Cade mind?"

Gone now to deliver the Allards' supplies, Cade had assured her he'd seen no sign of Mr. Parrish in Sycamore Shoals. But somehow word that a piedmont merchant was roaming the French Broad River settlements, seeking his abducted stepdaughter, had reached as far as Jonesborough, where Cade had parted company with his settlers.

"What of my mother?" she'd asked, freshly stabbed with grief. "Who took care of her? Where has she been buried?" But Cade had

256

had no answers to those questions. "Am I truly safe here?"

Cade had gripped her shoulder. "Listen. You are under the wing of this man who is a son to me." He'd bent a nod to Jesse, one that spoke of confidence and deep affection. "And he is under the wing of the Almighty. Mine too. You are safe here."

The intensity of his gaze was disconcerting, yet the words had reassured.

"Let's put everything where you're accustomed to keeping it," she told Jesse now. "If it seems better to change things, I can do it later."

Besides, she didn't know how long she'd be the one managing their hearth.

The arranging of supplies took the afternoon, since Jesse sorted through every sack and cask to be sure she knew the contents of each. Cade hadn't returned when Tamsen came down from the loft a final time and found Jesse at the table, reading. Jesse told her that along with bullet lead, sugar, coffee, and the rest, Cade never failed to bring home a new book each autumn, when one was to be had.

"*Gulliver's Travels,*" he said, looking up from its pages with a brow quirked. "You read it?"

"I have." And never felt more sympathy

257

with the titular character in his outlandish travels as she did now. She moved to the hearth to take stock of the utensils with which she had to work, putting from her mind the kitchen house in Charlotte Town, richly appointed by comparison.

Behind her Jesse said, "Don't go telling me how the story ends. I best stop now, though. I told Cade I'd milk that cow."

Tamsen faced him as he stood, closing the book almost reverently. "I can do the milking."

"You can milk a cow?"

She hadn't milked a cow since she was little — they'd had Dell for such chores. "I told you, I don't expect to be waited on hand and foot."

It came out sharper than intended, but Jesse only paused a beat before he said, "I'm coming with you all the same."

"I don't need company."

"You might need this." He reached for a low stool set near the hearth, used to spare a back when bending over pan or griddle. Then he took up his rifle. "And I'll show you where the piggin's kept."

The milking took longer to master than she'd hoped, but finally her fingers remembered the way of it and the creamy liquid squirted into the piggin. The cow proved as gentle as its eyes, taking to her awkward handling without fuss.

"She likes you." Chewing a blade of straw, Jesse leaned one shoulder against a post.

Tamsen glanced at the rifle propped beside him. "Did you mean to shoot her if she didn't?"

He laughed. "No. I never leave the cabin without my rifle."

"Even to go to the necessary?" She'd found that needful structure, set back behind the stable.

She'd been trying to lighten their mood, but his tone sobered. "The Overhill Cherokees know me and Cade and none got quarrel with us. But it don't do to let your guard down. There's others none so peaceful, like the Chickamaugas."

Tamsen's fingers fell slack on the cow's teat. "You're talking about Indian raids?"

"I'm talking about paying heed to what's around you. Never assuming that stick-crack you hear when fetching water at the creek is a harmless coon or deer. And never striking off into the woods without me or Cade alongside you."

Unnerved, she turned back to the milking, temple pressed against the cow's warm side. "I won't go into the woods."

259

"Not till I teach you to shoot."

She raised her brows at that but decided not to argue. Maybe learning to protect herself wasn't a bad idea. "What was that word you said? Chick-something?"

"Chickamaugas."

"I've heard that name before. Who are they?"

"Cherokee, most of 'em." Jesse laced his arms across his chest. "A few years back some of the warriors split off from the Over-hill chiefs who wanted peace but kept making treaties that just got broke over and over. A warrior called Dragging Canoe leads them. They settled on Chickamauga Creek and took that name for themselves. There's others joined 'em now. Creeks. Some Shaw-nees from up north."

It sounded as complicated as Franklin and North Carolina, though more terrifying. "Is there something in the water hereabouts that makes people turn against their own?"

Jesse gave a low chuckle. "I'd say you were on to something — if we hadn't just come through that war with the Crown. Seems it's human nature, taking sides. Only one thing brings folk together, preacher says."

"What's that?"

"Love."

She turned her face toward him and saw

260

his eyes widen. Blushing faintly, she looked to the milking. "Coming from Reverend Teague, I suppose —"

A flit of movement at ankle height made her jump. A gray cat slithered between the stall boards and took up post near a cloven hoof, tail curled over paws, gaze expectant. It licked its mouth with a pink tongue.

Tamsen smiled as her heartbeat settled. "Presumptuous creature."

"You fancy cats?" Jesse asked, sounding glad for the distraction.

"Better than dogs." In truth she'd never called either a pet. Animals in the house had made Mr. Parrish sneeze.

"Cade must've told this one we got us a cow. It's from over the ridge. One of the Allards'."

"I'm getting the milk into the bucket but doubt I can aim at a cat's mouth. That seems to be what it wants."

"Likely so. Janet keeps cows and goats. She made the butter and cheese she brought us."

The cow brushed its tail across Tamsen's head and shifted its stance, making the cat leap to a safer spot. Tamsen stroked a warm flank, her thoughts sliding away from cats and cows. They settled on Jesse's father.

He put her in mind of the mountains, did

Cade. Earlier he'd reassured her with such strong and touching words, yet she sensed much of what went on in his mind he chose to conceal, like the misty haze that often wrapped the mountains they'd crossed. She'd learned how treacherous those mountains could be, up close. How much of Cade was still that warrior, Wolf-Alone?

"I was wondering . . . about your father." Her words broke into the shuffling of contented stock, the liquid spill of milk.

Jesse tossed away the straw he'd been chewing. "What of him?"

She averted her face while she moved to the last teat. "How old is he?"

"Forty, maybe, give or take. Why not ask him?"

"I wouldn't dare."

A beat of silence passed. "You aren't afraid of him, are you?"

Afraid wasn't the word. But before she could reply, the horse nearest the barn door loosed a whinny. Jesse snatched up the rifle so fast it seemed to leap into his hands. As Tamsen rose to see what had alarmed him, he lowered the weapon.

Bethany Allard, capless and barefoot, stood in the stable doorway, bathed in the light of sunset, much as Tamsen had last seen her. With one difference. Instead of hostility on her peaches-and-cream face, there was a tentative smile.

Jesse exhaled a breath. "What're you doing here, Beth?"

"I've come to say a thing to your . . . wife," the girl said, faltering over that last word.

Jesse glanced at Tamsen. She moved the piggin so the cow wouldn't overturn it, drew herself straight, and nodded. He looked back at the girl. "She's listening. Go on and say it."

Bethany took a step inside the stable. The gray cat bounded over to coil itself about her ankles, ignored. The girl's face was shadowed, her voice childlike as she tossed back her unbound hair. "I'm sorry for my meanness yestereve. I come hoping you'll kindly look past it so as maybe . . . we two could be friends?"

To Have and to Hold

22

The man who abducted Miss Littlejohn had done a passable job of throwing him off their tracks. That much was clear to Charlie Spencer.

They'd crossed to the French Broad's north bank by ferry, needing several trips to get horses, mules, dogs, men and their kit over safe. A day out from the crossing, stopped near the remains of a blockhouse once enclosed by a ridge-top palisade, Charlie fessed up to what was weighing on his mind. "Well, see, I ain't certain for a fact now he *said* he was bound for the French Broad. As I recollect 'twere me named the place. All the feller did, best I remember, was say nothing to the contrary."

Thunder grumbled among the lowering clouds, but the heavenly muttering was nothing to the storm gathering on the brow of Hezekiah Parrish, who flung a pointing finger east at the peaks they'd crossed. "Are you telling me my stepdaughter could be anywhere west of those mountains?"

Charlie clenched the lead mule's rope, aware of the dogs ranging up along the crumble-down fort, leaving little squirts to mark the place. "Reckon so. Anywhere but on the French Broad."

With pinched-set face and burning eyes, Kincaid looked toward the Tennessee country, spreading out to the north. "Much as I am loath to admit it, I believe someone would have given her up by now, was she here."

Kincaid had got the notion to offer a reward for the girl's return, hoping to spur help from folk inclined to hold their peace and protect a neighbor in his wrongdoing. Charlie's brows had soared at the amount named, thinking he could skip a winter's trapping on such a windfall. Twice Kincaid had upped the prize, but nary a man had claimed it, though Charlie had seen a heap of want-to in many a hardscrabble farmer's gaze.

Kincaid was no happier with him than Parrish, but he did what Charlie had seen him do a dozen times and more — swallowed back his anger and held himself in rigid silence.

It'd take a bigger fool than Charlie to

expect the same from Parrish.

"You reckon so?" Parrish spat, dropping his horse's reins and advancing on Charlie. "Why didn't you *reckon so* back in Morganton, you scruffy, inept —"

Weren't no knowing what Parrish meant to do with no weapon but his raised hand, on account of Kincaid bursting out of his rigid stance to step between them, catching Parrish by the arm. One of the dogs rushed over and pressed against Charlie's knee, hackles raised. He needn't glance down to know it was Nell, showing sharper teeth than Parrish could boast.

Kincaid strong-armed Parrish back a pace. "How well are you able to recount the speech of the man who ferried us across that river yonder?"

Parrish snatched his arm free. "To what purpose should I recall his blather at all?"

"Precisely so," Kincaid said with better grace than Charlie could've mustered. "What reason had Mr. Spencer to recall the exact words of a stranger met in passing, knowing naught of the need?"

Parrish grudgingly accepted the point as fair but was no less livid for it. "What, then? Do you both mean to abandon me — and her?"

It was a chill wind blowing those heavy

clouds overhead. A cold spatter of rain pelted Charlie's face.

"We'll find Miss Littlejohn," Kincaid said. "It will simply take longer than anticipated."

Taking leave to doubt the *simply* part, Charlie saw the question coming before Kincaid put it to him. Was he willing to act their guide through the settlements to the north, perhaps along the Nolichucky? There would be compensation for his services . . .

"To that we ought both to be committed." Kincaid cut a look at Parrish, whose face closed up tight, leaving nothing to read but resentment careening across his eyes like rocks down a slope.

Parrish's lack of answer didn't escape him, but Charlie had seen enough of Kincaid to trust he was a man of his word. If he said he'd pay Charlie for the aggravation they were asking of him, he would pay. If he said he'd find Miss Littlejohn, by heaven or the other place, he'd do that too.

"I aim to be on the Holston afore snow falls," Charlie said, reminding himself this was for the sake of that suffering girl he'd seen back in the mountains. "But I can go by way of Greenville. That'll take us back along the Nolichucky."

As they led their animals down off the ridge into the trees, moods darker than the weather, Charlie resolved that, girl or no girl be found, beyond Greenville he'd be done with these two.

The cabin was no better than a shack, a tiny porch tacked across its front. In the middle of the porch stood a strapping woman with hair red as Kincaid's and a rifle aimed square at Charlie.

He'd called a greeting when they glimpsed the cabin set back off the trace. Even so, it wasn't the first time they'd been greeted by a gun muzzle. It *was* the first time anyone had demanded to know whether they stood for the New State or the Old before so much as a *mornin', ma'am* was offered.

"Neither, praise God" would've been Charlie's answer, had Parrish not put himself forward with his usual grace and shouted that he hailed from North Carolina and would she look at a portrait of his stepdaughter and tell them if she'd seen the girl and if so when, where, and with whom.

The first shot went high. Charlie was wheeling his mules back toward the trail as the woman followed it up with a taunt.

"What she done, your girl? Growed the good sense t' run off with a Franklin man? Hope she's well on the way to raising up a passel o' sons for our side. Now clear off

271

my land!"

Kincaid and Parrish, having other notions, started for the woman as if to rush the porch and lay hands on her person while she was reloading.

Charlie knew better. "No time — do like she says. Clear out!"

Sure enough, she'd rammed patch and ball to powder and was aiming down that barrel again afore the fools got halfway to her. Charlie was already into the trees. Seconds later came a rattle of loose stones, and Kincaid passed him on his horse. Behind came Parrish huffing on foot, leading his mount and cringing at the rifle's crack and the thud of a bullet smacking a tree a foot from his head.

"She weren't shooting to kill," Charlie gasped out, far enough down the trace to stop and catch a breath.

"What the devil ails the woman?" Parrish demanded.

"Saying you was from Carolina. The Nolichucky's John Sevier's territory. Most folk hereabouts is Franklin to the bone."

Parrish slapped his hat against his thigh, raising dust. "Backwater hooligans! Who's to know a Franklinite from a Tiptonite by the cut of his coat — or petticoat?"

"Ye can't," Charlie said. "And as they take

their politics with a side o' lead here, best never let on your being from Carolina till ye know it's safe to do so."

Morose and shaken, they pressed on, Charlie keeping watch for the dogs. They'd gone tearing after a deer some while before they'd spotted the cabin. When Charlie didn't follow, they'd give up and wander back. He wasn't worried. Not about the dogs.

About a mile down the trace, the scalp-creeping feeling came over him, putting him in mind of two summers back, on the Cumberland, when a Chickamauga got him in his sights unawares. That feeling, and fast feet, had spared him an arrow through the neck.

Traveling last with the mules, he looked left and right into the sunflecked woods. Glanced at their back trail. Over the ridges between them and the cabin they'd been chased from, smoke was going up. He halted the mules. Parrish and Kincaid turned their horses back and saw the smoke.

"Chimney fire?" Kincaid asked.

The smoke was too dark, too thick. A dirty great pillar. "That cabin's burning. Likely fell on 'em just after we left."

"Fell on them?" Parrish echoed.

"Chickamaugas. Like to be coming this

273

a'way next. Ain't no sign of their passing the other way."

Weren't nothing for it but to get off the trace. It mightn't save them, but short of abandoning his mules to leg it out of there, he'd no other recourse. Spying a rock outcrop high up a wooded draw, Charlie pointed. "Get up among them rocks. Keep hid and your horses quiet. I'll find ye once the danger's past."

"We'd do better not splitting up," Parrish argued, wasting precious seconds. "Meet them together, if it comes to it."

"He's trying to prevent it coming to that." Kincaid edged his horse off the trail. Parrish threw a distrustful look at Charlie and then followed, weaving his horse upslope between the trees.

Charlie concealed what he could of their passing. Hiding himself and the mules wouldn't be as easy. His heart bumped along as he pondered letting himself be overtaken. He'd full packs. Spoke passable Cherokee. Might be he could barter his way out of a scalping.

Or they'd lift his scalp and then his goods. You never could tell with Indians, and these were raiding.

Picking a spot of rocky ground with no brush to trample, he got the mules up into a hazel thicket, hitched them, and hurried back down to see he'd left no sign Indians on the run couldn't miss.

He almost made it.

Sighting them coming along, painted and befeathered, Charlie dropped behind a tree-fall. He belly-crawled to the log's end to peer at the warriors passing below. They'd come with no whooping or popping of gunshots, so he reckoned they'd missed Parrish and Kincaid. He heard their labored breathing, the thud of moccasined feet. The first one passed, russet skin agleam, musket clenched. The second. Third. Ten in all, three with fresh scalps at their belts. The last was one of these, the scalp dangling from his waist uncommon bright. At first Charlie thought they'd got Kincaid, after all, then saw the hair was far too long for a man's. The woman from the cabin porch.

A second later he forgot the woman. Back down the trace, a dog set to barking.

The last Chickamauga drew up short. Charlie's guts seized tight. He knew which dog it was like he'd know his ma's voice. Nell, always first back from roaming.

To a man the Indians had stopped, alert and muttering. The one with the red scalp aimed his musket back down the trace. Charlie couldn't see if Nell was nigh enough to hit. He watched the Indian sight along that barrel, knowing he'd seconds to act. Kill that one, then die with Nell?

Another of the party grabbed the musket barrel, shaking his head. Charlie waited, gripping his sweat-slicked rifle. His dog went on barking. The Indian who'd stopped the shooter squatted on the balls of his feet, put out a hand, made a cupping motion.

Nell hushed her noise. To Charlie's everlasting amazement, she came into view, belly to the ground, tail tucked. Come creeping in at an Indian's call. Letting an Indian fondle her ears. And showing her teeth in that smiling way she had, right afore she sometimes bit.

It went on for an eternity — four, maybe five seconds — before the lead Indian barked a word. The one petting his dog stood, made a motion with his hand and a gruff noise in his throat as clear as "git."

Nell didn't budge. The other Indians laughed. The one who'd petted Nell scooped a rock off the trail and hurled it. Nell leapt like she'd springs for legs. The stone sailed by, harmless. More laughter from down the trace, but the Indian trotted after his fellows, leaving Nell milling, fretted and confused.

Charlie raised his head, then sat. His

knees were too weak to stand him up. He made a *tch* sound with his tongue. Seconds later Nell plowed into him, dirt caked and wiggling. He hoisted his rifle clear of her flailing paws. With his other arm he pinned her to his racing heart.

"Good girl," he murmured into the silky spot between her ears. "What say we find them other varmints and see did *they* die of fright?"

A body couldn't help hearing the argument raging at the edge of the firelight, though Charlie fixed his gaze on the pot of squirrel meat simmering on the coals. Nell had made herself his shadow since the run-in with the Chickamaugas. Now and then he'd drop his hand to touch her head when a harsh tone from the camp's edge flattened her ears.

". . . all well and good, but you have the resources to neglect your affairs. I have not."

That was Parrish, still heated over getting shot at by a Franklinite and chased into the brush by Indians — so heated that other matters he'd been stewing on were boiling over.

Kincaid was finding them bitter to his taste.

"Do you put the concerns of your purse

above your daughter? Will you now abandon her to the very perils we narrowly escaped?"

"I've said nothing of abandonment. I won't rest until I've heard what she has to say for herself."

"Say for herself?"

He'd been about to give the stew a poke, but this was a question Charlie wouldn't mind hearing answered. He waited.

"I mean," Parrish said, voice shaking like a man who has imagined the worst, "while we have spent weeks traipsing these hills, what do you imagine the girl has been doing? Will you be as keen to have her to wife as you were in Morganton? She's bound to have been sullied — repeatedly."

Charlie cringed.

"She was taken against her will," Kincaid replied in a voice so tight it was hardly recognizable. "Whatever has befallen her, she is not to blame."

"That remains to be seen!"

Charlie sensed, in the silence following, that Parrish hadn't meant to speak that thought aloud. A breeze rattled the turning leaves in the surrounding thickets as he shot a look at the pair. Smoke fanned across his eyes, leaving no hope of reading Parrish's face, even if he could've seen it in the dark.

He stirred the stew.

"Do you imply she had a hand in her mother's death?" Kincaid's voice shook. "I have spent all of an hour in your daughter's presence, yet I know that to be impossible. How it is you do not?"

"I misspoke." The bite had bled out of Parrish's tone. "In my frustration, I misspoke. Of course the girl isn't to blame."

Another silence, then Kincaid said with chilling resolve, "I will find Miss Littlejohn and avenge her honor and her mother's murder — on the body of whomever holds her captive. As for your monetary concerns, Mr. Parrish, if what you've been attempting to extract from me is a promise of remuneration, then you have it. Now let us be finished with the subject until she is found."

Despite Kincaid's words in the girl's defense, Charlie sensed the exchange had shaken the younger man, as if Parrish's insinuations had stirred up doubts he'd been denying for some time. *Sullied.* What man who cared at all about the girl wouldn't be thinking on it? Even that woman on the cabin porch, God rest her feisty soul, had jumped to a like conclusion. If pretty Tamsen Littlejohn was still the marriageable miss who stared at Kincaid from that portrait . . . well, Charlie wouldn't have laid odds on it. But even if, in the end, she proved ruined goods to the likes of a Virginia gentleman, she was still Parrish's stepdaughter. All this cold-blooded talk of finding the girl sounded less like a man seeking his kin than a master tracking a runaway slave.

Parrish ate his stew in thankless silence. Kincaid avoided the fire, seeing to the horses, till the merchant rolled himself in his blanket.

Charlie shared supper with Kincaid while the dogs gazed on. Clouds overhead broke apart to show stars. Kincaid stared into the flames, stirring his stew with a wooden spoon, seeming to forget he was meant to eat it.

"You actually see the dead woman — the girl's ma?"

At Charlie's question, Kincaid shook off his brooding. "Sadly not until after her death. Strange you should mention it. I was thinking of her just now."

"About Parrish's wife?"

"Something about her has bothered me." Kincaid lowered his voice, glancing at Parrish's sleeping form. "He'd entreated me to see Miss Littlejohn again, that she'd had a change of heart toward me. I confess I was relieved to hear it and accompanied him readily to the house where they were staying, wanting a more private exchange than

our first had been. There we found chaos —
furniture overturned, that glorious gown
Miss Littlejohn had worn burnt to ashes in
the hearth, Miss Littlejohn vanished, and
her mother . . . The woman was laid out on
the bed, hands folded, composed as though
she'd lain down to sleep. Aside from the
blood, of course, and her battered face."

Charlie pondered that, then said, "Don't
sound like what a murderin' rascal would've
done, kill a woman, then lay her out decent
afore hauling the daughter off into the
night."

Kincaid set his bowl on the ground. He
made no move when Nell crept to it. He
leaned forward, hungry for word of the girl.
"Tell me again of your encounter with her.
Tell me everything you recall."

Charlie humored the man, closing his eyes
to bring up the details, adding at the end,
"Afore we parted, the feller asked to buy a
deerskin off'n me. Meant it for the girl, I
reckon. Her shoes were banged up. I give
him the hide, thinking 'em just married and
all."

Kincaid frowned. "You didn't mention
that before. About the shoes."

"Guess it didn't seem much to the point."

"But Miss Littlejohn — you said she was
disheveled, under duress, and spoke not a

word during the exchange?"

"If by *duress,* ye mean she looked like being forced off where she didn't want to go . . . At the time I thought so."

Granted, Charlie knew little of women and less of marrying, but could she be the first bride to wind up dazed on the heels of her wedding night — church blessed or no? Might she have gone off with the man full willing, only to have belated second thoughts? Could that suffering, bruised-eyed girl he'd seen have had some part in her own mother's murder?

He couldn't credit it, but he couldn't put the pieces of the story together and make them fit snug either, and wondered if similar notions were chasing circles in Kincaid's brain. He'd pulled out that portrait and was back to mooning over it, while Nell licked up the squirrel meat from his bowl, pinned between her paws. Thinking their conversating done, Charlie got up to put the camp in order.

"Nevertheless I shall find her," he heard Kincaid say low under his breath, eyes devouring the tiny painted face. "And avenge whatever she has lost."

Charlie felt his neck hairs lift, then reached for the stew pot to portion the leavings to the dogs.

23

Darkness had fallen outside the cabin. Jesse was stretched out long on his bearskin beside the hearth, engrossed in *Gulliver's Travels.* Cade sat cross-legged in the corner where he'd slept since Tamsen's arrival, a pair of leggings in pieces around him, hands busy with needle, beeswax, and sinew. At the table, Tamsen stitched a shirt for Jesse by taper-light. The fire popped, spraying sparks onto the hearthstone. Jesse snuffed them, then went back to his book.

In the silence, tension simmered. Mostly it was coming from Cade. He'd had little to say in her presence since his arrival three days past. He left the cabin to hunt at dawn. What daylight remained he spent in the yard, butchering meat, tanning hides, seeing to the stock. His avoidance left her feeling like a guest who'd overstayed her welcome — or maybe had never been welcome at all, despite his words the day he rode in.

She tried to focus on the sleeve she was attaching to the shirt yoke, but her attention kept straying to Jesse's enigmatic foster father. A man plying a needle was no novel sight. Mr. Parrish had male slaves trained in the art. It was the man himself who drew her gaze. Even sitting still, engaged in domestic routine, Cade radiated alertness, as if the slightest hint of anything amiss would launch him into action.

A piercing pain in her fingertip recalled her. She whipped her finger to her lips, chary of spotting the linen with blood.

Jesse looked up, golden eyes inquiring. "You all right?"

"Just a needle prick." The firelight softened his features, making him seem almost handsome, in that hawkish way of his. Not the sort of handsome she'd ever found attractive, yet when he gave her half a smile, she grew flustered and dropped her gaze to her sewing, thoughts spinning back to their mountain crossing, that day the thunderstorm swept over. Not the near drowning, but what Jesse told her afterward, by the fire. How he and Cade were once called Wildcat and Wolf-Alone, then left to become Jesse Bird and . . . Cade Bird? She'd never heard the name Bird applied to Cade. He was just . . . Cade. Was it his name from before he was Wolf-Alone? If he'd no other name but Cade, perhaps he'd been a runaway slave seeking refuge among the Shawnees. Some slaves were Indian, though her stepfather had never owned any.

She glanced across the cabin. This time Cade was looking back at her. "Is there something you wish to say to me?"

Jesse put down *Gulliver's Travels* to look at her as well. More than flustered now, embarrassed, she hurried to say something — anything. "How — how did you come to be among the Shawnees?"

Surprise glided across Cade's features, gone when he raised a brow at Jesse. "What've you been telling her?"

Jesse sat up, book balanced on a knee. "I told her how I became Shawnee. I didn't tell her your story. Leastwise not the start of it."

Cade pulled a stitch through the legging pieces draped across his lap, then shrugged. "Tell it, if you want."

Marking his place in the book, Jesse drew both knees up. "Cade's something of a legend among the Shawnees. Or he was at Cornstalk's Town, up on the Scioto River."

"Cornstalk? He was your chief, wasn't he?"

"Aye, you remember. *Hokolesqua* is his

name said proper, though." He sounded relieved to be talking, and Tamsen knew he'd sensed the tension in the cabin as well.

"So it happened on a morning just after sunup, at the creek where the women bathed," he went on. "The creek wasn't wide. Hardly deep enough to swim most seasons. But it was spring and the water was high when Cade came floating down the current in nothing but a breechclout. A girl saw him first, but she'd hardly cried out that a dead man was coming down the creek when Cade stood up and came wading toward the bank. They seen he was Indian — a big warrior, streaming wet, staring over their heads like he was searching for someone in particular."

Tamsen couldn't help casting another look at Cade, ignoring them now as he worked. She'd no difficulty imagining the sight he must have presented those women and girls.

"They all fell back. Most to gape, a few running to warn the town. Cade passed by the gapers, following the ones that fled. He walked right into Cornstalk's Town and didn't stop till he reached the *msi-kah-mi-qui*, the council house. He wasn't armed, but not a soul made to stop him. The tale of his rising up from the creek like a fish sprouting legs had swept ahead from mouth to ear. It was Cornstalk himself, tall and fierce, still in his prime, come out to confront him."

At last Cade had something to add. "I wondered could *Hokolesqua* see how my knees shook."

Grinning, Jesse went on to tell how Cornstalk, his lined face impassive, had listened to the tale of what the women had seen, staring hard at Cade all the while. Then the Shawnee chief asked what his business there with the People was.

"Cade didn't speak a lick of Shawnee then, but it was clear enough what was being asked. He told them — in Lenape, which most of them understood — that he'd come to make himself Shawnee, by whatever means the chief deemed fitting. The audacity of it was enough to win over some right there."

"Did you see this yourself?" Tamsen asked.

"I was there, but can't say as I recall it. This wasn't long after I was adopted. But I'm told even Cornstalk looked impressed. Even so, the means settled on was the one they most often use on captives."

"The gauntlet?" Tamsen stared at Cade with amazement and horror.

"That's right." Jesse's voice recalled her gaze. His eyes held the memory of that night above the draw, when he'd explained the practice. "For all he'd made himself a marvel, they didn't go easy, even fell on him at the end when he made it past the sticks and clubs with barely a stumble. He wrested a club from someone and fought 'em off. In the end, the warrior who'd given him the worst of it put himself forward to adopt Cade as a brother. Falling Hawk made a fine speech of it there under the sky, with Cade all bloodied up and welted and the town looking on, saying as how the Great Spirit had sent him a man to replace the brother he'd lost in a raid a year back. So Cade was taken back down to the creek he'd come out of, and the women washed him down and made him Shawnee. Then he was marched back up to Falling Hawk's lodge and given a meal."

"I still bear a mark or two from that day." Looking up, Cade gave Tamsen what could almost be called a smile.

"I should imagine so." In truth she was stunned to think this man sitting before her, placidly stitching clothes for himself, had been through such an ordeal. By choice.

Jesse rose and poked up the fire, adding more wood.

Cade started on the other legging.

Tamsen picked up her needle but didn't

make a stitch. Neither man had said why Cade had come floating down that creek in the first place nor where he'd floated from. He hadn't sprung into being from that creek. He'd had a life before. Some twenty years of it — if she had the timing of it all straight. And he was Delaware. What made him want so badly to become Shawnee?

Time for storytelling seemed past. Jesse sat back on his bearskin and drew a blanket close. "Think I'll turn in. Don't stop your work; it won't bother me none."

But Tamsen wasn't ready to bear Cade's presence without Jesse awake to shield her. She snuffed her candle, gathered up her sewing, and retreated to the back room.

Listening to the fire hissing as it started to die, Jesse slid into his nightly ritual of calling up the distant past. Futile as it always proved, it usually slid him into sleep. Tonight it did the reverse. Wide awake, he stared at the dying flames thinking on how oddly Cade had been behaving since coming home to find Tamsen sharing their cabin. Despite his seeming support at the outset, Cade wasn't happy with the situation and made it clear without a word said. It struck Jesse that words needed saying. He rolled away from the fire to face the room.

"You as tired as me of bunking on the floor?" he asked, knowing Cade was as comfortable on bare ground as on a tick. "What would you say to adding on a lean-to, before Tate's harvest?"

Cade's eyes flicked sidelong. He let a beat of silence pass before he asked a question of his own. "What's to come of the long hunt this year, Jesse?"

Was that what was bothering him? The long hunt? Since living on Tate's land, he and Cade had stuck around in autumn long enough to help bring in the corn, but directly after would close up the cabin and head out to harvest the furs that supplied them through the year. They'd be gone into January. Later, depending how far they ranged.

"No telling when Parrish or that suitor of hers will catch on to where we are," Jesse said. "Or if. I'm not saying I won't do the hunt, just . . . I don't know yet."

"Best get it figured."

Jesse tried to catch resentment in Cade's tone, but he was impossible to read when he wanted to be. "Let me study on it, Pa. By time we're back from White Shell's wedding, I'll have thought of something. Maybe Tamsen could stay on with Tate and Janet."

"You still meaning to go with me to

Chota? I'd planned to work it into the hunt."

Jesse sat up, all thought of sleep shaken off. He'd blunted his answer about the hunt. Truth was, thought of leaving Tamsen for the winter, even if he knew she'd be there safe and sound when he got back, was a blade between his ribs. Cade's pointed look drove it deeper.

"Face it, Jesse. You won't be on the hunt with me this year."

Though he'd give up the winter hunt and more for Tamsen, Jesse felt a wrenching in his chest. "Pa, I been thinking . . ."

Cade didn't look at him. "About?"

"Being done with it for good. Maybe laying hold of more'n a cow and a few acres in corn."

Cade's hands fell still.

"I want something more'n this." Jesse waved at the tiny cabin, lowering his voice so it barely rose above the fire's crackle. "More to offer *her.*"

Cade's mouth pressed tight before he said, "She's not your wife."

"I know it," he hissed, worried Tamsen was hearing every word they said.

"Might never be."

Jesse bolted to his feet. "Can we take this outside?"

"Ki Shawano aatowe," Cade said — speak Shawnee.

Jesse opened his mouth to do so, then shook his head. *"Ma-tah* — no. She'll hear our tones. Please, Pa."

Cade was slow in following him out to the yard. When he shadowed the doorway at last, he had his pipe in hand, freshly lit. Jesse gave a nod toward the stable. They walked in silence down to where the creek burbled a stone's throw off.

"Exactly what do you aim to with that girl, Jesse?"

"Let her catch her breath for now. Hide her. If the hunt dies down, give her time to decide what it is she wants to do."

"She hasn't told you what she wants to do?"

"I don't know that she knows." Jesse's raised voice made one of the horses start with a ruckle, muffled through the stable logs. "Why'd you tell me to keep her safe, back on the trace, if you didn't want her around? What did you think I was going to do with her? Wisk her over the mountains and set her loose?"

"I never said I begrudged her shelter, Jesse. Don't go putting words in my mouth."

"Then I don't see what's got you riled."

"Abduction? Murder? You forget about those?"

"Not hardly." Jesse struggled to tame his rising anger. "But I promised to keep her safe. Reverend Teague bid me give her time. That's what I aim to do."

"With us two fixing to leave? One of us has to, if we want to keep eating."

He couldn't see Cade's face to read it, just the set of his brows in the glow of the pipe he finally brought to his lips. "If it's a matter of trusting me alone with her, you can do that, Pa. That promise I made to keep Tamsen safe — I meant from *me* as well. I won't touch her. Not unless she wants me to. Not even then till we're married before God. That put your worries to rest?"

Cade blew out smoke, and what might have been a laugh, save it held no humor. "What if she never wants that from you?"

"Then she can leave. Go back to the Teagues or wherever she wants to go." His voice had risen again. One of the horses kicked at its stall. Jesse held his ground. "But *if* once she knows what she wants, and *if* that's me . . . I want something of worth to offer her."

"I'm of the opinion that, had you nothing but yourself to give, it would be more'n most deserve."

Cade spoke so stiffly the meaning of his words took a moment to sink in.

"Pa . . ." Jesse's throat clamped tight. He didn't know how to put it into words, to make Cade understand how Tamsen had stirred up the embers of a longing he'd kept hidden. The longing to know where he came from. How to say it without sounding like who he was wasn't good enough, or that he disregarded all Cade had done for him. Neither thing was true and yet . . .

"I been meaning to tell you. When her mother died, Tamsen found out some things, things kept secret from her till then."

Cade's pipe glowed, a tiny sun in the darkness. He coughed a bit on the draw, and his voice rasped as he asked, "What sort of things?"

Jesse told him about Sarah Parrish having been a slave, freed by Tamsen's father, a truth concealed so her parents could live together and raise their daughter without the stigma of slavery hanging over her. "It got me wondering, if I could learn where I come from, who my people were — or maybe *are* — it might turn out I've something to give her. I don't know what. Land. An inheritance. Something more'n living season to season." He hurried to add, "It's

294

been good for us, Pa, and I wouldn't think of changing except I don't reckon it's the life to be asking a wife to lead."

He'd said it. Poorly, no doubt, but it was out.

Cade had let the pipe fall to his side, forgotten. "I never knew you thought on that. About where you come from, before the Shawnees."

"Didn't seem talking would do anyone good. But I think on it. I've thought on it most every night I can recall. Guess Tamsen's talk of her parents started me thinking in the daylight hours too."

Cade drew on his pipe but found it had gone out. He tapped the bowl against his thigh, looked out to the open land where the dark-shadowed hills rolled away to the west. "So you fixing to turn farmer on me?"

"I'm fixing to do what it takes to win her. And now I come to think on it, right before we met Tamsen, that day in Morganton, weren't you the one talking about planting more corn, getting that cow? Sounded to me like you were the one thinking on turning farmer."

Cade blew out an exasperated breath. "I hardly remember what I was thinking then. We got a different set of circumstances facing us now, and sounds to me like you're risking an awful lot for this girl you've hardly had the chance to know."

"Maybe I am," Jesse said, heart sinking under the strain come between him and Cade. "And call me a fool for it. But I think I've known her since I first looked into her eyes. I love her, Pa."

Cade didn't call him a fool. He stared at Jesse through the dark for a moment, then went into the stable to check the stock, leaving Jesse alone under the stars.

24

In the covered dogtrot between the cabins, Tamsen perched on a bench, letting Janet Allard rub salve into her hands, which were cut and blistered after helping harvest corn in the fields. "It's lard," Janet said of the salve. "With sweet-balm and mallow-root from my garden."

The same Jesse gave her, in the mountains. She caught a softer fragrance beneath the grease and herbs. Rose petals, doubtless from the trellised canes climbing both cabins, still producing blossoms into October. Though across the nearby slopes sparks of red and gold heralded autumn's blaze, nearer the cabins late vegetables and herbs thrived in sprawling plots that must have presented a veritable Eden in the warmer months.

With the flora of the Allard homestead came fauna aplenty. Tamsen had counted four cats, two dogs, six goats, an ox team, two horses, a milch cow, a flock of hens, and, in a large wicker cage mounted under the dogtrot, a pair of birds the size of doves. Upon spying their brilliant green and yellow plumage and ruddy-feathered heads, Tamsen had exclaimed in delight, making Bethany ask, "Ain't you ever seen a parakeet? They flock about these parts, driving farmers to distraction. These 'uns would be shot dead long since if I didn't keep 'em to myself."

Tamsen watched the pair now, preening with their curved beaks, until Janet turned her hands over for a last inspection.

"Keep them out of water if'n you can. Come morning they'll feel better."

Bethany stepped from the cabin, mixing seed in a pan to feed her captive birds. The girl had been in motion since Tamsen and Jesse arrived that morning for the harvesting, yet looked as lively as ever, pale hair falling in a smooth sheath to her waist.

Tamsen had yet to see her don a proper cap.

"You do have the prettiest hands. Or did till today." A giggle accompanied Bethany's words as she turned to tend her birds. The parakeets fluttered to the bottom of the cage as she cast the seed. "Reckon you'd slaves to do for you, back in Morganton."

"Beth," Janet said. "Don't go making assumptions."

As assumptions went, it wasn't wholly inaccurate. Tamsen had never worked as she'd done today — or every day since her arrival in Greenbird Cove, and blistered palms weren't the only change that work had wrought. Even now she could feel the sunburn across her cheeks. Her hair was in a simple braid, pinned and covered in a plain cap. Her homespun gown was a far cry from the lace-trimmed silk she'd been painted in.

No doubt Mr. Parrish was out there somewhere, toting around that wretched miniature, showing her image to any who'd stop and look. How much did she still resemble that ringleted girl in the portrait?

Lord, keep him miles and miles from this cove.

She stood as Janet corked the salve. "I didn't live in Morganton, and I wasn't wealthy. Not really."

"No?" Bethany drew one of the parakeets from the cage, clipped wings extended, clawed feet clinging to her finger. She stroked the bird's bright head, eying Tamsen. "You never churned butter afore coming here. Never brought in corn. Bet you never strung shucky beans or plucked a

299

chicken or put up any kind of food at all."

"Not since I was small," Tamsen admitted, then smiled at Janet. "Except for plucking chickens, which I've never attempted."

"Then how d'you mean to do for Jesse?" Bethany asked.

Janet had started inside the cabin but paused to level a look at her daughter. "Tamsen will do just fine. Besides, she has us to show her anything she might need to know."

A breeze wafted through the dogtrot, wisping pale hairs against Bethany's cheeks. "Mama, you ain't got time to sit for the sewing you pine to do. Where you gonna find time for teaching Tamsen how to be the wife Jesse needs?"

"It's Tamsen could teach us a thing or two about sewing." Janet appraised her gown. "I'd give you the linen and a year's worth of cheese if you'd borrow my good jacket and petticoat again and make another along their pattern for me. I'll never match your skill with a needle."

Tamsen smiled, deciding not to mention that they were the plainest clothes she'd ever worn. "I wish you might have seen my mother's creations." A burn of tears pressed behind her eyes as she added, "I'd be happy to stitch a gown for you."

Bethany's mouth twisted, as if the conversation hadn't gone according to her liking. "What did your mama think, you coming Overmountain to marry our Jesse?"

"My mother died not long ago. She never met Jesse."

Janet expressed her sympathy, until Bethany cut in, "So Jesse met your pa in Morganton?"

Tamsen turned to the girl, wondering at the probing questions. "Papa died years ago. I was . . ." She searched for the line between truth and discretion. "I was alone in Morganton when Jesse offered to take me west with him."

Bethany wore a puzzled look, those big blue eyes of hers far too innocent. "You weren't one of them . . . What's the Bible call 'em, Mama? Those women that charge men for their favors?"

"Beth!" Janet's face flamed with mortification. "Of course Tamsen was no such thing."

"Indeed not." Tamsen surprised herself by laughing, causing Janet visible relief.

Bethany frowned. "An orphan? Jesse and Cade took you on out of charity?"

Tamsen bit back her grin. "Wrong again."

"Bethany Ann Allard," Janet said in exasperation. "It is none of your business why they chose to marry. Tamsen isn't obliged

301

to share it with you if she doesn't choose. Now hush."

Bethany returned the bird to the cage and shut the wicker door. "Sorry, Mama. I was just curious."

Tamsen wished she could tell them the truth. Despite Bethany's apology and offer of friendship, she clearly hadn't reconciled herself to Tamsen's status as Jesse's wife. *Supposed* wife. But truth — as pertained to her and Jesse — had become a thing too muddled to pin down in words. Since Luther Teague talked her out of marrying, she'd had time to be relieved she and Jesse hadn't taken such a drastic measure. Time to wonder what it would be like for them now if they had. Time to wish she'd never left the Teagues, never come to this isolated cove at all. Time to think that if she hadn't, there just might be another gaping hole in her heart where Jesse Bird had, to her surprise, begun to fit himself.

If only things could have been different. If only Cade —

"Why don't I teach Tamsen how to make butter?" Bethany turned with a brighter countenance, small hands brushing off a residue of birdseed. "What else can't you do? You got a kettle for boiling laundry in the yard, a battling stick?" When Tamsen

302

said she'd neither, the girl's brows shot high. "How're you keeping your clothes clean?"

"Rinsing them in the creek." Jesse did his own washing thus. Unless he'd come straight from working or riding, he always smelled clean. She'd surmised he bathed himself in the creek each morning too.

"You'd do better boiling your laundry," the girl pronounced.

"One thing at a time, Beth." Janet offered Tamsen a conciliatory smile. "Keeps busy as a bee in clover, my girl. Just like her brothers — Lord help their tired mama."

As if they'd waited out of sight for this herald, Bethany's little brothers came swerving around the cabin from the direction of the barn.

"Pa's coming!" seven-year-old Nathan announced, white-blond hair in straggles over stick-out ears.

"And he's hungry!" Zeb, a year younger, plowed into his brother's back. He grinned up at Tamsen, who was close enough to playfully yank a lock of his shaggy hair, dark like his father's.

Jesse appeared next, quiet in his moccasins. Bethany greeted him with a blazing smile, but he came straight to Tamsen and took up her hands, turning them palms up.

303

"How are they?"

Tamsen felt a tingle on her skin at his touch — something deeper at his focused concern. Sensing every other eye on them, she blushed and pulled away. "Janet tended them."

Jesse smiled and lowered his voice. "You want to share supper with the womenfolk or head back and have our own? Tate invited us, but I said I'd ask you first."

It had been a good day, even with the unaccustomed work, the awkward moments with Bethany. On the whole, Tamsen found the lively Allard clan good company, but she was ready for a space of quiet.

"What would you like me to fix for our supper?" she asked.

The dusty smell of corn chaff lingered in Tamsen's nose as she trudged the path behind Jesse. Long, papery leaves waved brown in memory's breeze. Husk-covered ears thudded into the wagon bed, punctuated by the laughter of little boys. The pair had tried repeatedly to climb Jesse like a tree until he'd given in to their mischief and, growling, entered into a bout of roughhousing that flattened a row of corn before ending in shrieks on the ground.

"Whenever he's by," Tate had told her,

"they stick to him like stink on a skunk."

She'd laughed at the expression, hiding what the sight of Jesse at play with the boys had done to her, tugging at her heart without due warning. Laughter hadn't banished the worry she'd carried around all day. That worry weighed on her now, dulling her eyes to the forest around her as they climbed the ridge. For the first time since he and Jesse raised their cabin on Allard land, Cade hadn't come to help with the harvest. And Tamsen was sure it was her fault.

The morning after Jesse shared the story of Cade's adoption by the Shawnees, rounding the cabin on her way to the necessary, she'd run smack into Cade coming the other way. He'd reached to steady her, as he had on the street in Morganton.

"Oh!" she'd said. "I'm sorry. Where . . . where's Jesse?"

"At the stable. I need to ask you a thing or two."

She'd blinked at Cade, before grasping the sudden shift of his words. "Ask me what?"

"That suitor of yours. What sort of man was he that you didn't take to him?"

"Mr. Kincaid? I . . . He . . . We only met the once."

"And?"

"I thought at first I might like him," she blurted. "Aside from his owning so many slaves and knowing that would be the life I'd have to lead if I married him." Words had come tumbling then. She couldn't seem to stop them, not with Cade's eyes fixed on her from under those fierce brows, as if he was looking for a reason to doubt her. "But then I thought, maybe he'd be a kind master. Kinder than Mr. Parrish. Maybe I could bear it. Then his own slave came in."

She couldn't look away from those steady eyes. She sensed disapproval. Resentment. Or thought so. Did Cade wish she'd never involved Jesse in her troubles? Never come between them like a wedge? That was what she'd begun to feel like.

Quickly she'd told him the rest, of Toby, and the slap, and Ambrose's unconcern for the slave who'd been raped.

"What was he doing in Morganton?"

She hadn't thought on the details of that conversation since she'd stormed out of the ordinary. "It was something about land. On the Yadkin River, I think. Really all he wanted to talk about was Long Meadows, his grandfather's plantation."

Cade studied her, making her feel like she was holding something back. "You're certain he'll not give up the hunt for you?"

"I'm no wise certain about anything, though I've every reason to think Mr. Parrish means to find me."

Cade had started to say something to that, but merely grunted as if in agreement and stepped around her.

Before Tamsen woke the following day, he had left them, taking more than a day's worth of gear and provision.

"Off hunting, more'n like," Jesse told her when she found him out back of the cabin, chopping wood and looking as troubled by the desertion as she felt.

Deep in her thoughts about Cade, moments passed before Tamsen realized they were climbing through unfamiliar woods. Jesse had taken a side trail while her eyes were trained on the back of his shirt, the damp spot where the straps of his rifle and bag crossed.

"Where . . . are we . . . bound?" she asked, out of breath.

Jesse paused, standing a little above her on the trail. Beyond him the path twisted up through rock-studded forest. "Thought I'd show you a spot up-creek. 'Less you'd rather go home directly?"

The day was cooling toward evening, but she was heated from the climb. Sweat trickled from beneath her cap where her hair lay coiled and heavy. Jesse looked every bit as hot, and filthy from their work.

"What about supper? Aren't you hungry?"

"As a bear," he said. "But reckon you'd like me to wash first. Anyway, we're nigh there."

Nigh was a relative term, she decided, some while before a faint rushing she'd taken for a breeze in the hardwoods grew louder. It couldn't be a wind, for the trees barely shivered. Then they rounded a bend in the trail, and there beyond was the creek, spilling over massive, moss-flecked stones in a little fall. It dropped in a glistening sheet and rippled out to the edges of a wide basin. Sunlight speared the surrounding trees, striking the pool's surface in stripes of translucent green and shadow.

When Tamsen would have stepped past Jesse for a better look, he put out a hand. Sliding the rifle off his shoulder, he went forward a step, looked upstream, down, scanned the clump of rusty serviceberry on the far side, the dark laurel thicket above the fall, then turned. "The falls mask noises. 'S all right, though."

The path descended to a rock that rose out of the pool, long and flat. Tamsen stood at its edge, faint mist off the fall cooling her face. Birds flitted among the brush surrounding the basin. Along the low bough of a sycamore, a squirrel ran out, scolding. She barely heard it. Nor did she hear Jesse, behind her, stripping to his breechclout. The first she knew of it was the splash of his dive into the pool. She saw the shape of him moving beneath the water before his head broke the surface in a patch of sunlight, sleek as an otter's.

He grinned up at her, treading water. "Coming in?"

"Me?" He moved closer, propelling himself toward the rock, only his head above the water's surface. His arms were long. Maybe long enough to reach her ankle. She stepped back.

"It's nice. Cold, but you get used to it." His lips were turning purple.

"I don't swim, remember?"

"I'm not likely to forget. But I can teach you. It's not hard."

She shook her head.

"Suit yourself." Still grinning, he sank under the rippling surface.

She watched him stroke around the pool, knowing he had to be freezing. Finally he swam back to her. He put a hand over the stone's lip and clung on.

She'd been right about his reach.

She knelt, tucking her petticoat close, so as not to have to shout. "Is this where you and Cade come to bathe?"

"It is. You want to come too?" He ran a hand down his face, sluicing away water, then dipped his head so his hair slicked back over his scalp. She found herself fascinated by the fine shape of his skull, usually hidden under that thatch of hair he wore tailed back. Her heart was going at a trot.

"I'm happy hauling water to the cabin. That way I can heat it."

Jesse gripped the ledge with both hands and vaulted onto the rock, streaming water all around. The breechclout covered him front and back. Not a bit at the sides. His long, lean belly and even longer legs were slick and bare, his shoulders and chest stippled with cold.

Fearfully and wonderfully made, he was.

Cheeks blazing at the thought — and sight — she tore her eyes away and looked at the pool, the trees, the sky. Shock, mortification, admiration were threads in a hopeless tangle around her pounding heart. She was tempted to plunge into the pool after all — clothed, of course — just to cool her face and calm her rioting thoughts.

Apparently untroubled sitting there nearly naked, Jesse shook his hair like a dog would

310

shake, giving her an excuse to scramble to her feet and put her back to him. After a moment she heard him dressing.

"You worked hard today. Tate told me he was pleased to have you helping. I'm sorry 'bout your hands."

Tamsen swallowed but had no words — only the image of golden skin and lean muscle seared across her mind. His gaze was hot on the back of her head. She felt a trickle of sweat run down her nape.

"You don't have to wear a cap all the time," he said, as if he'd seen. "Janet's given up on making Beth wear one."

Tamsen faced him. Shirt and leggings covered most of that disconcerting skin now. "You don't want me to wear a cap?"

"Wouldn't bother me if you didn't."

"But my hair . . ." Twice as thick as Bethany's, her hair could curl past taming when the weather turned humid. "It'd be a bramble thicket if I don't at least keep it plaited."

Her hands were trembling. She clenched them, wincing at the sting of blisters as Jesse squeezed the water from his own hair. Gaze locked with hers, he stepped closer. "I didn't mean to fret you none. Wear your hair any way pleases you. That's all I meant to say."

Tamsen looked away. It wasn't only Bethany, or her hair — or sight of his impressively knitted frame — that had her knotted up inside. "Jesse . . . I know Cade left because of me. You don't have to pretend otherwise."

Vines grew thick among the trees below the pool, draped scarlet among greenery nipped with brown and gold. Insects danced in the sunlight shafting through the trees. She couldn't look at any of it now, only at Jesse and the pain seeping into his gaze.

"Cade keeps a lot to himself. Always has done. He'll come back. And come 'round to accepting the way things are now."

"He shouldn't have to. I wish . . ."

"Don't say you wish I'd never helped you," he said, a look in his eyes now she couldn't read. "Don't say that."

"Then I wish it hadn't cost you so much. I wish you didn't have to lie to your neighbors, or that Cade felt driven out of his home, or that he's upset you can't go hunting this —"

"You weren't meant to hear that." Jesse closed the space between them, then touched her face. She froze, though his hand had already warmed, and for an instant she almost let herself press against it.

She stepped back. "I did hear it."

Jesse held her in his gaze. "You let me worry about Cade. Ain't nothing happened between him and me to cause any lasting upset. It's only . . . We've all reached a spot where we got choices to make, soon as the dust settles. It'll be all right."

He was trying to reassure her, drawing from a well of comfort she hoped wasn't as shallow as her own. Tamsen forced a smile. His in return was so relieved and full that it did something alarming to the pit of her stomach. Alarming, but nice.

Then he went and shattered the moment.

"There's another thing we need to talk about." He bent to pull on his moccasins. The hem of his shirt had darkened, wicking up water off his breechclout. "Back when Cade and me were bringing the beeves to market, before Morganton, we got ourselves invited to a wedding. Friends of ours. Cherokees."

She was fairly certain she concealed the jolt that went through her. She remembered now, that first day she milked the cow, his saying that the Cherokees knew him and Cade. She hadn't translated that into *friendship,* though. "Do they ever come here, your Cherokee friends?"

"Not often. Ain't safe. It ain't always safe

for us to go to them. There's miles of hazards between. But we promised to be there, Cade and me — for White Shell's wedding — not knowing things would change."

Her presence had complicated everything for them.

"You should go," she said, then before she lost her nerve, "I'll go with you, if that's what you mean to ask."

"Not exactly." He shot her a half-worried look as he reached for his bullet-bag. "It's at Chota — the principal Overhill town. A few days' riding for me and Cade, if we don't run into trouble on the way."

Hostile Indians, she supposed he meant. Dragging Canoe's braves, the Chickamaugas. Or were they Creeks? Not that she'd be able to tell the difference if either knocked at their cabin door.

She studied his face in profile, trying to guess what he wanted her to say, finally deciding he didn't want to take her to Chota. She'd slow them down, or maybe be seen along the way, recognized, bring down worse trouble than Indians on them all.

"When will you go?" she asked, as a sliver of unease pierced her.

"Once the corn's in. Or Cade comes back." He stood and slung his rifle across

314

his shoulder, searching her face. "I don't have to go. Cade can make my excuses to White Shell and —"

"I want you to go. I'll be fine on my own."

She'd managed to shock him. "I don't aim to leave you alone. You'll stay with Tate and Janet till we come back. They know who's looking for you, and I trust Tate to keep you safe."

The sliver of unease worked deeper.

"That's settled, then," she said with as firm a nod as she could muster. "I'm ready for supper. How about you?"

Without waiting on his reply, she started back the way they'd come. His hand on her arm halted her. He nodded toward another path descending along the creek. "Cabin's that way."

Chin high, Tamsen started down the right path with a stride she hoped looked fearless.

25

Shoulders aching, Tamsen shifted the lid aside and tilted the churn toward the firelight to check her progress. Instead of lumps of gathered butter, a disheartening puffy mess floated in the milk.

The churn was an old one, stored in the Allards' barn until the family's cornhusking a week past, which Tamsen and Jesse and neighbors from down along Stony Creek attended. Janet had wiped the churn clean of cobwebs and presented it to Tamsen who, after watching Bethany dash gallons of milk into butter, thought it a task she could accomplish without strict supervision.

She might have been a tad too optimistic about that.

Hearing a sound, she raised her head to listen. Bethany was hallooing the cabin. After fitting the lid back in place, Tamsen grasped the dasher and resumed churning until the girl's slight form shadowed the doorway.

"Thought you might've waited till I got here." In seconds the girl was at Tamsen's side, pale braid swinging in the firelight. "How long you been at it?"

"Nigh on an hour."

"You ought to be long done. Let's have a peek." Bethany took the dasher from her grasp, removed the lid, and bit her lip to keep from laughing. "Your cream's too warm. It won't firm up. You need cold water. Be back in a shake."

The girl snatched up a bucket from the hearth, then hurried out. Back so quick she must have sprinted to the creek, she poured water into the churn and took up the dasher. "Let's see can *I* make it come right."

"That's kind of you. I could use a rest." Tamsen kept her tone bright as she relinquished the stool, drawing a brief twist of Bethany's lips and a dimming of her pleasure in catching Tamsen on the edge of domestic disaster. Again.

In the past two weeks, Bethany had arrived at the cabin in time to save Tamsen's first attempt at soap making, candle dipping . . . the list was long. On those occasions when nothing needed salvaging, the girl could be counted on to arrive armed with a gathering basket and a rifle as long

317

as she was tall. She'd taken Tamsen into the woods to harvest late cherries, rose hips, persimmons, ginseng ('sang, she called it), walnuts, hazelnuts, hickory nuts, chinquapins — all while keeping up a running chatter on their preparation and uses.

Once she'd shot a turkey.

At times this relentless onslaught of proficiency did make Tamsen feel embarrassingly obtuse. And at times, it mattered.

"Your butter's ready for rinsing."

Tamsen started. She hadn't noticed Bethany leave off churning and come to stand beside her at the table, where borrowed butter molds waited.

"Think you can manage getting it into the molds?"

Tamsen forced a smile. "Of course."

Bethany frowned, openly dubious. "I only ask because —"

"Because you are determined to make me look incapable in Jesse's eyes." Tamsen instantly regretted the words. Though she'd spoken calmly, Bethany stepped back, blue eyes flashing.

"I am determined to do no such thing. And if'n I was, I needn't try . . ." Bethany let her words trail, defiance freezing on her face.

They both turned toward the door. Men's

318

voices, easy and companionable, reached them from the stable. Tamsen felt her heart leap. *Let it be Jesse and Cade.*

The silent prayer was barely formed before Bethany rushed to the open door, doubtless eager to boast of her latest domestic rescue. But the girl's posture slumped. "It's the Trimbles, come a'calling."

Tamsen joined her in the doorway, thinking she had to be mistaken. But it was the Trimbles, whom she'd first glimpsed in Jonesborough, racing to the courthouse brawl. The pair had shown up at the Allard corn-husking. Dominic, the elder, had danced with Bethany when a fiddle was played, under Tate's narrowed gaze.

The brothers hitched their mounts and started for the cabin. Looking for Jesse? There could be no other reason for their presence. Unless since the husking, when Jesse had introduced her as his wife, her stepfather had reached Sycamore Shoals and they'd seen her portrait — put her face with that likeness. Panic fluttered beneath her ribs.

"Best see to your butter." Bethany tossed the words with a mingle of pride and pique as she stepped from the cabin, voice brightening as she said, "What's brought you rascals back to our neck of the wood?"

Tamsen stepped back inside. From the yard came Bethany's laughter, Seth's and Dominic's deeper tones, while she transferred the perfectly firmed butter to a wooden bowl to rinse, then kneaded in the salt. She'd pressed the last of it into the molds before Bethany stuck her head in the door.

"You done yet? Come out and greet your guests." She turned her face to the dooryard. "You boys thirsty? We got fresh buttermilk here if'n you fancy a taste."

Seth stepped into the doorway, brown hair shining in the sunlight. "It'd be welcome, ma'am, if it's no trouble to ye."

Tamsen wiped greasy hands on a rag and fetched two tin cups. She dipped them full of buttermilk and carried them to the door.

"There she is — Mrs. Jesse Bird." Dominic grinned as she came into the light. He was leaner than Seth and taller, with a sandiness to his hair. Little resemblance marked the brothers, aside from both needing the attentions of a razor. Dominic reached for a cup. "Never took Jesse for such a sly fox, finding himself a beauty and getting hitched afore anyone hears peep."

"And here's us thinking he was sweet on Bethany," Seth added. Dominic shoved him with an elbow, sloshing milk onto the ground. "Look what ye made me do!"

"Now, boys," Bethany said, charmed by their play, or pretending to be. "There's plenty buttermilk to go 'round."

Tamsen cringed at the girl's suggestive tone. Was she taking out her resentment by flirting with these two?

"Dom's just happy you ain't Jesse's drink of choice," said Seth. "Reckon he'd have dragged me up this cove sooner than the husking had he known."

"Now you know." Bethany watched them drink, speculation in her gaze.

"Jesse isn't home," Tamsen said. "Are you here to see him?"

"Aye. Allard too," Seth replied. "Governor Sevier's calling up militia for a winter campaign. The Georgians are going against the Creeks. Franklin's sending fifteen hundred volunteers. By Christmas, most like."

"There's land promised every man that musters," Dominic said. "Land in the bend of the Tennessee River. We know the Injun won't muster but thought Jesse might. He's got no ties with the Creeks."

The Injun. Cade. And Tamsen hadn't missed the flash of mistrust in Dominic's eyes as he'd said it. "Jesse isn't here," she repeated.

Bethany shot her a look, then smiled at

the Trimbles. "Y'all come over the ridge and sup with us. You can bring your news to Jesse after. He'll be along."

"I'm sure he will." Seth touched his hat, but his gaze swept Tamsen in a way that made the blood rise to her cheeks. "I'd not stray far with a wife like you waiting on me — if'n ye don't mind me sayin'."

She minded, but merely pressed her lips tight and glanced toward the creek, the ridge, across the cleared cornfield to the woods, anxious for Jesse. Nothing moved through the fiery autumn foliage but a flock of crows.

Bethany seemed to mind Seth's comment too, or the attention directed at Tamsen. "Jesse might even be at our place. He was over early, then out with Pa, rounding up our hogs."

The brothers downed the buttermilk and handed Tamsen the cups. Seth went to fetch the horses.

"I don't think you should go off with those two," Tamsen whispered when both Trimbles were busy with their mounts. "Stay here; wait for Jesse to come home."

Bethany wrinkled her nose at the suggestion and didn't bother lowering her voice. "If you want folk to stick around, you might try being more neighborly, make a body feel welcome in your home."

"Never mind it, sweetheart," Dominic told her, coming around his horse to mount. "You're welcome enough for two."

Tamsen's stomach tightened. "Bethany, truly, you ought to wait here with me."

But when Dominic swung into the saddle and reached down for her, Bethany allowed him to lift her up to sit behind him. She tucked bare feet under her petticoat and wrapped her arms around Dominic's middle, and the horses started off.

"I'll be by tomorrow," she called over her shoulder. "If'n I find the time!"

They'd barely disappeared into the bright skirt of the woods, heading up the ridge, when Jesse's voice called out behind Tamsen, down at the stable. She turned to see him swing off his horse and jog up the slope to the yard. Instinctively she moved toward him, wanting the shelter of his body, the reassurance of his touch. Realization of the need — unthinking, visceral — drew her up short.

"Who'd Beth ride off with?" Jesse's hair was damp. He'd been by the swimming hole before heading home to her.

"The Trimbles." She watched his face darken. "They rode up a bit ago, looking for you. It was something about a muster.

Against the Creeks. Franklinites are joining up with Georgia. Bethany invited the Trimbles home for supper."

Jesse's mouth compressed as he gazed toward the ridge, as if he debated riding after the girl and her chancy escort, to be sure she reached home safely.

Tamsen ventured, "Maybe you should, just to be sure."

"I better." Jesse caught her gaze then, his softening with surprise and pleasure that they'd come to agreement without ever speaking the words. "I appreciate the kindness you show her, given she hasn't exactly returned it."

Bethany's jealousy still rested uneasy on her mind, but Tamsen couldn't bring herself to say anything — like the fact that she'd lost her patience with the girl today — that might erase that look from his eyes, a look of approbation and warmth that made it hard to breathe, much less speak.

"No sign of Cade?" he asked her.

Tamsen found her breath. "Still no. I'd hoped he'd come riding in with you. Did you get Tate's hogs rounded up?"

"We did." He was turning to go for his horse when their stomachs growled in chorus. "Now I'm hungry as —"

"A bear? I'll have corn mush waiting for

you." It was the only dish she'd yet to produce with anything like consistency.

"I'll be quick as I can," he promised, the anticipation on his face exceeding all hope of what he knew she could manage at the hearth.

She went into the cabin, flushed with warmth, yet still wishing they could admit their lie to the Allards.

Half-wishing it wasn't a lie.

26

Despite all her efforts, one thing was evident
— she wasn't going to save this meal. The
beans were hard pellets, roiling in the pot.
The cornmeal cakes had scorched, but it
hardly mattered since they were hard as
rocks. While her back was turned dealing
with them, the venison began to char. Now
in a sweating panic, she was trying to
salvage *something* from the mess to feed the
Reverend Teague, waiting outside the cabin
with Jesse.

Since the harvest season prevented his
scattered flock from traveling to meetings,
Luther Teague turned itinerant in the
autumn. This was to be his last night in
Greenbird Cove. He'd spent the previous
two across the ridge at the Allards', praying
for the family's needs, telling Bible stories
to the children, serving their elders meatier
fare. The reverend had refused her attempt
to repay him for the linen, shoes, and

sundry items Molly had purchased for her in Sycamore Shoals, yet Tamsen wished at least to thank him for his care of his far-flung congregation — of which she felt a part — in the only other way she could, by offering him a roof and a meal.

There would be no meal. As for the roof, it was fast filling with smoke from the meat on the spit. She was reaching with a towel to yank it from the flames when Jesse poked his head into the cabin.

"Smoke's coming out the door. Everything all right?"

She whirled on him, tempted to hurl a few choice words she'd have blushed for the reverend to hear.

Jesse's eyes widened. "Your skirt!"

She barely had time to register the smell of scorching linen before he'd bounded into the cabin, snatched up her petticoat, and smothered the kindled hem.

Not only had she ruined supper and smoked the cabin, she'd also managed to set herself aflame.

Reverend Teague came inside, face taut with concern as Jesse hastily brushed down her skirt. "Are you all right, my dear?"

"Bit charred is all." Jesse's face was chalky. With a hand that shook ever so slightly, he pushed back a strand of hair that had slipped from her cap to curl in the hearth's warmth. "*Are* you all right?"

"I've ruined everything." Smoke and tears stung her eyes. She'd so wanted to get this right.

Jesse moved the venison off the spit. "The meat's all right. Look, if you cut away the burnt part —"

"But everything else. We can't have just meat to our supper."

"Of course not." Reverend Teague came around the table. "This bowl of apples looks inviting after the filling meals I've had of late." He patted his waistline, which *was* thicker than when they'd met weeks ago. "Why don't I slice a few, you serve the venison, and we'll all enjoy what matters most, each other's company in the Lord?"

Stillness settled over the smoky cabin as they awaited her response. Tamsen felt the urge to cry for pure relief. Maybe the meal — better yet, what she'd meant by it — was salvageable after all. "All right. I'll just —"

"Good heavens," said Bethany Allard, appearing in the doorway as if by dark magic. She tilted her small nose to sniff the air. "Mama, was I right? We're just in time."

Behind her, Janet looked less certain of their welcome than her daughter, who marched across the cabin, took up the towel, and lifted the lid from the bean pot.

"Didn't you soak 'em first? Never mind. We've brought biscuits, jam, pie, chicken, and I can't remember what. But this smoke! We'd best move the table out-of-doors. Don't you think so? Jesse, can you and Pa tote it out?"

"This is the first chance we've had to talk, you and I," Reverend Teague said as Tamsen joined him at the edge of the yard, away from the activity around the table where the Allards were clearing the supper leavings, preparing to head back over the ridge.

"So it is." She smiled as they stood side by side where the cabin yard began its slope toward the harvested cornfield, staring out over the break in the hills to the ridges rolling away westward, a bright, rumpled crazy quilt of red and green and gold. Part of what she'd hoped to accomplish with her supper was time alone to speak to Luther Teague. The Allards' arrival had curtailed that part of the plan. Until now.

"How are you here, with Jesse?" the reverend asked.

"He's worried over Cade being gone so long." The answer didn't speak to what he'd asked, but Reverend Teague didn't press.

"Cade's a grown man. And a capable one.

If there's anything troubling him, more than likely he's gone off to work it out or pray it through. Rest your mind easy about Cade."

She nodded, wishing she could.

"I've had opportunity to watch you with your neighbors." The reverend bent his head toward the voices in the yard behind them. "There's been some strain from that quarter, I take it?"

"They've been kind," Tamsen hurried to say. "Bethany's been a help to me."

"So I have observed." His wry tone made Tamsen look more closely. Humor sparkled in the reverend's eyes, and understanding. "I suppose it would be worse if she knew the truth, that you and Jesse aren't married."

How he'd discovered they'd been pretending to the very commitment he'd counseled her not to make in haste or fear, she didn't know. Perhaps Tate or Janet had given it away.

Tamsen crossed her arms. The day was bright, the sky vibrant blue, but the air held a nip. Everyone's noses were tipped in pink, and fingers not kept busy grew chilled. Over the farthest ridges to the west lay a blanket of cloud. A change in the weather was coming. Maybe it wasn't so bad she'd driven them all outside to enjoy the sun, while it lasted.

"Jesse let the Allards believe we're married for my reputation at first, and it seemed a good thing he did so when Cade left. But, Reverend, you need to know that we aren't . . . I mean, Jesse hasn't . . ."

"I know he hasn't," the reverend said, "and that you aren't."

"You do?" Tamsen asked, surprised, but could tell by his face he understood what she was trying to say, and believed her. Too embarrassed to ask *how* he knew, she hurried on, "I'm just not sure misleading everyone was the best thing."

"I take it you're no more inclined to make it truth?"

She'd hoped he wouldn't ask that.

Everything the reverend had said of Jesse, that day she'd let him talk her out of marriage, had proved true. He was a good man. A godly man. She was grateful to him. She cared for him. More than cared, she thought, minding the feelings he stirred in her when their gazes met. At the same time, she felt she'd traded one cage for another, that she was stuck there at the cabin — hidden away, waiting with her breath held in unspoken dread — unable to decide her future while her past might yet pounce from the shadows, tearing Jesse to pieces for daring to help her.

There was still that abduction charge.

"I don't know." Tamsen smiled ruefully, adding in a lighter tone, "All I do know is that I ought to have stuck with corn mush for supper. It's the one thing I can get to the table without leaving disaster in my wake."

She laughed weakly, as the reverend started to reply. But she never learned what he might have said to that.

Behind them a throat cleared. "Tamsen? Reverend? Pardon my interrupting."

Though Jesse had addressed them both, it was Tamsen he fixed in his gaze when they turned. How long had he been standing behind them? Her face heated, until she read the contrition in his eyes.

"I didn't know letting the Allards think us married was causing you such upset. I'll set it right. I'll tell Tate before they head for home. He can tell Janet if he thinks she needs to know."

"You'll tell him everything?" Luther Teague asked, with emphasis on the last word.

Jesse's gaze sharpened on the reverend, a look almost of warning in his eyes. "Yes," he said shortly, then swung his gaze back to her, his expression softening. "I'll have a talk with Bethany as well. I'm not best pleased with her at the moment, and I think she ought to know. It's high time she did a bit of growing up, showed you the respect you deserve as my —"

She'd been about to ask what they were inferring, and why they didn't want her to know about it, but mention of Bethany — and what Jesse had almost called *her* — distracted Tamsen. She saw the blood mount in his face to match her blush. "Jesse, no. That might hurt her worse. Go ahead and talk to Tate, if you want, but . . . not Bethany. Not yet."

"All right. If that's what you want." Jesse's eyes on her were intent, questioning.

"It is," she said.

He nodded, took a step away, then abruptly turned back and closed the space between them. The cabin and the yard and the Allards and the reverend ceased to exist as far as Tamsen was concerned as Jesse took her shoulders firm between his hands and leaned his head down, until their foreheads nearly touched.

"You listen to me," he told her, his voice a low, brusque rumble. "I'd rather take corn mush from your hand — morning, noon, and night — than chicken and apple pie from any other. And that's the plain truth."

Then he was gone, striding off and calling to Tate, leaving her breathless and staring straight ahead at nothing . . . and inwardly at everything. Staring and smiling through the pressure of tears nothing like the ones that had threatened before.

Then she blinked, coming back to her surroundings, and remembered she wasn't alone.

Luther Teague, who'd missed nothing of that exchange, was looking at her with a gentle knowing in his eyes.

27

Hickory leaves sifted down like sparks at the clearing's edge, quickening to yellow-brown flurries as a chill breeze gusted. The target fastened to the shedding hickory was of crude construction, deerskin stuffed with grass, a charcoal circle drawn large in its center.

Ten paces away, Tamsen raised the pistol, steadied it, drew back the hammer, and squeezed the trigger. There was the tiny pause as flint struck frizzen, then noise exploded and the pistol jerked in her hands. She opened her eyes, squinting through powder smoke.

"Did I hit it?"

Beside her, Jesse fought a grin. "It must've jumped again."

"No!" She'd fired three times and had yet to graze the target. She restrained the childish urge to stamp her foot.

"Next time," Jesse suggested, "try keeping

your eyes open."

"Did I shut them again?"

"Squinched tight with your nose wrinkled up. Cutest thing I ever saw."

It was hard to be nettled in the face of his teasing. His teeth were near white as a child's, straight save for the bottom front pair, crowded close. She liked how his smile softened his features, how his eyes, golden brown as autumn leaves, sparkled on the verge of laughter, even if it was at her expense.

She recalled of a sudden how those features had unnerved her back in Morganton. How could she have thought his a reckless face — his character too, by implication? Brave he surely was, and daring with it — enough to turn his life heels-up to help a near stranger. But reckless? Jesse Bird was the steadiest of men, and if his face was disconcerting to her now, it was only because it was captivating. And hawk-wild beautiful.

"Here. Let me reload it for you."

Tamsen handed over the pistol, then drew chilled hands beneath her cloak, watching Jesse retrieve ball and patch from his bullet-bag. He'd opted for the pistol, since she'd been unable to hold the rifle steady enough to aim. Though Cade had yet to return,

White Shell's wedding was drawing near. Jesse wanted to leave her able to defend herself. "Keep nigh the Allards, and there oughtn't come a need for it. But you should know how to shoot, in any case."

Mist had blanketed the creek when they set out to practice. The sun hadn't risen far before a grim line of clouds scudded in, threatening rain. November was nigh upon them, the flames of autumn cooling as the trees on the ridges bared their limbs to the coming winter. Wedges of geese had arrowed over all morning, honking their way southward — all save one that Jesse brought down, destined for their table.

"Watch me while I load," he said now. "You'll do it next time."

She wrung her fingers to warm them as he half-cocked the hammer, then poured a measure of powder down the short barrel. Though she'd watched him load the pistol when they'd begun shooting, his movements had been fluid, too fast to follow. This time he paused between each step so she could memorize it. He wrapped the lead ball in a papery scrap of wasp nest and rammed it in after the powder. "Nice and tight fitted." He fixed the ramrod beneath the barrel. "Keep the muzzle up . . . Put a bit of powder in the pan . . . Snap the frizzen in

337

place, and you're set."

He handed her the pistol. Determined to keep her eyes open, she took aim on the target. This time when she pulled the trigger, Jesse gave a whoop.

"That's more like it!"

Excitement surging, Tamsen hurried forward through the pluming smoke to see not only had she hit the target, she'd hit inside the circle. The very edge, but still.

"You've a good eye," Jesse told her as she fingered the hole bleeding grass onto the leaf-strewn ground. "All you need do is keep it open."

Thrice more she hit the target before Jesse reached for the canteen he'd brought along, tilted it to drink, and then handed it to her. Her fingers were dark with powder soot. She tasted the residue on her lips as she drank. "Am I all begrimed?"

"Shooting's messy business." He fished a kerchief from his bag. "Ought to have seen me and Cade after Kings Mountain. Couldn't tell which of us was white."

She thought he meant to hand her the kerchief, but he cupped her face with his hand and wiped at the smudges himself. The touch of his fingers, warm against her wind-chilled skin, chased all thought of pistols from her mind. His knuckle brushed her lip. Their eyes locked. His fingers on her stilled. She heard him swallow. He started to bend toward her, then he pulled away and knelt, returning the kerchief to the bag.

Flustered, breathless, she blurted, "Kings Mountain? That's the battle where Reverend Teague lost his arm."

"And his son." Jesse took out another ball and wad of wasp nest. He looked up at her, squinting a bit. "Did your stepfather fight in that battle?"

She hadn't expected the question. "He managed to do no fighting at all." In war or business, Hezekiah Parrish was on no side save his own. She tried to quell all thought of him, the lingering dread it brought. She didn't want it crowding out other feelings. Not now. Just now she wanted Jesse to touch her again, to do what it seemed he'd almost done. Kiss her.

He stood, extending the pistol to her. Their fingers brushed as she took the gun. She nearly dropped it for the jolt it stirred. Jesse wouldn't meet her gaze.

"Why'd your mother marry such a man?"

Now she was grateful for the distracting subject. "She had to. Papa died, leaving Mama with me and no way to provide. Mr. Parrish is Papa's cousin." She'd lost the fleeting memory of his touch and was thinking instead of the bruised clouds spreading across the sky, of her mother lying dead in a near-stranger's bed. "Have you heard something you haven't told me, about Mr. Parrish?"

"There's been no word of him," Jesse was quick to reassure. "Or of Kincaid. Not in Sycamore Shoals. Seth or Dominic would've mentioned it."

The Trimbles had visited twice since delivering the summons to muster against the Creeks. Sniffing after Bethany, who did little to discourage the attention.

"It's a long way from Jonesborough to come courting so often."

Jesse's gaze lifted toward the creek and home. "They happened to be in Jonesborough that day we nearly signed us a marriage bond, but they live in Sycamore Shoals."

Not even a full day's ride away.

"Haven't they farms to tend?"

Jesse snorted. "Those two farm? Not hardly. Seth works at the smithy, Dom at the tavern — when they keep off the liquor and don't get distracted by a horse race or a game of loo."

"Or a courtroom brawl?"

Jesse pursed his lips and shrugged, then

340

seemed to put the Trimbles out of mind, searching her face as if he sought to read her thoughts. "You still worried about Parrish and Kincaid?"

"Not to lie awake at night, but yes." If only they could discover whether her stepfather had given up the hunt without revealing themselves in the process.

"Just remember, when I go —"

"Stay close by the Allards." She smiled as she said it, wanting to be brave for him in this one thing at least, because the thoughts going through her mind — thoughts she was too much a coward to share with this man who'd risked so much to help her — were all about wanting even more from him. If her stepfather gave up hunting her, could they have a chance at a true marriage? Could she become the kind of wife a man like Jesse Bird needed?

She reached for the powder horn he held ready. "I'd best fire this pistol a time or two more, if I aim to be a sharpshooter before you come back from Chota."

"If Cade hadn't taken you away from the Shawnees, would you have become a warrior?" Tamsen's voice rose above the creek's chatter as she strode behind him, returning from the shooting.

341

Jesse paused on the path, letting her catch up. She hadn't worn a cap today. With the hood of her cloak thrown back, her hair was curling up around her face with the damp of coming rain on the air. He admired her hair — everything else about her too, but that hair was a glory, near-black and shiny, pinned up off her slender neck and looking so heavy he wondered she could carry her head so proud.

"I mightn't have had the chance," he said in answer to her question. "I told you we left the Shawnees not long after the fighting with Dunmore's troops?" He steered her ahead of him on the path so she'd hear without his having to shout. "The Shawnees were forced to talk peace. One price of that peace was handing over their children born white."

"Their captives?"

"Aye." He tightened his grasp on the goose he'd shot and frowned at the trail ahead, sifted over with russet leaves. "But that don't mean what you might think. Some were glad enough to go back. Most weren't."

"But why not?"

"Anyone the Shawnees adopt is well treated, cherished like the family member they're meant to replace. Don't matter if

342

they're white, black, or red."

"Like you, for Split Moon and Red-Quill-Woman?"

Behind her Jesse smiled, pleased she'd remembered their names. "Aye. Those adopted young, like me, didn't recall their white kin. Or if they did, most had no inclination to stop being Shawnee. Some were grown and married, with children of their own."

She glanced back at him, looking as if such a thought had never crossed her mind. "And the Shawnees gave them up that easily?"

He tensed, then reminded himself there was no way she could understand. In his heart he would always straddle the red world and the white, even if he never saw another Shawnee face, but he was getting on in the white world mostly on account he let folk forget he'd ever been anything but a frontier hunter, who happened to have a half-Delaware man looking out for him as a pa would do.

"Weren't nothing easy in it," he said, keeping his tone even. "Many of the Shawnees were desperate for peace. Too many were dead. Hearts were on the ground in those days."

Every day since, he reckoned. Peace

hadn't lasted long, despite all the Shawnees had given up for it. Peace never did last, it seemed.

At a lip of stone jutting across the path where the creek made a little fall, Tamsen stopped and looked at him, the tip of her nose pink from the chill. "Hearts on the ground?"

"You understand what that means?" he asked, then looked into those dark eyes of hers. Of course she knew.

"But Red-Quill-Woman. Didn't it put her heart on the ground when you and Split Moon failed to come back from that hunt?"

"She'd died the winter before." He'd been orphaned for the second time that day Split Moon's chest was blown open by a white hunter's musket. That day Wolf-Alone saved him.

"What would you have done," Tamsen asked, "if you'd been one the Shawnees were forced to give back?"

Jesse stepped off the rock and turned to help her over the drop with his free hand. He didn't let go when she was steady on her feet, just went on down the trail, reaching back and clasping her hand, like it was a thing they'd done countless times. She didn't pull away.

"I'd have run off, hidden till it was safe to

come back." It amazed him he could sound normal with her small chilled hand in his and his heart banging away with the thrill of it. "Done whatever I could to stay with the People."

"You hadn't any white family to go back to."

Her hand was warming in his. He thought of twining their fingers together but feared to go too far.

"Not without knowing the name I was born with," he said, thinking of that ritual on the edge of sleep. Always the memories ended in a canoe on a broad river, brown shoulders all around him, strong arms dipping paddles, feathers in scalp-locks twirling in the breeze. In the wake of that canoe lay the unknown country, his first years on earth, a dark brink that drew him to stand at its edge and gaze into the void. If a bridge existed across that blackness, he'd yet to find it. He wanted to. Even if his admitting to it was likely what upset Cade enough to drive him away.

"Truth to tell, in my heart of hearts, I'm still that little Cat-That-Scratches. What think you of that?" He looked back to see her lip caught between her pretty teeth. She wouldn't return his look, but she still held his hand.

345

Possessing his soul in patience was a lesson coming hard. He didn't want to be talking about himself, but of her. Her soul was a country he longed to explore and know as well as he did every stone that pocked that creek path. "Now I've told you something of my past, it's only fair I get to ask something of yours."

"What do you want to know?"

They were nigh the cabin clearing. He glimpsed it through a fringe of red sumac and wished they'd miles yet to walk.

"How 'bout, what's the first book you ever read? Or had read to —"

They'd come out of the trees. With the corn harvested, the line of sight up to the cabin was unobscured. Two horses stood outside the stable. Sitting in the cabin's open doorway was Seth Trimble.

Jesse halted, letting go of Tamsen's hand to grasp the butt of the rifle slung across his back. Two horses. One Trimble.

Thunder rumbled as Seth caught sight of them. He shot to his feet.

"Company," Jesse muttered.

Tamsen's face showed no more pleasure than Jesse felt. He started up the slope with the dead goose dangling and heard her following.

Seth called out something, a greeting

346

perhaps, but thunder murmured again; whatever he'd said was lost. He took a step toward the side of the cabin, then checked, looking back at them approaching.

Unease gripped Jesse's chest.

From somewhere out of sight, there came another sound. A sound like a muffled scream.

A sheet of red slashed across his vision.

"Stay clear of this," he said, catching Tamsen's puzzled gaze. There was no time to explain. He slung the rifle off his shoulder, dropped the goose at her feet, and broke into a sprint.

28

Jesse was halfway up the slope before Tamsen unfroze in a shattering of comprehension. Leaving the dead goose on the ground, she hurtled after him. Ahead she saw Seth Trimble hesitate, seeming torn between racing for his horse and meeting Jesse head on. When Jesse was nearly upon him, he broke and ran for the stable.

Jesse let him go, disappearing around the cabin.

Thunder grumbled, louder now, reverberating in her bones. A raindrop pelted her scalp. Then another. Sounds of struggle met her in the yard. A shout. A hollow thud as of something hitting the log wall. Then Jesse staggered around the side of the cabin, half-dragging Dominic Trimble, and she saw in Jesse's face what must have sent Seth running — the warrior Jesse might have been, furious and implacable.

She didn't wait to see more but ducked

around the cabin on the opposite side. Bethany Allard lay sprawled on the ground by the woodpile, petticoat and blond hair awry. "Bethany!"

The girl's mouth hung open, spilling drool and blood down a smear of dirt, as though her face had been shoved into the ground. She was bloodless save for that torn lip and a red patch across a cheekbone swelling up to close one blue eye.

"It's all right now. Jesse's got hold of him." The girl was shaking as Tamsen got her to her feet. Rain pelted down, hard fat drops that struck the yard in dusty spurts. They rounded the cabin to the thud of fists on flesh. Dominic was fighting back, blinking away blood from a cut through one eyebrow, hurling every foul name she'd ever heard at Jesse, who ducked and struck in focused silence.

Bethany leaned on Tamsen, limping toward the cabin door. Dominic saw her. Worse expletives spilled from his mouth until a roll of thunder, and Jesse's fist, silenced them. The blow landed under Dominic's jaw, jarring his head back with the click of teeth. The man went to his knees.

Jesse glanced her way. "Take her inside!"

In that instant of distraction, Dominic

launched off the ground with a snarl. Caught in the chest by Dominic's shoulder, Jesse staggered back but didn't fall.

Tamsen pushed Bethany through the door while behind her the combatants grunted under another exchange of blows, breath coming hard. A shout of satisfaction rose.

On the threshold Tamsen spun, dreading what she'd see. In those seconds her back was turned, Dominic had gotten hold of Jesse's knife, the long hunting blade he wore at his belt, and sprung away with it. Where Jesse's rifle had gone she didn't know. He pulled free his hatchet and beckoned, grinning with a fierceness that jolted fear and admiration through her.

Movement in the distance caught her eye. It was a horseman, down at the base of the slope, halted at the very spot she'd left the goose lying. A horseman with a rifle raised, trained on the cabin yard. Had Seth not ridden away as she'd assumed, but only to where he could get a shot at Jesse? They were rain soaked now, Jesse and Dominic. Hair plastered. Faces streaming. Their feet had churned the earth to mud.

Tamsen opened her mouth to scream a warning when she recognized the horse. It was Cade across the empty field, leveling his rifle. Lightning flashed and thunder rolled a second before gunfire cracked.

Bethany was frantic. "Who was shot? Who?"

Tamsen had gotten the girl to the back room. Bethany sat clutching a blanket to herself while Tamsen dipped a rag in the water basin on the tick beside them and, by the light coming through the open door, tried to clean the blood and dirt from her chin. "No one was shot. Cade fired a warning to run Dominic off. It worked."

Bethany's eyes welled. She winced as the tears stung the darkening weal across her cheekbone. The eye above was swollen half shut, but the other held enough pain and humiliation for two. "Why'd you have to be so nice?"

Tamsen's hands stilled. Then, smiling sadly, she went back to cleaning the girl's face, careful of her wounds. "When I needed it, someone was kind to me."

Bethany's lashes lowered. "Jesse?"

"Yes."

A shudder went through the girl. Her shoulders curled inward. "I'm sorry."

Tamsen poised the rag again. "Why are you sorry?"

"You were right about me. I tried so hard to hate you, to make you look small in Jesse's eyes. I *am* sorry. I know I said it

351

weeks ago, but I mean it now."

At the mention of Jesse, Tamsen closed her eyes, yearning to be near him, to see to his injuries, or relieve herself if they were only minor. She sent half her attention back through the cabin, out to where he and Cade stood under the eave, sheltered from the rain, talking in low tones. Giving her and Bethany privacy. Was Cade explaining his long absence? Or were they discussing the Trimbles and what had just happened? A violation of Bethany, but also this cabin. This home. *Her home.*

She let that notion wrap itself around her heart.

"I know," she said. Bethany looked at her, uncertain. "How about we put that behind us and start fresh?" It mightn't have been the best way to phrase the question. Bethany started crying again.

"Did he rape you?" Tamsen asked softly.

Bethany made a face, like she might be sick. Tamsen put a hand to the basin, ready for it, but the girl firmed her broken mouth. "Jesse got him off me in time." She shot a glance at the door. "I don't want to see him."

"Who?" Did she think Dominic was out there still? He was long gone, bloodied and battered and cursing Jesse all the way, while

352

Cade, still down the slope on his horse, kept that rifle trained until he'd mounted his horse and ridden after his brother. "Who don't you want to see?"

"Jesse."

The whispered answer surprised Tamsen. "All right. I'll help get you home."

Bethany shook her head. "Pa's away hunting, but I don't want to see Mama either. I just want to die!" She ended in a wail, and Tamsen didn't know what to do except take the girl in her arms and cry with her, thinking of a mountain clearing and an unbearable weight of grief, and a young man with his head on his knees praying over what to do for her.

She let Bethany sniffle and cry into her hair until the girl was done, then asked, "Do you want to stay here in this room with me tonight?"

"Could I?" It came out a little sob.

Tamsen stroked the sleek blond hair she'd helped brush into order. "Of course. Don't you worry about a thing. I'll bring you in some supper later. Jesse shot a goose today."

"And rescued another." Bethany pulled away, hands falling into her lap to twist the blanket. "I came here thinking to see if . . . Oh, I don't even remember now what I had in mind, but there they were, those two, riding up the creek trail. Should've turned around and gone back home the second I saw them, but I thought . . . Jesse might be jealous if he found me here with them flirting . . . I been so *stupid.* He'll always be faithful to you."

Tamsen's mouth fell open . . . and just in time she remembered. Bethany didn't know the truth.

He'll always be faithful . . .

She managed a smile for the girl. The very worst hadn't happened; they could be thankful for that. But when Tate Allard saw his daughter's face, worse might yet come of it.

Bethany seemed to be listening to the low murmurs drifting through the darkening cabin. "Cade's back. That's good, right? Y'all been worried about him."

"Yes, we have been." Tamsen had crossed the mountains to escape one encompassing worry but seemed to have gained a whole new set besides. Jesse had gotten himself wound around her heart so tight that she didn't know where her concerns ended and his began. Maybe they were one and the same now. But were the two of them twice as burdened, or twice as strong to face it all?

"I should go speak to them. Let them

know you're staying. Will you be all right if I leave you for a bit?"

Bethany lay down on the tick, pulling the blanket across herself. "All right. Just don't shut the door."

Cade was changed. Something in his spirit was lighter, though he'd avoided explaining where on earth he'd been so many days. He'd stabled his horse, unloaded a pack of fresh hides — proof he'd spent at least part of the time hunting — and was leaning now in the cabin doorway while the rain tapered off in the yard and dusk crept up from the creek.

Jesse leaned opposite, watching the clouded night steal in, glancing aside at his pa as their conversation drifted along. Even the scene he'd come home to hadn't ruffled Cade, once he knew Jesse and Bethany hadn't come to any lasting hurt. Jesse's jaw was bruised. He'd be sporting a black eye for White Shell's wedding. But he'd given worse than he'd got.

"Thanks for bringing that goose up." He nodded at it lying against the doorstep. "I best get to plucking it. Tamsen will want to get it over the fire."

Cade's brows rose. "Her cooking's improved, I take it?"

"Practice makes perfect," Tamsen said close behind them. "Tolerable, anyway."

Jesse turned to see her standing in the fire's light, hair down and shadowing her shoulders, brow furrowed as she took in his face.

"Jesse . . ." She lifted a hand to his temple and stroked down along the side of his face to his jaw, where Dominic's fist had caught him hard.

The touch left him breathless. He took her hand and gave it a squeeze, feeling Cade's eyes on him as he forced himself to let her go and step back. "Looks worse than it is. How's Beth?"

"She wants to stay here tonight. I told her she could."

"Doesn't she want to be home?"

"I think . . ." Tamsen lowered her voice, glancing shyly at Cade. "She's not ready to face anyone just yet. She'll go home tomorrow."

"I'll head over," Cade said. "Tell Janet what happened. She'll be worried Beth's not come home."

"Thanks, Pa."

"Yes," Tamsen said. "Thank you. Will you tell Janet I'm looking after Bethany and to come over in the morning when she can? And Cade . . . it's good to see you. I'm very

356

thankful for your timely return."

Cade pushed off the doorframe, holding her gaze. Tamsen met it, though Jesse read uncertainty in her eyes. Cade looked down at her, and for the first time Jesse could ever recall, smiled at her. "You look well. Better than he does," he added, with a teasing nod at Jesse.

Tamsen's face fell blank, then slowly her mouth curved in an answering smile so full and sweet Jesse's whole body responded in a riot of longing he could barely restrain.

One smile from her had him more rattled than an all-out brawl with Dominic Trimble.

"At my best she does, Pa. Go on over the ridge. We'll talk more later." He spoke lightly enough, but he was thinking Cade had got himself home just in time to save him utterly failing to keep that vow he'd made to their preacher.

Jesse watched him go through the tapering-off rain. The storm had been brief, violent, but the earth was giving back its cool breath in a mist gathering along the creek, the smell of soaking leaves. Night coming down. The peace flooding over him now made what happened in the dooryard scarce an hour since seem hard to credit, were it not for his throbbing face and half a dozen other aches taken limb to limb.

"Jesse?"

He looked at Tamsen, taking in her tired eyes, her worried brow. "She really all right? He didn't . . ."

She shook her head. "She's upset and hurt, all the same." Her lower lip quivered, and the distress that wracked her face cut him to the soul.

"Are you all right?" he asked her, but even as he was speaking, she'd walked straight into his arms, wrapped hers around his waist, still wet from the rain, and heaved a sob against his chest. He swallowed back a groan and stroked her hair, whispered her name, but didn't try to stop her crying.

Finally she said into his chest, "Was it our fault?"

He leaned back, sliding his hands around to cradle her face. "What?"

She didn't lift her gaze. "She's been flirting with Dominic trying to make you jealous."

He pressed her head against his chest, where it rested as snug as if she'd been made to put it there. "She may be young, but Beth's old enough to be accountable for her actions."

He felt her heave a sigh against him and held her tighter.

"Lord," he said, and it was a prayer. "I'm

sorry as I can be this happened, and we're asking You to set it right. Protect that girl in there and heal her, body and soul." *Protect this woman in my arms,* he added silently. "Amen."

"Amen," she said and pulled back, but not far, still touching him. "Thank you, Jesse."

He wanted badly to go on holding her, but he put her from him gently, firmly, worried she'd think he was trying to take advantage. Worried he might do so. It was near dark now, the only light that from the cabin spilling out. No stars. No moon.

She looked at him, eyes dark and fathomless as the heavens. "It was *One Thousand and One Nights.*"

He stared, understanding the words plain but finding no context for them. He opened his mouth to say something full of brains and dazzle like "Huh?" but she'd already read his confusion.

"That's the first book ever read to me," she said. "You asked, remember? I used to pretend that Mama was Scheherazade."

29

A venison ham roasted on the spit. Tamsen, seated on a bench drawn near, kept a close eye on it. The other eye was on the cloak spread across her lap. It was uncomfortably warm thus, but soon enough she would appreciate the rabbit fur lining she was stitching to the garment's inner side.

Jesse had given her the pelts. In the morning, he and Cade were leaving for Chota. They were gone now to the Allards', taking the extra horses and the cow to stable. Tate was back home and promising to stay close while Cade and Jesse were away. He'd spent the past two days hunting the Trimbles, who'd abandoned their cabin near Sycamore Shoals and lit out for parts unknown, no doubt anticipating his wrath.

Alone with the door open, Tamsen glanced with longing at the sunlight streaming in. It would be easier to see her work outside, but she was determined not to budge from the

360

hearth and risk burning the last meal she would make for Jesse. At least for a fortnight.

Holding up the cloak to the firelight, she examined her work with satisfaction. If not for variations in the small pelts, it would have appeared a solid fur.

She'd begun the task after supper the previous night. With Jesse out tending stock, it had been the first time she and Cade were alone in the cabin since his return. He'd sat at the table, rifle across his knees, cleaning the weapon with a rag and grease, pausing now and then to peer through the spectacles set across the bridge of his nose at the Bible open on the boards, illumined by taperlight.

Despite the spectacles, she'd had to remind herself that Cade was only half Delaware. Apart from his eyes, his white blood hardly showed. At least to her, who'd never seen a full-blooded Indian that she could recall. Surely such a one couldn't look more fierce than Cade. She'd dropped her gaze to her sewing, wondering what he thought of her now. Was he resigned to her presence?

"Jesse tells me you've a keen eye."

She'd jerked her gaze up to find Cade no longer attending to rifle or Bible but to her. She glanced quickly at the pistol on the table, waiting its turn with rag and grease. "So he tells me too."

Cade studied her in silence, then said, "When Thunder-Going asked us to come to Chota, none of us knew our paths would cross with yours. If it troubles you to be parted from Jesse, I'll go alone."

With all her heart she wanted that. "I don't want that," she said. "I'm fine staying with the Allards for a spell."

They'd talked about it, she and Jesse. Cade, he'd told her, had been in Sycamore Shoals before coming home. There'd been no fresh word of an eastern merchant searching for an abducted stepdaughter. Winter wasn't far off. Soon snow would seal off the mountains, sundering east from west, making travel between a hardship she doubted her stepfather would risk. Dared she hope that he'd returned to Charlotte Town . . . that he'd never find her . . . that he'd never seek to harm Jesse for helping her escape?

If only there was something she could do to lift this burden of *not knowing.*

The crinkle of turning pages joined the fire's fluttering. Just when she'd thought Cade had gone back to reading, he'd spoken again. "I've something to say to you. Will you hear it?"

She looked up to find him waiting for her response. Warily she nodded. To her surprise Cade put aside his rifle, wiped his hands on a rag and took the Bible onto his lap.

"Teach me thy way, O LORD," he read, "and lead me in a plain path, because of mine enemies. Deliver me not over unto the will of mine enemies: for false witnesses are risen up against me, and such as breathe out cruelty. I had fainted, unless I had believed to see the goodness of the LORD in the land of living. Wait on the LORD: be of good courage, and he shall strengthen thine heart: wait, I say, on the LORD."

Cade raised his face, and the gentleness in his eyes was that of a father, meant for her. It brought her to the swift brink of tears. *Wait on the Lord, be of good courage, and he shall strengthen thine heart. Wait . . .*

Wait and do nothing? She blinked back the tears, searching for words to ask what had prompted him to read that passage. Jesse's presence didn't register until he spoke.

"Tamsen? You all right?" He stood in the doorway, head bared, brow furrowed.

She sprang to her feet, wanting to go to him, hold him, beg him to stay with her, but she'd just told Cade she was fine with his going.

"I'm fine," she'd blurted, and because she wasn't, and couldn't hide it, she'd taken the unfinished cloak to her room.

Now, as the venison juices sizzled on the embers, she tied off the final stitches of the lining, while her heart ached with wishing she'd been courageous like the passage admonished. In the morning Jesse would leave, and she vowed she wouldn't cry again. At least, she amended, wiping at a defiant tear, she wouldn't be *found* crying.

She almost missed the scurry of movement at the edge of the sunlight streaming through the open door. When she saw what made it, she forgot the venison. Forgot Jesse's leaving and Cade's surprising tenderness and the cloak she'd spent hours lining.

A bushy-tailed squirrel had gotten into the cabin.

At first she didn't move, disbelieving her eyes. A squirrel so brazen as to come into the cabin in the middle of the day? But there the creature was, flitting through the sun patch into the shadowed corner where Cade kept his things, including the sack of dried venison and parched corn he'd put together for their journey. She couldn't let the squirrel get that corn, yet an irrational fear of its invasion held her frozen to the bench. For the tiniest instant, she wished

Bethany were there.

Then something rose up in her, an indignation so great it shoved such immobilizing thoughts from her mind. Hurling the cloak to the floor, she snatched up the nearest weapon to hand, a long-handled twig broom. With it she rushed the corner where the squirrel had retreated.

It was no longer there. In the seconds she'd taken to grab the broom, it had scurried for the loft ladder and was climbing it like a tree, heading for their stores.

"No, you don't. Shoo — get out!"

The squirrel froze at her advance, clinging to a rung halfway up. Brandishing the broom, she darted at it, hoping it wouldn't climb higher but leap to the floor where she could swat it toward the door.

The squirrel did neither. Defying expectation — not to mention gravity — it sprang straight up the cabin wall, streaking up and over, higher than her head, scuttling across the logs like a giant furry spider.

Tamsen screamed. Broom extended, more shield than sword, she rushed after it. The squirrel leapt from the wall, narrowly missing her head, and dashed beneath the table.

Tamsen followed, overturning a bench with a clatter. The squirrel darted from under the table and dove beneath her discarded cloak. With a bark of triumph, she threw down the broom and scooped the creature up, muffled in wool and rabbit fur.

She had it trapped, but not subdued. It struggled wildly against the furs she'd painstakingly stitched. The horror of a live squirrel with teeth and claws in her hands overcame her nerve, and she hurled it away with a screech. Squirrel and cloak hit the puncheon boards and parted company.

Surely now it would make for the door and escape.

It didn't. It darted back to Cade's corner and whirled to face her, tiny legs splayed, chittering at her, scolding as if *she* were the intruder.

Fury drove out fear, and maybe all good sense as well, for afterward she wondered why she didn't pick up the broom again instead of going for Cade's pistol, still on the table after last night's cleaning.

Perhaps by then she'd lost all sense of proportion.

After snatching up the weapon like a club, she hurtled toward the squirrel. It made another dash — for the door. With a curdled scream Tamsen flew after it and nearly sprawled over her own feet at what she saw blocking the creature's exit — a man, silhouetted against the sunlight. The breechclout, leggings, and long shirt were right for Jesse or Cade, but the head wasn't crowned with a hat or thick hair pulled back. It was plucked smooth save for a crest on top, tied with feathers and something that flashed and glinted.

As the squirrel ran a panicked circle in the doorway, the man spoke a word. It sounded like "see you." He took a step inside the cabin, where she could see *him* better. Bronzed face. Black eyes. Silver ear-bobs. Tattoos. An Indian.

The squirrel leapt.

The Indian gave a startled cry, grabbing for the doorframe as the squirrel clawed its way up one fringed legging, launched itself into the air, and was gone — leaving Tamsen nowhere left to spend her fury save on this new and more ominous intruder.

Still screaming, she came at the doorway, pistol raised, while a part of her brain calmly informed her that she'd been dead wrong about how fierce a full-blooded Indian could look. Then she swung the pistol at his head.

He ducked. The pistol swept through empty air, throwing her off balance. A sinewy hand shot out and plucked the weapon from her grasp.

Tamsen scurried to the corner where the

squirrel had sought refuge. The Indian straightened and faced her, pistol clenched. She thought of trying to reach the hearth, grabbing for tongs, poker, frying pan — but it was too far. They stared at each other, Tamsen with her heart galloping, scalp prickling at sight of the gleaming hatchet at the Indian's belt. He didn't reach for the weapon. Aside from her pistol, he seemed to have no other on his person.

"I do not know you, little squirrel chaser," he said, wariness in his jutting face, something else dancing in his eyes. "But if I give this back, you promise not to hit me with it?"

Grasping the pistol by the barrel, he offered her the stock. Struck dumb by his flawless English, Tamsen moved to take the proffered weapon. The Indian didn't loosen his grip.

"Or hit me with any other thing?" he added in addendum to his terms. "We have peace between us, you and me?" He waited until she nodded, then released the weapon to her.

"*Osda.* Good. I seek Wildcat — known as Jesse Bird. This is his cabin still?"

Tamsen worked her mouth, soundless as a landed fish at first. "I — He — You know Jesse?"

368

The Indian's brows were plucked clean, but the place where they should have been arched high. "You are his woman? Ha! A wildcat and a squirrel chaser have joined blankets? Or maybe it is two wildcats. Ha-ha!"

It dawned on Tamsen then — what she'd seen dancing in the Indian's eyes before was laughter. He was fizzing with it now, his whip-lean frame convulsing. Shock and bewilderment swirled around her like stars, but uppermost in her mind was relief — brought on as much by the sight of such a terrifying face crinkled in glee as his speaking Jesse's name.

"*Osda,*" he said again. "It is only too bad the squirrel got away."

Tamsen felt a smile tug her own mouth. Then a giggle rose in her throat, born half of hysteria, irrepressible.

That was how Jesse found them, Tamsen clutching the pistol, giggling in helpless mirth with an Indian in the cabin's front room.

"Bears? What're you doing here?"

The Indian turned to Jesse, blocking the light from the doorway. "*Siyo,* brother. I am making peace treaty with your woman."

It was amazing, in a day of amazements, the shade of red that bloomed in Jesse's face at the Indian's words. And that he didn't correct the assumption. "Sounds like you're making headway. But how'd you know I had a woman here to be making treaty with?"

"I did not know. It is why Creator sent me, maybe. My father sends me for another purpose."

"Sit and tell me about it." Jesse glanced at Tamsen, the fierce color ebbing from his still-bruised face. He started to smile at her, perhaps in reassurance, then sniffed the air and looked to the hearth. Tamsen set down the pistol and rushed to tend the roasting meat as Jesse said to the Indian, "You've arrived in time to fill your belly, as usual. No dead cows this time. You'll have to content yourself with venison."

"It is good," the Indian said, then added with a sliding glance at Tamsen. "Since I cannot get squirrel."

She muffled the urge to break into hysterics again. Jesse looked between them, then shook his head and ducked out of the cabin. He brought in a rifle and bow, which the Indian must have left outside the door. As they were seated, Jesse explained for Tamsen's benefit that Catches Bears was the brother of the woman whose wedding they were shortly to attend.

She felt Jesse's gaze as she took up a platter and began carving the venison to fill it.

"You all right? You weren't fixing to shoot Bears, were you?"

"No. I meant to club him."

Bears threw back his head and laughed. "I will have a story to tell my father about this one. He will be amused."

Jesse glanced at her, but his attention was soon diverted as Bears explained his presence. His father, it fell out, had moved his family away from Chota. Others had followed. "Dragging Canoe has Chota's warriors all stirred up," Bears said. "We found a new place where my father thinks we can be left in peace. I am to show you the way."

The Indian angled a look at Tamsen as she set the meat platter on the table, the teasing glint back in his eyes as he said to Jesse, "It is a thing to wonder at, finding such a woman as this to put up with you — despite your misfortune to be found by Shawnees before a Cherokee could come along and make a proper man of you."

Jesse suffered the ribbing with a wry smile. "I wonder at it with every breath I draw," he said and leveled her a look of such unabashed admiration it rooted her to the floor, unable to look away.

Cade came into the cabin then, breaking the moment, Tate Allard on his heels.

371

Tamsen turned to fetch a pot of corn soup left from dinner, heart pounding with joy for what she'd seen in Jesse's eyes, wishing desperately that her cabin wasn't suddenly full of men, when she wanted only one.

30

The clouds hugging the sodden hills had sunk as low as Charlie Spencer's spirits. Bedeviled by a cold and cheerless rain the length of the Nolichucky, he, Kincaid, and Parrish had found no trace of Miss Littlejohn. Despite his vow to the contrary, Charlie had agreed to stay the course to Jonesborough.

Inside the hamlet's log tavern, a cup of applejack cradled in reddened hands, from his bench by the hearth, Charlie half-listened to the talk of patrons in the smoky taproom, while Kincaid showed 'round the portrait — a scene reenacted too many times to recount. Parrish had left them to it, gone to the courthouse to make inquiries.

Sick to death of the fruitless mess, Charlie sent his thoughts scouting down other trails, one of which, to his surprise, still headed east — down the Yadkin River to his farm in the Carraways. It was years since he'd seen it, tucked up in those hogback ridges rising from the piedmont . . . But the Holston, the long hunt, buffalo, beaver, bear . . . that was the second trail unspooling before him. Yet the more Charlie gazed down it, the fainter it grew. He faced his mind east, considering. He'd dipped deep into his supplies, but there was the promised payment from Kincaid to make it up. Maybe wintering back east wasn't a bad proposition. Might be right peaceful after the past few weeks.

Going east to find peace and solitude — who'd have thought such a notion would cross his mind? Maybe fire and applejack had fuzzed his thinking. He ought to go outside, clear his head. Too much damp hide and woolens stinking up the place.

"Spencer!"

Kincaid stood over by the cage bar, next to a table where a man and woman sat, grizzle headed both, gesturing as if at odds. Charlie thought at first it'd been more time and breath wasted. Then he knew their luck had changed. Kincaid wore the look of a man shaken from fretful dreams.

Charlie crossed the room, cup in hand. Half-cleaned stew plates and crumbled bread littered the table. At the edge of the boards was Miss Littlejohn's face, staring up from its tiny oval frame.

"She was there," the woman was saying, not for the first time, going by her tone. Fleshy cheeked and sharp nosed, she jabbed the board next to the miniature. "Perched on the end of that bench inside the door."

The man grimaced, showing a string of meat stuck betwixt his teeth. "Which time? We been to that confounded courthouse thrice trying to square that deed."

"I don't recollect which time, but I do mind *her*." The woman's gaze swept Charlie and fixed on Kincaid. "She'd a feller with her. I figured them for marrying, the way he was looking at her, all nervous-like."

Even had he taken leave to doubt Parrish's version of events, Charlie hadn't gone so far as to imagine Miss Littlejohn walking tamely into matrimony with the villain who'd whisked her away before her mother's blood was cold. Neither had Kincaid, judging by the color draining from his face.

"Don't pay my wife no mind," the man began, then jumped in his seat and scowled.

Kicked under the table, Charlie reckoned.

"Hush. Let a body *think*." The woman squeezed shut her eyes, deepening their crinkles, till they popped wide again and she snapped her fingers. "The day Colonel Tipton raided the courthouse. That's when we seen her. Long about the end of September, 'twas."

The man stopped scowling and ogled the portrait, tongue working at the meat in his teeth. "Hang on; maybe I do recall. But the girl I seen weren't all done up like that."

"That's right," the woman said. "She was got up plain as a Quaker. Not with that fancy-dressed hair and silk and all. She'd moccasins on her feet."

So he'd been right about that deerskin, Charlie thought. A small thing to take satisfaction in, but it weighed on him, his having led Kincaid and Parrish so far astray at first. And if the girl had married her kidnapper, willing or no, he supposed that was partly his blame. Miss Littlejohn might be lost to Kincaid — that'd depend on what sort of man he proved once they saw the feller who killed her ma strung up.

"If'n that was your girl we seen," said the man at the table, "no telling where she and that feller went, or if they got their business seen to. Like my wife says, Tipton came with a passel of Carolina boys and raided the place, directly we left. If there was any papers signed, they'll be long burnt to ash."

"Nobody took lasting hurt," the woman added, seeing Kincaid's alarm. "Reckon her man got her out 'fore things turned ugly.

We'd have heard tell otherwise."

Parrish's visit to the courthouse would be in vain.

Kincaid drew up straight, frustration chasing over his face. He took up the portrait and turned to speak to Charlie, then whipped his gaze to the tavern door, where a man had come in, pausing to shake the wet from his hat.

Raining again was the thought at the back of Charlie's mind. The front of it was fixed on the man — younger than Kincaid, sandy headed, blue eyed, lean. Naught to make a body stand at gaze or his face go chalky like Kincaid's was doing.

The man looked up, locked eyes with Kincaid, and went every bit as white and still. Then he lunged for the door he'd just come through. Kincaid was steps behind him, shoving the portrait into his coat, leaving the couple at the table staring, mouths agape.

Charlie put his to better use. "That who ye seen with Miss Littlejohn, by chance?"

"No," the man said. "That's Dominic Trimble, from over Sycamore Shoals. Thought the other fellow hailed from Virginy. What's he got against Trimble?"

Charlie plunked his cup on the bar and went to find that out.

It *was* raining again, a mizzle so fine it clung to the skin, drifting rather than falling, but Charlie ceased to notice once he spotted the grappling figures.

Trimble, caught midflight at the hitch-rail, broke free and sprinted 'round the side yard, Kincaid on his heels. The dogs rose up excited, ready to abandon the mules Charlie had set them to guard. He shot them a collective "Stay!" and hotfooted it 'round the building to see Kincaid snag Trimble in the rear yard. Paying no heed to dignity or mud, he wrestled Trimble down and pinned him, forearm across his neck.

"Where's the other one — your brother?" A wheeze came from Trimble's mashed throat. Kincaid eased up. "Where?"

Trimble's face contorted as he sucked in air. "Don't know — get off me, Brose!" The younger man twisted in the mud but couldn't break Kincaid's hold.

Few were about in the dismal weather, but even in the rear yard, they were drawing more of an audience than Charlie. Kincaid lurched to his feet, dragging Trimble up with him. Both were mud-plastered, bristling like tomcats, hats on the ground.

Trimble sported a freshly cut lip, but this wasn't the first scrape he'd been in of late. Charlie hadn't noticed inside the tavern, but now made out the bruise fading around one eye. A cut through an eyebrow looked to be inflamed.

Trimble spat a gob of blood, glaring at Kincaid. "What took you so long?"

Kincaid clutched the front of Trimble's soiled coat, cold fury in his face. "My business here wasn't to do with you — until now."

"Dom!" Another man came pushing through the small ring of onlookers, brushing roughly past Charlie. He halted when Kincaid turned. Recognition washed the newcomer's features, and the same urge to run that had come into Trimble's eyes. This one didn't scratch that itch.

"Hey, Brose," he said, like one braced for a blow long feared. "How's things back home? Your pa still looking to wring our necks?"

Parrish found them out back of the tavern in time to help detain the Trimbles, who Kincaid took no joy in making known to them.

"Horse thieves, the pair. I know several court justices who'd appreciate knowing where these hell-jacks have been hiding the past few years — after Alexander Kincaid is through taking out our loss on their hides."

Flinching at that, the brown-haired one, Seth, said, "That's your grandpa, ain't it? What about your pa? It was his horse we —"

"Shut up!" Dominic growled, though he was kept from reaching his brother, who was held firm by Parrish.

Kincaid leveled his glare at them with equal loathing. "Collin Kincaid is dead. But your crime against my family is very much alive in my grandfather's mind."

Despite his bloodied lip, Dominic smirked. "He's got to be eighty, if he's a day. It was your pa scairt us out of Virginy, but now he's gone, can't you just —"

Kincaid backhanded him across his broken mouth. Seth made a garbled sound and struggled, but Parrish gripped him with surprising strength.

Dominic let the blood run down his chin. He'd quit his smirking, but his eyes mocked. "Seems you've inherited the family temper, much as you always claimed otherwise."

Kincaid's mouth thinned. Before he could speak, Parrish cut in. "What is it you plan to do with these two? We've precious little season left before winter and no leads on

380

my stepdaughter's whereabouts."

Most of their audience had drifted away, gone back in out of the rain once the drama sputtered out. Charlie stepped forward from the few that were left, clearing his throat. "Well, now, looks like maybe we have."

Parrish's gaze sliced toward Charlie. "Are you telling me you've found Tamsen?" He shoved Seth Trimble away as if he was of no further consequence. "Why, then, are we wasting time with these ruffians?"

Kincaid related what they'd learned from the couple in the tavern. Charlie watched Parrish's face work itself from surprise — he'd almost have called it alarm — to calculation, to something darker.

"Tamsen?" It was Seth Trimble who repeated the name.

Charlie caught a look of confusion in his eyes before his brother shot him a quelling glare.

Dominic turned to Kincaid, no longer fighting his hold or seeming concerned about his capture. "Look, Brose, tell us what it is you come all this way for. Must be a powerful reason to draw you off those precious acres of yours. Something about this man's daughter gone missing?"

"My stepdaughter," Parrish supplied. "She was abducted from Morganton in September — the very hour her mother was murdered."

Lines Charlie had heard a hundred times from the man's lips, delivered without feeling.

"You don't say?" Dominic looked from one to the other. "Happens we been 'round these parts a good while now, me and Seth. Might be we know something could help you find the girl. But what's she to do with you, Brose?"

Hesitation tightened Kincaid's jaw, but the need to leave no stone unturned in his hunt for Miss Littlejohn — no matter what might crawl out from under it — proved stronger. He told the tale in brief.

Dominic gave a low whistle. "And you been hounding her all these weeks since? She must be something, Brose. What'd you say was her name?"

"Tamsen Littlejohn," Parrish said.

Charlie saw the skin around Seth's eyes tighten. Dominic pinned his brother with another look.

"Uncommon name. What's she look like?"

Charlie and Parrish exchanged a glance while Kincaid reached into his coat and brought out the portrait. The Trimbles crowded close to look. Seth drew in a breath, but Dominic spoke first. "You know who it was took her off? To name him, I mean?"

"No," Parrish said. "But he's wanted for the murder of the girl's mother, as well as her abduction. Spencer has seen him."

"Murder?" Seth said, frowning.

"Murder," Dominic said, as if musing on an interesting notion. He flashed a grin at Kincaid. "Well, Brose. You can count on us to keep an eye out for her."

"You'll do more than that." Kincaid stowed the portrait out of the rain. "You pair are going to help us find Miss Littlejohn and see her safe, or it's you I'm taking back to Long Meadows."

"You sure it ain't a case of her choosing this other feller over you?" Seth Trimble cut in. "Some sort of elopement?"

The suggestion didn't ruffle Parrish's countenance, but scarlet rose from Kincaid's muddied neckcloth. "A woman of that quality would never throw her life over for some backwoodsman she barely knew. And never for the man who killed her mother in front of her eyes."

Dominic's bleeding mouth rose in a smirk. Maybe to give himself time to think — maybe just to goad Kincaid — he said, "How's it any different, Brose, you chasing after a woman who don't want you, and

383

how your pa was with your uncle's wife, sniffing after her till they fled Virginy to be shed of him? Or that's the story we heard. You come off so high and mighty, looking down your highbred nose at us, but the apple ain't fallen far from —"

Charlie doubted the fool saw the blow coming till he was doubled over gasping, clutching his gut.

Kincaid lunged forward, but Seth got hold of his arm and hauled on it hard enough to throw him off balance, giving Dominic time to stagger for the front of the tavern. "No — Brose, we'll help, all right? We'll look out for Ta— for your girl. I promise we'll help."

Kincaid had lurched to a standstill, staring after Dominic as if he was the one gut-punched. "I am nothing like Collin Kincaid," he said under his breath. "Nothing whatsoever."

"Sure," Seth hurried to agree. "You never touched a drop of the hard stuff. We all knew that. Dom was just tryin' to get your goat."

Kincaid eyed Trimble. "Is this where you live, Jonesborough?"

"Naw, we got us a cabin, up by Sycamore Shoals. Or we did." Something like regret twisted Seth's face. "I best git afore Dom leaves me behind. Can I go?"

man. Counting that trapper, three men hunted Tamsen. Why hadn't he sent his regrets to White Shell and stayed?

You are a man of your word. It had filled him with strength, knowing Tamsen saw him so, and maybe this longing that troubled his sleep, his peace, was merely that of his heart and loins. Just the natural ache to get back to her that any man blessed with such a woman would feel. But what if it was something deeper? What if holding to his word was running crosswise to what the Almighty was trying to tell him to do?

He'd seen Tamsen tested in so many ways, seen her failures, her triumphs, learned her weaknesses and strengths, and he was as sure of her now as he'd been on that street in Morganton. What was he doing away west while she was waiting on him to get back so they could make this fragile bond between them a solemnized and witnessed union?

Timing. It was a thing they hadn't mastered yet.

"It is about my wife," he said.

Bears nodded. "You feel the want of her. She is easy to look at, for a white woman."

"She is so, brother. I will never deny it. But no. It is not that." He laughed softly. "Not just that. I have had a dream of her. Two times in the night, I had the dream, waking between them."

Bears's plucked brows rose. "The same dream twice? Will you tell me the dream?"

Jesse did so as they walked back to the village, goose flesh rising on their damp skin. Others were stirring now, passing on the path with murmured greetings, including White Shell and the warrior she was to wed, their glow of content defying cold and snow. At Thunder-Going's lodge, the smell of wood smoke and the murmur of voices welcomed. Beneath the arbor Jesse reached for his bearskin. Bears put a hand to his arm.

"If you tell this dream to my father," he said, conviction taut across his face, "I know what he will tell you. He will tell you to heed it. He will tell you to go back to your woman, and be quick about it."

32

Tamsen pushed the cabin door open. The air within was chilled, motionless after the leaf-blown breeze that had swept her over the ridge. The smells of old grease and wood ash, Cade's kinnikinnick, and the mustiness of hides hung in the shuttered space. Leaving the door half-open for light, at first she simply relished the silence.

Not an hour ago they'd all been in the barn, she and the entire Allard clan, plucking a brace of geese, sorting feathers for quills and ticks and pillows. In the midst of laughter and sneezes and floating featherdown, she'd been pierced with a longing for her quiet home — and for Jesse — so acutely that she'd slipped away to the loft she shared with Bethany.

But a brief spell of solitude, all she was liable to get, hadn't been what she needed. She'd loaded the pistol Jesse insisted she keep, on impulse retrieved her mother's box

— tied shut with cords — from under Bethany's bed, put on her fur-lined cloak, and made fast for the ridge path, knowing had she told anyone where she was bound, she'd never have gotten away.

She'd brought the box with the notion of reading over her parents' secrets again, but here in the cabin, it was the future her thoughts swirled around, not the past. She set box and pistol on the table and crossed to the hearth. It was swept clean as she'd left it at their parting just over a week ago — a day alive in her memory, every word, every touch.

She hadn't known a kiss would be like that, that it could make her ache for wanting more. Awaiting Jesse's homecoming was a torment, but there was a sweetness to the blade of anticipation that sliced through her, morning, noon, and night. It was easy to pretend the shadow that pursued them had vanished, blown away on a freeing wind, leaving behind clear skies and sun. She let herself believe it as she wandered the cabin, touching books, spare clothing on the walls, the table where they'd shared meals — most of them hardly edible at first. She'd never cook as well as she sewed, but she was getting better, learning her way. She remembered the squirrel, and laughed.

It was a lonely sound in the chilled cabin, but it made her decide to check their stores in the loft, to be sure no varmints had come raiding. She climbed the ladder. All was as she'd left it, but she didn't climb down directly.

Crouched under the roof, among casks and sacks, Tamsen closed her eyes and filled her mind with Jesse, how the firelight played over his sun-streaked hair, how his golden eyes and lean, angled face contrived to make him seem hawk wild, forbidding even, until a smile would come like sunlight and soften his edges, melting all of hers.

She was going to spend the rest of her life letting him know how thankful she was God brought him to her, as Reverend Teague once said, at the very moment she needed him. But the Almighty had done so much more. He'd given her her heart's desire before she knew she wanted it or had the eyes to see the treasure standing in front of her. Before she'd come to love Jesse Bird.

"Jesse," she whispered, "I wish I'd said those words to you."

They'd be the next he heard out of her mouth. She knew now what she wanted. A life with Jesse Bird, whatever shape it took, wherever they lived it.

Down below, the cabin door creaked, as if

a wind had pushed it inward. Or a hand.

She'd left the pistol on the table.

"Tamsen? You here?"

Tamsen's heartbeat slowed. "Up here, Bethany. Just checking on things. I'm headed down."

"Why'd you run off without a word?" Bethany came into the cabin with a gust of chilly air, looking and sounding almost timid. "You worried Mama when she found you gone. Pa was about to come running over the ridge with rifle and hatchet, but I said I'd come fetch you back."

Tamsen halted at the foot of the ladder. "They needn't have worried so."

Bethany frowned. "What would Jesse say if they didn't? Pa promised to look after you."

"There's no one here going to bother me."

"I thought that once." Though Bethany's mouth had healed and the bruise under her eye was all but faded, more lasting scars left by Dominic Trimble showed in her gaze.

It occurred to Tamsen this was the first time Bethany had visited their cabin since that day. The girl had her arms crossed, holding the ends of a shawl together across her breasts.

"I'm sorry." Tamsen came around the table to give her arm a squeeze. "It was brave of you to come after me."

Bethany smiled, but her eyes were haunted. Clearly she didn't want to be there. "You're missing Jesse. I understand."

Tamsen wasn't sure how to answer, how to admit the rawness of her feelings, her hope, when the girl assumed they'd married weeks ago. "I do miss him. We haven't been parted like this since we left Morganton. I almost wished I'd begged him not to go."

She leaned on the table, heart aching.

"I'm not sure which would've been safer for him," Bethany said. "Staying or going."

Tamsen stared, puzzled by the remark. "Safer?"

"With the charges and all hanging over him." Bethany looked at her as if expecting her to understand. "That stepfather of yours is a right scary piece of work, ain't he? Trying to pin kidnapping and murder on Jesse, who'd never think of doing either thing."

Feeling her knees go weak, Tamsen kicked out a bench and sat, landed crooked, and nearly toppled to the floor before she caught herself. *Kidnapping and . . .*

"Murder?" She met Bethany's quizzical stare and felt her heart plunge to her belly. Why had she never thought it? Of course Mr. Parrish was going to blame someone else for her mother's death. And who was there to blame but Jesse?

It was Bethany's turn to gape, blue eyes going wide. "You didn't know about that? But you're Jesse's wife, and it was your mother. How could you not know?"

Because Jesse had kept it from her. So very carefully kept it from her. But not from the Allards.

She opened her mouth but could make no sound.

Bethany came to her, put a hand on her arm as Tamsen had moments ago done her. "Pa knows. So does Mama. I heard him telling her about it. Reckon they didn't mean me to hear, but I never thought you didn't know."

Tamsen's desire for solitude earlier was nothing to the screaming need for it now. "It's all right." Somehow she made her voice steady, though it sounded thick to her ears, unnatural, like talking under water. "But will you please go?"

Bethany licked her lips, gaze swinging to the door, then back to Tamsen, uncertain. "But I promised Pa, and he promised Jesse —"

Tamsen forced a smile of reassurance. "Just start back home, all right? I'll be along."

The girl needed little more persuasion.

■ ■ ■ ■

Bethany was barely out the door before Tamsen knew her mind. She couldn't let the charge of murder fall on Jesse. How long had he known about it? Why hadn't he told her?

"Oh, Jesse." Did he think her so frail? She was afraid — shaking with it. But she knew what she must do. Luther Teague had known Jesse half his life. He would vouchsafe his character. Along with her account of what truly happened in Mrs. Brophy's house, it had to be enough to counter whatever outrageous lies her stepfather had concocted. It had to be.

If it wasn't, she still had the coins in her mother's box. Money was all her stepfather cared about. Maybe it would be enough to make him go away — if he was still looking to force her back under his control. Looking to harm Jesse.

That's what she had to find out. They couldn't go on living with this shadow hanging over them, this ax waiting to fall. Jesse had done so much for her, caught her up like an eagle on its wings and carried her off to where she could rest and heal and find her strength. And her heart. The least she could do was try to clear his name — and convince Hezekiah Parrish, and Ambrose Kincaid if he hunted her too, to forget she ever existed.

She packed a few provisions, donned her warmest clothes, gathered more shot and powder for the pistol, and made it a mile from the cabin before she heard the hollow beat of hooves on the trail ahead, coming along at a clip, on the far side of a jutting boulder that loomed above the trail.

Jesse. Cade. A rush of joy and relief carried her swiftly forward. She was halfway to calling out, "Jess —" when two horses rounded the boulder, and all three of them drew up short in surprise.

It was Seth and Dominic Trimble. Their gazes shifted beyond her, as if looking for anyone else coming along the trail. Fear coiled in her belly, a writhing snake.

Dominic's brow and lip still bore the faint marks of Jesse's fists. A fresh wounding too. The slow grin spreading across his broken face was a chilling sight. "Look who's come to meet us, Seth. Mighty obligin' of you, Tamsen Littlejohn."

The snake in her belly tightened its coils, slithering up to squeeze her throat. *They knew.* Through the buzzing of alarm that filled her brain, a small voice was telling her she was going to have to run or fight. Or maybe — just maybe — she could bluff her way back to the Allards' and safety. She narrowed her eyes and raised her chin.

"What are you two doing in Greenbird Cove?" she demanded, hoping the shock at hearing her name hadn't showed on her face. "If Tate Allard catches sight of you —"

"Where is ol' Tate?" Dominic cut in, unconcerned. "Where's Jesse, for that matter? What you doing out on this trace alone?"

Tamsen swallowed, desperate for something to say, some means of threat. She had the pistol. It was loaded and primed. It was also tucked into her pocket, deep beneath her skirt.

The Trimbles urged their horses forward, moving to opposite sides as if to cut her off. Fear spurted through her, chill and sharp. She fumbled for the slit in her skirt, but couldn't get the pistol free before the horses were strides away from hemming her in, trapping her between them. She'd seconds to flee, and only one way to go that horses couldn't easily follow. One way she might have a chance.

Clutching her box, still fighting to free the pistol, she scrambled down the stony bank into the water, leaving curses — more annoyed than alarmed — behind her.

The water was shockingly cold and swift, no higher than her knees, but the bed was a jumble of ankle-turning rocks and she hadn't a hand free to keep her cloak and petticoat from trailing, slowing her, threatening to stumble her. She lost both shoes before she reached the other side.

The Trimbles were off their horses, pounding down the bank, plunging into the creek. She heard them coming and pushed on, up the far slope through half-leafless trees, hampered by the drag of wet linen and wool. She drove her stockinged toes into the hillside, stabbing her soles with twigs and debris, too numbed from the cold creek to feel anything but the slam of her heart and the burn of her lungs and side and the blood pumping through her veins like liquid terror.

She heard heavy breathing, louder than her own gasps, louder than the noise of her flight. One of them was almost upon her.

With a ripping of seams, she wrenched the pistol free and whirled on the slope. Her mother's box tumbled from her grasp as she gripped the weapon in both hands and fired.

33

They'd gagged her, bound her wrists, and taken her into the hills. It had come on to rain, fat drops that smacked through the leaves still clinging to the broad oak she was propped against, beating the acorn-littered ground. Chilling her.

Already half-soaked from the creek, Tamsen felt the cold working deep, aching in the bones of her feet and legs still encased in torn, wet stockings. Her nose ran freely. She tried to clench her teeth, feeling the urge to chatter them, but the gag prevented both. She cracked her eyelids for a look. The Trimbles hadn't yet realized she was conscious.

"It ain't but a scratch," Dominic muttered, kneeling beside his brother, who'd removed his coat and torn aside his shirt sleeve to bare a deep red scoring above his elbow, bleeding scarlet runnels down his rain-wet forearm.

She'd done that. She remembered Seth, spun to the ground by the pistol's shot, tumbling back toward the creek. Unbalanced by the recoil, she'd sat down hard, unable to scramble up again before Dominic wrested the pistol from her and slammed it against her head.

What happened after was a blur. She'd been hauled off her feet, carried back over the creek, thrown across a horse, too dizzy from the blow to fight. Next she recalled was the horses plunging off the trail into cover, Dominic holding her fast across the saddle. Had she heard another horse pass? Someone calling her name? Had it been Tate? Jesse? *Jesse* . . .

The Trimbles had moved higher into the hills, to avoid being seen with her, she guessed. They knew who she was. Knew she was sought. Was there some sort of reward in the offering? Did they hope to turn her over for money? She had money. They'd taken her mother's box as well as the pistol and satchel, but they hadn't untied the cords that held it shut. She saw it, sitting on the ground just out of reach.

"It's deep enough, blast it!" Seth said through gritted teeth. "Will you hurry up and bind it? We need to get home, out'n this rain. Find Kincaid."

A whimper bubbled in her throat at the name. The Trimbles looked at her. She shook her head, making it explode with pain. She squeezed her eyes shut until it receded, then made motions toward the box, trying to communicate her intention. Dominic rose and came to her, rain dripping off the brim of his hat onto her already soaked lap. He saw where it landed, then met her gaze.

"Don't think I ain't tempted," he told her with a loathing that left her shaken. "But there's folk got other plans for you, and we got our reasons for helping them. So be good, come along peaceful-like, and no one need get hurt."

"I'm hurt," Seth gritted out behind him. "Jesse must've taught her to shoot that thing." He jerked his chin at the confiscated pistol, lying with her box.

Dominic turned back to finish wrapping a length of torn shirting around his brother's arm. "This ain't the kind of hurt I mean," he muttered.

Tamsen's mind spun, trying to work out what was happening. They were taking her to Ambrose Kincaid. And her stepfather? Had they even mentioned him? A shiver worked through her and didn't stop. Her brain felt thick and sluggish.

"We get her to Brose," Dominic was saying in reply to something she'd missed. "Then you'll see. He'll keep his word and forget he ever saw us here."

" 'Cept it ain't no good," Seth retorted. " 'Cause you gone and made it as hot for us on the Watauga as it was in Virginy. We ought to be moving on, not helping Brose get his girl back."

That jarred her into sharper focus. She made a noise of protest in her throat. She was not and never had been Ambrose Kincaid's girl.

Dominic cast her a withering look. "Get used to the notion. Jesse's gonna hang for murder." He made a tsking sound, mocking her. "What sort of woman spurns a man like Kincaid for one that kills her ma and carries her off Overmountain?"

Even in her misery, Tamsen could tell Dominic Trimble didn't believe a word of the accusation he'd just spoken. Nor did he care. He wanted to see Jesse come to harm.

Seth got to his feet and winced back into his wet coat. "Get the horses. We'll have to pick our way from here, can't take the trail."

The shiver had become a shudder by the time she was hoisted back onto the horse, dripping wet and numb with cold.

■ ■ ■ ■

Leaving the dogs and mules at the Trimbles' cabin, Charlie Spencer backtracked the mile or so to Sycamore Shoals, with more coin to spend than he'd seen in many a season. The fellow in the trade store was happy to take some off his hands. He chose his supplies while thinking over the route he meant to follow come morning, up the Watauga. He only wished he felt better about what he'd be leaving behind.

He wasn't easy about the latest turn the hunt for Miss Littlejohn had taken or that Kincaid knew nothing about it, having stayed in Jonesborough to do his asking 'round. Charlie didn't know what Parrish told Kincaid to explain his setting out for Sycamore Shoals without him, but Charlie had been forced to agree with the man — those Trimbles knew more'n they'd let on about Miss Littlejohn. Following them to Sycamore Shoals made a certain sense, never mind how badly Charlie wished it hadn't when Parrish asked him to lead the way. He could hardly refuse, having admitted he was headed there directly. So off they'd gone, Parrish on horseback, Charlie leading his long-suffering pack train, the dogs happily roaming the trace's borders, looking to scare up something to chase.

The Trimbles might've ridden hellbent out of Jonesborough, but they hadn't gone far. They overtook the pair five miles out, camped off the trace behind a scrim of buttonbush. The two sprung up from their fire at Parrish's call of greeting but eased seeing Kincaid wasn't in their company.

Twilight was creeping in thick, but the clouds had parted to show stars. The Trimbles had shot themselves a turkey and seemed inclined to share the bounty. Parrish put his horse to graze, then he and Charlie and the dogs joined the brothers at their fire.

"See you parted ways with Mr. High-and-Mighty," Dominic said once they'd settled down to eat.

Charlie, parceling out bits of turkey meat to the dogs, glanced at Parrish. He didn't take offense on Kincaid's behalf, though Charlie felt unease cinch his belly. The girl-dog, Nell, whined to him. A string of drool dropped from her lips. He tossed what remained of his turkey to her.

He hadn't unloaded his mules right off but hobbled them near the horses in good grass. He hadn't made up his mind about staying the night in that company.

"Seems he's set on marrying your girl," Dominic pressed. "Guess you agreed to the match, coming all this way together. I take it she didn't?"

Parrish had been about to put meat in his mouth. He lowered it and stared with level brows at Trimble. "You would be mistaken in that assumption. The last words I heard out of her mouth were of an agreeable nature."

The pair across the fire exchanged a glance, heavy with meaning.

"Well, then," Dominic said after taking a swig from a flask. "What's the story about this kidnapping and murder business? Did Kincaid tell us everything? Who is it you think done the deed?"

Dominic kept his eyes on Parrish, who calmly tore off another bite of turkey from a leg, then nodded toward Charlie. "He's the one you ought to ask, though I've a fair idea I had a run-in with the villain myself. I caught him menacing my stepdaughter in the stable the day prior to her disappearance. I never learned his name."

"But you've seen him too?" Seth asked, looking across the flames at Charlie.

"West of Morganton," Charlie admitted. "Miss Littlejohn in tow. They looked to've been travelin' the night through. The girl never spoke a word — she was plain done in. The feller claimed they'd just been married."

"A lie." Parrish said it with such venom that both Trimbles raised their brows. He met their gazes square. "I think you both know it to be."

Charlie mistrusted the mocking eyes of the sandy-haired Trimble. He'd a cunning look, that one. He caught Charlie's gaze and the look vanished, washed out by a ready grin. "Can't say as we do or don't. We're late coming into this tale. There's a lot we ain't got straight yet. Like what's Kincaid doing now, hanging back in Jonesborough?"

"We figured he'd be the one hot on our trail," Seth added.

They were hedging, unwilling to admit whatever they knew, or thought they knew. Charlie reckoned they wanted to get the girl to Kincaid so he'd keep his word and not haul them back to Virginia.

"He thought to stay on another day," Parrish said. "Make further inquiries before he heads for Sycamore Shoals. He talked of gathering a posse. My guess is such won't be necessary."

The brothers shared another speaking look. Seth asked, "What're you thinking, Dom? Ought we to ride on up —"

Dominic tossed his flask at his brother, who broke off to catch it — and his brother's glare.

Parrish watched them close, a cat waiting to pounce.

Charlie let on like he hadn't noticed. "Reckon I'll see to the mules."

When he rose, so did the dogs. He motioned them back and went into the dark beyond the firelight's reach. He unloaded the mules, piled their burdens beneath a spreading oak tree, and started back to find himself a dry spot to sleep — could such be found — when he saw first one Trimble, then the other, rise from the fire and head in different directions, as if to answer nature's call. Parrish watched them go, then went back to finishing off the turkey remains while the dogs looked on, hoping in vain.

Paused in the dark beneath the oak, Charlie heard Seth Trimble first, a faint crackle of movement through the brush. Trimble paused. Half a minute later, a second set of footsteps came out of the forest. Dominic had circled 'round to his brother. The two stood close, shadows in the starlight, too far off for Charlie to catch all their words, but scraps of their talk reached him. He dared not take a step lest even moccasins on wet leaves betray him.

". . . meanin' to steal her out from under Jesse's nose? How?"

Charlie strained to hear an answer, but it was too low to catch. He glanced over to see Parrish tossing bones into the fire.

A breeze shifted, carrying its secrets.

"You know Jesse Bird didn't murder no one, 'specially not a woman."

"Her old man thinks it. That's good enough odds on him gettin' paid for what I know he did."

Jesse Bird. Was that the man he'd seen in the mountains, leading Miss Littlejohn on his horse?

He shifted his weight. A stick snapped under his foot.

The voices hushed.

Charlie came walking out from under the oak. "Think I'll be turning in," he told the Trimbles.

The younger of the pair stepped across his path. "Name's Spencer, ain't it? I reckon Brose won't ever admit to it, but maybe you will. Did that girl y'all are after really get taken, or did she run?"

"Can't say as I know for a fact," Charlie admitted. "I'd reason enough to think she was kidnapped at the time. Why? You fellers know the man?"

That had ended the conversation quick.

They'd passed through Sycamore Shoals next day, with its old fort and shallow ford, and on to the Trimbles' cabin. Around midday the pair rode off without a word.

Charlie waited a bit, wanting to see what would unfold, but Parrish was ill company at the best of times. Finally he'd gone for his supplies, back the mile or so to the trade store near the fort, taking one of the mules. It had come on to rain again while he was inside the store, and though it was already letting up as he headed back, the air had taken on a deeper chill. Likely it was snowing in the high passes. Charlie hoped it wouldn't be more'n a dusting as yet. Fair weather or foul, he was heading out in the morning. Weren't nothing going to persuade him otherwise.

The barking of his dogs greeted him as he came in sight of the Trimbles' place — a clearing hacked out of forest, little more'n a lazy shack raised with a lean-to tacked on back, a clay chimney, a pole corral out back where the mules and Parrish's horse grazed.

It was the Trimbles returning that had his dogs in a state. They hadn't come by road, but over hill, leading their horses afoot. On the back of one rode a woman in a sorry state, looking ready to tumble from the saddle.

Face ghastly white. Eyes half-glazed. Dark hair straggled down. Clothes sopping wet.

Charlie's chest constricted. First in shock. Second in outrage. Third in recognition.

Stopped in the yard with his mule nuzzling his shoulder, dogs rushing over to sniff him in greeting, Charlie felt like he'd come full circle, only the men who had Miss Littlejohn in custody now had bound and gagged her.

On second glance, Seth Trimble wasn't looking well either. Both the brothers were rain soaked, but Seth's face was clenched in pain, nigh as white as the girl's.

All that suffering was nothing to match what Charlie saw as the cabin door opened and Hezekiah Parrish stepped out. The man stood, arms crossed, rage and satisfaction chasing across his glowering face. Miss Littlejohn's head snapped up, swaying on its slender neck. Though she was gagged, Charlie read the terror that cleared her widened eyes at sight of her stepfather.

The man had nary a smile for her. No sign of pleasure. No question for the Trimbles as to where they'd found her. No cry of protest at the state in which they'd brung her in.

All Parrish said was, "Look at you. You've undone it all." And to the Trimbles, "Bring her inside. Leave her bound."

34

The sun was in the west when Jesse, rain-wet and wearied as his horse, crested the trail from the creek. The forest rose beyond the cabin, gray and piney green. No sound broke the stillness but the swollen creek, and the *cruck* of a raven in the dripping wood. He rode up to the dooryard, dismounting long enough to step inside.

The cabin looked as he'd last seen it. For the first time since leaving Thunder-Going's village, relief took root in his mind.

He'd ridden hard for days. He ought to wash, change into a clean shirt, but he couldn't wait. Eagerness propelled him back into the saddle, and he rode up the ridge to the Allards'.

"There's no good way of saying this, Jesse." Janet, not Tamsen, met him in the dogtrot between the cabins, features strained with worry. "She's gone."

His heart dropped clear to his heels before his mind could take in the words. The place was still, no sound of boys at play, no Bethany bustling about. Even the parakeets stared from their perches, voiceless. In the unnatural quiet, Jesse echoed, "Gone?"

Janet sat on a bench beside the door, slumped as if a yoke straddled her shoulders, mouth opening, closing, opening again.

Alarm raced through Jesse's veins.

Bethany came to the cabin door, looking more wretched than her mother, who was still sitting there struggling for words. "It's my fault, Mama. Let me tell it."

"Someone tell me — and quick," Jesse ordered. "So I can be after her."

Janet's face lost its color. "Tate's already looking, Jesse."

"Looking? You mean she's *lost*?" He clenched his teeth. "When did she leave? Why did she leave?"

"Today, long about dinnertime." Bethany stepped into the dogtrot, tears welling in her eyes. "I didn't mean to tell her."

"What did you tell her?"

Bethany flinched at his tone. "I thought she *knew.*" Her face crumpled in misery.

He was making this worse with his anger, upsetting them more than they already were. Drawing a calming breath, he got himself in control, though dread was nearly choking him. "Start from the beginning and tell me what's happened."

Janet found her voice first. "We were all in the barn this morning, sorting feathers from a brace of geese. Tamsen slipped out — we figured she went to rest a spell, but she didn't. She went over the ridge."

"Alone?"

"It weren't long afore we knew. Beth went after her."

"I found her at your cabin," the girl said through her tears.

Jesse wagged his head, looking from mother to daughter. "Then where is she? What was it you told her?"

"About you being accused of her ma's murder. I overheard Pa telling Ma, and I know you meant to keep it hushed, but I thought surely Tamsen knew." Bethany's eyes pleaded. "After I told her, she bid me start for home, so I did."

"You *left* her?"

Bethany's eyes welled afresh. "She said she'd be along behind me, only she never came."

It occurred to Jesse to wonder if the girl had spilled that secret on purpose, but he dismissed the notion. The anguish in her face was real. He paced to the edge of the dogtrot, gripped by bewilderment and rising panic till he thought he would be sick. Sweet fool woman! What was she doing?

"Jesse, do you know where she might've gone?"

Janet's question made his head stop spinning long enough to realize he did know. Or had a notion. "She's gone to the Teagues'. Gone to try and . . . She's gone to try and clear my name. That has to be it."

Janet rose and came to him. "But if that's so, Tate ought to have found her on the trail, afore she reached Sycamore Shoals, and been back with her long since."

Anxiety and need pierced like shards through his vitals. Blood pounded in his head, building pain behind his eyes and a red haze before them. Where was Tamsen?

"I'm so sorry," Janet said, mouth trembling. "You trusted us to look after her and —"

"Don't." He couldn't hear their apologies. Not now. "Just pray. I'm off to find her, or Tate."

Please, God, the both of them, was his own prayer as he vaulted into the saddle and turned his tired horse back toward Sycamore Shoals.

420

■ ■ ■ ■

Two miles from the cabin, Jesse met his neighbor coming back along Greenbird Creek, horse lathered, Tate grim-faced.

"I rode to Sycamore Shoals, asked all over the place, even the fort — you must have passed by while I was there, else I'd have seen —"

"But Tamsen?" Jesse interrupted.

"No one's seen hide nor hair, or heard tell of her neither."

"She might be making for the Teagues'."

Tate said exactly what his wife had. He'd have found Tamsen on the trail, still close to home, if that was so.

Another explanation, one Jesse had held at bay till now, made a full-on assault on his mind and heart. Perhaps she'd started that way, but someone else found her first.

After all this time?

His dream. The one where he'd failed to pull her from the swollen creek. It *had* been a warning. And he'd been an utter fool ever to have left her, to trust in her safety.

"They've got her, Tate. Parrish and Kincaid. I don't know how, who helped 'em, but they've got her."

It was all he could do to draw his next breath.

Tate nudged his horse close and grasped his arm. "I aim to help you, Jesse. You left her in my care, and I won't rest till you get her back. Now let's get on, retrace my steps, watch the trail close with the light we got left. Maybe you'll see something I missed. Don't give up hope."

Hope, it seemed, had given up on Jesse. Dusk was thick by the time they reached Sycamore Shoals, having carefully scouted the trail. But there'd been hard rain that day, and if Tamsen or anyone else had left sign of their passing, it was long since washed away.

Still, Jesse went through the tiny hamlet, asking the same folk Tate had asked if they'd seen a young woman, dark of hair and eye, traveling through on foot, maybe in company with two men, one of them red of hair . . . But not a soul had seen her, alone or in such company — as if the trail or the creek or the weeping sky had swallowed her whole.

Jesse left the trade store, mind in a turmoil, body strung like an empty bow. He saw Tate coming from the smithy, but knew before his neighbor reached the rutted yard that he'd found no sign of Tamsen either. "Nothing, Jesse. I think we best ride for Luther —"

Tate broke off when Jesse clamped a hand to his arm, looking past him at a sight that drove a spike of cold down his spine. Coming into town from the west, at the head of his mule train, looking dead set on passing through fast, was a scruffy little trapper with three spotted hounds at his heels.

Charlie Spencer should've known he wouldn't get free of this Miss Littlejohn business so easy. Heaven — or the other place — had snared him in this coil and hadn't seen fit to free him.

He'd left the Trimbles' place as fast as he could load the mules, doubting whether anyone inside that ramshackle cabin noticed his going. Too busy arguing over what to do with the girl now they'd got her. They'd put her in the lean-to. Locked her in with whatever stores they kept. Shut her up still shivering, wet through, hands bound behind her back. They'd taken off the gag, but only so Parrish could give her a chance to bow to his will, demanding she swear up and down to Kincaid she was still fit to marry, soon as the man made his appearance.

Charlie had stood in the cabin doorway as

Miss Littlejohn — pried off the horse and dragged inside — made an attempt at defiance. She'd plenty to say to Parrish, but forced through chattering teeth, it proved a pitiful show. While Dominic Trimble saw to his brother, who dropped onto a cot in a corner, fevering up from the pistol shot the girl had dealt him, Miss Littlejohn told Parrish what he might do with his demands, Charlie growing colder in his gut with every word she stuttered.

"Can you p-possibly imagine I would give you any f-f-further authority over m-m-me, after what you d-did to —"

That was the last she got out before Parrish clamped a hand over her mouth and tossed her into the lean-to, ordering Trimble to deny her food, water, warmth, anything else she needed. Charlie had been too stunned to protest, but not Trimble.

"Hang on. Soon as I see to Seth, I mean to get her to Brose. Y'all can fight it out what you do with her after that, but let her out by the fire else she's liable to sicken. Plus I gave her a clout for shooting Seth. Might be her head needs tending."

"And it's plain wrong, treating her that way," Charlie finally interjected. "She's your daughter."

Parrish dealt with him first, striding across

424

the cabin and shoving him bodily out the door. "What I do with her is no longer your concern. You're finished here."

Charlie stumbled backward but righted himself and drove his shoulder into the cabin door. Too late. A bar had dropped into place on the inside.

He'd stood back, listening as Trimble and Parrish argued. Trimble wanted to take Miss Littlejohn straight to Jonesborough. Parrish was adamant she stay where she was till she proved amenable to marrying Kincaid — if the man would have her.

Miss Littlejohn wouldn't prove amenable. Charlie had seen that right off. What was the man going to do with her once he figured it out? And where was this Jesse Bird, the one who'd taken her from Morganton? Hunting for her even now? Lying dead somewhere at the Trimbles' hands?

While they argued, tended to Seth, and ignored the girl they'd gone to such lengths to find, Charlie knew someone had to go for Kincaid, and fast.

That someone was going to have to be him.

By time he had the mules roped and ready, the dogs were milling, eager for the trace. It was late in the day. He'd be traveling through the dark, and it was looking like to rain again. Maybe snow. He was sorry for the mules, forced on another sidetrack. But that poor wet shivering girl . . . He couldn't leave and do nothing for her.

He reached Sycamore Shoals for the third time that day as dusk was falling. As he passed the trade store, the thought of stabling the mules and hiring a horse for the trip crossed his mind. On impulse he turned down between the store and the smithy, trying to think where he might find a horse.

Out of a shadow along the building's side stepped a man, blocking his way.

Charlie drew up short, pulling back hard on the bridle of the lead mule. Two of the dogs were near. They stopped in their tracks, one of them growling as the man approached. He was young, clad in buckskins, in need of a shave. What light remaining between the buildings showed his face with its thin-bridged nose and eyes of a peculiar shade, almost golden.

Even in the failing light, having seen him only once before, Charlie Spencer would have known him anywhere. He was bigger than Charlie minded, harder looking, fierce as a hawk about to snatch its prey.

"Hold on, now." Caught between relief

and alarm, Charlie backed away — and ran smack up against another body bigger than his own. A second man had moved up from behind, swift and silent. Charlie hadn't time to draw a breath before his arms were grasped and wrenched up sharp behind him.

Rage and fear had Jesse by the throat. "Where — is — she?"

Spencer's eyes bulged, filling with fear. "I . . . She . . ."

Jesse's hand was around the man's neck before thought of putting it there registered. "You tell me where she is, or so help me I'll wring it out of you." The dogs were bristling, whining. The mules stood placid, dumb and patient. Jesse started to squeeze, feeling tendons give beneath his fingers. "You got seconds to start."

"Jesse, wait," Tate said, easing his grip on the trapper. "Hush a moment."

Jesse heard it, the pound of hooves coming fast.

They were half in shadow between the smithy and the store, unnoticed as yet. Jesse looked behind him as a rider passed the gap between the buildings, headed for the Jonesborough road.

Dominic Trimble.

He eased up on Spencer's neck. The man

let out a gust of breath and choked out, "He's gone for him. I got to tell —"

Jesse turned back, giving Spencer's neck a shake. "They're in on this, the Trimbles? Where is she? Here?"

Tate released the man. "I think he's trying to tell you, Jesse. Take a breath and listen."

He let go of Spencer's neck. "Talk."

Spencer did so, his hoarse words broken with coughing. "Parrish has her . . . mile or so off . . . Trimbles' cabin. That one just rode past . . . he's gone to Jonesborough for Kincaid."

Jesse grabbed the man again, this time by the arms. "Have they hurt her?"

Spencer shook his head, but the words he next spilled demolished what little relief he'd offered. "Not bad, but it ain't good neither. There was a scuffle. She shot the other Trimble. A graze, but he's already taken fevered."

Jesse stared, trying to take it in. "She *shot* Seth Trimble?"

"She did," Spencer said. "But she was sopping wet when they brought her in, shivering like to rattle her teeth loose. Parrish has her locked in the lean-to." The little man gazed up at Jesse, face twisting with remorse. "I'm sorrier than I can say I'd any

part in her coming to this pass. I thought
—"

"I know what you thought," Jesse said
through his teeth. "It was Parrish killed his
wife. You been helping a murderer track
down the one person who could tell what
he did. You think he won't do the same to
her, if she defies him again?"

Spencer looked sick at his words. "I'd
about got that worked out for myself. Best
we three figure out how to make sure it
don't come to that."

Was Spencer offering his aid, after weeks
of working against them? Jesse let go of the
man. "You said she's bad off?"

Spencer bobbed his head. "They come
down with her from the hills, through the
rain and chill. I seen the like afore. I've *felt*
the like. She's been cold and wet for hours.
Dominic said he hit her too."

Jesse stifled a groan.

"She mightn't last the night, Jesse, we
don't get to her quick," Tate said.

"I was going for Kincaid, in Jonesborough," Spencer said. "He'd never countenance treating her like this, whether or not
he still means to marry her."

To Jonesborough and back would have
taken most of the night.

"You'd have been too late," Jesse said

under his breath. But it did put Dominic out of the reckoning for the time being. He looked at Tate. "We could bust straight through that door, take her by force."

"The Trimbles got a lot to answer to me for," Tate said. "Dominic's the one I want, but I'm willing to go in fighting if that's what you decide."

"You'll do it without me, then," Spencer said. "Won't have no part in killing. No sir."

Jesse turned on the man, furious. "You been aiding a murderer for weeks!"

"Which I repent me of heartily," Spencer retorted. "But it ain't the same as doing the deed. Look — Seth Trimble might be in shape to fight ye, but I doubt it. Might just be Parrish to contend with here, so let's try it my way first."

"Your way?"

"Aye," Spencer said. "Here's what I'm thinking, if'n ye want my advice. There ain't no outer door to the lean-to where they got her, but there's a window slit, high up. Now, Parrish knows me. I can go right up to that cabin door, get his attention — loud-like — and hold it long enough for you to find a way through that lean-to wall and pull Miss Littlejohn out. Simple as that."

Simple as that. Jesse was about to lose all semblance of control. Every second wasted felt like a drop of blood from his veins. Simple as that. *Lord, let it be so.*

"How fast can those mules move?"

35

The only thing keeping her conscious now was terror. It certainly wasn't hope. Charlie Spencer had gone. Dominic Trimble had gone. Seth's voice had tapered off soon after his brother left. She'd seen how inflamed the wound she'd dealt him had become in the hours they'd trekked through the cold wet hills, making their cautious way to their cabin. How long had he been silent? How long had she cowered in the dark?

Her thoughts came thick as sorghum syrup — save for when she heard Mr. Parrish moving about in the cabin. Then her heart would lurch. She'd rouse, straining to listen. He told her she could stay there until she reconsidered her obstinacy. She knew what would happen if she didn't. He'd leave her as she was, until she succumbed to cold or sickness. Or he'd do what he'd done to her mother, end her life by violence. Why had she left the Allards'? Why had she gone against Jesse's warning to stay put? She'd had compelling reason. Something about murder . . . ? Murder . . . Jesse . . . Jesse accused of her mother's murder! That's what she'd been trying to rectify.

Wedged between barrels and crates, she huddled on the dirt floor, petticoat clinging, wet and muddied, cloak heavy on her shoulders, wool and rabbit fur soaked through. Now and then she struggled at the cords pinning her wrists but had no way of knowing whether she loosened them or drew them tighter. Her hands — feet too — might have been lumps of wood for all she could feel them.

Beyond the door, a kettle clanked against stone. Liquid poured. Longing for whatever hot thing that hateful man was drinking, she swayed, nearly toppling into a pile of sacking.

Her body's jerking stirred her, helped her to focus. The cords around her wrists — she had to get free of them. Was there something, anything, in that tight space sharp enough to cut through rawhide?

First to get some feeling into her hands. All she could do at first was twitch her fingers, but a painful tingle soon indicated progress. When finally she could sense the touch of objects again, she hitched herself around, feeling among splintery crates and barrels. Her fingertips found metal. She knew the shape. An animal trap, the sort with serrated teeth. A broken one, the halves of its jaws lying in a heap.

It took an age to find an angle that worked, backed up against it, but at last she positioned her wrists over the teeth and began an awkward sawing at her bonds. Keeping the trap from shifting and clanking proved tricky. She ended up half sitting on it to keep it anchored. She'd lost her cap in the struggle by the creek. Long wet curls straggled down from their pins, tangled in her efforts to cut the rope. She tossed her head, trying to sweep her hair out of the way, but it clung to everything it touched.

Pain lanced her wrist. Something warm trickled down her palm, slicking her fingers. Blood.

Shudders wracked her. She clenched her teeth. Just as she'd repositioned herself for another try, shouting erupted, along with a pounding on the outer door. She stilled, dread and hope clutching her chest. *Jesse.* Oh, if only . . .

"Parrish? I know ye're in there! Open up, else I aim to go on banging till cockcrow!"

It sounded like that trapper, Charlie Spencer. He'd been shocked when the Trimbles brought her in. Even through her stupor she'd registered that much. By now he ought to know what sort of man he'd been leading. What had he expected, that she'd be treated like a princess when they finally caught her?

Mr. Parrish growled something in reply to the banging and shouting, but Tamsen was no longer listening. She strained again at the cords, reckless now, unheeding of noise. Urgency drove her. If she could just . . . get . . . free . . .

She felt the first of the bindings snap.

Charlie Spencer went on shouting, fists pummeling. Mr. Parrish argued through the door. Then she thought he'd opened the door because the banging stopped and the trapper's voice grew suddenly clearer. He was fussing about payment for his services. Payment! While she was being treated like an animal.

She'd set to working on the bindings again when she heard another sound, separate from the two men shouting.

She froze, staring into the dark. Had she imagined . . . ?

Her gaze lifted to the window slit, high up in the lean-to wall. It was only a few inches wide — invisible now with a clouded night fallen. Had the sound been from there? A scrabbling noise, like a varmint trying to get in. *Lord, not another squirrel . . .*

"Tamsen?"

For a moment she didn't believe her ears. The whisper came again, urgent. "Tamsen!"

"Jesse." Thirst and fear and hope knotted in her throat, choking her voice. She'd no idea if he'd heard her above the commotion Spencer was making.

A distraction. That's what the shouting was about. Spencer was covering up what Jesse was trying to do. And now she could hear hands pulling at the timbers around the window, breaking down the very wall to get to her. The wood in places had rotted. It was coming away by bits. She sawed at her bonds with renewed vigor, ignoring the pain.

The cords snapped. A new pain shot through her shoulders as her arms came around, free for the first time in hours. She rubbed at her limbs, willing strength and feeling into them, then tried to stand. She made it to her knees. The scrabbling at the window paused.

"Tamsen, can you hear me?"

She had to work the spit into her mouth to force sufficient sound. "Jesse . . . I love you."

Silence. Then his voice again, warm as the sun pouring over her in its relief. "Thank God Almighty — I love you too."

She heard him murmuring to someone out there with him, then the soft thud of his hatchet as he cut away a timber in the wall. It came away with a crack. They all stilled, waiting. Parrish and Spencer went on arguing.

"I'm getting you out of here, sweetheart," Jesse hissed down at her. "Are you free to move about?"

"Yes. But . . . I'm cold. I can't stand up."

"What's by you? Anything to help you stand? I need you to reach high as you can. I'm going to pull you through."

She could do this. She had to do this. She didn't know how he'd found Spencer, got him to help, why Jesse was even here at all, but she was going through that hole in the wall to him if it killed her.

She found a barrel and used it to push herself to standing. Leaning hard on it for support, she tried to curl her toes, move her ankles, anything to work the feeling back as she'd done her hands.

It wasn't happening fast enough. Could she get up on the barrel and reach the window on her knees? It was tall, broad, a hogshead. She clambered onto it, hampered

437

by her clinging garments, tempted to shed the cloak and leave it behind . . . but she'd need it in the cold . . . and it was raining again . . . misting on her face.

She saw movement at the opening. Jesse. He'd pushed himself through to his shoulders. He was reaching down to her.

"There you are. Take my hands. I'll pull you up. Tate's got the other end of me."

On her knees, balanced precariously, she stretched as high as she could, felt the brush of his fingertips, then fell back, grasping the barrel's lid to keep from tumbling to the dirt floor.

Jesse's voice reached down to her again. "A bit farther. Come on now, I'm getting you out of here."

She tried again. This time their fingers clasped. He groped for a better hold, strong hands clamping her wrists, stinging fresh cuts. As he pulled, she got her feet under her and stood, then was grateful for layers of wet clothing as, with a grunt of effort, he dragged her through the ragged hole he'd made and into the night, into his arms, onto the back of the horse he'd knelt on to reach the window slit. His beautiful, blanket-rumped horse.

Then they were moving, rain was falling cold, and the voices still shouting fell into

the distance, until she no longer heard them
at all.

■ ■ ■ ■

To Love and
to Cherish

■ ■ ■ ■

36

Jesse stepped from the Teagues' stable, where he'd sheltered his exhausted horse, to find Tate Allard waiting for him in the yard. With nightfall, the temperature had dropped, turning rain to snow. In the lantern light, it fell in soft, fat flakes, dusting the ground and Tate's hat brim.

"Jesse, I hope you'll forgive us letting her get away."

Jesse glanced past him to the cabin across the clearing, where Tamsen was ensconced by the fire, with Molly and the preacher busy getting her warm. Relief, joy, and concern were a tangle in his chest. He set the lantern down and took his neighbor by the arm.

"What happened to Tamsen, it's on me," he said, voice cracking. "I ought to have told her everything, long since, and never let her out of my sight. I was riled when I left Janet and Beth. It was mostly at myself, but . . ."

443

"I'm sure they know that, Jesse."

"Just tell them I'm sorry. I don't blame you or them, Tate."

"I'll tell 'em you're safe and together." Tate gave his shoulder a thump. "That's all they're going to care about."

Jesse stepped back, relieved, grateful. "Sure you want to head home in this?"

Determined to ride back to Sycamore Shoals, then make for home, Tate waved off the gently falling snow and swung into the saddle. "If'n it gets bad, I'll take shelter. Go on; get back to Tamsen now."

"I plan on it." Truth to tell, the lion's share of Jesse's mind — and the whole of his heart — were pulling him toward the Teagues' cabin like a tether. He bent for the lantern. "Just one more thing, Tate. You see hide or hair of Charlie Spencer again, you give that man my everlasting gratitude. He's got himself a mighty set of lungs, for his size."

Tate grinned down at him. "You thanked him half a dozen times afore we reached the Trimbles'."

"Did I?" Jesse couldn't recall a single instance. It was all a blur of terror and hope and need till he'd heard Tamsen's voice floating up weak and hoarse from the musty chill of that lean-to. *I love you.*

"He's likely a mile up the Watauga by

444

now," Tate said. "You best not linger long here either."

"Don't mean to. I got in mind someplace to take her."

He meant to say no more than that. Tate seemed to sense it. "All right, then, Jesse. God keep you both."

As Tate rode into the falling snow, Jesse hurried across the clearing to the cabin. Inside he found Molly at the table pouring something steaming into a cup, the preacher adding wood to a fire already going strong.

Tamsen was curled in a chair by the hearth, her feet tucked up under a quilt. Her hair fell in long damp strands, but she was out of her wet clothes, which were spread over another chair to dry. She wore one of Molly's shifts, he presumed, but was so swaddled it was impossible to tell. Her eyes were closed, head resting against the chair back.

He set down the lantern and went to her, kneeling beside the chair. She didn't open her eyes.

"I think she'll be fine, Jesse." Molly crossed the cabin and put a cup of hot tea into his hands. He sipped it absently. It felt good going down. The cold in him went deeper, but it wasn't from the weather. He'd known Parrish capable of violence. He'd

445

feared Parrish meant to see him hanged. But Jesse knew now that he hadn't truly believed the man would throw Tamsen's life away so easily, that he was prepared to let her die, if not outright murder her.

With shaking hands, Jesse set the teacup on the floor and felt along the quilt's folds till he found a foot. It was cold, though swathed in Molly's wool stockings. He took it between his hands, commenced to rubbing, and glanced at Molly standing over him. "Her feet look all right when you helped her change?"

"No frostbite," Molly assured him. "Drink that tea, now. You need warming up yourself. And when you're done there, peel off your wet things. I've laid out a shirt of Luther's for you."

Reverend Teague rose from the hearth. "Tate headed home?"

"Aye." Jesse switched to Tamsen's other foot. "He tell you what's happened, why we need a place to rest a spell, before we move on?" After the preacher affirmed Tate had caught him up on all that had transpired, Jesse asked, "Would it be all right if we dry our things, give Tamsen a few hours' sleep?"

"Anything you need, Jesse," the preacher said, but his gaze was questioning, troubled. "But why run again? Why not stay, try and clear your name, like Tamsen meant to do when she set out?"

Jesse stood and peeled off his heavy woolen hunting shirt, knowing there was little enough time for the garment to dry.

"No sir. The man nearly killed Tamsen. I'm getting her away from him, never mind what he thinks he can pin on me." He draped the shirt over another chair Molly drew near the fire's warmth and proceeded to shrug out of the shirt he wore next to his skin, soaked through as much as the outer had been.

Luther Teague stood by, arms crossed, Molly beside him looking concerned. "Isn't it time to bring in the law? I'll speak for you."

"Again, sir, no. I won't risk it, or her. What if Parrish or Kincaid has the law on their side already — Franklin, Carolina, or both?" Jesse stood in breechclout and leggings, shivers racing up his bare back, though his chest was hot from the roaring fire. "Besides, you weren't in Morganton. You weren't a witness. No one was, save Tamsen — and it's clear to me now the man wants her silenced."

Molly spoke. "What about this Mr. Kincaid? Surely he doesn't want her dead."

Jesse snorted. "Just me, more'n likely." He

447

rubbed the back of his neck, gazing at Tamsen, wishing he'd a better plan. "When I have her safe away, maybe I'll come back then, see if between you, me, and Tate Allard we can make these charges go away."

Spencer would have been a help with that, but the man was gone his way and God bless him for all he'd done this night.

"Whose will are you heeding, Jesse? Is it the Almighty's or your own?"

Jesse jerked his gaze to the preacher. "Truth to tell, Reverend, if I heeded my will, I'd leave Tamsen here with you, ride back to Sycamore Shoals, and make that charge of murder one in truth."

"Jesse," Molly said, clearly shocked.

Jesse ground his teeth. "I ain't going to do it." Hard as that was to say with the need churning in him, rage burning like a cold blaze, another look at Tamsen's sleeping face and he knew she was all he must think of now. "I'm giving over vengeance."

"Good," Molly said. "It's the Lord's anyhow. He'll repay."

"I'm counting on it."

Neither Teague replied to that. There came a silence, tense, waiting. Finally Luther spoke. "Where do you mean to take her?"

Jesse sat down to pull off his wet moccasins and untie his leggings. "West. To Thunder-Going's town."

"No, Jesse. Not yet."

Jesse whipped his head up, gazing at the mound of quilt in the chair beside him. Tamsen was awake, peering from her patchwork nest, dark eyes fixed on him. He put a hand to her. Hers snaked out of the quilt to grasp his tight. "Tamsen, we can't stay this nigh to Sycamore Shoals. If the hunt's not on already, by morning it'll be. Thought we'd get us a few hours' rest — the horse too — then be on our way before sunup."

"I understand." Her voice was hoarse, but she sounded otherwise in possession of herself. Holding the quilt around her shoulders, she let go of his hand and rose from the chair, setting her feet gingerly on the puncheon floor. Molly was beside her in an instant to help, but Tamsen was steady.

She took them in, looking back at her, and lifted her chin with a determination Jesse recognized well. "I'll go anywhere you see fit to take me, Jesse Bird. But I won't set foot out of this cabin again till I'm a married woman. This time I'm going to insist."

Though he was bone-aching tired, Jesse knew there'd be little sleep for him this night. Not with the day's perils still swirling

449

cold through his blood, the hunt they'd yet to evade weighing on his mind, and the sight and feel and smell of Tamsen nestled like a spoon beside him in the firelight doing its best to distract him from everything else.

"Ulethi equi'wa . . . ni haw-ku-nah-ga," he whispered. Beautiful woman . . . you are my wife.

They'd stood before the preacher scarce an hour past, Tamsen swathed neck to heels in Molly's shift, he in breechclout and borrowed shirt, and pledged their vows to each other: to have and to hold . . . for better, for worse . . . for richer, for poorer . . . in sickness and in health . . . to love and to cherish . . .

"Till death do us part, according to God's holy ordinance." He'd been unable to stem the tears, seeing his joy reflected in her weary, happy eyes. "And thereto I plight thee my troth."

It had been quick and to the point, as was the kiss they'd shared when the preacher pronounced them married before God. For all her insistence, Tamsen barely made it through her vows still awake on her feet.

Jesse might've believed he'd dreamt it, but here she was lying next to him, the curve of her shoulder bared by the wide neckline of the borrowed shift, smooth skin an inch below his lips as he lay propped on an elbow, arm curved around her, watching her sleep, and marveling. She was bone of his bone, never mind they'd yet to consummate their vows. Soul of his soul, for the moment he'd known her missing, something inside him had wrenched crooked, like a joint torn from its socket.

That part of him was slipping back into place now, leaving but a memory of crippling pain. He held his wife, and the refrain singing through him was no less profound for its plainness. *Thank You . . . thank You.*

After they had spoken their vows, Luther Teague put a hand to their bent heads and spoke a blessing, a prayer for safety, as they held each other, Jesse feeling the beat of Tamsen's heart against his own, knowing by then his arms were the only thing holding her upright.

The preacher had been right, all those weeks ago. It was worth waiting to know she'd married him for the wanting of him, first and foremost. He'd seen it in her eyes when she gave her ultimatum . . . or proposal. *I won't set foot out of this cabin again till I'm a married woman.* He'd gone to her, touched her face, her hair, then led her into the Teagues' bedroom where he found the promised shirt waiting for him.

Alone, she'd turned to him and said, "Don't ever keep a thing like that — the murder charge — from me again, Jesse. Just don't. I want to be in this with you, right beside you in everything. I'm stronger than I look."

"You are," he'd said, then taken her in his arms, felt her lips press against the skin of his chest. "Let's pray there never is another thing like this for us, but aye, no more secrets between you and me. From this day forward."

From this day forward.

He listened now to the Teagues murmuring in the room beyond, to the pop and hiss of the fire, to Tamsen's breathing, till he couldn't stand it anymore and pressed his lips to the spot where her shoulder curved into her neck . . . and bit back a groan.

Lying with her chastely was as much trial as pleasure, but they'd another journey ahead of them, in the cold and snow. She needed sleep. Once they were settled again, they'd have their time . . . But she smelled so sweet, and the touch of her was making his nerves sing, and he couldn't stop himself nuzzling his face against her hair, pressing another kiss behind her ear.

She stirred beneath his arm, murmured something he didn't catch. "What did you say?" he whispered near her ear.

She shifted onto her back. Her eyes opened, looking into his, tiny flames reflected in their depths. She reached up and touched his face. "Did I ever say it?"

He pressed her fingers to his lips. Her eyelids drooped, as sleep sought to claim her again. "Did you say what?"

Beneath the quilt she shifted against him, making herself comfortable. Making him stifle another groan.

"Did I say I love you?"

"First words out of your mouth, when I found you." He kissed her brow. The tip of her nose. "I love you too. Go back to sleep."

Hours passed over them. The fire settled and sank. The cabin grew cold. When he could wait no longer, he kissed her gently until her eyes fluttered open. "Wake up, Mrs. Bird. Time for us to fly again."

Snow lay six inches deep before Jesse could see well enough to ride. They'd left the Teagues' place before dawn, making for the Holston, meaning to follow the river west toward the Overhill country. Till now Jesse had kept to a well-worn trace. It was easier on the horse but bad for leaving a trail, though the rising sun was hidden behind ragged clouds not done with spitting snow.

He prayed their back trail would fast be covered. He needed to put better distance between them and Sycamore Shoals. They'd yet to meet another soul out so early. The snow they crossed bore only the tracks of critters. Still Jesse busied his eyes scanning ahead, the snow-laced trees to either side, the telltale signals of the horse, while his mind scoured its own landscape. Had Cade left Thunder-Going's town? Had he reached their cabin, learned of Tamsen's capture? How strange not being together on the hunt when the first snow fell . . .

Would Dominic risk coming back to Sycamore Shoals or make for that muster against the Creeks in order to keep clear of Tate? What would Kincaid do when he learned Tamsen had eluded them again? Would he finally give up, even if Parrish didn't?

Jesse ground his teeth over having let Parrish go unscathed for what he'd done to Tamsen. There were times he wished he'd come to manhood among the Shawnees, that he could dance the war dance and strike the post, then go out and take bloody revenge on those who'd wronged him and his, and be counted right in doing so. It was a hard thing to beat down, that yearning to be the instrument of heavenly recompense, but he put the craving from his heart, remembering what manner of man he was. Remembering the God who wouldn't be mocked, who in time would serve up justice, even if the law of the land failed in that regard.

A twitch of the horse's ears, swiveled to catch some sound behind them, sent a crackle of awareness up his spine.

He didn't look back. Or hesitate. "Hold tight."

Tamsen squeezed his ribs as he urged the horse through a break in a thicket, plunging down to a runnel the track had hugged. Ice cracked beneath them, then they were up into the hardwoods beyond. The maneuver wouldn't aid them if pursuit was close, not with the snow declaring their passage clear as a blaze mark. He wove a path upslope through woods where the snow lay thin. When they broke out onto clear ground, he crossed it quick, glancing back before naked trunks enfolded them again.

No sign yet, but he was nigh certain someone pursued.

They rode on, Jesse urging the horse to a pace just short of reckless. Unable to hear above snow-crunching hooves, he kept watch on the horse's ears and in moments lost all doubt.

He pressed his calf against the rifle in its sling. He didn't want to stop, didn't want it to come to fighting. "Tamsen, can you look back without losing your grip on me?"

The pressure of her arms shifted, then she stiffened against him. She'd seen their pursuers.

He scanned the terrain for barriers to put between them. A boulder. Then a stand of birches. They struck a game trace he hadn't expected, and he urged the horse to speed. It was snowing harder, enough to sift through tangled limbs.

"How many?"

"Two riders. Jesse, I think one of them —"

She broke off at a shout behind them. A rifle's report cracked the air. The horse missed a step, then surged forward, panic in the bunching of its muscles.

Blood spattered Jesse's hands. At first he thought Tamsen hit. Then he saw where the ball had grazed the top of the horse's neck, taking out a chunk of cinnamon mane behind the ears. Blood writhed from the wound, drops of it flinging out behind. Beneath him powerful muscles churned. Hooves flung up earth and snow.

Before them a clearing widened. Snow fell thick in the open. Across it pines beckoned.

He took the chance of racing straight across, letting the horse have its head, praying he could slow it when they reached the trees. Praying for the snow to come hard.

No more gunshots. No more shouts. They were into the pines. They were passing through them. Ahead the land rolled downward. Not too steep. If he angled it right, they could —

The horse stumbled, pitching them both into empty air.

Pain burst like a mortar in Jesse's side. Then he was rolling downhill through snow and brush, a shattering in his ribs like the earth itself was stabbing him. The bole of a tree halted his tumble. Covered in snow, half-dazed, he caught a searing breath and looked frantically for Tamsen, spotting her higher up the slope, crumpled in a heap, dark against the white.

Pain pierced his side, robbing him of breath, as he crawled up through snow and churned leaves, past the rock that had broken his fall, jaw locked to keep from groaning.

Tamsen sat up as he reached her, disheveled, snow dusted, stunned, and unhurt. "Just bruised. I'm all right."

He looked for the horse next, expecting to see it lying on the slope, else crippled and struggling.

It was neither. The beast stood on the crest above, reins trailing, peering down at them from the pines. It hadn't fallen at all, nor lost any of its baggage. Just its riders.

"Tamsen, could you — fetch him — down?"

She caught the wince in his voice. "You're hurt?"

"Broke a rib, I think." He forced himself to his knees, then his feet, where he pressed his arm to his side, struggled to breathe, and waited for a starry blackness to pass. When it did, Tamsen's eyes were wide.

"Jesse, your hands — your face. There's blood!"

"Not mine." There was no taste of blood in his mouth. The ribs hadn't pierced anything vital. He hoped. "Get the horse?"

She struggled up the slope, caught the trailing reins, then picked a careful way back down, leading the animal. Jesse moved to meet her, gaze going to the crest of the slope with every other step. Nothing but pines. Snow fell thick and fast, laying down a fresh blanket over the churning they'd made in their tumble. He took the reins from Tamsen.

"It's been shot." She looked at him in concern.

"A graze. He'll be all right. Can you mount up?" She made to do so, climbing awkwardly with no help from him. His hands were shaking. "Stay in the saddle," he said when she started to make room for him.

He glanced up-slope again. Still no sign. That didn't mean someone wasn't casting about up there, seeking their trail. Wincing, he bent for a handful of snow, packed it, and handed it up. "Press it to the wound. It'll slow the bleeding."

She did so, the snow and her hands quickly reddening. "Can you walk?"

He looked away from her anxious gaze. "Got to."

He started out through the trees, all his thoughts on putting distance between his wife and their pursuers. Had she seen their faces? He would ask. For now all he could manage was one foot before the other, while daggers stabbed his side with every breath. He faced his mind forward, tried to make a plan. Escape first. Then shelter. Then . . . But whatever lay beyond that aim was lost in a haze of red.

37

Shelter proved a limestone cave along the Holston, not near enough to the river to risk travelers stumbling across them. Little more than a dank recess in the face of a draw, it was still high and wide enough to let the horse within, and drew enough air through fissures in the rock for a small fire.

Snow lay twice as deep on the ground as when they'd started out. Having trudged through it half the day in pain barely short of intolerable, Jesse groaned in relief once he lowered himself to the old bearskin Tamsen spread in the scanty space the cave provided.

She saw to everything: horse, fire, provisions, though neither had appetite for the latter. Then she knelt beside him, spreading the sopping hem of her skirt and cloak before the fire. "Now you."

He eyed her resolute gaze. "Now me what?"

"Your side. I mean to have a look at it."

"There's no need." Ignoring him, she tugged at his hunting shirt, trying to raise it. He caught her hand. Her fingers were icy. "Tamsen . . ."

She was having none of his protest. Too tired to resist, he rucked up his shirts, letting her see the bruises darkening his ribs.

"Likely just cracked, else I'd never have made it this far." If it was worse than a crack, the bones could still do damage with all their moving about. Even if they didn't, it wasn't good. He'd cracked a rib before. It was going to be some time till he could draw a proper breath, or walk a full stride, or defend his wife as a man must in that country. Thunder-Going's town was nearer than Chota, but at the rate he'd moved today, their provisions wouldn't last. Worry dark as river flood engulfed him. "Nothing you can do for it."

She lowered his shirt and raised her eyes. "I can walk come morning, let you ride."

"No."

"Jesse, this isn't the time for manly pride and stubbornness."

"Not pride," he said too forcefully, and hissed in a shallow breath. "Not *all* pride. I couldn't get myself into the saddle if I wanted to."

461

Come morning he'd be doing good to stand to his feet.

Tamsen brushed his face with cold fingers, then turned from him to feed the fire. She arranged her cloak and lay down in the cramped space, shoulder brushing his. A shelf of rock rose between them and the horse, hobbled at the mouth of the cave, creating a heat reflector, warming the small space. He lay on his back, face turned toward her. She was between him and the fire, as he'd insisted. Its light limned her nose, the curve of her lips, her firm chin. A different sort of ache filled him.

She turned her head, then rolled onto her side to face him. The fingers that touched his cheek were still chilled. He brought his hand up to hers, kissed her knuckles, warming them.

"Tamsen . . ."

"I think the storm's passing. Perhaps it will clear up."

"Maybe so." He stared at the fire shadows dancing across the cave's pitched roof, where smoke collected before trickling out through the slope above. "What were you fixing to say, afore that shot?"

"Oh," she said, as if only now remembering. "It *was* Ambrose Kincaid — I saw his hair — and Dominic. Mr. Kincaid had hold of Dominic's gun, as if to wrench it away."

The pair must have been on their way from Jonesborough and caught sight of them. Jesse pondered her words, listening to the fire's snap, the horse shifting. It would've been Kincaid that shouted. Objecting to the reckless firing? That made sense, seeing as Dominic could've hit Tamsen — as he had their horse.

Anger suffused him, but he willed thoughts of what he wanted to do to Dominic Trimble to the edges of his mind. They made it harder to breathe.

Tamsen stiffened beside him. "Jesse. I just realized something else. I don't have Mama's box."

He hadn't seen the box since back at the cabin, before he and Cade rode off with Catches Bears. "Did it fall out on the trace again?"

"No. The Trimbles took it. And your pistol. It must still be in their cabin."

He reached for her hand, found it fisted. "I know what it means to you, being all that's left of your parents. But whether you're white or red or brown don't matter to me. You know that. We're married now. Nothing's changing that."

She unclenched her fingers, letting him take her hand. "I know. But remember, papers aren't all that's in there. There's the coins Mama hid away."

He tightened his grip on her hand. "Just shiny metal. They don't mean nothing."

"Oh, Jesse. I wanted you to have them — for us. Our own land, if that's what you wanted."

Lying in a cold cave with broken ribs, an injured horse, and a healthy fear of pursuit, he already felt himself a rich man.

"I admit to entertaining the notion of late," he said, hoping she heard the smile in his voice.

"Mr. Parrish will have taken the coins. If he found them."

"And maybe Kincaid will get a look at your mother's free papers and that'll be the end of it for him. That's worth a trunk of silver right there now, ain't it?"

By morning the storm had blown east, but the temperature had dipped. They woke shivering to an ice-encrusted landscape. In the gray of dawn, Jesse crawled from the cave, dizzy and sick, and vomited into the snow. The retching stabbed like knives. Judging by Tamsen's pinched face, he hadn't stifled the animal whimpers that rose with the bile.

There was no blood at least, and the horse

was faring better. The ball had grazed a raw scar, but the bleeding had stopped. Hobbled through the night, the horse had left the cave of its own accord to graze on winter-brown grass it had pawed through snow to reach. Tamsen saddled it in the time it took him to claw his way to his feet against the cave's face, side screaming like his guts were shredding.

On his feet, his vision darkened, swirling with spots. Dimly he heard Tamsen say his name, but he was lost in memories of when he'd broken his leg running from Cade, trying to get back to the Shawnees, across the Ohio. Cade had carried him agonizing miles before finding those settlers. What had happened to that family, to that boy whose name he'd borrowed . . . ?

"Jesse! Can you hear me?"

He blinked into Tamsen's frantic face with the sense she'd asked the question more than once. Bright points still danced at the edges of his sight. "I'm . . . all right."

"No, you're not. Let's stay put, for today at least."

He knew by reason a day would make no difference, yet he faltered at the fear in her eyes. Stay or go? Either posed a risk. But staying would be giving in to weakness, and he couldn't fail her. Not hours after he'd stood holding her before God and the Teagues, promising to protect and provide for her. Till death did they part.

He wasn't dead. Not yet. Though he longed to hunch into his pain, curl up and escape it if he could, he stiffened his spine. "I'm on my feet. The horse is saddled. Let's go."

Tamsen didn't budge. "What if I went for help? I'll follow the river to a settlement —"

"No . . ." He leaned against the cave entrance, trying to draw breath. Trying not to puke again.

Tamsen crossed to the horse and set her foot in the stirrup. He lurched after her. She got her foot back down and ended up supporting him while he sagged against her. "You don't know this country, Tamsen. You're as like to find harm as help."

He groped for the saddle while she clutched at his sleeve, exasperated. "And you're going to kill yourself out of stubbornness and —"

The horse whinnied, high and loud — in greeting. From nearby another horse answered. Jesse thrust Tamsen behind him and reached for his rifle in the saddle sling. It caught on the leather halfway drawn. The horse shifted, and next he knew he was sprawled on his back, pain ripping through him, the rifle out of reach. Tamsen's cloak swirled near. Then she cried out and ran out of his range of vision. He found breath enough to bellow her name, then nearly screamed with the agony that tore through him. She shouted again. They had her. Would they murder him or leave him to freeze while . . . ?

His ears at last made sense of *what* she was shouting. A name. *Cade.*

Jesse raised himself enough to see his pa's winter moccasins hit the snow in time to be rocked back as Tamsen threw herself into his arms. Cade grabbed her to steady them both.

Astride another horse was Catches Bears, on his head a cocked hat with a rakish white plume of a feather, a blanket edged in red draping his shoulders.

Jesse struggled to sit up, but his head spun and his ribs shrieked. He fell back in the snow, knowing Bears would never let him live this down — and frankly not caring. He closed his eyes and thanked the Almighty from the depths of his being.

Tamsen's voice made his eyes open. "How did you find us?"

Bears snorted. "How do you find two wildcats quarreling in the woods?"

"Listen for their yowling," Cade said

dryly. He knelt beside Jesse, lips pressed tight, worry in the slant of his brows. "We were headed for Greenbird Cove, but stopped in at the Teagues' first. Saved us the trip."

"So you know everything?"

Cade nodded. Jesse saw the anger his pa was keeping in check. Then something like a grin twitched his mouth. "Except why I find my son on his back in the snow with his wife threatening to ride off and leave him."

Absurdly pleased by the word *wife,* Jesse allowed them their amusement. "You're busting to laugh. Don't hold back on my account."

"Don't you dare laugh, either of you." Tamsen's cloak swished into view again, but it was clear by her tone she was nearly laughing herself — from relief, he hoped. "We're trying to reach your father's town," she told Bears, her tone sobering a bit. "His ribs are broken — worse than he wants me to think. I feared we wouldn't make it."

Swathed in his blanket, Bears looked down at Tamsen.

"You will make it, Little Wildcat. But," he added with a chin-jerk at Jesse and a feigned solemnity ruined by the bobbing of his jaunty white plume, "*he* will not enjoy the journey."

38

Late December 1787

The old woman, called Blackbird, sat with legs crossed, back hunched in a bow, as her crooked fingers wove the strips of river cane spread before her. She was making a mat, like those scattering the dirt floor of the lodge. Some of the strips were the cane's natural tan, others dyed shades of rust and black, the varying hues woven into an intricate diamond pattern.

Blackbird's granddaughter, White Shell, newly married sister of Catches Bears, set aside the basket she was weaving to tend a pot of corn soup bubbling over the central fire.

Tamsen took the opportunity to examine the young woman's work. The basket was actually two, one nested inside the other, but woven of a piece. White Shell had begun with the inside base and worked up the sides, where the canes bent downward, forming the rim. Then the outer basket was woven down toward its own base, enclosing the inner basket. She'd used only tan and rust shades, creating a simpler design than her grandmother's, but the double construction was a feat of skill, the weave dense enough to hold corn flour.

Tamsen, who knew something of dyes, touched a cane of Blackbird's mat, a russet one, still damp from soaking. "Is this color from bloodroot?"

White Shell peered past rising steam. "Yes. And the black? You know?"

"Butternut?"

"That is English word, I think. You make color?"

"Not for this manner of work." Tamsen spoke slowly so the young woman could follow her English and brushed a fold of her petticoat. "For cloth."

Blackbird, who spoke no English — or none she would admit to — raised her bead-like eyes from her work and said something that sounded like *i'hya.*

"That is word for this." White Shell pointed to the cane strips. "All colors, *i'hya.* Cane, you call it."

"*I'hya.*" Tamsen had learned a smattering of Cherokee in the fortnight she and Jesse had taken refuge in Thunder-Going's town.

Though at first she'd been afraid to leave Jesse's side, eventually she'd come to see that the town's inhabitants were welcoming. She was, however, still a little awed by Blackbird. She leaned again to touch the old woman's mat and said, *"Uwoduhi,"* hoping she'd said *beautiful.*

Hands never stilling, Blackbird spoke a stream of Cherokee.

"My grandmother thanks you for kind word." White Shell gestured at the mat. "But this is simple. Not what she make before hands . . ." Lacking the words, she crooked her supple fingers into claws.

Blackbird nodded toward a sleeping bench, and the women began pulling out basket after basket, Tamsen marveling at the designs, the sturdy construction, the skill and time each had demanded. White Shell held up an oblong basket with a fitted lid. "This is make when my father is in belly."

Before Thunder-Going-Away was born. Yet the basket was still tight enough it likely could hold water. "Your grandmother is what my people call a master craftsman. Or crafts*woman.*"

White Shell translated. Tamsen was gratified to see her words pleased the old woman. It was difficult to imagine, looking at her bent frame, whitened hair, eyes nearly lost in crinkled beds, but Blackbird had in her younger days gone on the warpath with the men. She'd fought Creeks, Chickasaws, and the French. Now she was what the Cherokees called *Ghighau,* Beloved Woman. She had a voice in the council, and her presence brought prestige to Thunder-Going's settlement — still small as far as Cherokee towns went, comprising a mere dozen thatch-roofed lodges.

Tamsen, Jesse, and Cade had been given places in Thunder-Going's lodge, since White Shell and her husband, along with Blackbird, had moved into their own. There Jesse had spent much of the past weeks flat on his back, his ribs healing. Gradually, as she'd ventured from his side, Tamsen had overcome her shyness with the *Ani-yun-wiya,* or the Real People, as the Cherokees called themselves, and accustomed herself to the rhythm of yet another strange way of life.

Every morning the women went to a nearby creek to bathe — even in winter, breaking through ice to reach the water. Once Tamsen accompanied White Shell but stopped short of joining the bathers, not just for dread of the cold. Going about with her hair uncovered was one thing, but bathing in the open?

This lack of privacy in a Cherokee town, for bathing and other intimate activities, was a thing she hadn't yet reconciled with her own sense of modesty.

"Then where bathe?" White Shell, aglow in the first weeks of pregnancy, had asked in a cloud of frosted breath, standing knee-deep in frigid water, naked save for a short stroud skirt.

"In your father's lodge, behind a buffalo hide. But only when no one's there," she added hastily.

The women tittered when White Shell translated her words, slipping wet feet into moccasins and wrapping themselves in blankets for the trek back through the cold.

"Even with Wildcat you not bare skin?"

Through a heated blush Tamsen tried to explain. "Jesse is my husband, but we . . . We've never . . ."

Tamsen faltered at discussing such matters, but White Shell's curiosity was piqued. She widened her doe-brown eyes. "Never . . . ?"

"Never done what you and your husband did to make that baby in your belly. Not yet." If she'd hoped White Shell would fail to follow her blurted English, Tamsen hoped in vain. The woman's round face scrunched in disbelief.

"I see why some *unega* — white men — take wife of *Ani-yun-wiya*. If as you say, from where so many *unega* come? Pop from the ground like mushrooms?"

Since that day at the creek, Tamsen had caught herself glancing at White Shell's belly, distracted by thoughts of babies, and of making them with Jesse.

They slept each night beneath the same furs, barely touching, a restraint fallen between them. First his broken ribs had been the barrier, but as she'd struggled to adjust to the communal living of the Cherokees, the thought of finally consummating their union while Thunder-Going — often Cade as well — lay within full sight and hearing of them . . . It was just too much. Yet it was all she could think about.

"You try, with basket?" White Shell's question snatched Tamsen back to the present. She was pointing at the cane strips spread between them. "You try weaving?"

"I — I'd like to try. But right now, I need to see Jesse." Her cheeks warmed, though White Shell couldn't know the ache of wanting breaking over her in waves, the pull she felt to go to Jesse, if only to see him and hear his voice. But as Tamsen rocked back on her heels to stand, she caught the watchful eyes of Blackbird and sensed, despite the barrier of language, the old woman understood perfectly.

Cracked ribs had to be the most confounding nuisance Jesse had ever put up with. The bruising across his midriff had faded to a sickly yellow brown. He could sneeze now without thinking it was like to finish him. Still the ache would catch him unawares while reaching for a stick of wood or standing to his feet, leaving him frozen in place till it eased. So it didn't surprise him when, sitting on his sleeping bench in Thunder-Going's lodge, restless as a tethered hawk, he mentioned his aim of joining Cade on his next hunting foray and Cade said, "I'm going to pretend I didn't hear that."

His pa didn't even look up from the bearskin he'd taken on his way back from Greenbird Cove, where he'd gone after seeing Jesse and Tamsen settled with Thunder-Going, to gather more of their winter supplies and clothing.

"I can't sit another day doing nothing, Pa."

"Healing ain't nothing." Cade meant to use Thunder-Going's town as a base for the winter hunt, but between Jesse's injury and the late start, it promised a spare harvest. "Cracked ribs take their time mending. You

476

know as much."

Jesse glowered. Cade glanced up and glowered back.

The door-hide moved aside as Thunder-Going ducked within. He let the hide fall, eying them. "Look at the two of you, scowling at each other like bears awake in winter."

Cade snorted. "This son of mine insists I take him hunting."

Thunder-Going came to the fire and settled on a mat, taking up his pipe. Tamping fresh tobacco into the bowl, he said, "You might let this impatient one have his way, but here is what will follow: the woman who is my mother will come hunting too — to drag one of you back by his neck scruff." Thunder-Going's eyes crinkled. "I will let you guess which of you that will be."

Jesse, who could have overpowered Blackbird with both arms tied behind his back, felt a quelling. At first Blackbird had bound his ribs and fed him foul teas and clucked over him like a fretful hen, but never had a colonel of militia possessed so reproachful a glare as that bent and wrinkled *Ghighau* turned on him days later, catching him too soon on his feet.

"That ought to put paid to the notion, Jesse." Cade unearthed his pipe and joined Thunder-Going at the fire. The pair fell back into *Tsalagi,* discussing the doings in Franklin . . . North Carolina. *Wherever.*

Stifling an urge to grind his teeth, Jesse eased himself down on the sleeping bench, half-listening to his elders talk.

The muster against the Creeks that the Trimbles had tried to entice him into had come to nothing. Franklin's governor, John Sevier, had expected to be out on campaign before Christmas, but so far no firm orders to march had come.

Jesse was glad. Always with these campaigns it was the women and children — on both sides — who suffered, which made him realize Cade was right. He needed to stick close by. Not on account of his ribs, or not the broken ones. His heart's rib, Tamsen. He wished she'd come back from White Shell's lodge. He wished they had their own small hut . . .

"Having no orders to march has not kept Sevier to home," Cade was saying. "He has kept busy with his militia, raiding Dragging Canoe's towns."

"What is it your Book says?" Thunder-Going asked. " 'A wise man sees trouble coming and gets out of the way.' Sevier is not such a man, but one who goes running to make trouble. If he is not careful, he will stir up the rest of the *Ani-yun-wiya* to war."

478

Watching his pipe smoke tendril upward, joining the fire's thicker column rising to the roof hole, Thunder-Going said, "I am for peace if it can be found, but I am like this trickle of smoke from my pipe, one voice among many, easily swallowed and lost. Most of the people may be for war. If that is so, it will be a fire not easily put out."

He met Cade's gaze. "And what of the new *unega* state? Have our troublesome neighbors been given leave by the Thirteen Fires to call themselves Franklin?"

Cade shook his head. "Sevier lost a supporter over to the Carolina faction, a judge called Campbell. Jonesborough was overrun by Tipton's men again, and the Franklinites driven out. Most have rallied down on the Nolichucky, in Greenville."

Jesse perked up at that news. *Down on the Nolichucky.* Had Dominic and Seth made for thence? Greenville was far enough removed from Sycamore Shoals to keep them out of Tate Allard's sights. And what of Kincaid? Might the unrest have persuaded him to forget Tamsen, go back to Virginia?

Could *he* have forgotten Tamsen, having met her but the once, if he'd thought her carried off against her will? He'd have done what Kincaid was doing, soliciting the

479

strength of any and all who would aid him — even a couple of ne'er-do-wells like the Trimbles — to get her back.

As for Parrish, the man had much to lose while Tamsen had a voice to raise against him. He'd proven his ruthlessness already. Jesse knew in his gut the man hadn't left off the hunt.

He waited for Thunder-Going to speak, but the man sat contemplating the fire, apparently having nothing more to say on Sevier's travails or the infant State of Franklin. Jesse let a few seconds pass to be sure, then cleared his throat.

"Pa? Don't reckon you've heard aught of Kincaid or Parrish?"

Cade seemed to have some trouble with his pipe, for he fixed his attention on it as he spoke. "Tate says they've cleared out of Sycamore Shoals. He hasn't seen them, or the Trimbles, since the night you got Tamsen away."

Had the light streaming through the smoke hole been brighter, Jesse would've known for certain, but it almost seemed Cade wore an evasive look.

"There something about Parrish you ain't telling, Pa? If he's gotten wind of where we . . ." Jesse let the question trail off, as the door-hide swept aside and Tamsen came in.

Talk of her pursuers was dropped by silent consent. Not that Jesse could've minded what they'd been talking about with his wife standing there ravishing his eyes. When he finally looked away, dazzled, he noticed Cade and Thunder-Going exchanging long-suffering looks. Wordless, they rose and took their pipes out-of-doors. Tamsen stepped aside to let them pass but lingered in the doorway, looking at Jesse almost shyly.

"Come here," he said, reclining to an elbow, barely wincing at the pain it caused. She came, kneeling beside the bench so their faces were on the level.

"How is it today? May I check the bruising?"

Jesse grinned. "Blackbird sent you in her stead, eh? I like this arrangement." In the warm lodge, he wore only a breechclout and long linen shirt, easily rucked up to bare his ribs.

He sucked in a breath at her touch. While she kept her gaze fixed on the remnants of his bruises, he devoured her with his eyes. Her glossy hair was pulled back and braided, but a few curls had worked loose to frame her face, still faintly golden from the autumn. Her lips were red and soft, and

481

close . . .

He croaked a mite when he asked, "Have a good visit with the women, did you?"

"It was nice." The tip of her tongue passed over her lips. He stared at it, wanting to lie back and pull her atop him, though it'd set his ribs back a week.

"You give the weaving a try?"

"Not yet." She moved her hand beneath his shirt — not a mere touch this time, a caress — and a jolt of pleasure shot through him. He held his breath. "Jesse?"

"Aye?"

At last she let their eyes meet. Hers were hungry, exposed. "I missed you."

Next he knew he had her across his lap, so lost in the touch and taste of her he barely felt the ache it caused his ribs. She returned his kiss with the hunger her eyes had promised, fingers stroking through his hair, down his neck, his shoulders. He pulled back long enough to say, "I missed you too," then kissed her again, heart leaping like every one of his ribs might crack wide to let it out to dance with hers.

"Tamsen —" Their lips met between words he'd barely breath to speak. "D'you want to . . . now?" His mind spun with notions on how they could proceed, grasping one idea and flinging it aside for another while his hands moved down her back, unraveling her braid.

She pulled back, and her gaze swept the lodge, settling on the doorway, where nothing but a hide prevented anyone walking in. "I don't want to wait another second."

There was hesitation in her voice, but she hadn't said no, and he couldn't stop grinning like a fool. Still there was that swaying hide, and no way to bar it. "We could hang the buffalo robe. Like when you bathe. If Thunder-Going or someone else comes in and sees it hanging, they'll likely go back out."

She frowned, considering this, but even as she did so, he knew it wasn't right. As much as he longed for her, had waited for her . . . this wasn't how he wanted it to be. Not hurried and furtive, half their senses trained on that swaying hide.

"No," he said. Confusion bloomed in her eyes. "Not *no*." He brushed her face with his fingertips, thinking he was like to drown in those dark-blossom eyes. "I want to make love to you — every day for the rest of my life starting now. But not like this."

She bit her lip at his declaration, lashes sweeping down as color suffused her cheeks. "I've wanted it too, Jesse. But . . . I don't know. Even if Thunder-Going and Cade stayed away, something about it feels wrong. Why should it feel wrong?"

He thought maybe he knew. "More'n once I've started to ask you . . . Do you even remember that night at the Teagues'? You'd been through so much."

She bit her lip, frowning. "Some of it, but it's foggy." Her eyes glistened. "I want to remember. A bride ought to remember her wedding day. Are you disappointed I can't?"

"No." He touched her face, knowing she was disappointed. "I wish I could change that for you, but I don't know . . ." He paused, as the solution dropped into his mind, perfect as a sunset. "Wait. I do know. Let's get married."

She responded to his lightened tone, the anticipation he knew must be in his eyes, with a ravishing smile. "Jesse, we are married. You remember it, surely?"

"I do, for a fact." He let her see in his eyes what wanting her every moment since had cost him. Her eyes went all melting . . . yielding. It took all the self-control left him to refrain from kissing her again. "But hear what I'm thinking now. We could be married in the way of the people here, then we'd both have that to remember."

She leaned back against his arm, blinking. "A Cherokee wedding?"

"Why not? It's a fine ceremony. Simple, respectable. There's a feast goes with it. I'll just have to bring in a deer before it can happen."

"A deer?"

"I'll explain the details, if you say yes. It won't make us any more married than we are, but maybe a ceremony's what we need to mark it — since one of us slept through the last one."

Seeing he teased her, she made a fist and gave his shoulder a thump. He pretended she'd hurt him, but his grin spoiled it. "What do you think?" he asked, though he could tell she was liking the notion.

"When?"

"Once I ask Thunder-Going, if he agrees . . . seven days."

"Seven?"

"They'll want to bless the council house, prepare the feast."

She sighed. He sighed.

"On the bright side, it gives these ribs more time to heal." He didn't say why that was important but knew she read it in his eyes.

That a man's own wife he'd slept beside, worked beside, argued with, swum nearly naked in front of, and just thoroughly kissed could sit on his lap blushing for shyness was a wonderment.

But then, he reckoned, not many men went about pursuing a woman as backward as he had Tamsen Littlejohn.

■ ■ ■ ■

TILL DEATH
DO US PART

■ ■ ■ ■

39

February 1788

Jesse reckoned himself in danger. From the looks of it, so was his horse. "Growin' fat and soft, the pair of us."

He leaned on the top rail of the paddock where Thunder-Going's folk kept their small herd. At his whistle, the horse tore itself from the cornhusks strewn on the snow-dusted ground and ambled to him, breath ghosting in the air. Jesse took the white-splashed head between his hands while the animal chewed its mouthful. The wound where the ball had clipped its neck had healed, though the scar would never grow mane again.

The horse's ears perked. Jesse turned as Tamsen, wrapped in her cloak, cheeks pink with cold, joined them. She slipped out a hand and presented a winter apple to the horse's reaching lips.

"I see who's to blame for his going round

as a barrel. The one doing the same to me."

Tamsen batted her lashes, a picture of innocence. "Does that mean you've grown partial to my cooking?"

He blinked back at her. "You've always cooked just fine."

"Liar," Tamsen said, taking his hand in hers. "I didn't come here just to feed the horse." With her other hand she held her cloak open, revealing what she wore beneath. A pale deerskin tunic bedecked with shell beads fell to a matching knee-length skirt, fringed leggings, and high winter moccasins patterned with dyed quills.

"You finished," he said.

"White Shell did the quillwork, but the rest is all mine." She nibbled her lip, awaiting his verdict.

"They're beautiful." Wearing such clothes, with her dark hair and eyes, she could pass for having Cherokee blood herself.

Spanish, he thought, pierced unexpectedly with a stab of envy. His wife didn't know all she wished to about her past, or her parents . . . but what he wouldn't give to know as much about himself. Maybe when they finally put down roots of their own, questions about his white parents would stop haunting him.

Tamsen was fingering the beads she'd

stitched across the tunic's front. "I'd need to work at this for years to come close to what White Shell can do. But I couldn't resist the challenge."

"It makes you happy, sewing clothes?" He hardly needed to ask. She glowed with the accomplishment.

"I never thought I'd sew, much less wear, clothes like this, but yes, it makes me happy. And reminds me of Mama." Sorrow brushed her face, a passing shadow. "I wonder what she'd think if she could see me."

It had been her wedding garments — a near-white doeskin tunic and skirt borrowed from White Shell — that decided Tamsen on attempting the construction of Cherokee old-style clothing for herself. Most Cherokee women wore stroud cloth and calico anymore, but she'd been taken with the soft deerskin.

Truth to tell, he hardly recalled what she'd worn at their wedding feast, held in the council house more than a month since. Tamsen had eaten with the women on one side of the structure, Jesse with the men on the other. Eaten what, he couldn't have said either. He did recall Bears and two of his friends gleefully seating themselves shoulder to shoulder, blocking his view of Tamsen, until the feasting ended and the wedding proper had begun. Cade stood with Jesse before Thunder-Going, White Shell and Blackbird with Tamsen. He'd given Tamsen a venison roast — *perfectly cooked,* he'd teased her with his eyes. She'd given him full ears of corn, symbols of their promise to dwell together, seeing to each other's needs. Then they'd each been given a blanket, which they draped together around their shoulders, whereupon Thunder-Going pronounced their blankets joined. Jesse had led Tamsen, amidst laughter and teasing and Bears' ululating turkey call, to a tiny lodge newly built for them, warmed and stocked. There, finally alone, he'd held her face between his hands.

"I wake each morning," she'd said, her eyes luminous in the light of the fire laid for them, warming to him, drawing him into their depths, "thanking the Almighty you were there in Morganton. I needed you but didn't know then that I would love you too."

"Then 'the Lord do so to me, and more also,' " he'd quoted, " 'if ought but death part thee and me.' Ever again."

Not Hezekiah Parrish. Not Ambrose Kincaid. Thought of them reflected briefly in her eyes too, then vanished, and it was only the two of them and the buffalo rugs and the fire's warmth.

The morning after the wedding, Cade had left to hunt, waving off Jesse's halfhearted attempt to ride with him. "Stay. Enjoy your wife. You waited long enough for her." He'd tugged at the straps of the packhorse's saddle, not bothering to suppress his grin, though there was something melancholy about his eyes. "Come spring, we'll leave the Watauga."

Jesse had held the horse's bridle as Cade swung into the saddle. "I know you been thinking on it, but what decided you? Think this Franklin business has come to more'n court raids and fisticuffs at last?"

"A feeling's all." Cade looked to the east, worry on his brow, then dropped his gaze to Jesse. "Franklin's troubles aside, I wouldn't want to see you taking land west of the mountains to farm. There's good land still where the waters flow east."

Land the Cherokees have no hope of re-claiming. Jesse finished the thought Cade wouldn't speak, not with the eyes of Thunder-Going's people glancing at them as they passed. Was this Cade's way of compromising with the life his choices were leading him toward?

It had struck Jesse then . . . he might have changed, but what of Cade? His pa was a roamer, a hunter, a man even more than Jesse caught betwixt two worlds, walking the shifting line between. Would he want to settle with him and Tamsen, or was a parting of the ways looming? He'd had a notion that something more weighed on Cade's mind than the complexities of land claims in the Watauga, or its feuding political factions.

A redbird lighted atop the paddock rail and trilled its liquid song, bringing him back to the present. Together with his wife he watched the bird till it winged off toward the wood, a red spark against the gray and green.

Tamsen squeezed his hand. She searched his eyes, her own questioning. "Are you wishing you were out with Cade?"

"I was thinking on him," he admitted.

"Jesse Bird, are you restless with married life already?"

"Come back to the lodge and I'll show you how restless I am." He bent to nuzzle her ear, breathing in the smoky scent of her hair. "Much as I fancy these new clothes of yours, I fancy 'em off you more."

He felt her shiver and melt against him. Forgetting Cade, the horse, the people throwing them grins as they passed, he guided his wife straight to their lodge, not stopping to speak to a soul.

Tamsen watched from the sleeping platform as Jesse stirred the fire and added wood. Flames blazed up, snapping sparks toward the smoke-wreathed ceiling. Feeling the tickle of a draft on her shoulder, she edged away from the wall and tugged the buffalo rug higher. Only in the center of the lodge — or beneath the furs — was it anything resembling warm. Yet Jesse knelt there in nothing but a breechclout, staring into the flames with distance in his eyes. "You *are* wishing you were with him."

He looked at her, having come but halfway back from wherever he'd been. "With who? Cade?"

He rose to sit on the bench. She sat up, wrapping him in the buffalo robe that warmed her. He kissed the tip of her nose, then lay back with her on the bench and held her in the crook of an arm, her head on his chest. With his heart beating strong beneath her ear, a sense of wholeness washed over her so complete it stung her eyes with tears.

"It was easy to stay." His words rumbled beneath her ear.

She moved her hand across him, feeling the contour of hard muscle, the slope of his ribs — no longer hurting him — reveling in the sinewy strength of his body. "But?"

His chest heaved beneath her cheek. "I'd hoped to take this last crop of furs to put toward some land, if you think you could abide being a farmer's wife."

She knew what he wasn't quite asking. She'd been reared to finery, intended for the pampered wife of a wealthy planter — if only to broaden her stepfather's business and line his pockets. Did she miss it, the silk and lace, the pretty linens on table and bed? For that matter, the table and the bed?

She did not. Not with the price they'd carried — a price exacted from the hearts and backs of slaves, and her soul. Besides, what was such needless frippery compared to the treasure of the man lying entwined with her now? Whether it was his singular raising or simply the manner of man he'd have been in any case, Jesse Bird didn't see her as a possession to be used. He didn't want to dominate her or drive her to some end suiting his own purpose. He wanted to pull *with* her, whatever furrow they chose to plow. How rare and priceless a man was he.

She raised her head to meet his gaze. "Wherever you settle, Jesse, whatever work you set your hand to, I'll be beside you. Trading corn for venison."

He had lovely eyelashes for a man, thick and dark. His eyes, keen in the firelight, reflected his pleasure as he took her hand lying on his chest and pressed it to his lips. "I chose well."

"As did I." She ran her thumb along his lower lip, knowing he liked that, but he didn't respond as she'd expected. He kissed her fingertips, then returned her hand to his chest, holding it there. That far-looking glaze stole over him again. He was worried over more than whether or not they'd be farmers, poor or otherwise.

Not since their second wedding had they spoken of her stepfather or Ambrose Kincaid. By mutual consent they'd held those shadows at arm's length, wrapped in the cocoon of their intimacy. But they couldn't hold back the rumblings of pursuit forever.

"You're thinking about them, aren't you? Mr. Parrish and Mr. Kincaid."

Jesse reined in his gaze, a corner of his mouth curving. "You turning mind reader on me?" He closed his eyes. "Reckon we got to face it, sooner or later."

"But not alone." She raised up on an elbow, hair spilling onto his chest. "Remember what Cade and Thunder-Going were talking about last night?"

Jesse took up a strand of her hair and

looped the curling end around his finger. "They talked on a lot of things, those two."

On the eve of Cade's setting out again to hunt, the two men had been having one of their God Talks, as Thunder-Going called them. As far as Tamsen could discern, Cade had been hoping to win his Cherokee friends to faith in Christ for years, to no avail, though it made for what seemed like lively discussions. Last night's had gone on for hours, and because it was mostly in *Tsalagi,* she'd barely followed it. But whenever Cade read from his Bible, it had been in English.

" 'He that spared not his own Son,' " Tamsen quoted, " 'but delivered him up for us all, how shall he not with him also freely give us all things?' All things, Jesse. He knows what we need and when. He'll deliver us and find us a place — a good place — to settle. That's what I have to believe." Even when the trail toward that hope seemed buried deeper than the mountain passes, there in the midst of winter.

"Amen to that." Jesse pulled her close by the tether of her hair, enfolding her in his arms. His heart beat steady and strong against her cheek. "I don't know how to put this any plainer, my Little Wildcat, save that you make me whole."

■ ■ ■ ■

The warriors from Dragging Canoe's town stood outside Thunder-Going's lodge, making their final case for war to Catches Bears. Or that's what Tamsen presumed they were doing as she peered past the door-hide. She couldn't follow their words, but their gestures spoke of urgency, and with their faces painted black, war was clearly why they'd come. And it looked as though Catches Bears, listening intently to their urgings, might finally have been swayed to their cause.

"Tamsen," Jesse said behind her. "Bears'll tell us what he means to do when he's ready."

She let the hide fall shut. Though the formal talk with the Chickamaugas had ended some time ago, Thunder-Going was still at the council house with Blackbird. Tamsen and Jesse were alone in his lodge, where Jesse had come to work one of the hides Cade last brought them. She watched him at the smelly work, marveling at his calm amidst this stirred up, knife-edged atmosphere that had invaded the little town, despite Thunder-Going's hope for peace. Jesse pulled the scraper across the stretched pelt, wiped the blade clean, drew it again. The fire crackled beneath a pot of boiling beans and corn she was meant to be watching.

The Cherokees observed no formal mealtimes. Food was kept ready at every hearth for anyone who happened to be hungry.

Tamsen gave the stew a cursory stir. "Thunder-Going doesn't want Bears to fight with Dragging Canoe . . . right?"

"That's right."

"And Bears will do as his father says, because he's chief of this town?"

"Bears'll keep his father's wishes in mind 'cause he respects his wisdom, but in the end he'll do what seems best to him."

What seemed best to Bears, who came in with a gust of frigid air, remained an issue in the balance. "Georgia will not go up to fight the Creeks. It is settled. The Thirteen States big council . . . What is it called, all of them together?"

"Congress," Jesse said. Cade had brought word of the grand convention in Philadelphia that had taken place over the previous summer, where men from each of the states had gathered, presided over by the celebrated General Washington. Months of discussion and debate had produced a Constitution, laws to govern all the states.

Copies of this Constitution were making their way Overmountain. Cade hadn't seen it for himself, but he'd spoken with a man who had.

"In Order to form a more perfect Union, establish Justice, and ensure domestic Tranquility," Cade had said, quoting the opening words of the document the man had recalled for him.

Jesse couldn't imagine a less perfect union — or domestic tranquility — than what was afoot in the west where, as far as Cade could discover, Franklin still hadn't been named the fourteenth state. "It goes worse for Sevier," Cade had told him. "North Carolina levied a tax on his property. While he was away training his militia for spring campaigning, Colonel Tipton ordered a sheriff to seize Sevier's slaves in payment of the levy. They're being held at Tipton's house on Sinking Creek."

"This Congress," Bears said now, "told the Georgians to put down their muskets. But Sevier still makes ready for a spring raid against the Chickamaugas. Even in this cold he drills his soldiers. One of the two who spoke in council with us saw him at it, saw with his own eyes. That is why they have come. To tell all the *Ani-yun-wiya* of this, and to ask these questions — Do you think it will stop with the Chickamaugas? And how will these soldiers know a Chickamauga town from a peaceful town? In the heat of killing, will they even care?"

Jesse made a noise of acknowledgment. Too many times settlers, acting on their own, had taken revenge for deaths and thefts on the nearest Cherokees available, whether or not those Cherokees were the guilty parties. So had the Cherokees done to the settlers. "They're certain Sevier isn't drilling his men to fight with Tipton's Carolina troops? Not just more Franklin trouble on the boil?"

"That one who saw them, he went to a trading post and spoke with the white man there. This man warned of Sevier's plans for the spring."

Tamsen could no longer stand the suspense. "Will you fight with Dragging Canoe?"

Bears glanced at her, eyes narrowed. At first she thought she'd overstepped some bounds in interrupting. But Bears said, "This may be the time, if the *Ani-yun-wiya* are ever to take back our hunting lands in the Tennessee. Now, while the Wataugans fight among themselves over what they are to be called — besides Wataugans."

"Has your father changed his mind on the

502

matter?"

"He has not."

Jesse paused in his work, waiting.

"For now I will stay. There are not enough men here to hunt for our old ones. Maybe in spring . . ." Bears stood, radiating restlessness, clearly not at the end of his thinking on the matter.

Tamsen heard the scratch of moccasins on the frozen ground. Thunder-Going ducked beneath the buffalo hide, trouble on his brow as he looked across the fire at his son, who wore the warrior's scalp-lock.

"I will pray and make ready to hunt," Bears said and brushed by his father on his way out of the lodge.

Though expected to be gone for days, Catches Bears returned before nightfall with news that he had met a hunter from Chota who'd brought down two woods buffalo and needed help bringing in the meat. For the use of a horse and travois, he would give one of the buffalo to Thunder-Going's people.

"Take my horse," Jesse told him at the stock pen. "He'll welcome the exercise."

Bears eyed him. "What of you? It is many sleeps since you hunted. Not since you got your deer for your wedding feast."

Reminded of that day, Jesse glanced at the lodge where Tamsen was tidying away the day's work, where soon they would seek the warmth of their bed, weighing that against a cold trek through snow to bring home buffalo meat. Turning back, he caught Bears in the act of rolling his eyes.

"I see it will be some time yet before you can be torn from the arms of your wife. So it was with my sister's husband. Useless for two moons at least. But I will take the horse."

40

Tamsen had fallen asleep to the howling of wolves. Their distant voices, at once blended and discordant, followed her into slumber to haunt her dreams through the night, jarring her awake at last and resolving themselves into the voices of men, speaking in low tones outside the lodge. She lay still, listening. One of the speakers sounded like Bears. But that couldn't be right. Bears had taken Jesse's horse to bring in a buffalo and wouldn't be back until the morning had passed. She put out a hand to wake Jesse. He was gone.

A hint of dawn streamed through the half-covered smoke hole in the roof. Below it the fire was nearly out. The air felt like ice crystals in her lungs as, wrapped in her cloak, she knelt to feed the fire, still listening. She recognized Jesse's voice now, and it *was* Bears. They were conversing in *Tsalagi*.

With the fire going, she tied her moccasins

and leggings and hurried to the doorway, nearly colliding with Jesse coming in. She looked past him, but Bears was gone into the graying dawn. "He's back awfully soon," she began, but Jesse took her by the arm, his gaze stricken. Alarm flared beneath her breastbone. "What is it?"

"My horse is dead."

Shock gripped her. "How? Is Bears all right?"

Jesse led her to the fire. He'd gone outside in only a breechclout but didn't reach for shirt or leggings as he settled on the edge of the sleeping platform. She draped a fur around his shoulders. His hand came up to hold it there as he stared into the flames. "Bears met that hunter at dusk yesterday. It was bitter cold. There were wolves — you hear 'em in the night?"

"Wolves killed it?" She shuddered, not wanting to picture such a horrible end for the horse.

"No." Jesse sounded as if he wished they had. "Bears and the other hunter were working to finish the butchering in a meadow where the herd had been grazing. They had my horse hitched to a travois, nearby." A shiver passed over him, raising gooseflesh up his legs. "There was a shot. From a ridge to the east."

It had taken his horse between the eyes, he told her, dropping it where it stood. Jesse met her gaze, eyes darkened to amber in the firelight. "They never saw the shooter but didn't stay to make themselves easy targets. They took the other horse, left the rest of the meat, and ran. Bears traveled through the night to get back."

Tamsen felt grief for the animal that had carried her over the mountains, into another life. More than sorrow clouded Jesse's gaze. The look in his eyes made Tamsen's heart thump with foreboding. "There's more?"

"Bears thinks the shooter didn't aim for him or the other hunter. My horse was the target."

"Why would anyone shoot a horse and not . . . ?"

"The Indians with it? To send a message. Dominic or Seth . . . either of 'em knows my horse on sight."

There was a thump on the doorpost. With a rush of cold air, Bears stuck his head past the drape, panting for breath as though he'd run back to their lodge.

"Cade is here," he said. "Men on horses come behind."

They'd dressed in haste, Tamsen donning her doeskin tunic and skirt over her shift.

The frosted ground beneath her moccasins felt hard as fired clay as she ran to keep pace with Jesse. Morning was brightening around them, but clouds were coming in fast, obliterating the fading stars. Outside lodges, people stirred. Voices queried as they made for Thunder-Going's lodge, where Cade was unloading one of the packhorses. They converged there with the few warriors not out on their winter hunts — a grand total of three, counting Bears. Tamsen glanced aside as White Shell appeared at her shoulder. She'd brought her grandmother out of her winter house, blanket wrapped, to hear what news Cade brought.

"They've come. Kincaid, the Trimbles, maybe Parrish too, with half a dozen men they've rounded up besides." His gaze swung to Tamsen. "They're searching the Overhill towns, showing around that portrait of you."

Tamsen's stomach lurched. "Do they know we're here — here and not some other village?"

"My horse," Jesse said. "They'll know I'm close by, and you with me." He grabbed for Cade as he straightened from tossing down the last of the hides. "How close?"

"Very." Cade's face, shaded by the brim of his feathered hat, was as fierce and impas-

508

sive as those around them taking in their words or listening while others translated. He turned to Thunder-Going. "We'll go, and pray we don't bring our trouble down on you. I leave you these hides." He gestured to the pile outside the lodge door. "And the others I have stored here. What the other horse carries we'll take."

Thunder-Going gave a short nod. "There are not enough of us to fight, even if you stayed, but still we will know nothing of you here."

The two clasped arms.

"God be with you," Cade told the older man.

"As He is with you."

It seemed to take a moment for Cade to register Thunder-Going's words. When he did, Tamsen saw a thing that by now she never truly expected to see. A full-blown grin crossed Cade's features, blazing joy in its wake.

Amusement lit Thunder-Going's eyes. "For many moons now."

"Then I leave you with peace in my heart." Features radiant despite their urgency, Cade turned to remove the pack-saddle from the horse, meeting Jesse's gaze. "We got to move fast while we've still a lead. Pack your things and —"

A new disturbance across the town —
barking, shouting — drew their attention.
Tamsen spotted a figure coming toward
them, running full out. It was White Shell's
husband, who had left to hunt days ago,
coming with his rifle held low. The crowd of
mostly women and children outside
Thunder-Going's lodge parted to admit
him. Jesse grabbed Cade's horse as it shied
from the arrival, who staggered in, gulping
breath and releasing it in clouds. White Shell
was at her husband's side, speaking rapidly
in *Tsalagi*. He responded, still gasping. She
raised her face and looked at Tamsen, her
features frozen. "There is no time. They are
just behind him. A mile, maybe."

White Shell's husband had spotted their
fires across a valley and raced to warn the
people, who were already melting away in
the burgeoning dawn, racing for livestock,
vanishing into lodges and hurrying out
again with packs, baskets, bundled children.
Before Tamsen could grasp what was happening, Jesse had her by the hand, running.
With her heart pounding and her blood racing, she no longer felt the brutal cold.

"What are they doing?"

"Same as us. Getting out of trouble's
path."

"Everyone?" Her foot hit an icy patch, but

Jesse bore her up, pulling her along. They reached their lodge. He held aside the door drape.

"There ain't enough men left to put up a fight. If all the hunters were here . . . but I wouldn't risk their lives. They need every man they got to survive the winter. Best thing we can do for them is clear out — fast."

Tamsen needed no further urging than the panic nipping at her heels. Inside, Jesse doused the fire with creek sand. He donned his buckskin coat over his hunting shirt, while she wrapped her cloak around her shoulders. There was jerked venison in a knapsack; Jesse's rifle, bullet-bag, and horn; his bearskin rolled tight and tied to shoulder straps.

"Leave the rest," he told her from the doorway. "God willing, we'll be back for it."

Looking up at him, for a moment she was thrust back across time and distance to Morganton, to Jesse standing in another doorway urging her to haste, her mother lying dead, her dazed and brittle thoughts scattering like leaves on a fearful wind. She heard hooves on icy ground, the snort and blow of horses. The sound froze her until Cade's voice called from outside. "Jesse — now!"

Tamsen forced her limbs to move, legs to carry her out into the cold. Cade was in the saddle, holding the reins of both packhorses, one still loaded. They'd be riding bareback.

Jesse hoisted her astride the horse, then handed up his rifle and mounted in front of her, agile as a panther.

Women and old men were leading children and horses up into the surrounding forest, where little shelter waited. Blackbird, led by White Shell, turned back at the forest's edge, seamed face drawn in frustration as though she still felt the call of the warrior beating within her withered frame. White Shell looked across the clearing at Tamsen. The young woman's fear snapped on the air like the breaking of creek ice.

The same fear twisted Tamsen's belly.

"We can make for home," Jesse was saying. "Gather what's left there, head into the mountains."

Tamsen broke White Shell's parting gaze to see Cade shaking his head. "We won't go back to Sycamore Shoals."

"We can't light out in this cold with nothing but our rifles and a stack of hides," Jesse argued as the horse beneath them fidgeted.

"We won't go back," Cade said again.

The horse danced sideways, made nervous

by their tension. Jesse fought it around to face Cade. "Why?"

"Thanks to the Trimbles, they've put a name to your face. Every county sheriff's looking out for you. Franklin, Carolina both. You can't go back to Sycamore Shoals or show your face anywhere Kincaid's been."

"Don't you mean Parrish? Or is there something 'bout that redheaded varmint you ain't told me?"

"Jesse!" Cade's tone was harsher than Tamsen had ever heard. "We got seconds to set our course."

Jesse relented, his voice edged too. "Make for the Cumberland Gap?"

Cade looked at Tamsen, misgiving in his eyes. The horse shifted again, swinging her nearer. "Haven't I proved I can live anywhere I must?"

She expected argument, but it didn't come. Perhaps she looked the part of a frontier wife, dressed in deerskins, clutching her husband's rifle. Jesse chose that moment to pluck it from her grasp and settle it across his thighs. She raised her chin and aimed every ounce of determination she'd earned at Cade. It must have been enough.

"Kentucky, then. Something happens, if we're parted, make for that bend in the

513

Holston — last winter's camp."

"I mind it." Jesse kicked the horse to follow Cade through the emptying village.

They were heading into the wilds again, this time in the heart of the coldest winter Tamsen could remember. As were Thunder-Going's people. Guilt thickened in her throat at the memory of White Shell and Blackbird fleeing to the woods. She pressed her face to the bearskin crossing Jesse's back as he guided the horse between trees, leaping deadfalls, skirting those too large to clear, following Cade along the base of a bluff, then up the side in a break where a deer path climbed.

They'd gone but a mile through ridge-cut forest when Cade pulled up, a hand raised. Jesse reined in. Tamsen's grip on his waist tightened to keep from sliding off the saddleless horse. He and Cade swung their rifles, pointed back over an icy stream they'd just crossed. Jesse heard the branch-cracking thud of a rider coming fast, heedless of stealth. He raised his rifle, finger twitching on the trigger.

A shout rang out. Horse and rider came into view. Jesse whipped the rifle's barrel skyward. "Bears!"

Catches Bears hurtled his horse across the

stream. "They come behind me. *S-qui:ya.*
He-ga!" Too many. Go!

They whirled their horses, Tamsen clutching Jesse hard enough to pain the ribs he'd
broken weeks back. Bears flew past them.
They followed, letting the Cherokee pick
their route through pine thickets and hardwoods, fallen timber and stones. A half mile
on, another shout rose behind them. Jesse
glanced back to see the trunk of a beech
explode in a shower of bark yards from
Cade, bringing up the rear with the packhorse.

He could hear their pursuers as Bears led
them up a thinly wooded slope, across the
crest of which a massive sycamore lay fallen
in twisted chunks over outcrop rock, skirted
by a growth of laurel. It was a natural
palisade, thicker than a fort wall, yet when
he saw what Bears intended, instinct
screamed against it.

Fight or flight. The impulses warred. But
the riders were too close to elude. They'd
make a stand, try to warn them off. Failing
that, pick them off.

Cade and Bears had dismounted. Jesse
slid down and pulled Tamsen to her feet,
shoving the reins of their horse at her. Scanning their position, he saw no better cover
for her than the looming wall of rock she

sheltered behind. "Keep the horses near. They won't bolt at gunfire."

"But if they do?"

"Let 'em go. Stay in cover, no matter what happens."

She clutched his coat sleeve. Fear trembled her voice. "Jesse . . ."

He pulled her to him and kissed her, hard and swift. "I love you."

Rifle in hand, he dodged a break between the rock and a section of the sycamore and crouched beside Cade. Back to the downed tree, he checked his priming, heaved in an icy breath, and whirled to take aim.

Bears popped up from behind a stone several paces beyond Cade, aimed his rifle down-slope and fired, then ducked back to reload. The breeze bore sulfurous powder smoke across their faces, stinging Jesse's throat.

A shot from below nipped the stone that shielded Bears, sending slivers of rock flying. They missed Cade, crouched low to aim through a gap under the fallen sycamore, but struck the side of Jesse's face like needles. One missed his eye by a hair. He swiped a hand across his stinging cheek, smearing blood.

Another shot cracked. Cade's rifle answered. Through the rising smoke, Jesse looked to Tamsen. She was pressed against the stone, white face staring from her hood. The horses shielded her from behind.

Silence fell, ringing with gunfire's echo. Smoke hung over the hilltop. Cade fished out ball and patch. "I hit someone. Winged or felled, I don't know."

Jesse edged to the left, taking up position at the same gap Cade was using, gaining a better view of the terrain below. A drift of powder smoke marked where the last shot was fired. Rifle trained on the trees near the smoke, he looked for a scrap of clothing, a shift of movement. "They got to know Tamsen's with us. They can't be firing to hit."

"Maybe trying to flank us. Cut her out."

Like wolves with a herd.

"I will see." Bears started to rise, but Jesse waved him down.

"Stay in cover," he began, then Tamsen's urgent voice made him look away from Bears.

"Jesse! Let me go down to them."

He looked down-slope, pretending he hadn't heard, chest constricted with fury and fear.

"No," Cade said for him, ramming patch and ball down the muzzle of his rifle.

"We can't keep running this way," she

persisted. "Let me go talk to —"

"I won't let you go to him." Jesse pressed his shoulder against the bulwark of the sycamore and took his eyes off the forest below. "There's nothing you can say would make me trust you to your stepfather."

Tamsen's face was torn with pleading. "Mr. Kincaid may listen."

"Pa," Jesse said, turning in desperation. "Maybe if *I* go down —"

"No, Jesse," Cade said with unsettling conviction. "That's a worse idea yet. He'll take you in custody for murder, abduction, whatever else Parrish wants, if he doesn't kill you first. He'll take what he wants — your wife — and won't heed even her pleading. Not if he's anything like —"

Jesse was staring at his pa, baffled at how he could know such things, when another report shattered the cold. Not from below, but along the crest of the slope.

Bears was no longer beside them. Jesse saw him several yards off, on his feet, spinning . . . falling. Shot.

Rising to a knee in the rimed duff, he raised his rifle toward the distant telltale patch of smoke and fired. Whether or not he hit the shooter, there was no return fire. Bears was up on an elbow, trying to drag himself toward his fallen gun. Jesse started to go to him. Cade yanked him back.

"Take her and leave. Before we're surrounded."

Jesse jerked free. "Bears —"

Cade grabbed him again, wrenching him nearly prone. "I'll see to Bears."

It sank in like a dagger's thrust, what his pa was telling him to do. "I'm not leaving you either."

There was no relenting in Cade's face. Only his eyes showed any hint of what he'd settled with himself, what he was offering. "Get her away. I'll hold 'em off."

Jesse felt his heart wrench. "Pa . . ."

"I saved you for more than what you'll get at their hands. Make for the Holston. God willing, you'll see me there." Cade thrust him toward the rock where Tamsen hid.

"Wehpetheh!" he all but shouted.

Go.

41

Snow sputtered from the hurrying clouds as they reached the foot of the ridge, where cane grew tall, spreading away for a winding distance as the land dropped toward a frozen creek bottom. Jesse guided the cantering horse along its edge until they struck a game trail leading in.

"Keep your knees in tight and hang on," he told her and plunged them into the brake.

Behind the shield of his back, Tamsen made herself small, arms around his waist, shoulders clenching at the crack of gunfire behind them on the bitter air.

Even in the low-lying canebrake, the ground was iron hard, sheeted with ice that cracked beneath their passage. Jesse slowed the horse to a jostling lope, letting it pick the path — one Tamsen prayed wouldn't peter out and leave them stranded in canes towering over their heads, growing too thick to see beyond a few yards in any direction.

Another shot rang out. Though its distance was reassuring, anxiety for Bears — and gut-wrenching dread for Cade — gripped her. Jesse reined the horse to a walk and pushed aside a leaning cane. As they passed beneath, he put a hand over hers at his waist. "We're clean away. You hear me, Tamsen? We'll be all right."

She realized she was crying, that he'd felt her sobbing against his back. She dreaded asking. "Is Cade dead?"

In the circle of her arms, Jesse heaved a breath but didn't answer at once. The horse bore them deeper into the brake.

"He's come through worse," he said at last, but his voice held the dread that choked her own throat tight.

They found their way out of the canebrake miles from the ridge where they'd left Cade and Catches Bears. In thickening snowfall, they traveled east, keeping to dense forest when possible, crossing streams, once a river. Already several inches of new snow blanketed the clearings. Jesse wrapped the rifle to keep its firelock dry but was too alert for threat to let it ride snug in its sling. They spent that first night shivering against a rock face near a frozen waterfall. Jesse built a screen of hemlock boughs to hold the heat of a small fire near, and Tamsen picked stone slivers from his cheek, cleaning away the blood.

"We're some ways south of where we need to be," he told her the next day, pausing to let the horse drink from the center of an ice-crusted stream. They were out of Cherokee territory now, near the north bank of the Nolichucky — at least he thought so. It wasn't a place he and Cade had ever hunted. Following a river — any river — would take them in the right direction but over terrain peppered with settlements, which was both good and bad. Good, because if Tamsen needed shelter from this cold at some point, he could find it fast. Bad, because such shelter might prove harder to get out of than into, if their identities were discovered. At some point Jesse meant to pick a trail north to reach Cade's rendezvous. How long they would wait for him there was a question Tamsen didn't voice.

"One thing at a time," Jesse said, reading her thoughts. "First we got to get there."

At least the bitter cold would limit the chance of running across anyone who might admit to seeing them. Sensible folk would be inside their cabins with the chinking patched and a fire blazing. Tamsen longed to be one of them.

When they started again, Jesse adjusted the bearskin slung around his shoulders so she could bury her hands in its warmth. She pulled her hood close and clenched her jaw to keep her teeth from chattering, wondering if she'd ever be warm again.

They gnawed on jerked meat as they rode that second day, stopping only to let the horse graze in a clearing where wind had scoured the ground bare in patches. Jesse bade her dismount and conceal herself in a stand of pine, while he stood at the end of the lead line.

Even with the pines for a windbreak, the cold bit deep. It began to snow again. Tamsen clutched her cloak tight while heavy flakes sifted down, making a shushing as they clung to dark needles all around. Flexing her toes inside her fur-lined moccasins in hope of warming them, she peered through the boughs at Jesse. He faced away from her, rifle nested in the crook of his arm, moving only to keep pace with the horse's grazing. It was a darker horse than Jesse's that had been shot but as hardy and used to the cold. As was Jesse. He stood as though indifferent to the elements, scanning the falling snow, turning so she caught the angle of his jaw, shadowed with a day's beard.

What was he thinking, staring out into the snow? Fearing for Cade? Looking for pursuit? How did he bear this cold with such stoic patience?

She remembered the swimming hole and that he was raised Shawnee. "Wildcat," she whispered. Love for him came surging to her throat as she glanced across the clearing.

Through the snow, the tree line at the far edge was an indistinct blur. Something moved against that blur, stabbing her with alarm. When she trained her gaze on the spot, whatever it was had vanished.

"Jesse," she hissed. "Someone's out there."

He had his rifle raised before she'd ceased speaking. He didn't look her way. "Where?"

"Across the clearing. Something moved."

He shifted to see past the horse's rump. Tamsen's heart pounded. She wanted to edge closer to Jesse, even if it meant leaving cover, but was too frozen to lift a foot.

Movement came again, near where she'd seen it before. Jesse sighted down the rifle . . . as a rack of antlers lifted, emerging from the snowfall.

Jesse lowered the gun and darted her a look of relief. Her quickened heart had sent blood surging to her numb extremities. Now warmth flooded her face as well, a disconcertingly delicious feeling. If this was the price of embarrassment, she hoped a deer would jump from behind every bush to fool her now until spring.

They spent another freezing night, only to have the temperature drop even further the third day. By early afternoon, Tamsen's feet were again benumbed, though Jesse had unrolled the bearskin to swathe them both. She huddled inside its shelter, pressed against his back. She wondered what they were meant to do come nightfall. They were exhausted, miserable, hungry, and with the temperature fallen, they'd never make it through another night in the open.

Sometime later the horse beneath her stopped, jarring her awake to the most bone-aching cold she'd never known. She'd missed the sun's setting. Barely a hint of gray showed the massive, snow-dusted trees spreading away on every side. She must have dozed for hours, clinging to Jesse in her sleep. Her back and rump screamed with soreness, and her ankles were too stiff to bend.

"What?" she managed through cold-chapped lips.

Jesse, apparently *not* frozen with cold, got a leg over the horse's withers and slid to the ground. He tried to hand her the reins, but her fingers wouldn't grasp them. He led her forward and hitched the horse to a bare-limbed sapling.

"A cabin's yonder, through the trees."

She made out a wall of hewn logs, a snowy roof, a zigzagging line of rails. Wood smoke tainted the air. No glimpse of firelight. The window, if there was one, was shuttered.

"Are you g-going to ask f-f-for shelter?" Her voice stuttered and slurred, as if she'd drunk too much hard cider. Oh, what she'd give now for some cider, spiced with cloves and warmed with a poker red from the hearth. What she'd give for a hearth . . .

"Can't risk it." Jesse's low voice snatched her back from the edge of a lovely dream. "Aim to see if there's a barn we can shelter in. Bide here."

Before she could muster protest, he'd slipped away. The horse rocked her, shifting uneasily, as miserable as she. She looked down at the snowy ground and wondered how she'd ever reach it.

Of a sudden Jesse was back.

"Cowshed's empty." His breath billowed as he untied the reins. "Reckon they lost their stock, else Sevier's militia's been by to requisition."

She wanted a fire, not a cold, deserted shed.

Jesse put a hand on her knee. She felt the pressure of it through leggings, cloak, and snow-crusted bearskin, yet the sensation seemed removed from her, as if she watched from a distance. "Can you get down? Best we come at it on foot."

A plan formed in her mind. Once off the horse, she'd run for the cabin, hollering for help. For warmth. The idea overwhelmed her with yearning. Only one problem. She couldn't bring her leg up to swing it across the horse. She was stranded, all her joints frozen.

Jesse pulled her, bearskin and all, off her shifting perch. He steadied her, then turned to lead them, whereupon she crumpled at his feet. Her legs might have ended at the knee for all she could feel them.

"Should've left m-me on the h-horse," she murmured as he bent to hoist her up again. "Now you'll have to c-carry me."

Grunting, he scooped her into his arms. She turned her face into his neck, felt his lean cheek against her brow, rough-whiskered. "Like a bride over the threshold, eh?"

"A b-bride with cold f-f-feet."

He led the horse inside and loosed it while he set her down in a strew of hay, cold and prickly. The wind ceased when Jesse shut the door, closing them in. The weight of the bearskin came down on her, as did the scent of old manure, thick and stale. The blowing of the horse as it found the hay sounded in her ear. Very near her ear.

"Don't let the horse eat my hair," she murmured, too near sleep to turn her head.

Jesse's breath brushed her cheek, warm enough to make her shiver. "Your hair's inside your cloak, sweetheart. The horse can't get it."

His body came around her. He found her hands and chaffed them between his own, until something resembling feeling prickled back into her flesh. Then he moved to her feet.

"So much for my plot to reach the fire," she tried to say, but she might only have dreamt it.

For a time Jesse resisted the images that spiraled through his thoughts, holding them at bay. Instead, he focused on the physical, on those parts of him most chilled — those not touching Tamsen — and the horse that had eaten its fill and stood dozing near enough he could reach out and grasp a fetlock. He listened for noises beyond the shed. All was quiet. No reason the inhabitants of yon cabin should venture out on such a night. Not to an empty cowshed.

When such distractions lost their power, he set his thoughts on Thunder-Going's people, praying for each by name. Especially Bears. Had Cade gotten him to safety? Did he live? Did either of them live?

He had no fitting words to pray for his pa, only groans that tore through him with gutting pain. The Almighty heard those, Cade himself had assured him when, still a boy, Jesse'd grieved hard for a dog he'd briefly loved. God spoke that tongue, as He did all others.

At the end of his groans, the images still beckoned, drawing him to look . . . to wonder at the toy that spun away from him across a puncheon floor, its defection provoking him to squawk in protest and reach stubby fingers for the . . . *twirly-top.* That was its name. A much larger hand reached down, stopped the toy midflight, and put it back into his greedy fingers. It made him happy, though it was a crude, homemade thing, the ridges of its whittling rippled to the touch.

Was it his? From before?

Lord, let me finally remember. He concentrated, giving himself over to the memory — if that's what it was — mining it for detail. The hand that had fetched the twirly-top was a man's, work-roughened, smelling of . . . *deerskins.* And there was a hearth. He could almost feel the heat on his face. That buzz and rumble beyond its crackle . . . the cadence of voices. A man's and a woman's.

His heart skittered a beat, jolting something through his bones that felt like recognition. If only he could *see* them. He couldn't make this memory-child turn its head, look up at their faces. *Jesse,* he willed one of them to say. Only that was wrong. He hadn't been *Jesse* to them.

"Say my name. Say *something.*"

He came to himself blinking in the dark and cold, stunned at what had transpired. The twirly-top . . . the reaching hand . . . Was it a true memory at last of his life before the Shawnees? Or was it only that those warriors had told the tale of finding him so often — described what remained of the cabin, the things they found there — that he'd merely stitched together a crazy quilt of secondhand memories into something resembling whole cloth?

Maybe so. Because the hand that had grabbed the renegade top and given it back to him hadn't been a white man's hand. Against the tender skin of his own pudgy fist, it had been brown as an Indian's.

Jesse jerked his head up, alert. Somewhere beyond the shed, hooves crunched the snow. The horse snorted awake. He rose to calm the animal before it did something foolish like whinny in greeting. Tamsen stirred at his absence but didn't wake. He went to the shed door, heard the chink of harness, the blow of horses. More than one. From the cabin came the muffled bark of a dog — thank the Almighty it was *inside* — then a *thud* like a musket's butt against a door.

He was half out of the shed before he wondered if he should wake Tamsen, make a run for it in the dark. If it was Kincaid, Parrish, there wasn't a moment to lose. If not . . . the night was brutal cold. He didn't want to force her out into it unless he must.

Someone opened the cabin door. Voices rose.

Jesse eased the shed door shut and crept around the structure, ducking along the gap between it and a woodpile blanketed in snow, the dog making racket enough to cover his footfalls. The snowfall had tapered to a flurry. He edged around to the corner of the shed, far enough to see across the cabin yard.

There were five of them, bundled for riding in bitter cold. Four mounted men with baggage heaped behind their saddles, and a fifth, dismounted. The latter was speaking with a blanket-wrapped man who barred the doorway, thrusting out a smoky pine torch as if to ward off the nocturnal visitors. Behind him the spill of firelight showed the lithe shape of the collie still barking its head off.

"My shed's empty, thanks to Sevier," the man was saying in a tone devoid of neighborliness. "You boys done took my mule weeks back. Now ye want more?"

The man fronting him spoke over the racket. "Militia's got John Tipton's house under siege. Tipton's harboring property belonging to Governor Sevier — and upward of forty-five Carolina troops holed up with him. I've authority to requisition for the Franklin men waiting him out."

"Hush yer noise!" the farmer shouted, turning on the dog and a wailing child that had joined the din.

Jesse felt the news run like ice through his limbs. It had been hard to judge distances with the falling snow, so many detours. They were farther east than he'd reckoned. How nigh the besieged Tipton home? He didn't know this region well.

The farmer gave the militiaman on his doorstep no ground. "Sevier's property? Back-owed taxes to Carolina more'n like. But Franklin ain't getting no more help from me. I got no more to give."

"You've a cow," said the man on his porch.

Panic seized Jesse at the thought of Tamsen lying asleep in the shed, but the farmer stoutly denied the assertion.

"Do not."

One of the riders in the yard spoke up. "I can smell it from here, Cap'n. He's got it in the cabin."

"I brought her in out th' cold!" the farmer thundered. "My wife's done lost her milk, and the least'un ain't weaned. You'd take the milk out'n my baby's mouth?"

Silence. Then, "Have you aught in the smokehouse to spare?"

"Empty."

The captain nodded to one of the riders, who turned his horse toward the side yard. The farmer shut the cabin door and hurried out with his torch. "I'll fetch ye a ham — and hope you choke on it."

The man had shut the dog inside. Jesse drew back into shadow as the farmer passed with his torch not a dozen feet away, trudging through unmarked snow to a smokehouse behind the cabin, returning with the promised ham, cursing under his breath as he passed.

"Keep your worthless Franklin paper," Jesse heard him grumble seconds later. "Just git!"

Saddle leather creaked. Hooves crunched the snow. Jesse heard the farmer's boots clomp onto his porch, where he paused to offer a parting shot. "If Tipton's got a lick o' sense, he'll pick off ever' last one of ye from the comfort of his upstairs winders!"

The cabin door opened, loosing the chorus of baby, dog, and bawling cow. Then it shut with a *bang,* and the inside bar slammed down.

Jesse waited till he could no longer hear the riders, then returned to Tamsen, feeling like a rabbit diving head first into its hole. Not that the shed was much refuge. She was his refuge, he realized as he flung an arm over her for their mutual warmth, comforted by the sound of her breathing while his mind sorted through what he'd overheard.

Sevier had Tipton's house surrounded. Something about stolen property . . . or was it taxes? He supposed it depended on which side of the great divide of Franklin one stood.

Slaves. He remembered Cade telling them that slaves had been taken from Sevier

— Tipton forcibly levying a North Carolina tax. So, Sevier hadn't let such an affront go unanswered. No surprise there.

Other things his pa had said came back to him in snatches. Things about Ambrose Kincaid. The way his pa had talked, it seemed he knew the man, knew what he'd do if he caught them. But how could that be?

Jesse dozed, once hearing riders pass again. Franklinites patrolling the roads to Tipton's farm? Or a more personal threat? He wished he knew how far it was to Tipton's.

Hounded by enemies. Hemmed by fractious neighbors. Somehow, between them, he had to get his wife north to the Holston, in hopes Cade was still alive to meet them.

42

The slamming of the cabin door had him springing out of the hay, jerked from sleep, thoughts spinning with memories of Franklin militia and barking dogs and men determined to take his wife and see him hanged for murder.

Tamsen sat up, face pale and creased in the gray of dawn.

"Jesse?" She gave a startled yelp as he pulled her to her feet, no more than half-awake.

"We have to go." He snatched up the bearskin, flung it over the horse, then cupped his hands to help her mount. He checked the priming of his rifle, then slung it over his shoulder. Cutting short the horse's feeding on the hay Tamsen had vacated, he led it from the shed. Tamsen ducked to clear the doorway as the farmer came striding around the shed to his woodpile, carrying rifle and ax.

The man halted, gaping. "Who in tarnation — ?"

Jesse was running before the man could collect himself. When they'd cleared the woodpile, he thrust the reins at Tamsen and vaulted onto the horse behind her, grabbing his rifle to keep it from slinging off his shoulder.

"Where do I go?" Tamsen's hood fell back, and her hair, loosed from its braid, streamed in his face.

"Take to the wood." Jesse held to her with his hands and the horse with his knees, frantic to keep them both astride.

A shot cracked. The ball struck a tree beyond them, shattering bark across the snow. Before the farmer could reload, they'd put too many trees between them to make a target. Jesse had her slow the horse, fearing a tumble now more than a shot in the back. He looked ahead through the lifting gray, scouting the snowy wood.

"See that fallen oak? It's pointing north. That's the way we got to go." And fast, he thought, as the snowfall thickened around them again.

It took every scrap of concentration Tamsen possessed to pick a path through the maze of trees and stumps and outcrop stones

537

obscured by the slanting snow. Cold stung her eyes, blurring her vision further. At first the sound, a distant crackling, barely registered. It was Jesse, behind her, who drew attention to the noise. "Gunfire. Tamsen — hold up."

She hauled back on the reins. Jesse slipped off the horse and took its bridle in hand. He walked them forward along the edge of a draw, scanning the trees enclosing them, pausing every few paces to listen. Tamsen's heart bumped against her ribs, trapped and panicked. "What is it? Who is shooting?"

Jesse didn't answer. He led the horse on, making for a sheltered spot ahead where a pine on the lip of the draw had fallen against a neighboring tree. Its roots hadn't pulled completely free of soil; the tree lived, creating a green, thick-needled wall. Jesse led them behind it. He reached for her then, touching her hand, squeezing her moccasined foot. She thought he meant to help her down, but he cautioned her to stay in the saddle.

"Militia stopped at that farm overnight, a party out requisitioning for Sevier." He tugged the dangling bearskin free and rolled it tight, tying it with whangs from his knapsack. She reached for the rug to sling around herself so he'd be less encumbered.

"Sevier — Franklin's governor?"

"Aye. Just now he's got John Tipton's house surrounded, with Tipton holed up inside." Jesse paused at another ragged volley of gunfire, far enough away to echo through the hills, near enough to make her flinch. "Maybe they've broke out. Or in."

It took her a moment to put the name of Tipton into proper context; Colonel Tipton, leader of the Old State faction, the man they'd seen in the Jonesborough courthouse, back in September. She shivered, certain the world had gone mad again with war, with every man at odds with his neighbor, red or white. "How close is Tipton's house?"

"Too close by the sound of things." Jesse's face was grim in the half light, wet from snow. "Whatever's afoot, I've got to skirt us around it, get us headed north. With attention fixed down this way, maybe we can slip past Jonesborough and . . ."

Jesse's head lifted. Tamsen heard it too. Another horse, maybe more than one, coming behind them, snorting in the cold. And it wasn't snowing hard enough to have covered their trail. She met his gaze. "The farmer?"

"He didn't have a horse. Scoot back." Jesse handed up the rifle, then mounted in front of her. Before the horse could take a

539

step, an explosion of noise rent the air.

Jesse jerked against her.

Tamsen nearly dropped the rifle but clung to it one-handed while the horse churned snow and pine needles and snorted clouds of breath. While Jesse fought to restrain it, she craned around his shoulder, looking for blood. And found it — soaking his thigh, bright against his legging.

A voice shouted from beyond the leaning pine, sending waves of shock along her spine — a voice she'd last heard in a cabin near Sycamore Shoals. Dominic Trimble.

"Jesse Bird! You hit?"

Terror skittered down her limbs. "Jesse, you are. You're bleeding."

His voice was tight. "A graze. Give me the rifle."

She handed him the weapon.

"I reckon you winged him," a second voice called — Seth's, sounding well recovered from his own winging at her hands. "He ain't took flight again!"

Jesse cocked the rifle, aiming it back along the draw. Snow obscured any movement, else the pair was hunkered behind cover.

"Where's Kincaid?" Jesse shouted. Tamsen could detect no hint of pain in his voice now but knew he only masked it.

"With us," Dominic hollered. "He's come

for the woman you done stole out from under his nose twice now."

"If he's there, let him speak!" Jesse edged the horse forward a step, peering through the snow-laden boughs, trying to pinpoint their location through the shifting curtain of white. "You're lying. He wouldn't shoot so near to Tamsen."

Silence.

Finally Seth called out, "That was a warning shot. We ain't going to hurt the girl, just give her over to Kincaid. He's over with Sevier's militia, waiting on us to flush you out."

"Militia that's swarming these woods," Dominic added. "They're busy with Tipton, but they know to be looking for you. Ain't no getting through 'em."

"There's no getting through *me* for you," Jesse called back. Tamsen could feel him shaking, though he was rigid with the effort to control it. "I won't let 'em take you," he said, gaze fixed down the barrel of his rifle.

"Look, Jesse." Seth's voice cut through the blinding snow. "You're a wanted man in most every county west of the mountains, but turn her over and we'll let ye go. You can take your chances with the militia."

Tamsen felt the growl rise up from Jesse's chest. "You'll take her over my dead body!"

She saw the flash in the pan as Jesse fired, felt the rifle's kick through his shoulder as they were enveloped in the throat-stinging reek of burnt powder.

There came a second blast, sounding farther away. At first Tamsen thought Jesse's shot had echoed back from some nearby bluff, then realized a second weapon had fired hard on its heels.

Jesse passed the spent rifle back to her, and the horse surged from cover. Clinging to Jesse, she struggled to prevent the heavy thing being snatched away by reaching brush. She risked a glance behind but could see no pursuit through the snow. Hanks of icy hair straggled across her face as her thoughts spun — half-formed, fragmented things. How could the Trimbles have found them? Had they been tracking them all the way from Thunder-Going's town? Did it mean Cade and Bears were dead? Would this running and hiding never end? Would the snow never end? If anything, it was thickening, on the verge of becoming a violent blow.

Jesse slowed the horse to a trot. He'd found a path, which quickly broadened to a wagon track, but it was impossible to see more than a few yards in any direction. He reached back for the rifle, then dug in his bag for the means to reload it.

Blood was spreading, darkening the buckskin covering his thigh.

"Jesse, your leg. That's no graze."

The crack of gunfire sounded again, a broken series of shots, rolling through the hills in echo. Jesse drew the horse up, turning a circle, scanning the forested slopes. The shouts of men — many men — mingled with the firing, indistinct in the falling snow. "God Almighty . . . where?"

The shooting, the disembodied shouting, seemed to be all around them.

From out of the confusion came the thud of a rider coming fast on the track behind. Jesse urged their horse on again, its hooves slipping in the snow, digging for purchase.

"Peshewa!"

Tamsen nearly lost her seat as Jesse wrenched them to a halt. She saw the rider emerging from the snow, tall in the saddle, black hat pierced with a hawk's feather.

"Pa!" Jesse reached for his father as he drew in his horse. The two clasped arms, beset by relief. "Bears?"

"Alive when I left him. I've been on your trail since I got him back to his people." Cade saw the blood staining Jesse's leg and blanched. "Bad?"

"Won't credit my chances on foot. Long

as I stay on this horse, I'll do. Was it you shooting back there?"

"I pinned 'em so you could slip free, but they'll be coming."

Tamsen's stomach lurched, the relief of Cade's presence fading. The intermittent shots, the cries, the shouts hadn't ceased. It was maddening, hearing but not seeing, fearing the impact of a stray ball at any moment. Or one not so stray.

Cade turned his horse into the trees. Jesse followed behind but soon as he could urged his horse in close.

"You know about Tipton?" Cade said.

"We do. Tamsen — duck!" They bent in time to avoid being swept off the horse by a low bough, but the stock of Jesse's rifle banged her nose. She hardly felt the impact for the numbing cold, but when she wiped a hand beneath her nose, it came away bloody.

"I've been all over these hills looking for you," Cade said. "Ran across Carolina militia coming down from our way. Tipton got word through the Franklin lines. Sounds like an all-out battle now."

How were they to keep clear of it? The question flashed through Tamsen's mind, but the thought was driven out as shouts rose behind them. These voices she recognized. Seth and Dominic had found where they left the track. She squeezed Jesse's ribs in her fright. "They're right on us!"

"Battle or no, we got to shake those two." Cade plunged his horse down an incline to the bed of a narrow creek, even as a musket ball whiffled through the limbs above their heads. "Pray we find a way through this hell."

The riderless horse came plunging through the snowfall, reins trailing, sides heaving. At sight of them, it swerved with a plume of snorted breath and was gone again into the swirling white.

Tamsen smelled the smoke of battle on the air.

Seconds later, the first fleeing soldier blundered out of the swirl, dressed in butternut woolens. White-eyed, powder-blackened, he seemed barely to register them until he slipped and sprawled to a knee, crying out as Jesse wrenched the horse sideways to avoid trampling him. The man was up and running again.

Another crashed through a stand of laurels, cursing, whimpering. They saw him weaving through the trees before the snow swallowed him as well.

Gunfire continued, sporadic but unnervingly close, each shot a blow to Tamsen's senses. She was first to spot the clearing ahead. "Jesse — look!"

He saw where she pointed and called to Cade. Beyond a scrim, of leafless trees, they could see the edge of a fallow field, a line of rail fence, and through the driving snow a log house in the distance, two-storied, outbuildings crowding close. Between the house and their position, a line of men was breaking, a few pausing to fire their weapons before turning to flee again. Straight into their path.

Other figures gave chase, some streaming out of the house, some from the surrounding woods, mounted and afoot.

"Back!" Cade shouted. "Go back!"

A bullet spit past, cracking through tree limbs. A trio of horses, one mounted, raced into the trees, and a man, astonishingly barefoot, nearly collided with them running at cross direction. They whirled their horses to flee. Someone coming behind the barefoot man yelled Sevier's name, but Tamsen hardly registered it. Her mind felt suspended, thoughts shuddering to a halt at the horror of having blundered straight into the battle.

Not a battle anymore. A rout. And she couldn't tell in which direction safety lay.

"There!" Jesse pointed at a stony outcrop looming out of the snow — a refuge, at least while they gained their bearings. He groaned as he hit the ground but turned and pulled Tamsen from the horse. He hurried her to the lee of the rock before he staggered to the snow, clutching his rifle. Cade took the horses in hand. Jesse put his back to the rock and reloaded his gun. His fingers shook, lacking their usual smooth efficiency.

Tamsen was shaking too, a bone-deep trembling she couldn't restrain. She pressed against the stone, conscious of its lichened face, cold and rough and wet. In breaks in the gunfire, she heard the shouts of men in retreat and pursuit, the occasional scream of a horse. Twice, men ran past within yards. One paused behind a tree, knelt to aim, and fired toward the house. Then he was up and reloading as he vanished in the snow.

Jesse sat pressed to the rock, rifle ready, wounded leg extended. Spots of crimson blotted the snow beside his thigh. Tamsen knelt, shielding the wound with her cloak. "Jesse, you're still bleeding."

"Like a stuck pig." The face he turned to her was fearfully leeched of color. She tried to spread the torn legging to see the wound, but he pushed her hands away. "Pa, what do you see?"

Peering over the edge of the rock, toward the field and house, Cade shook his head. "Too little in this snow."

"Maybe if we try and circle the farm, just walk the horses . . . take it slow?"

Cade put the reins into Tamsen's hands. She stood to take them as he took her place in the snow beside Jesse. "I'm seeing to that wound first."

To Tamsen's irrational vexation, Jesse didn't protest Cade's cutting open the legging to inspect the wound. She took the opportunity to get a look for herself, and her knees nearly buckled. The ball had passed across the muscle atop his thigh, but the scoring went deep.

"Bloody mess," Cade muttered, stripping down to the linen he wore beneath hunting shirt and coat. His tawny shoulders stippled against the blowing snow as he used the shirt to bind Jesse's thigh. "Got to slow this bleeding, or you won't make it far, whichever way we go."

Jesse's jaw bulged as the binding tightened. By dint of will, Tamsen didn't swoon. "Can he make it at all?"

"Aye, he can —" Jesse grabbed hold of Cade's bare arm to wrench himself to his feet. While Cade donned his hunting shirt and coat, Jesse got a look at her. "You're hurt." He drew her close, cradling her face in bloodstained fingers.

"The rifle banged my nose, is all." She could barely breathe through the swollen tissues now. "Forget about me."

"Never."

The intensity of that word pulled her straight into his soul. She clung to him, every fiber fixed on one hope — to find a way through this turmoil of blood and snow to a life in the sun with Jesse Bird, to bear his children and keep his hearth and make for him a haven from the world's calamity. She poured it into her eyes, giving back the unreserved devotion he'd shown her all along.

"I love you," he said, lips trembling blue.

Before she could reply in kind, Cade thrust between them, leading the packhorse over. "All right, you two. No time for —"

Tamsen heard the click of a hammer cocking behind them, but Cade was faster to react. He lunged in front of her and Jesse as the shot fired. Blood spattered Tamsen as Cade bore them both down into the snow.

43

The horses shied, revealing Hezekiah Parrish striding out of the snowfall, tossing his spent pistol back to Dominic Trimble and pulling another from his belt. He halted with it aimed. Sprawled in the snow and half-tangled with Jesse, Tamsen was frozen, though not now with the cold. Only her heart careened inside her, frantic with the paralyzing fear.

"Pa!" It tore from Jesse's throat like an animal cry as he struggled to extricate himself from Cade's inert weight, fresh red blooming on the linen binding his leg.

The ball had taken Cade in the chest. He lay still, his blood bright in the snow now too. Red and white. The whole world was red and white, and the cold black of a pistol barrel. Grief and helpless rage tore through Tamsen's chest.

"You didn't have to do this!"

Ignoring her, Mr. Parrish said over his

shoulder, "The Indian's down. Bird's wounded. Get the horses and find Kincaid — I can deal with them alone."

"Do what you want with those two." Dominic jerked his head at Jesse and Cade. "But we got us a deal with 'Brose. *She* goes to him."

"Then find the man!" The pistol in Mr. Parrish's grasp swung a few inches sideways. Dominic cursed and sprinted off through the trees.

Tamsen got to her knees, but Jesse grasped her arm as she tried to stand. "Stay down."

"Just let me go with him. Let this be over." She fought his hold. "Jesse, please. I'll make Ambrose under —"

"Wasted breath, girl," Mr. Parrish cut in. "Months ago you had that chance, but not now. And since you are of no more use to me, I cannot let you live with what you know."

The pistol hammer clicked.

"No!" It was a moan, low in Jesse's throat. His rifle had fallen too far out of reach, but too late Tamsen realized that beneath the cover of Cade's out-flung arm, Jesse'd worked loose the hatchet at his belt. Too late she saw a third man emerging from the swirling white, a man with a red blaze of hair spilling below his hat, a pistol of his own aimed.

Ambrose Kincaid roared something incoherent.

Shoving her off balance into the snow, Jesse raised up and drew back his arm. The report of a shot fell across Tamsen's heart like a thunderclap, as Jesse hurled the hatchet.

Bullet and blade each found their mark, but Tamsen hadn't another thought to spare her stepfather. Neither did Jesse. He was too busy clasping her, running his hands over her shoulders, arms, face. "Are you hit? Did he fire?"

"No. I'm well — but Cade!"

They turned as one to peel away Cade's blood-soaked coat. The ball had pierced his chest, high on the right side. Tamsen pressed her hands to the wound, hoping to staunch the bleeding.

Jesse bent his face to Cade's. "He's breathing." Fear tempered the relief in his voice. There was so much blood, and Tamsen's efforts weren't stemming the flow. They had to find him shelter and help.

In unison they raised their heads, seeking the enemy that had so long pursued them. Yards away, Ambrose Kincaid knelt over her stepfather. In contrast to their frantic hovering, his stillness told her Hezekiah Parrish was beyond aid. Mr. Kincaid was staring at the body sprawled in the snow as if he couldn't credit what had transpired, or his own part in it.

There would be time for coming to terms, but not while Cade's life was seeping into the snow. "Mr. Kincaid — please — help us!"

His bright head lifted at her plea. Stiffly, he rose and came toward them, gaze fixed on her. His face beneath its coppery stubble was the dingy white of unbleached linen, his blue eyes almost feverish as they darted over her buckskin garments, her unbraided hair crusted with snow, her swollen nose, all of her spattered with gore.

"Miss Littlejohn . . . ?"

Amidst dread and cold and crippling anxiety, a giddy spark leapt within Tamsen. The man wasn't sure he recognized her. Then Jesse's hand gripped her shoulder. Pressing down on Cade's bleeding chest, she said, "My name is Tamsen Bird, and I mean to keep it so."

Mr. Kincaid flinched, but she had no delicacy of feeling to spare him. She'd had no attention to spare the battle these last moments either. The sporadic din had faded. The Franklin militia that had surrounded Colonel Tipton's house had scattered into the hills or fallen. Her scrabbling mind latched on to the one pertinent result of this development. "Where are they taking the wounded?"

Mr. Kincaid halted. Beside her Jesse stilled, waiting on the word of this man who had long loomed a threat in their minds. Tamsen took Jesse's hand from her shoulder and placed it over Cade's wound, pressing down on it.

Covered in the blood of her menfolk, she stood. "Please, Mr. Kincaid. Will you help us?"

Ambrose's gaze flicked hard at Jesse, as though taking him in fully for the first time. Something darted across his features, a spurt of startlement Tamsen couldn't fathom. He looked toward the Tipton farmhouse, then met her beseeching gaze.

"I have found you. The rest will wait. Can we get them onto the horses, do you think?"

Daylight fell in wan stripes through the parted curtains of the room in Colonel Tipton's house, where some of the wounded were being tended. Cade lay on a folded quilt, blanketed against the unrelenting chill the fire across the room couldn't dispel.

The ball had been dug from his chest by a harried surgeon who'd arrived in time to pull some of the gravest injured in the skirmish back from death's door — for now. The torn flesh was dressed with a poultice, but Cade had bled out alarmingly before they'd gotten him across the snowy field to shelter. He'd yet to speak with anything resembling sense. For now he was gone away to some place Jesse couldn't follow. A fitful place, troubled by pain and dreams.

Others besides wounded came and went, bustling through the room with its fine furnishings in contrast to its log walls. Women of the house, neighbors, servants — a blur of petticoats and bending backs and basins on hips. A man lying on a pallet near the fire moaned. Two others on a bed slept, or tried to. A fourth sat against the wall, arm in a sling, taking food from a woman helping him eat one-handed.

Jesse's wound had been tended. He sat on the hardwood floor beside Cade, back to the cold wall, bound leg bare below his breechclout. Movement caused him throbbing pain, but not as consuming as the need to will his pa to draw breath, and again, and yet once more.

Kneeling nearby, Tamsen dipped a cloth in warm water. She'd ceased trying to coax him to eat the venison stew someone had left beside him, congealing in its bowl. He watched his wife gently sponging away the crusted blood from his pa's flesh, and through the capstone of his worriment came bursting up a love for her that stung his eyes. He let the tears fall unashamed, warm on his skin. Her nose was still swollen from its run-in with his rifle stock, her beautiful doeskin clothing bloodstained, but with her face washed and her hair braided, she looked otherwise recovered from their ordeal. He'd yet to thaw, though he'd spread his coat over his bare leg. Blood loss and exposure. He'd come right in time. But Cade . . .

"The boy!" His pa's frame jerked as he cried out. Breath hissed through strong teeth bared in pain. Fingers fumbled at the blanket drawn to his waist. "Taken . . ."

"Cade, it's all right. We're here." Tamsen stroked his brow, smoothing back his hair. For the first time, Jesse noticed the white mingled in the long black strands streaming from his pa's temples. How many of those had he put there? He was up to his neck treading guilt when Cade spoke again.

"Peshewa . . ."

Tamsen shot him a questioning look. "My name," he said, reaching for Cade's restless hand. "Pa, I'm here. Nobody's taken me. I'd do more'n scratch now, did they try."

He bent his cheek to the shoulder of his shirt to wipe it dry.

Tamsen reached across Cade and clasped their joined hands with hers. She prayed, plain and direct as she would speak to him. "We commit Cade into Your hands, Father. His trust is in You. So is ours. Let Your will be done on earth — in the body of this man lying here between us — as it is in heaven. Amen."

With the knot of pain and hope lodged in his throat, it was all Jesse could manage to add his own "amen." The clearing of another throat intruded like a raven's croak.

Jesse had done his best to ignore Ambrose Kincaid, seated in a chair pushed against the wall, staring at them each in turn like a buzzard come to pick the battle leavings. After helping them to the house, he'd gone off again for a while but returned moments ago to sit and stare. He'd removed his greatcoat and hat. His coppery hair was damp at the ends, the crown of it fiery in a shaft of window light, his watchful eyes unreadable.

Jesse shot the man a look — in time to see those eyes widen. He whipped his gaze back to find his pa awake, head lifted, giving back Kincaid's stare with eyes like molten amber, ablaze with recognition.

With a strangled groan, Cade flung an arm at Jesse, as one might shield a child from onrushing danger — an arm too weak for the purpose. Jesse caught it and eased it back to his side.

"Pa, be still. You're hurt." Jesse thought sure Cade would pass out from the pain he'd caused himself, but his gaze steadied, fixing on the red-haired man as if to burn a hole straight through him.

"Collin."

The name was barely a rasp. Baffled, Jesse looked to Kincaid. He was staring at Jesse's pa like a man thunderstruck, eyes aglitter in the slanting gray light.

"I never thought I resembled him," he said.

Tamsen, clearly as puzzled as Jesse, was quicker to find her voice. "Resembled who?"

The man glanced at her, a haunting in his eyes. "Collin Kincaid."

Tamsen shook her head. "*Who* is Collin Kincaid?"

Hearing the name, something almost clicked into place in Jesse's mind, but like stars reflected in water, his thoughts shimmered and rippled, refusing to align. He stared at his pa's taut face, light from the window glossing bold bones, tawny skin, eyelids closed now. He swung his gaze to the man sitting straight in coat and stock, white hands splayed on the knees of fine woolen breeches, narrow features exhausted, disturbingly intense. There was no resemblance in their faces. Not in coloring or the bones beneath. Why had he thought there might be?

"I told you of Collin Kincaid when we met in Morganton," Ambrose was telling Tamsen. "You don't remember?"

Her face went as white as the rag she still clutched.

"He was my father." Ambrose turned his stare then on Jesse, as if he were some piece in a puzzle the man was finally fitting together. "And I begin to suspect he was something to you as well."

Tamsen stood with Ambrose Kincaid in a chilly corner of the front room, while servants and members of Tipton's household bustled around them, trying to look as if they weren't eavesdropping as they passed.

"I have the Trimbles in custody," he informed her. "I mean to take them back to Virginia, with the assistance of a Carolina militia captain and a few of his men."

So that was what he'd been about, those hours he disappeared after helping them bring Cade to Tipton's house for tending.

Tamsen was glad to hear it but also curious. "However did you manage that?"

"With surprising ease. I know them of old — they committed a crime against my family, back in Virginia. I'd agreed to stay quiet as to their whereabouts if they helped in searching for you. They found me soon after I'd left you here, thinking to present you as a prize — far too late, of course."

Since they'd stepped from the room where Cade and Jesse rested, Ambrose hadn't taken his gaze from her. He stood now with his hat in hand, nervously rotating the brim. "Miss Littlejohn —"

"Mrs. Bird," she corrected. "And I think I know what you're about to say. You didn't know my stepfather meant me harm. You didn't know he was the one who caused my mother's death." She sighed, not wanting to relive those memories, but here at last she had her chance to let the truth be known. So she told him. Everything. "I wanted only to escape him — at first. And Jesse was there, offering to help me, asking nothing in return."

Ambrose pressed his lips tight, a thin slash amidst the bronze stubble of his unshaven beard. "Yet you've given him everything."

She met his gaze unflinching. "Yes. And you need to understand," she added. "I

560

didn't marry Jesse simply to elude you or to thwart my stepfather. I married him because I love him."

Acceptance struggled on Ambrose's face. "I wish I might have been the one to offer you the help you needed. Had I but known. Had I understood . . ." He swallowed hard, as if the loss of her was a stone going down. "I hope one day you will find it in your good heart to forgive me."

"For shooting Mr. Parrish?" she asked in surprise. "His brutality and neglect killed my mother. He held me prisoner, meant to kill me as well since he couldn't silence me any other way."

Ambrose shuddered. "You mistake me. I meant can you forgive my making it possible for the man ever to find you again. For the distress I've caused you in aiding his pursuit. And for encouraging the Trimbles to aid us. Not that I enlisted them to harm you in any way," he hastened to add as she drew breath to respond. "Such was never my intention. Please know that even at the start, when your mother was found dead and you vanished from Morganton, I wanted foremost to see you safe, and justice — as I understood its need — served."

Not blind to the sincerity in his eyes, Tamsen relaxed in his presence for the first time. Though she hadn't believed he would tear her from this refuge and spirit her back over the mountains, it had taken courage to stand and face him alone.

On the heels of Ambrose's enigmatic comment concerning Collin Kincaid, Jesse's father had awakened and again grown agitated at the sight of him. Despite Jesse's protests, she'd herded Ambrose from the room, leaving the door wide between them. She glanced now at that doorway, longing to be back with them.

"I believe you," she told him. "But you said my safety was your foremost concern. Had you others?"

Ambrose rubbed a hand across his mouth, regret tormenting his eyes. At first she thought he didn't mean to answer her, then he blurted, "Could you truly be in ignorance of the spell you cast upon me at our meeting? Your beauty, your charm, those eyes of yours dark enough to drown a man . . . I was so lost to you that I was easily persuaded you'd been borne away against your will by a half-savage stranger, the same who slew your mother to get at you. There was no mountain I wouldn't have crossed, no danger faced, to see you restored — to me, I had thought."

Tamsen blinked, not immune to such

words, though they couldn't touch her as perhaps their speaker hoped they might. She fixed on the salient point, saying as gently as she could, "The only true peril was the one you brought Overmountain with you." Seeing the clench of his jaw as he absorbed her words, she added, "But in the end, you accomplished what you set out to do."

The guilt that haunted his eyes wasn't banished. "Yet how near a thing it was."

Tamsen closed her own briefly, remembering Mr. Parrish, the snow, the pistol, the blood — then she pushed the images from her mind, distracting herself with a question needing to be asked. What had Ambrose meant, moments ago in the room with Jesse and Cade, by that comment about his father?

Before she could gather her thoughts, the man raised a question of his own. "Your husband . . . his name *is* Jesse Bird?"

Frowning, Tamsen opened her eyes, puzzled that he should need to ask. "Yes, Mr. Kincaid. I've said so."

"And the Indian. He's your husband's father?"

"Cade is his adopted father. Jesse was taken from his family's cabin when he was small, little more than a baby."

"Taken?"

"By Shawnees." When Ambrose's eyes darted toward the bedchamber, Tamsen hurried to add, "Cade wasn't one of them. He's Lenape — Delaware. I'm not sure why, but he came to be adopted by the Shawnees too, at the same town where Jesse was living. When Jesse was ten years old, Cade brought him away from the Shawnees. They've lived west of the mountains since."

Rather than satisfy Ambrose's curiosity, her answer seemed to deepen it. "From where was he — your husband — taken as a child? Do you know?"

"Somewhere in the mountains east of here. Jesse has no memory of his parents. They died in a fire."

Surprise flared in the man's blue eyes. "A fire? Then Bird is some sort of Indian name?"

"It was the name of settlers who helped them after they left the Shawnees. Cade sort of borrowed the name of Jesse Bird. Before that, Jesse was called by a Shawnee name. It's the first he can recall."

Ambrose's brow was furrowed, as if with great concentration. "Did he — Cade — know your husband before he found him among the Shawnees?"

"I don't think so. Mr. Kincaid, why so many questions?" If he meant to disparage

Jesse's upbringing, persuade her of his unsuitability as a husband, it was far too late for such tactics. She opened her mouth to tell him so, but Ambrose shook his head, abruptly dismissing the topic.

" 'Tis enough for the moment to know you are free of constraint." Despite his words, there was something in his eyes, something he was less eager to reveal but seemed compelled to do so. "There is another matter," he began, then paused as two women passed behind him, carrying linens. "There is another matter that has long weighed on me. I'm aware of the poor impression I made in Morganton because of Toby — my slave." Color stained his cheeks. "When I saw how you looked at me afterward, it was my mother I saw, looking out from your eyes as she once looked at my father, in his drunken rages. I was undone. Undone that I'd lost control and struck a man who'd served me faithfully since childhood, and done so in your presence. Believe me when I say that such behavior isn't habit with me."

The unlooked-for confession both touched and intrigued her. "Why did you do it?"

The query took him aback. "I — I wanted desperately for you to be at ease with me, untroubled in mind at our first meeting.

When Toby approached, I took offense for your sake."

"Did you think me such a fragile flower?" Tamsen hid her amusement as his gaze passed over her now, doubtless drawing comparisons. And if he was, whose fault was that? All he'd ever seen of her were those fragile petals, never the woman within — save in those moments before she stormed out of the ordinary. Perhaps he understood that now.

But instead of giving answer, he put a hand into his coat and withdrew an object, small and oval framed. "This belongs to you."

Tamsen took the tiny portrait and gazed at the girl staring back at her. "Am I so very changed?"

"Not all for the worse." When she looked up, biting her lip to keep from smiling, Ambrose reddened to the tips of his ears. "That is to say —"

"All for the better, from where I stand," she said, before he could sputter the needless apology. It swelled her heart with gladness to know she was no longer the sort of woman to fire his imagination with dreams of wedded bliss. That woman had possessed little more substance than the portrait she now held.

Regaining self-possession, Ambrose said, "I have also in my keeping a box to which I believe you have claim. 'Tis with my saddlebags, in Tipton's stable. Its contents have been unmolested. I have Seth Trimble's word on that, for what it's worth, but I shall let you be the judge." He started to raise his hat to his head but checked the action. "It may please you to know that, after your rather dramatic exit that day in Morganton, I saw straightaway to Toby's concern."

"Your servant who was attacked. What happened to her, if I may ask?"

"I sent her home to Virginia in the care of a physician, with Toby. After some necessary issues are seen to regarding the Trimbles, I shall look forward to joining them at Long Meadows."

Long Meadows. His beloved plantation, where she would never be mistress — thank the Almighty and His ministering angels.

Minding her manners, she curtsied to the man, wondering if she was the first woman ever to do so wearing deerskins. "I really must return to my husband. Please bring my mother's box to me here before you take your leave." She turned to go.

"Mrs. Bird, there is yet a matter — a troubling matter — the particulars of which I feel compelled to acquaint you with. The

567

injured man, the half-breed your husband calls his father . . ."

She smiled patiently as she turned back. "Yes? What about him?"

Ambrose's ruddy brows drew tight as a servant approached with a chamber pot, entered the sick room, and shut the door behind her. Tamsen would have moved to open it again — for Jesse's peace of mind — had Ambrose not said what he did next.

"I cannot yet be certain, but I believe he is not who he claims to be."

44

Cade was resting quietly with Ambrose gone from the room. It was anything but quiet in Jesse's soul. Or his flesh. The wound in his leg was a fire, wavering betwixt a crackle and a roar depending on if he moved. The floor hurt his backside, making him *want* to move. He fretted for Tamsen, beyond the closed door with Kincaid. But it was his pa who claimed his deepest anxiety.

Reaching for the trust his wife had professed in prayer, Jesse laid his hand across the callused brown fingers that had taught him to handle bow and rifle, to fish and hunt, build a cabin, work a hide, gentle a horse, everything a boy needed to know to be a man in that world they'd straddled, somewhere between white and red.

"Don't leave me, Pa." He stared at Cade's face, its bones sharp beneath the skin, and willed him both to drink of healing sleep and to wake and speak as a man in possession of wits and strength. Cade's lips stayed taut with pain, the deep-set eyelids closed in their hollows. Brows that normally soared hunched like ravens' wings in the cold.

No matter he wasn't blood of his blood, what Jesse felt for this man ran as deep as any son could feel for a father. Maybe more. Cade had had every choice in the world but to take on the raising of him, yet he'd done it. With all his heart.

God Almighty forgive him, Jesse thought, for every time he'd yearned for more. All those nights he'd lain awake, summoning buried memories. Cade was his pa. He needed no other. *Just let him pull through so I can tell him so* — and ask what in the nation he'd meant by calling out to Ambrose Kincaid by the name of that man's father.

Jesse couldn't wrangle sense out of it. They'd never met Collin Kincaid. They'd had no connection to his red-haired son before Tamsen. And *what* was his wife doing out there, still talking to the man? He couldn't have forced her out of Tipton's house, not without Jesse hearing it. She'd have made a scene, fought him like the little wildcat Bears had named her.

The room was devoid of servants, the physician moved on to deal with casualties elsewhere. The last to come and go had been a girl with a chamber pot. Said pot sat by the door, reeking of troubled bowels. Only the wounded lay about, adding the stink of blood and sweat to the fetid air.

Who could heal in such quarters? Soon as he could move about, he'd go into the wood, build a shelter and a clean fire, and bring Cade out by stretcher. Open air. That's what was needed. Long as they didn't freeze to death, and *why* didn't Tamsen come back?

He determined to get to his feet and find her.

Moments later, drenched in pain and clammy sweat, having made little headway toward the goal, the door opened and she entered. Sight of her lifted his heart, but there was trouble in her face. He eased back down, wincing as his leg met the floor.

"Where's your lovesick suitor?"

His teasing fell flat. She crossed to him, unsmiling, and knelt. "Seeing to the Trimbles. He's taken them into custody." Her voice turned wary. "Jesse?"

Before he could reply, another voice, one a mere thread, said his name. "Jesse . . . am I dying?"

"Pa." Jesse leaned close, fussing with the blanket drawn up to the linen bindings at Cade's chest and shoulder. "You got shot, but nothing vital's hit. Reckon in a day or two, we'll —"

"I have to tell you . . . before it's too late."

Jesse shook his head. "You're going to live, you hear me? But you need to rest. Whatever it is can wait." Talk of dying gutted him, as did those eyes staring up, drinking him in as if for the last time.

"Jesse?" Cade's fingers fumbled for his.

Jesse held them tight. "Yeah, Pa?"

"Hush."

Something betwixt a laugh and a sob stuck fast in Jesse's throat. Tamsen squeezed his arm. Tears were on her cheeks.

"Fighting you is costing him more than if you just let him talk, Jesse. And you need to hear what I think he has to say." She touched Cade's arm, drawing his gaze. "It's about Collin?"

Cade swallowed. Nodded.

Jesse closed his eyes. He burned to know what his pa had to do with Kincaid but feared what the telling would cost. "All right. Say it. But set to bleeding again and next thing I'm binding is your mouth."

"Think you can take me . . . with that bum leg?" Cade countered, and Jesse beamed as though he'd risen up to dance a jig.

Cade's lips moved again in silence, mouthing a word. *Water.* Jesse lifted his head to let him sip from a horn cup, then eased him back. Cade's eyes never left his face, the look in them beseeching. It hollowed Jesse with dread.

"You aren't Jesse Bird," he said.

Jesse stared, then forced a chuckle. "That's no news. You're the one borrowed the name, remember?"

Cade blinked, languid and slow, as if even such small movement taxed him. "Time I gave you back . . . your rightful one."

Tamsen gripped his arm again. Jesse didn't look aside at her. "My *what*?"

"The name you were born with. Alexander . . . John . . . McLachlan . . . Kincaid."

Jesse waited, but there was no mistaking what he'd heard. Cade had formed each name with care, a strained breath drawn between. He looked at Tamsen. He looked back at his pa. A buzzing was in his head.

"Who told you that's my name?" He knew he'd asked the question, but the voice hadn't sounded anything like his.

"Your father told me . . . the day you were born." Cade swallowed again, lips cracking, showing tiny threads of blood. "It was Collin Kincaid . . ."

"Collin Kincaid was my *father*?"

"No. He . . . killed your father. He killed

573

Bryan and Fiona."

Cade's voice had faded to a rasp. He needed water, but Jesse couldn't move. It was Tamsen who pressed the cup to his parched lips. When he lay back again, blood spotted the bindings around his chest and shoulder. *Stop now,* Jesse wanted to say. *Don't say any more.*

What he heard himself say was, "That was their names? My parents?"

"Bryan and Fiona Kincaid. For nearly three years you were theirs . . . Alex."

Rooted to the floor, Jesse stared into the void that was his life before the Shawnees, waiting for a spark, a memory, a bridge for him to cross back to that name. *Alexander John McLachlan Kincaid . . .*

It was the name of a stranger.

Tamsen touched Cade's brow. "It's true, then, what Ambrose told me. Collin was Bryan's brother. Jesse and Ambrose are cousins."

"It's true."

Jesse could half-believe his pa was raving mad with wound fever. "How could you know this? How did you know these people — my parents?"

Cade's eyes closed. His face went so still, for a terrible moment Jesse thought he was gone. Then the linen-bound chest rose. The

574

throat cords worked. Jesse leaned forward. Suspended. Waiting.

"Beg pardon, suh."

Startled, Jesse turned at the voice behind them. Ambrose stood in the doorway, one of Tipton's slaves attempting to edge past him with a steaming pan. The man stepped aside, laying his hat and greatcoat on the chair he'd vacated earlier.

Jesse said, "How long you been standing there listening?"

While the maid picked her way past sleeping wounded and set down her pan on the hearth, Ambrose came to stand at the foot of Cade's pallet. He made no answer to Jesse's query.

Instead, he said, "Theophilus?"

Jesse gave serious consideration to whether *he* might be delirious from fever and dreaming this entire conversation, for there was his pa gazing up at Ambrose Kincaid, nodding as if this was making all the sense in the world. He braced himself, hands flat against the floor in case that decided to tilt catawampus next.

"Who in blazes is *Theophilus*?"

Ambrose pushed aside his coat and sat, meeting Jesse's gaze square on, looking almost as dazed as Jesse felt. But far less bewildered. He was slow to speak, as if

575

needing to gather his thoughts.

"To answer your initial question, I heard enough to confirm the suspicion raised when I first saw your face, again when I heard the name of my father spoken in this room."

Jesse's brows pinched tight. "What suspicion?"

Tamsen placed her hand over his. "Jesse, let him tell it."

He took his wife by the wrist and felt her pulse hammering away, though he didn't think it was with fear. His own blood was running wild, quickening the more as Ambrose raked him with that blue-burning gaze of his.

"You strongly resemble your mother," he said. "But there's enough of Uncle Bryan in you that I can see the likeness. I never met them, of course. But in the summer parlor at Long Meadows is a wedding portrait of Bryan Kincaid and his bride, Fiona McLachlan. And as well as bearing his name, Alexander, you have our grandfather's eyes. As does he," Ambrose added, bending a nod at Cade.

Our grandfather. The shock of it shuddered through Jesse's bones. "Are you telling me he's not fever-mad? You and me — we're kin?"

Ambrose's mouth twitched. " 'Tis unexpected, I grant you, and no doubt more than a little confounding." He glanced at Tamsen. "Your wife may recall that I possess a certain failing when it comes to recounting familial histories. Permit me to start at the beginning, as best I know it?"

While Ambrose spoke, Jesse watched the Tipton's maid bend for the chamber pot by the door and, nose wrinkled, flash them a curious look before taking the smelly thing from the room. Robbed of her, he fixed his stare on Cade, who before his eyes was transforming from the man he'd called his pa purely out of affection and respect into his genuine half uncle, born to a Delaware slave at Long Meadows, a plantation on the James River, fathered by her master, Alexander Kincaid — born a slave and given the outlandish name of Theophilus by his mother.

"Theophilus — Theo, he was called — and Bryan were friends from the time Theo was a tad, toddling about the summer kitchen, where his mother served. 'Twas no secret he was their brother, but Collin despised him — and Bryan, for not rejecting their connection. Then Fiona McLachlan came into their lives. Whatever brotherly bond Bryan and Collin retained was demolished when she fell in love with Bryan. By then my father was well on his way to becoming the profligate drunk he remained until the end of his days."

"I saw . . . his grave."

They all started at Cade's soft words.

"You did?" Jesse turned sharply in query. "How? When?"

"When I left you." Cade's eyes flicked to Tamsen, warming in a way that flooded Jesse's soul with comfort, even as his mind reeled. "You talked of settling . . . farming. Before I could trust in your safety, I needed to know."

"You've been to Long Meadows?" Ambrose broke in. "Does my grandfather know?"

Cade's head moved across the pallet. "Slaves hid me . . . I wasn't seen."

"Is this why we've been so long rootless?" Jesse demanded. "You didn't think it was safe to stay put for long with Collin Kincaid alive?" Though he nodded, Cade was clearly losing strength. Jesse looked at Ambrose in his chair. "Make me understand."

"I shall do my best." Ambrose looked from face to face, the thoughts behind his eyes assessing, questioning, as if he was still piecing together the truth from the scraps of history they each possessed. He raised a hand to worry the hairs at the base of his neck. "As Grandfather tells it, when Fiona married Bryan, my father lost what little restraint upon his wickedness he still possessed. Suffice it to say, he made life unpleasant enough that Bryan and Fiona fled Long Meadows. They left Virginia, choosing to homestead near the headwaters of the Yadkin River, in North Carolina. They took Theo with them. He was young still, fifteen, sixteen years of age. Grandfather agreed it was for the best. Collin would have made his life a hell, without Bryan to protect him. Do I have it right thus far?"

Jesse realized Cade was listening closely. His body must have been wracked with pain, far worse than Jesse's own. "Pa? You all right? We can stop this if you need to."

Golden hawk's eyes found him, eyes folk said were so like Jesse's, and what were the odds, them being no true kin?

"Jesse," Cade said on a shallow breath, and for an instant he *was* still Jesse. And Cade was Cade. Simple, sorted, and plain.

But it wasn't, and Jesse didn't know if it was anger roiling inside him, or wonderment, or just the dumbfounding shock of it all. He stared at the melting rivulets of snow on Kincaid's riding boots, wanting to lie down and sleep for a week and wake up

579

Jesse Bird again. Yet a part of him was beginning to be . . . not *used* to the idea of Alex Kincaid. Not *liking* it. But intrigued.

"Is there more to this tale?"

"Until I heard my father's name spoken here," Ambrose replied, "I'd have had no good answer to that question. Grandfather knows Bryan and Fiona died when their cabin burnt, some twenty years ago, for their land was left to Collin, in the event Bryan died without an heir. Bryan told Grandfather so in a letter not long after they established themselves in Carolina. I've always wondered why Bryan did so, given their history — an attempt at reconciliation, even if it would be from the grave, perhaps? Regardless, how the fire started and what happened to the child Grandfather alone knew had been born remained a mystery. Grandfather never told me I'd had a cousin until Collin's death. He believed the child — a son, his namesake — must have perished in the fire as well. But here you are."

Ambrose's gaze shifted from Jesse to Cade. He leaned forward in the chair, expression braced. "So it is true, then. My father started the fire?"

Cade's eyes answered, even before he added, "Covering . . . the murders."

Jesse felt a moment's pity for Ambrose as

580

something in the man's face shattered.

"I'd dared to hope . . . but I knew him too well, too long. Did you see it done?"

"I was . . . running traps . . . came home to ashes." Cade's eyes found Jesse again. "I combed that cabin . . . every cinder . . . every bone. You weren't there."

"But you found the tracks," Jesse said. "The tracks of the Shawnees that came on the scene, who took me. That's why you came to Cornstalk's Town and ran the gauntlet, became Shawnee? For me?"

"For you . . . for Bryan. He gave me freedom."

Of course. Ambrose had just told him Cade — or Theo — had been born to a slave. That would have made Cade a slave too. Bryan had given his half brother his freedom, as well as friendship. "How'd you know it was Collin who killed them if you weren't there to see it?"

"You know this part," Cade reminded him. "Shawnees . . . told of the man . . . what he did before they found you. By their words I knew him. I wanted to find him . . . kill him. But couldn't risk . . . losing you again. So I stayed with you at Cornstalk's Town."

Jesse tried to hold back the question, but it broke free. "Why didn't you tell me this

581

years ago? After we left the Shawnees. You could've told me then."

The pain in Cade's eyes deepened. "Remember . . . after we fled the Long Knife hunters, you broke your leg? I left you with those settlers . . ."

"I mind it." He'd been out of his head with pain and grief, thinking the warrior he knew as Wolf-Alone had abandoned him to white strangers. It had been a week, at most, then Wolf-Alone returned, calling himself Cade.

Kincaid. "You took on your father's name? Why? Why after everything?"

"It was . . . Bryan's name too." Cade paused, swallowed, went on. "When I left you with the Birds, I went to Long Meadows . . . Needed to know . . . did Collin live? Could he learn of us . . . hunt us down?"

"To cover his murders, like my stepfather tried to do," Tamsen said.

Cade met her gaze, understanding passing between them. "I saw him . . . drunk in the stable. By then . . . I pitied him. I let him be."

Ambrose gave an ungentlemanly snort. "I cannot begin to guess how many times Grandfather and I found him so. Collin Kincaid cast his shadow over every soul he touched."

"Yet he sired a son . . . with a good heart."

Cade's words took Ambrose by evident surprise. And pleasure.

Jesse frowned, unsure he was willing to extend such favor to the man. "Was keeping shed of Collin Kincaid the only reason you didn't tell me?"

Cade shook his head. "I was waiting."

"For what?"

"To see the man you'd make. A man who could forgive . . . or one to seek revenge."

"You saying I'm come up short?"

Cade's eyes took on a sheen. "You are your father's son," he said, with such pride in his exhausted gaze that Jesse couldn't speak a word past the tightening in his throat. "If I was wrong . . . holding the truth this long . . ."

"You made the right choice, Uncle Theo."

Jesse glanced at Ambrose, startled, then annoyed, at the familiar address. It rankled, like having his hair rubbed against the grain. It felt like . . .

Of all things. He was jealous of the man. Jealous of his having genuine claim on Cade, and Tamsen too — not because of some misguided obsession with her, but on account of *him,* his own blood that linked them.

With his next breath, he knew the foolishness of such thinking and saw instead another hand at work, one that had been weaving their paths for good. Not just Tamsen's and his. Cade's. Ambrose's too. Even that unknown grandfather for whom he was some sort of namesake. That man who'd lost his sons, one to murder, one to drink and darkness. And a third son, born a slave, whose fate remained to him unknown.

"And I suspect," Ambrose continued, still addressing Cade, "you've been thinking all these months I'd picked up where my father left off. That I was bent on a like persecution, pursuing you all as I've done."

"I was wrong." Cade closed his eyes, beyond exhausted now. "I pray there's time . . . for both of you . . . to forgive me."

"No." Tears were starting, but Jesse didn't care. "I don't need time. He's right, is Ambrose. You'd reason enough not to tell me. You were trying to protect me, like you've always done. Tamsen too, because I chose her, love her. And even if you are my uncle, I mean to go on calling you Pa. If that's all right."

A breath went out of Cade's parted lips, curving them in the faintest of smiles. But he didn't speak, and for another wrenching moment, Jesse feared he was that quickly gone.

But he only slept.

45

The day passed over them, and the snow fell, but whatever lingering concern with the Franklin skirmish that might have troubled the Tipton household was kept at arm's length by Ambrose Kincaid, who came and went throughout the day, making sure their needs were met. The rest of the battle wounded had been removed by kin, leaving Tamsen, Cade, and Jesse in relative solitude in the small parlor while the house was put back in order. They were offered food. Bandages and dressings were changed. Cade slept, woke, talked a little, slept and woke again. Though he mightn't have realized it yet, Tamsen could see that with each waking, the spark of life in him stretched taller, greedy as a candle flame reaching for the air that sustains it.

That air was Jesse, his brother's son. His son, in all the ways that mattered. In the silence of her heart, Tamsen pondered all she'd seen and heard and was certain what had turned the tide between life and death for Cade had been Jesse's swift forgiveness, his love. Aiding to a lesser degree — one of the greatest ironies she'd ever witnessed — was the presence of Ambrose Kincaid.

Watching them from across the room — Cade propped now on a bolster, Jesse and Ambrose seated on the floor beside his pallet — she could almost see the bond of kinship widening to embrace one until this day counted an enemy, as together Cade and Ambrose wove a picture for Jesse of his heritage. And as the shock of revelation gave way to acceptance, Jesse drank it in and asked for more, until the cup of his past was spilling over.

Tamsen watched, and she pondered, and the image that kept coming to her was that of a young woman's brown hands weaving . . . weaving many-colored canes into a basket that was really two baskets, just as their identities — hers and Jesse's — had proved to be two, one nestled inside the other, joined by the skillful hands of the Master Weaver.

Finally her wounded men both slept, and Ambrose left them for a time. A few tapers added to the fire's glow pushed back the shadows of dusk-fall to the corners, filling the room with the honeyed scent of bees-wax. Sound in body and with much to occupy her mind, Tamsen remained wakeful. Thus it was to her that Ambrose came the final time, greatcoat slung over his arm in anticipation of departure, to talk about the land that once belonged to Bryan Kincaid, which had precipitated his journey to Morganton, and their meeting.

" 'Tis your husband's land by right," he told her, looking at her with eyes that, while no longer dazzled, held a lingering regret. "Send word to me at Long Meadows, when the time is right. We'll meet in Morganton to settle the deed. For now, here's something that belongs to you."

Standing there in the clothes she'd made in Thunder-Going's town, still bearing darkened bloodstains, Tamsen took from him what he withdrew from beneath his coat. Her mother's box. She breathed out in relief and nodded her thanks. Then frowned. The leather whangs that had held it shut were gone. Her eyes sought his, asking whether he knew of its contents.

"The Trimbles had it among their kit. It took a spill as I was apprehending them." He'd seen and understood what it had held, his gaze told her. "Can you believe it wouldn't have mattered, had I known from

588

the beginning?"

The box tilted in her grasp, emitting the soft clink of coins. Even that he had preserved for her. "That my mother was a slave? I don't know you well enough yet to say, but I believe you a more honorable man than I once credited you with being."

Though never a man she would choose to marry — not when there was such a man in the world as Jesse Bird. Or would he be Alex Kincaid after today? Or simply Wildcat?

With love and satisfaction swelling beneath her breastbone, she gazed at her husband, asleep beside his foster father, whose name was as much in question at present as that of the orphaned nephew he'd devoted himself to raising. Whatever name Jesse chose, he was hers, and she his, and what God had joined together, no man — kin or otherwise — would ever put asunder.

"Before I take my leave," Ambrose ventured, "might I request the privilege of paying a visit on your behalf to Charlotte Town, to whatever persons might claim Hezekiah Parrish as next of kin?"

He had her full attention again.

"With the intent," he added, seeing her questioning look, "of setting right certain misconceptions concerning the death of your mother. It is the least that I can do for you, if you will permit it." Ambrose settled his hat upon his head, dimming the blaze of his hair in the taper-light. "I ask because I know Grandfather will have his own ideas of what to do, once he's heard the tale in full. For all that he's nearing eighty, he is not a man to suffer lightly the slings and arrows cast against those he holds dear."

Nor, Tamsen was quite sure, was his grandson and heir, who made her a bow and reached for the door. "You have my permission. But will you tell your grandfather the truth about the fire?"

Ambrose hesitated, turning to her with bruised, weary eyes. "Perhaps not at once, aside from the fact that Theo and Bryan's son are found. What I intend to do is set right my father's wrongs — and your stepfather's — as far as they can be." His gaze on her warmed. "Now a certain pair of horse thieves and I have miles to ride before we lodge this night. I bid you farewell, Mrs. Bird."

"Farewell for now . . . Cousin," she said to his departing back. "God speed you safely home."

Surprised by the address, Ambrose Kincaid turned back again, this time smiling.

He left her with his words full in her heart and the image of an old man she had never met rising up to her defense. She had lost a mother and would mourn her yet awhile and miss her always. But she'd gained a husband, and with him, a father. Now a cousin and that distant, shadowy figure of a grandfather. And before next winter's snow fell, there would be another to bind their hearts and blood together, God willing.

With a hand spread across the place where Jesse's child was cradled, she shut the door, crossed to her husband, and settled on the quilt beside him, setting aside her mother's box, smiling with her secret. She meant to tell Jesse when he woke, thinking it would be some hours yet, but he stirred now, turning toward her those features sharp and clear as a hawk's. He reached for her, voice rasped with sleep and lingering pain.

"He's gone?"

"Just now," she said, softly so as not to awaken Cade.

Jesse was silent, watching her face, mouth curving in response to the joy she couldn't suppress. "Is that why you're smiling?"

"No," she said, and bent to kiss the bridge of his nose. "But if you promise to go back to sleep right after, I'll tell you why."

■ ■ ■ ■

FROM THIS DAY
FORWARD

■ ■ ■ ■

EPILOGUE

Upper Yadkin River, North Carolina
Spring 1788

While support for the State of Franklin crumbled through the winter and into spring, enmity between Overmountain settlers and Chickamaugas grew ever more bloody and fierce, drawing in many of the formerly peaceful Cherokees. Catches Bears went to join Dragging Canoe's warriors, though Thunder-Going-Away still hoped for peace. As for Cade, Jesse, and Tamsen, they packed their earthly goods, saddled their horses, and left the Tennessee country to its troubles.

Jesse had an inheritance to claim.

Dogwood and redbud still bloomed on the high slopes as they crossed the mountains eastward, following the west-flowing Watauga to its headwaters, then striking the east-flowing Yadkin. Tamsen found the journey easier the second time, despite being five months heavy with child. This time she crossed the mountains with two men, three horses and a cow, provisions aplenty — and serviceable shoes.

It was a day filled with birdsong and the tang of awakening earth, when they reached the long-neglected parcel of land once chosen by Bryan Kincaid to make a life with his wife and infant son. Trailing behind her menfolk and the stock, Tamsen didn't see the cause of their halting on the trace they'd followed up one of the Yadkin's tumbling feeder creeks.

"Are we there?" Leaving off examining a patch of fiddleheads curling up tender from the forest loam, she hurried to where Jesse and Cade stood, one to either side of the lead horse's halter.

Cade passed a hand across his beard-shadowed chin. "We are."

"And we've a welcoming committee," Jesse said.

Ahead in a sloping clearing studded with saplings, two picketed horses grazed. Nearby stood a wagon, heaped high and covered in canvas, beside it an open-faced shelter, a fire ring, and the cookery and gear one might expect of a camp where men had lived rough for days.

At the fire the men in question were rising

to their feet, gazes fixed on the trailhead where Tamsen, Jesse, and Cade stood. One, hair blazing in the spring sunlight, dressed in shirtsleeves, neckcloth neatly tied, was Ambrose Kincaid. The other, slower to rise, was an exceptionally tall man, clothed in a coat of green, with white hair worn tailed back.

Tamsen found she was squeezing Jesse's hand, not knowing whether she or he had done the clasping.

"Did you expect this, Pa?" Jesse asked.

"I did not, but I reckon we're both man enough to meet it." So saying, Cade led the way down into the clearing he'd last seen the day he buried the remains of Jesse's parents and set off for the Shawnees in the north to find his brother's son.

They met Jesse's cousin and grandfather near the wagon, Tamsen bobbing a curtsy, blushing when their gazes went to her thickened waist. She managed a smile for Ambrose, then looked with something akin to awe into the more remarkable face of Alexander Kincaid. Jesse and Cade *did* have his eyes, though the golden stare of the old man put her in mind less of a hawk than an eagle. Unlike his hair, his brows were still dark and strongly marked, level like Jesse's but nigh as bold as Cade's.

"Theo," the old man said, gaze settling with hungry intensity on Cade. Then the man turned to Jesse. "Alex."

Jesse started slightly at the address. They stared, each waiting for the other to speak, but what words were there to begin? to bridge twenty years of separation?

Ambrose found them, though they blurred past Tamsen's ears, and before she quite knew it, she found herself taken aside and escorted to the wagon while Jesse and Cade lingered with the old man, speaking too low for her to hear.

Ambrose had kept his word. In company with his grandfather, he had paid a call on Hezekiah Parrish's kin, as well as his solicitor, in Charlotte Town. Confronted with knowledge of Mr. Parrish's culpability in the death of Tamsen's mother and his attempted murder of Tamsen — "and the ire of Grandfather" — all concerned had turned remarkably generous of spirit, eager to compensate Tamsen for her loss and trouble at the man's hands.

"Nothing could bring Mama back," Tamsen said, then at Ambrose's pained gaze banished the sorrow from her voice. "He had cousins, I think. I suppose one of them was his heir?"

"The son of a cousin, actually. He's attempting to salvage what remains of Parrish's estate, but with most of the slaves having absented themselves during *his* absence . . ." Ambrose shrugged, then drew back the oilcloth covering the wagon's contents. "He sent along these for you, in the hope they should be of some comfort."

Tamsen recoiled from the pair of wooden trunks at the rear of the crowded bed. "I want nothing from them."

Understanding curved Ambrose's mouth, but his eyes sparkled. "Open them before you decide. Their contents were chosen by one of your stepfather's slaves who remained at her post, one who held your mother in high regard and knew what of her personal effects — and your own — you would wish to have."

Tamsen stared, then reached to touch the nearest trunk. "These are my mother's things?"

"See for yourself."

Ambrose unclasped and raised the lid, giving Tamsen a glimpse of its contents. It wasn't the sight of them that brought the rush of tears. With the lid's lifting, a scent had wafted forth, faint but unmistakable. A smell almost of cinnamon. "Oh, Ambrose."

"Gowns, petticoats, quilts, linens, a great deal of sewing paraphernalia, a few books," he said, visibly pleased she was so moved. "The rest is from Long Meadows, and Grandfather, for your home." He tugged the oilcloth back farther, revealing a feather tick, a clothespress, another trunk, an array of household goods. "Speaking of home-making . . ."

Ambrose met her look with a determined cheerfulness as her hand went naturally to the child. It was but a fortnight since she'd first felt it move, like the flutter of tiny wings. Baby Bird, she and Jesse had taken to calling it.

"My congratulations," Ambrose said.

Behind her Jesse said, "Thankee kindly, Cousin."

Startled, Tamsen looked past Jesse to see Cade and his father standing alone beneath a copse of silvery birches, their backs to the clearing. Beneath the birches lay two stone mounds, clearly placed by human hands. Cade's, over twenty years ago.

"Thought it best to give them a moment," Jesse said.

Tamsen showed him his grandfather's gifts, though she didn't open the trunks that held her mother's things again. The three wandered over to Cade and Jesse's grand-father. As they came within sound of their voices, Tamsen noticed a larger stone at the head of each grave. One was scratched with the faint remnants of a *B,* the other, an *F.*

". . . hold to the hope that you will come again to Long Meadows," Alexander Kincaid was saying. "Not in secret this time."

"To live?" Cade turned to face the old man. "I couldn't."

The elder Kincaid didn't take his gaze off the graves at their feet, so all Tamsen could tell of his reaction to this refusal was through his voice, disappointed but persistent.

"Let us call it a visit, then." When Cade gave no reply, Alexander Kincaid put a hand, gaunt and rope veined, to his son's strong arm. "Spare it thought, Theo. Will you do that?"

Impossible to tell what Cade felt upon seeing his father again, free man to free, being called by that old name, presented a choice he clearly never looked for. "Maybe" was all he said.

The old man seemed to accept that, turning now to Jesse.

The look of the man was formidable — perhaps as Jesse might look should he see such an age. There was a resemblance beyond the eyes. It was in the way they stood, the set of their heads, the carriage of their straight backs. She knew her husband well enough to realize he sensed his kinship with the man, however untried was the ground between them.

"I should think, for you especially," said the old man, "this has come as quite the shock."

"It has, sir. Not necessarily a bad shock."

Cade's mouth curved at that, but he held his peace.

"One which I'm sure we'll all come to weather happily," Tamsen put in, drawing the eagle's gaze.

"Young woman, Ambrose has acquainted me with the particulars of your remarkable union with my grandson. If you'll permit an old man the observation, I've grown rather proud of you, though we'd yet to meet until today."

That eased her pounding heart a bit but sent warm blood rising to her face. "And I'm proud to be Mrs. Jesse Bird." A twitch of the old man's brows made her eyes widen. "Oh . . . I suppose I'm actually Mrs. Alex Kincaid?"

"That depends on my grandson." The old man looked amused, but behind the look Tamsen read a consuming interest in the question now raised.

Jesse cleared his throat, meeting it head on. "While I'm grateful to know you, sir,

602

and for your generosity . . ." He swung his gaze to Cade, who, Tamsen saw, was waiting with as keen an interest for Jesse's reply. "I'm rather partial to the name you gave me, Pa."

Cade did his best to hide the grin that sought to shatter his self-control.

"But I've no objection to adding a few to it," Jesse added.

"Jesse Alexander John McLachlan Wildcat Kincaid Bird," Tamsen said, "is a bit much for any man. Perhaps we'll save a few for Baby Bird, if it's a *he*?"

Ambrose spoke up for the first time since they'd joined his grandfather and Cade at the graves, asking Jesse, "What name will you sign to the deed, once we head down to Morganton?"

Jesse didn't answer the question until a fortnight later when — with a sturdy, three-room log house raised and roofed with the help of Cade, Ambrose, and his grandfather, still hale enough at eighty to split shingles — he and Ambrose made the journey south to Morganton, closing a circle he'd traveled unknowingly for twenty years. There, Bryan Kincaid's land passed to his son, who for the first time set down in writing a name that, to his mind, blended the life he'd had before, and the one a chance encounter with

Tamsen Littlejohn on the streets of Morganton had restored to him.

Alexander Jesse Bird Kincaid.

Though of course their meeting hadn't *truly* been by chance. Not to Jesse's reckoning.

AUTHOR'S NOTES AND ACKNOWLEDGMENTS

Until relatively recently I had never heard of the State of Franklin, often called the Lost State of Franklin. *Lost* seemed an apt description to me the day I stumbled across mention of this first post–Revolutionary War attempt at independent statehood by a group of veterans, politicians, frontiersmen, and citizens of the fledgling United States: Tiptonites and Franklinites; old State and New State; courthouse raids, fisticuffs, siege, and battle. For a little over four years (1784–89), the people of the Tennessee region lived under the jurisdiction of two governments vying for the same territory. How, I wondered, could such a situation result in anything but chaos — and a setting that begged for a story to be woven through it?

During the research that led me to "discover" the Lost State of Franklin, my primary focus was on a slightly later period in North Carolina's history. In order to keep track of those tantalizing hints of conflict surrounding the failed statehood attempt I'd come across in passing, I started a file and called it something like the Franklin Book. Creating such a file pretty much guarantees the setting, historical event, or story nugget it's built around will keep nudging me from time to time, suggesting further possibilities. This State of Franklin file was obviously no exception. Gradually a cast of characters clustered around it, they began to speak to me, and *The Pursuit of Tamsen Littlejohn* took shape.

In writing this story, I knew early on that I wouldn't focus on the political intricacies of the Franklin movement and its opposition, nor on the primary historical figures involved, such as John Tipton and John Sevier. Instead, I would show what it might have been like for those men and women attempting to wrest a living from that frontier land, to provide for and protect their families, during those few tumultuous years in the Tennessee country. It appealed to me not only as an intriguing and, I think, little-known era of United States history but also as a unique complication in the flight and pursuit of Tamsen Littlejohn and Jesse Bird. So I proceeded to discover everything

I could about the time and place, the key players and events, pinpointing as many occurrences in the historical record that could possibly, and plausibly, be woven into my characters' story without overwhelming it — including Tipton's raid on the Franklin courthouse, and the necessity to marry under both governments. I chose to end Tamsen and Jesse's story concurrent with the Battle of Franklin, the skirmish that occurred at the home of Colonel John Tipton on February 29, 1788. Afterward, the Franklin movement unraveled until its collapse early in 1789. John Sevier, war hero of Kings Mountain, was eventually arrested and brought east to Morganton to stand trial for treason. He escaped (or was released) before the trial, returned Overmountain, and eventually became the first governor of Tennessee when that state was added to the Union in 1796.

Just as I'd overlooked this brief but fascinating history, I was in store for another, more personal surprise in connection with the Franklin statehood movement. In the pages of one of my most helpful resources on the subject, *The Lost State of Franklin: America's First Secession* by Kevin T. Barksdale, I found mention of a relative of mine living the history that forms the backdrop of Tamsen and Jesse's story. From page 24 of Barksdale's book: "Captain Thomas Amis, one of the most successful early merchants in Tennessee, moved his family from Bladen County, North Carolina, and opened a small store and tavern in present-day Rogersville." Later, in August of 1787, during a hotly contested election that nearly brought the region to open war, Thomas Amis ran for a seat in the North Carolina legislature. He was my distant cousin. We're both descended from another Thomas Amis, who purchased land in the Colony of Virginia in the sixteen hundreds.

To learn more about Franklin and how the movement for statehood began and ended, I highly recommend Barksdale's book. Also, PBS has a program on DVD, *The Mysterious Lost State of Franklin: The Story of America's First Secession,* that's well worth watching. Other books I found helpful: Pat Alderman, *The Overmountain Men;* Brenda C. Calloway, *America's First Western Frontier: East Tennessee;* John R. Finger, *Tennessee Frontiers: Three Regions in Transition;* Samuel Cole Williams, *History of the Lost State of Franklin.*

My parents chose North Carolina as the destination of many family vacations during my growing-up years, building in me a particular fondness for the state from the Outer Banks to the Blue Ridge. Even with visits to North Carolina over the past forty years — more than one of them with novel research as the catalyst — this story required a great deal of study for setting and historical purposes, and insights I couldn't glean from books. Several individuals who live and work in North Carolina graciously responded to my questions over the past few years. For their helpful assistance, my thanks to Betsy Pittman, resident genealogist, Burke County, North Carolina, for information on marriage bonds and how people married in North Carolina in the 1780s; Gail Benfield, curator, North Carolina Room, Burke County Public Library, for information about Morganton in the late eighteenth century; Sandy West, for descriptions of Morganton and the surrounding countryside as it would have appeared in 1787.

The Cherokees, a people living in the Overmountain region long before the influx of white settlers, were tragically caught up in warfare and strife during the entire eighteenth century. The war chief, Dragging Canoe, is not my creation. His history — his opposition to white land purchases and the treaties many of the older generation of

Cherokee chiefs, including his father, had signed and seen broken, and his break with the Cherokees to form the splinter group, the Chickamaugas — as presented in this story is true. I'm thankful to the authors of the following books for sharing their insights and expertise, particularly on the history of Cherokee women and the life of the warrior Dragging Canoe: Sarah H. Hill, *Weaving New Worlds: Southeastern Cherokee Women and Their Basketry;* Theda Perdue, *Cherokee Women: Gender and Culture Change, 1700–1835;* Pat Alderman, *Nancy Ward, Cherokee Chieftainess, Dragging Canoe, Cherokee-Chickamauga War Chief;* Nadia Dean, *A Demand of Blood: The Cherokee War of 1776.*

A people whose history was essential in the creation of two characters, Jesse Bird and Cade, are the Shawnees, particularly the Mekoche sept, to which the famed peace chief, Cornstalk, belonged. The novels of James Alexander Thom (*Warrior Woman, Panther in the Sky, Follow the River*) first brought the Shawnee people and their history to life for me. My thanks to Samantha Holland for her help with some of the Shawnee words and phrases included in this story. For further research on Shawnee culture, I turned to Colin G. Calloway's

610

book *The Shawnees and the War for America.* I also extend my thanks to the folk at the Pickaway County Ohio Historical Society for needful information on Scippo Creek, near where Cornstalk's Town stood, and where Cade made his dramatic appearance among the Shawnees.

It's said it takes a village to raise a child; the same is true of books. A writer spends an inordinate amount of time alone with her characters, but eventually a host of people come alongside and offer invaluable insight and skill that takes a manuscript and improves it by leaps. For that refining process with *The Pursuit of Tamsen Littlejohn,* my deepest thanks go to my editor at Water-Brook Multnomah, Shannon Marchese, for input on the characters' emotional arcs both insightful and true. I'm amazed at her ability to see what was there, what was lacking, and how to knit it all together. Also my thanks to Susan Tjaden, Nicci Jordan Hubert, and Laura Wright for further refining many story elements. Kristopher Orr created another gorgeous cover for the original publisher's edition and allowed me a voice in choosing the Tamsen who would grace it, making this writer very happy. Amy Haddock, Kendall Davis, Lynette Kittle, and the rest of the WaterBrook Multnomah team who answer e-mails, provide graphics, bookmarks, publicity, reassurance, and countless other things behind the scenes, it's a privilege to work with you talented folk.

Pamela Patchet — thanks for sharing your hilarious squirrel-invasion stories. Tamsen and I are likely scarred for life.

Last but not least, thank you, readers, for making room in your hearts for my characters. Writing is a circular endeavor, and the writer is only half that circle. She needs readers to close it for her. Deepest thanks to each of you who've closed that circle for me in the form of letters, e-mails, reviews, and notes to tell me how my stories have affected you. God knows how you've blessed me. I hope you do as well.

READERS GUIDE

Jesse and Tamsen: An Uncommon Pursuit

1. From the moment he set eyes on her, Jesse senses Tamsen is the woman God fashioned for him. Have you experienced an instant connection with a new acquaintance? Are Jesse and Tamsen well suited to each other? Why or why not?

2. Jesse's vow to Reverend Teague to protect and provide for Tamsen without asking anything in return was as binding to him as a marriage vow, though it was Tamsen who first suggested the marriage. Were you as surprised by that proposal as Jesse? Did Jesse keep his vow?

3. Jesse and Tamsen both make star-

tling discoveries about their identities. What factors enabled each character to accept these discoveries and move on? Have you ever learned something about your past that came as a surprise? Did it change how you viewed yourself or your place in the world?

4. Both Jesse and Ambrose experienced strong reactions to their first sight of Tamsen Littlejohn. What did each man see in Tamsen, and how did that shape their subsequent actions toward her?

5. How many people were pursuing Tamsen Littlejohn? Name them, and explain the nature of each pursuit. Was God pursuing her as well?

Bryan and Collin Kincaid: A Father's Legacy

1. Which character was most impacted by Bryan Kincaid? In what way? How has Bryan's legacy of acceptance and loyalty been passed on to Jesse? How does Jesse reflect it at

the end of the story?

2. Ambrose Kincaid struggles with a temper like that of his father, Collin, who gave it such rein it led to destruction, bitterness, and grief. Did you feel sympathy or anger toward Ambrose? Did that change over the course of the story? Why or why not?

3. Cade risked his life to find his brother's son, then devoted his life to raising him. Did he always make the right decisions for Jesse? Should he have told Jesse the truth sooner, or do you agree he had reason to be cautious in that regard?

4. The Reverend Teague describes Cade and Jesse as godly men. No man is perfect, but would you agree with that assessment? Why or why not?

Tamsen's Quest: A Woman's Place in the Eighteenth Century

1. Tamsen longs for something more than the restricted existence her

stepfather planned for her. Was her snap decision to flee with Jesse based on something more than fear? If so, what might it have been?

2. Throughout the story Tamsen encounters women from walks of life different from her own: Molly Teague, Janet and Bethany Allard, White Shell and Blackbird. Which of these women do you think was the most influential example of the kind of woman Tamsen ultimately decided to become? Did they each contribute in some way to Tamsen's finding her path in life? How so?

3. Throughout the story, clothing is a metaphor for Tamsen's quest of self-discovery. Can you chart the progression of Tamsen's inner growth through the clothing she discarded, borrowed, or created? If you were to list the items, what inner change in Tamsen corresponds with each?

4. Tamsen's feelings for her mother were complicated. Did Tamsen gain a clearer insight into her mother's

choices? Do you think Sarah did the best she could, given the circumstances in which she was left after Stephen Littlejohn's death?

No Man Is an Island: Supporting Characters

1. Against his will, Charlie Spencer was drawn into the hunt for Tamsen, only to realize his initial perceptions of those linked to the situation were mistaken. Were you satisfied with the role Charlie played before he got his wish for solitude? Why or why not?

2. Tamsen's relationship with Bethany had a rocky beginning. Could you understand or sympathize with Bethany? Was Bethany more of a help or hindrance to Tamsen in the end? In what ways might she have been both of those things?

3. Two men stepped into the role of father figure for Tamsen. The second was Cade, but the first was Luther Teague. Were you surprised at the turn things took once Tamsen

and Jesse reached the Teagues' the first time around? Do you think Luther Teague gave the couple wise counsel? Why or why not?

Historical Backdrop: The State of Franklin and the Cherokees

1. Did you know about the Lost State of Franklin before reading this story? What about this attempt at independent statehood surprised or interested you most?

2. The turmoil in the Overmountain region in the 1780s extended beyond the borders of Franklin and North Carolina, to the Cherokee Nation and the Chickamaugas. Were you surprised to learn that Native peoples were struggling with divisions during this time period? Did the inclusion of the Cherokees and Thunder-Going-Away's town provide more to the story than a refuge for Tamsen and Jesse? If so, what?

618

GLOSSARY OF NATIVE WORDS AND PHRASES

Tsalagi — the Cherokee language
mata-howesha — not good; Shawnee
meshewa — horse; Shawnee
nooleewi-a — be quiet; Shawnee
Lenni Lenape — the Delaware Nation
Spay-lay-wi-theepi — the Ohio River; Shawnee
Lenawe nilla — I am Shawnee; Shawnee
msi-kah-mi-qui — council house; Shawnee
ki Shawano aatowe — speak Shawnee; Shawnee
ma-tah — no; Shawnee
osda — good; Cherokee
siyo — an informal greeting; Cherokee
ulethi equi'wa — beautiful woman; Shawnee
ni haw-ku-nah-ga — you are my wife; Shawnee
i'hya — river cane; Cherokee
uwoduhi — beautiful; Cherokee
Ghighau — Beloved Woman; Cherokee
Ani-yun-wiya — the Cherokee Nation, liter-

619

ally the Real People
unega — the white man; Cherokee
s-qui-:ya — too many; Cherokee
he-ga — you go; Cherokee
wehpetheh — go, leave; Shawnee
peshewa — wildcat; Shawnee

ABOUT THE AUTHOR

Lori Benton was born and raised east of the Appalachian Mountains, surrounded by early American and family history going back to the sixteen hundreds. Her novels transport readers to the eighteenth century, where she brings to life the colonial and early federal periods of American history, creating a melting pot of characters drawn from both sides of a turbulent and shifting frontier, brought together in the bonds of God's transforming grace.

When Lori isn't writing, reading, or researching eighteenth-century history, she enjoys exploring the mountains of Oregon with her husband and their dog.

The employees of Thorndike Press hope you have enjoyed this Large Print book. All our Thorndike, Wheeler, and Kennebec Large Print titles are designed for easy reading, and all our books are made to last. Other Thorndike Press Large Print books are available at your library, through selected bookstores, or directly from us.

For information about titles, please call:
(800) 223-1244

or visit our Web site at:
http://gale.cengage.com/thorndike

To share your comments, please write:
Publisher
Thorndike Press
10 Water St., Suite 310
Waterville, ME 04901